STEEL COFFIN

STEEL COFFIN

MALCOLM RAYMOND

ATHENA PRESS
LONDON

STEEL COFFIN
Copyright © Malcolm Raymond 2010

This is a work of fiction. Names, characters, places and incidents are either the product
of the author's imagination or are used fictitiously, and any resemblance to actual
persons, living or dead, events or locales is entirely coincidental.

ISBN 978 1 84748 709 4

First published 2010
ATHENA PRESS
Queen's House, 2 Holly Road
Twickenham TW1 4EG
United Kingdom

Printed for Athena Press

Note from the Author

I was born on 16 October 1926 in Cardiff and I still live here.

I attended the local elementary school and left at the age of fourteen in 1940. By that time my mind was focused completely on going to sea, and I joined the merchant navy as a deck boy in 1942. In November 1944 I was called up to the Welsh Guards and served for the duration of World War II. After serving just over two years in Germany, I left the Welsh Guards early in January 1948.

On release I formed the well-known Ever Open Eye Youth Club, through which I became well known in local sporting circles. The club played a valuable part in the social life in Cardiff, especially for the underprivileged boys. I received a special award forty years after founding the club. The club won many honours in the Cardiff and District Football League, and in Welsh baseball.

I retired from work and the Youth Club in 1992 through poor health. I devoted my time to writing, from which I was getting a lot of enjoyment, but now I have to curtail that as my eyes are failing me.

In the year 2000, many of the older boys grouped together to send in for the Queen's Award without my knowing. I found out three years after that I had been refused because they made the application too late after the time I retired.

So it only proves that forty-five years is not enough time given of your life in work for the youth of Cardiff to be acknowledged!

Prisoner

'Is there any more apple pie?' I said to Mam at the dinner table one Sunday.

'I don't know where you are putting it, John!' she said, cutting a small piece and adding a little custard, rebuking me in a kind way. I had eaten my dinner of potatoes, cabbage and peas, with Yorkshire pudding and roast beef.

'Kommen, kommen!' The voice pulled me in with a hook on a handle. Not knowing I was being taken aboard a German submarine, I was shouting, 'Mama, Mama! Some more pie, I'm starving!' The captain came down on the casing to see what all the shouting was about.

The captain, speaking good English, said to his officer, Kranx, 'He must be delirious. He is only a little boy. Bring him aboard, be careful with him. Go steady!' He said to one of his men, 'Take him down and put him in my cabin.'

As his men were obeying his orders, he turned to Kranx, 'Where the hell has he come from? He cannot be older than my boy. He is only fourteen, so I would say this boy is the same.'

As Captain Sturmer disappeared below, he told the watch to keep a sharp lookout. The captain then made his way to his cabin, where he shouted for the steward, who was also first aider and ammunition carrier. He told the steward to *überprüfen* (examine).

The steward, whose name was Heinze, gave me a thorough going over, with the captain and Kranx in attendance. My clothes in tatters, I was stripped and examined. Heinze turned to the captain. 'Other than not eating he is all right, but it looks like he hasn't eaten for quite a few days.'

'Wash him down and put ointment on those sores, which were caused by the salt water and the sun and wind. Put my pyjamas on him. I want you to look after him. When he comes around, I want to know straight away. Keep him in my cabin, and mop his brow, for he has a temperature.'

Six hours after being taken aboard, I woke up. I thought immediately that I was in heaven. Then I saw Heinze, who disappeared. The next time I saw him we were with the captain, which was actually a few seconds later. The captain looked at me, and spoke very good English. 'Now, my boy, how are you feeling?' Receiving no answer, the captain could see that I was disorientated, so he turned and went back to the control room, telling the steward to get the cook to make a broth soup, and for him to nurse him with it.

It was not till the next day that I started to observe where I was. The steward could talk English, not as well as the captain, but good enough to get by in talking with me. He told me that he was going to wipe me down, and that I should try to eat. I said, 'I'm starving.' The steward replied that he would get some sandwiches made, as it was in between meals.

The captain came in just as the steward brought the sandwiches. Captain Sturmer said, 'Good, that's what I want to see: you eating.' The captain sat down beside me, and showed me a photograph of his family. 'That's my boy. He is fourteen, and he is in boarding school. That's my wife, and that's my daughter. She is in school at Bensberg.'

I was eating as the captain was talking – only a little bit, for I had not eaten for ten days. I tried to swallow the sandwich that I was given. The captain asked my name, and I said, 'John Morgan.'

'Now, John, tell me in your own time where you have come from, when were you sunk and by whom. I want to know so that we can let your parents know that you are safe.'

'I am fourteen years and six months. I wanted to go to sea, and my parents had no objections, so I managed to get a boat out of Cardiff, a coal boat.'

'What tonnage?' asked the captain.

'I don't know. We left Cardiff on the eighth of July to go to George-town, Guyana, South America. We discharged our coal, and reloaded with general cargo, and sailed on the third of August. We were sailing to pick up a convoy, which we joined eight days out. Thirteen days later we were sunk.

'I was a deck boy with three others. When the torpedo hit us I was just coming off watch, and I went to make myself a cup of cocoa. I was having a pee, before I got to my cabin which was in the fo'c's'le point, when there was a big explosion which threw me off my feet into the water. I was lucky, for the order of the day on the ship was that on watches personnel must wear their life jackets.

'The ship was well on fire and somebody had lowered the lifeboat. There I was picked up for, although it was like daylight, I connected my light to the battery. I was seen through the fire on the ship. In my lifeboat there were only four of us. We got away from the boat and circled around to see if there were any survivors. We saw a lifeboat in the distance a length of the ship away on the port side, which we had now come to from the starboard side. We could make out people sitting in the lifeboat. It didn't seem all that many. We shouted to them but, with the crackle of the fire and explosions, there was no way they could hear us.'

I started to cry. The captain was trying to console me with Heinze the steward. Then the captain told Heinze to go to his war cabin and bring a bottle of schnapps. I was given a little drop in a glass, then Captain Sturmer said, 'Try to get a little sleep, and we will finish our talking when you are better.'

I woke up now to find that the submarine was moving. I said to Heinze as soon as I saw him, 'Where we are going?'

'I don't know,' Heinze said, 'we never know where we are going to. How are you feeling?' he asked, changing the subject.

I said to Heinze, 'I am frightened. I don't like being trapped in these steel coffins; I don't like being closed in.'

I was then given a dish of tinned fruit, which I enjoyed. Heinze was watching. He said, 'You enjoyed that, didn't you?'

'Yes,' I said.

It was my third day. The captain came and sat beside me. 'John,' he said, 'you are just like my little boy. Your parents had no right to let you go to sea at your age. I made sure my boy will not go into the forces yet, not until he is old enough.

'Do you feel like carrying on our talk? So, you were in the lifeboat with four others and you could not attract the attention of the other lifeboat. So what happened next?'

'We never had a clue. The chaps in the lifeboat were firemen, they had no idea how to sail a boat, nor did I. Then, when the dawn came, we were on our own.

'The firemen were very despondent now, and they started to argue, and that's what it was like all the time. We checked the water the first day, and found there was water enough for us, but there was no food. Someone, somewhere, had pinched the food and the sweets that were supposed to be there. Everyone now was really despondent. I started to cry, for where was the leadership? They just threw the towel in. They told me to shut up, or they would throw me over the side.

'The water was rationed out, half a cup, twice a day. If we had been lucky enough to catch a fish, which no one even tried, we could have eaten it. After a week we were right down. No one would talk. If they did it was a snarl. Then they started to eye me up. I heard one of them say, "Just leave him alone." I didn't know at the time what was meant by the remark. I think they were looking to eat me.

'The tenth day two of them started to fight. As weak as we were, for now we were all very weak, it was over to me. I had stopped crying the day before, and I was in a little shell of my own, just waiting to die. I was murmuring for my mother. I kept seeing Sunday dinners before me, with lashings of custard on apple pie for afters. I was now hallucinating, but I didn't mind – I was in my own world. The two that were fighting went overboard. Neither of the other two tried to save them. They had stopped fighting, but we had drifted away, and the other two couldn't care less. I looked up and saw them shouting. We could all hear, but no notice was taken.

'There was no talking at all in the boat. The one fireman I liked was in a very poor way. He died the next day after the two who were fighting had gone. There now was me and this other fireman. I didn't really like him, and he kept looking at me. I remembered that I had my sheath knife on my belt. I thought, *If he moves to me I will knife him.*

'My mind wandered. I thought, Mam, why didn't you stop me? But she never stopped me doing what I wanted, and my father was the same, they simply gave in to me. I left school at fourteen and I got a job as a tea boy on a building site. After a couple of months I thought to myself, this is not a job for me, and I decided then to go to sea. I wanted adventure.

'I unclipped my knife. I was ready if he came at me, although he was a big man. I felt very weak – I am sure he must have felt the same. I was determined to defend myself the best way I could. I looked up – he was just watching me. I felt very uncomfortable. I was trying to read his mind.

'I found that recapping what I had done from schooldays helped me, until it came to food – I was always a big eater. I was reminiscing again. I must have fallen asleep. I woke up and it was late in the afternoon. I looked at the other fireman in the boat with me. He was still looking at me, he hadn't moved. I was frightened. He just kept staring.

'Night came and the situation was the same. But the water started to swell, and the boat was going up and down, water splashing into the boat. It was very disturbing. A couple of times I thought we were going to capsize.

'This chap was still gawking at me. It only then came to me – perhaps he is dead. I plucked up courage and said, "I thought we were going to capsize when the next wave hit us." He never said anything. I stayed where I was because I was frightened I would turn the boat over.

'The weather kept like this for three days and nights and the chap was still in the boat. He was dead. I had been in the lifeboat for fifteen days, and the way I was feeling, I didn't think I would be long behind him. I started to cry again, thinking of my sisters and my mother and father. I cried myself to sleep.

'When I woke up, the weather was warm. I think it was in the morning for the sun was in the east. Remembering my schooldays, the sun rises in the morning from the east, and sets in the west in the evenings. I wanted to get that chap out of the boat. He was still hunched the same way, with his eyes looking at me, and it was driving me mad to see him like this. I moved across and started to handle him over the gunnel. I put his legs over first, one at the time, then I put his head and what I could of his shoulders over the gunnel. I had to rest then, for I was dead beat. It must have been about an hour before I tried to get his buttocks over, but in the end I achieved it, and in the water he dropped. Was I relieved: I just couldn't stand him. I had never spoken to him on the ship.

'I realised that now I was on my own. I was just going around in the boat, going nowhere. I didn't know where I was. All I had was water, of which there seemed to be enough for what I wanted. I thought I would wash myself, although I didn't have a towel or soap. It would be refreshing to use my hands to wash my body, for I had a couple of times peed myself, rather than say anything to the crowd in the boat. My clothes were smelling. So I put on the life jacket just in case I was too weak to swim. I tied a length of rope to my waist, and then lowered myself into the water.

'I was weak. I had one hell of a job to get back into the boat. I had washed myself in a fashion, before deciding to get back in. Because I was exhausted, it took me quite a time and effort to clamber back in, but I won.'

Under Attack

The captain said, 'Have a break, John.' He asked the steward to fetch three coffees for Mr Kranx, himself and me. The steward came back after about five minutes with three coffees on a tray. The captain was telling me about his son, only fourteen. 'The school leaving age in Germany is fifteen, but he is in a place like your Eton, where he stays. He comes home every weekend, as we don't live far from the school. He is a good boy.' I asked his name. 'Tomas,' the captain said.

The captain spoke German to Kranx, wondering how a boy my age could have survived. Although I could not speak German, the captain explained what he had told Officer Kranx.

'I was drinking a lot of water,' I told him, continuing my story, 'for in the days it was very hot, but I wasn't eating anything. I was starving. I kept having hallucinations and dropping off to sleep. I had now come to the end, I knew it, and the more I thought about dying, the more I cried, until I would wake up again, and think about my family. I kept seeing my mother and father.

'I prayed to God. As I could not cope without eating, I wanted the good Lord to take me. I was getting sores all over my body. I knew I had lost weight, for when I joined the merchant navy I was just over eight stone. I was proud of my body.

'The next thing I know was lying on this bunk. When I came to, I thought I was in heaven.'

'That will do for now,' Captain Sturmer said. He got up and said to Kranx, 'Kommen.' He then turned to the steward saying, 'He is to stay here, and you are to look after him.'

When the captain went, Heinze said in his broken English that I was to stay in the bed. If at any time I wanted a drink or food, I was to ask. Also I would be washed down every day, and he would get some clothes off the crew. 'To while away the time,' he said, 'I will teach you German and you can teach me English.'

We started our lessons there and then. By the time the week had gone through, I was feeling a lot better. Also Heinze was great, he really looked after me.

After eight days I was allowed out of bed, but was not allowed to roam the submarine, I was to stay in my cabin (the captain's); if I wanted to go to the toilet or showers, Heinze was to be with me. I had to promise the captain that I would stay in the cabin unless I was escorted.

I was very shaky and I had to be assisted to walk. The captain all the time was making sure that I had everything I wanted. He would pop in frequently. He was like a father to me, and now I was getting to worship him, and Heinze.

Heinze came into the cabin on the afternoon of the ninth day, and said, 'Keep it to yourself,' in good English (or I thought it was good). I replied in German, 'Was ist das?' (what's that?), mixing English and German he told me a convoy had been seen on the horizon, and the submarine was getting in position to attack.

It was 11.15 p.m. – we fired two torpedoes, after which the boat was very quiet. I knew it was two because the boat jumped – a funny experience. After a while Heinze said, 'We missed,' but there were further explosions at intervals.

I said, 'What are those bangs?'

He said, 'There are other submarines with us.'

After a while we let two more 'fish' go, and there was a result: we heard a bang, and the captain looked up and confirmed a hit.

'Dive, dive, dive!' shouted the captain, and the boat was dropping down into the unknown.

As she levelled off, the order went out, 'Silent running.' Heinze sat with me, for now I was frightened. 'No talking,' he said, 'Just lie on the bunk, and I will stay with you.'

There was an almighty explosion. I thought the submarine had blown up. It was a depth charge, quite awesome. The bang was terrific, and there were some more. It was as if they were dropping on top of us. Heinze could see I was really frightened; he started to smooth my forehead, and he kept whispering in my ear.

It was very quiet after a while so I thought it was all over. I said to Heinze in a whisper, 'Aren't you frightened?'

'Yes,' he said.

It was quiet for about five minutes. Then you could hear the engines of the ship above come right over the top of us. I grabbed Heinze, really frightened. You could smell Heinze was frightened as well. I desperately clung to him – I thought this time my time was up. He gripped hold of me in the same type of panic as I was in.

This straddle of depth charges was right on top of us. The bangs were terrible. The boat started to leak. All things that were not secured were soon on the floor. There was general mayhem in the boat. The two quietest people there must have been Heinze and myself. I was gripping him so tightly, frightened that we would be parted. He kept repeating 'Hilfe' (help), though at the time I didn't know what he was saying.

They were having a terrible time. In the control room area there was a small fire. All the lights went out. They were using strong torches. You could hear the warship above going away. I was praying that it wouldn't come back, and at one stage I thought that it wouldn't. But it did, and again was right on top of us. Since the time of the last attack, however, we had dived further down. I didn't know to what depth, neither did Heinze.

It seemed the charges were all around us. Whether we were too deep I didn't know, but they still sounded as if they were on top of us. The attacking ship passed over us and carried on. We heard no more from her.

Heinze and I sat alongside one another on the bunk. I asked him how old he was. Nearly nineteen, he told me, and he looked very young.

My German was improving all the time, though Heinze's English was a lot better. I was now leaning very heavily on Heinze. I found myself wishing at one point that he was my brother. Forget that he was a German – he looked after me. I also think that he thought the same way about me.

You could hear orders being shouted out here and there. Then the captain came in. 'Are you all right?' he said to me.

'Yes, thank you,' I said.

'What about you, Heinze?' he said.

'Very good, Captain,' said Heinze.

One by one, members of the crew were peeping into the cabin to see if I was all right. These were the ones who had given me some of their clothes.

We were back to normal the next day. I said to Heinze that I wanted to toilet and have a shower. I had an hour designated to me in which no one else was allowed into the ablutions other than Heinze. I now felt a

14

lot better. I could walk, I was putting on weight, so the captain took me to the control room to have a look around. I had now been on U-boat Number 201 nearly two weeks. I hated it, but the crew were brilliant and I was getting on very well, for they were all poking their heads around and saying something in English. By now they were all learning English.

Heinze would not leave my side. The captain had told him to stay with me all the time, except when he was getting my meals. I got to really like him. I could see a lot of activity going on. I asked Heinze what was happening. 'You will be going off the boat on to a ship,' he said, 'which we are tied up to. I am afraid that this is the end.'

I said, 'Don't leave me, Heinze, don't leave me.'

'I cannot help you,' he replied.

Heinze and I were both near to tears. 'I have written my address,' he said, and he gave me a slip of paper.

I said in tears, 'I will give you my address, and promise me that, after the war, you will come and see me, Heinze, and I will come and see you.' I was called to come up on deck. All the crew wanted to shake my hand, Heinze and I were in a clinch – I didn't want to let go. The captain separated us.

Tramp Steamer

'Captain Sturmer,' I said, 'I want to thank you for saving my life. I wish you and the crew the very best of luck. Also, I hope to come and see your son after the war. I hope to see you as well, if I survive this...' I pointed to the tramp steamer that I was about to board.

'Here,' he said, writing his name and address on some paper. I did the same on the paper that he provided. I then shook his hand and that of Officer Kranx. Although I had not seen much of him, he was all right.

The captain said, 'Be careful going aboard.' When I got on deck I turned to look for Heinze. He was wiping his eyes, as I was doing with mine. The captain of the ship I had now come on told one of the hands to take me to a cabin that had been allocated for me, at least for the time being.

While I was in the cabin I could hear a lot of orders being thrown about on deck. They were refuelling the submarine and Captain Sturmer was stocking up with supplies. We were tied up to the U-boat till the next day, and we cut adrift from the boat at 1100 hours.

When we left the sub I was taken out of the cabin to the captain, whose name was Jenks. At first impression he looked a nice chap. 'Ah,' he said when he saw me, 'and what have you been up to?' He spoke very good English. I did not answer. 'Never mind,' he said, 'we will have a little talk again. I don't know what to do with you,' he added, then, after thinking for a while, he said, 'Put him with the others.'

I walked with an officer to No. 4 hold. There was a sort of canopy leading to the hold, and when the tarpaulin was pulled aside, steps of a kind led to the twin deck, where there were quite a few English seamen prisoners on the boat. They were not put right down the hold, which was very considerate of the captain for, if there was an emergency, at least the lads had a chance to get out.

When the ship had been tied to the U-boat, the tarpaulin covered the hatch, but on released from the submarine or any other craft that this tramp steamer was servicing, the sheet would be pulled over the exit to the hatch. There was another exit from the hatch: from the twin deck there was an alleyway to the poop deck, where there were a couple of cabins or holds where ammunition was kept. This was also where they kept their big ropes and paints, and other things that help to run a ship. Furthermore it was an outlet to the toilet that was improvised on deck.

On deck all the time were two crew members who were on watch over the prisoners. We could come up at any time, but in numbers of no more than ten at a time. For the moment everyone obeyed the rules, for they knew the captain could be a lot stricter if they should break them.

Captain Jenks was a very considerate man, easy-going to the crew as well as the prisoners, of which there were 137, all spread around the twin deck. (A twin deck is a lower deck underneath the top deck; the reason for the twin deck was to carry anything rated as expensive, or a scarce commodity.) There was no cargo on the twin deck, only the bunks that were made for the prisoners.

The rest of the hold was full of provisions for the U-boats or ships that she was servicing. If the cargo was level with the twin decks you would be able to walk across the hold, but, seeing that the cargo was emptying, through supplying other ships, there was a fair drop, so you could not climb on to the provisions.

There were lights installed for the prisoners up till 2200 hours. Then most of the lights would go out, leaving just dim lights in the twin decks, with the hatch cover and tarpaulin left open for the prisoners to toilet.

The crew were all merchant navy chaps. There were forty-eight of them on the ship. Excluding the officers, they were all down in the fo'c's'le head. The firemen were on the starboard side (the left-hand side as you look at the bows from the bridge), with the donkeyman in a little cabin on his own. The firemen, including the coal-trimmer for each watch, were four to a watch, which was a four-hour watch.

The sailors were three to a watch, with the bosun in a tiny cabin next to the seamen, on the port side. Right into the point there were six men used for guard duty and loading the boats that needed supplies. There were three greasers, who were in with the firemen, and the carpenter, who had a locked space underneath the bridge.

The steward and the two cooks made up the complement, other than the officers. There were four deck officers, including the captain, and four engineers including the first engineer. No cabin boys – the duty was shared by the steward and the cooks. Then there were two wireless operators.

The ship had been at sea five weeks, in an area in the middle of the Atlantic where no ships go. Every time she refuelled, she would be right out of the way. Then, when she had all the prisoners she could carry, she would make her way to Spain, where sometimes she loaded up again and went back out, or she would make a dash for the French coast.

This time she was due to unload the prisoners and have a refit. The captain was a very methodical man. He would not hear of any mistreatment. He allowed a lot of scope to the crew and the prisoners. The prisoners were all, near enough, officers, for they were all the subs would bring to the steamer. After they had torpedoed a ship, they would take off only the officers, but at least most of the subs would tell the lifeboats which course to take.

I was put in the hold where all the English prisoners were kept. When they saw me coming down the steps, they all started to take the mickey out of me, with such comments as, 'Where's your napkin? Does your mother know where you are? I didn't know we had babies in the MN. A voice from below as I was coming to their level said, 'Leave him alone. Come here, son.' The whole place went quiet.

I moved to the voice. A chap who looked really old stood up and said, 'Come and sit on the bunk. My name is Commodore Timkins. I am the senior officer down here. Now, where have you come from?'

As I began telling the commodore, the other officers crowded around to hear what I was saying, keeping very quiet, just listening.

When I finished, the commodore said, 'You have been through it, son, haven't you?' And with that he asked one of the chaps who was in a bunk by him to, 'Move, so that this lad can have your bunk.' He wanted to keep an eye on me, in case any of the officers might try anything. There were no objections from the officer whose bed I was to have.

When one of the German crewmen called for me to go up to see the captain, I followed up behind him. The captain asked me the same as the commodore, and I told him the truth. He said, 'Would you like to be cabin boy for me and the officers?'

I said, 'No, I want to be with my own kind.'

The captain said something in German, which I could not follow. After about ten minutes there was a knock on the door. The captain, in

English, said 'Enter!' and the commodore came in to the cabin. I was very surprised.

'I have just asked the boy if he would like to be cabin boy for the officers of this ship,' said the captain. 'He has said no, but I thought with such a young chap on board, it would occupy his mind, and we could do with someone to clean the cabins, and make the beds. Also he could have the run of the ship from the bridge to the poop, without being tied down.

'I tell you what,' Captain Jenks said, 'you go and think it over, and give me your answer tomorrow morning.' With that I was dismissed. I and the commodore had got up to go, when the captain said, 'Would you stay behind, Commodore?' So I carried on to the hatch, to the other prisoners.

I came down the steps into the hold. All the boys were looking at me. I could see them trying to think what the captain had wanted me for. As I made my way to my bunk, one officer, whose name was George Brecon – he was senior to the others, next in line to the commodore – came up and asked if everything was all right. I said yes.

'What did the captain want?' he asked.

'He wanted me to be cabin boy,' I said.

He thought for a minute, then said, confidentially, 'Do you speak German?'

'Yes,' I said, 'pretty good.' And with that he walked away. He called another officer to him and they were soon deep in conversation.

When the commodore came back he went straight to his bunk. Seeing me lying down, he said, 'You all right, John?' to which I answered, 'Yes, thank you.'

Captain Brecon came up to the bunks and said to the commodore, 'Can I have a word, sir?' to which the commodore said, 'Certainly.'

Captain Brecon walked away, which enticed the commodore to follow him. Making their way across the deck, they came to some bunks where there were three other officers waiting for Captain Brecon and the commodore.

All officers who were hanging around were asked politely to vacate the area. That left Officers Wainright, Thomas and Powell with the commodore and Captain Brecon. These officers ran the prisoners and the prisoners were responsible to this committee.

The officers made themselves comfortable. Then Captain Brecon told the meeting, that I had told him that Captain Jenks of the German ship *Tri-Mark* had asked me to act as cabin boy to the Germans. 'Yes,' the commodore said, 'I was in the cabin when he was asked. John originally turned it down, but the German captain advised John to think about it, and give his answer tomorrow morning.

'John said he would, and left, but the captain asked me to stay, offering me a glass of schnapps, which I readily accepted. He then said the job would be good for John, seeing that he was only a youngster – something to occupy his mind, rather than hang around the ship thinking of home. "John doesn't look on us as enemies as you do," the captain said.

' "All right," I replied, "I will try and convince him. It would be better for him to be active than mope about." I left thinking perhaps the German captain was right. What if we can convince John to be cabin boy? He understands German, confidentially, so why not get him to accept the German captain's proposition? Perhaps he could help us a lot in picking up information. Also there might be papers around that he might be able to understand, which might tell us something. At least it will keep him occupied.

'Let's call him over and ask him.'

So Officer Wainright went over and invited me to come over to the commodore. 'Sit down, John,' the commodore said. I sat alongside him.

'I have been informed, John, that you can speak and understand German.'

'Yes, I was learning German on the U-boat. I was teaching the first-aider English and he was teaching me German. He could speak English a bit, which was an advantage for me, and in school I was very quick to pick things up. We always conversed with me in German and him in English, once I had grasped the German language. We were doing very well. It might be that reading German will be difficult, for I never had all that much to read, but I am not dull.'

'All right, John, I understand,' the commodore said. 'We want you to take the cabin boy's job, and we want you to listen to all the talk of the officers whenever possible. We don't want you to go opening drawers or anything like that. Just listen while you are working. Always pretend that you are working even though you are not – always butter the Germans up. Will you do that for us? We really want to know where we are going.

'You will report your findings to Captain Brecon, and Captain Brecon only. You will not speak to him with any other officers around other than those here now. You must not let anyone know what you are doing. Don't speak German to anyone, even if they ask if you can speak it.

'Besides doing the cabins for the Germans, we want you to keep the water situation going for us, for as you must know by now we get very thirsty down here. You will be allowed to roam the decks this side of the bridge, but you are not allowed to go the forward part of the bridge.'

As we were talking the ship started to roll with the waves, and before we knew it we were in a heavy storm. Captain Brecon said, 'You will be bringing the food down to us with the Germans. Your job is now to creep to the Germans. Get them to rely on you for something. Creep around the cooks – in other words, creep around the Germans.'

The weather was really bad, and the ship was tossing and turning. The trouble with the weather was whenever anyone wanted to go to the toilet they had to go on deck, to the improvised toilets, and you had to be very careful you didn't get washed overboard. Or you could get a real soaking – then you had one hell of a job to dry your clothes.

The guards during this bad weather would be on the poop deck, where the entrance to the twin deck was. They would sit smoking. They would talk in their broken English, and they were very good. Generally speaking, that went for the whole crew. But the captain was the influence there; he would not have any of his crew ill-treating the prisoners.

Next morning about 9 a.m. I went to the captain. 'I didn't want to do it,' I told the commodore, 'but I thought helping the boys out would be good for them as well as for me.' I asked permission in English to go up on the bridge. The officer on watch gave permission, and I said I wanted to see the captain. The officer took me to the captain's cabin, which was alongside the chart room.

The officer knocked on the door and spoke in German. It was a rough type of dialect, compared with the boys in the submarine, that the officer used, but I thought I would be able to cope with it. The captain said, 'Enter!' I went in and the officer left me. I walked in. The captain said, 'How are you feeling, John?' in perfect English, which really surprised me. I had heard him speak English when he had spoken to me the previous day, but now I had more time to digest it, for I wasn't so frightened. The ship was still rolling badly. The captain said, 'Have you ever been in weather like this before, John?'

'Yes,' I said, 'we were on the edge of a hurricane when we left South America. 'It was bad.'

'I don't know how long this will last for,' the captain said. 'Well, John, have you decided?'

'Yes, sir,' I said, 'I will do as you asked.'

'Good,' said the captain, 'but, John, I want you to promise me – if at any time any of my men try to interfere with you, or your own kind, you will come straight to me and report them or him to me. Will you promise?'

'Yes, sir,' I said.

He then called his steward to his cabin, by ringing a bell to the steward's cabin. The steward was there in a couple of seconds. When he came in, the captain said, 'Frederick, I want you to take John and show him the first, second and third officer's cabins, for he has agreed to clean them and make the beds. You will not touch mine,' he said to me, 'as Frederick always does mine. Don't forget, you are not allowed to open drawers or cupboards. Just dust the tops and clean the floor and make the beds, and fetch any little thing that the officers may want.'

I came out of the captain's cabin with the steward, and went down from the bridge to the bridge deck between the ordinary deck and the wheelhouse. Frederick asked me if I could speak German. I shook my head in an attitude that conveyed I didn't know what he was saying. He could speak very little English, so when he came to the officers' cabins, he held a finger up to indicate the first officer, then next door two fingers, then next door three fingers indicating the three officers.

He opened the door to show me the third officer was asleep, and said, '*Nein arbeiten*' (no work). I shrugged my shoulders. He was getting in a terrible sweat trying to make me understand.

We went next door to the second officer's cabin. I started to clean and make the bed. Frederick then indicated for me to leave the door open all the time, and showed me how to put it on a hook, an arrangement that was in all the cabins. This was probably to enable them to keep a check on me, and stop me searching.

He left me then, but I carried on doing the two cabins, and when the third officer got up and went out I cleaned his. There was nothing hanging about, but there again I was new and they were wary. But, I thought, the more I am down there, the less notice they will take.

I finished the cabins and went to the galley. The cooks were very jovial. They made a right fuss of me, and I am a proper 'guts', so I gestured for something to eat. There was coffee on the stove, bracketed by guards on the fire to stop anything falling off. A cook gave me some coffee, and a thick piece of bread and jam, and it was lovely. One of the cooks could speak English, while the other could not at all. I said to the cook that could speak English, 'What's your name?'

'Gunter, and this is Otto.'

I said, 'I am learning German, so each time I come with you, you give me a German word, and I will give you the same in English.'

The Storm

I helped in the galley for about an hour after my coffee. The ship was now in the grip of a very bad storm, I said to Gunter, 'I am frightened, I have never been in a storm like this. This started yesterday, but today it is worse.' I asked Gunter, 'Have you experienced anything like this before?

Around this time of year, towards the end of August, you will always get this type of weather as you get nearer *Spanien*.'

I thought, after he had said the word '*Spanien*', I had never heard of it before, I must remember it to tell the officers. So I kept repeating it as often as I could without the Germans seeing me. Although the storm was fierce, it was still very warm. You could walk about with shorts and no shirt, but for the waves lashing the ship. I had to try to make my way back to my English buddies in '4' hole.

I got back to '4' hole. The cooks wanted me to stay with them, and were even willing to put a bed up for me, but I wouldn't hear of it. I said, no, I wanted go back to 'hole 4'. The German sailors, without me knowing, had strung a rope down the deck; anyone wanting to go aft or for'ard just hung on to the rope. One of the German crew – I hadn't seen him before – saw me when I came down to the deck, stopped me and fixed a rope around my waist, and around the thick rope that straddled down the deck.

He couldn't speak English, but I knew what he was doing, and I said, '*Vielen Dank*' (many thanks), for that was one of the first expressions I was taught. I got to the hatch through the poop. I was soaking – the ship was still rolling terribly. It was like an oven in the hold. Everyone was sweating, and everyone was thirsty; they wanted water. I was supposed to keep water handy for them, but it was all gone. However, they would not let me go and get any.

Two other officers went and got some water. I was told by the commodore that I was not to go out in this weather, I was to stay in the hold. I told Captain Brecon about the talk I had with the cooks, telling him about the one German who could speak English, and how we were talking about the weather and the storms. 'He said, "Yes, it's always like this around this time of year around *Spanien*." '

I asked Captain Brecon where that was. He said, 'Spain, boy, Spain. You've done well. Keep your ears open all the time.' The ship was rolling very badly, and the cargo (the supplies for the U-boats) was rolling all over the place. Captain Wainright went and got the security guards to have a look, for if the cargo were to spill over to one side and stay there, it would unbalance the ship, which could have serious consequences.

The security guard went and got the officer of the watch, who came and didn't like what he saw. He left and reported to the captain, who immediately called the crew out to try to secure the cargo.

The commodore asked Captain Jenks if he wanted any extra hands. The captain was grateful for all the help he could get, for the ship was now on a list – only seven per cent but that could turn into enough to topple the ship, so desperation was creeping in. The commodore asked how many men Jenks wanted. 'About twelve,' he said. Everyone was really willing, but twelve went, and the rest of the men were told to bunch on the side opposite to the list.

The captain got all his officers off watch. He told the chief engineer to check Nos. 1 and 2 holds, although they were fuel for the U-boats, also 3 hold, though there was nothing much in there; it had already been more or less emptied, serving the U-boats.

The first mate went with the chief engineer and they checked the other holds. There was not much they could do about the holds with the oil in, but they checked that no water was coming in. They found there was some water in No. 3 hold – not much, but the point was, where was it coming in?

They found out that the cooling system ventilators were not turned away from the waves. When the waves hit the ship, the ventilators were taking a lot of water, so they were turned around. That saved an awkward situation.

They had levelled the cargo in the hold. The ship then came on an even keel, so that now everyone could breathe a little better. All of us, German and English, were happy together.

The weather lasted three more days. In the hold where the prisoners were it was stifling, and there was a lot of dissent among the prisoners. The ship itself was riding well in the water. I had not been out of the hold since the first day of me cleaning the cabins. When I went to do my chores, I tried to explain about the weather. The steward said, 'That's all right.'

I carried on doing my work. I saw or heard nothing. I went to the galley, where the cooks were not trying to cook: all through the bad weather we had tea, but the rest was sandwiches, with plenty of meat in the bread. The bread was the German type, but I liked it. I started to give them lessons as we were preparing the dinner, and they gave me German lessons.

After tea I had a shower. No one else was allowed to use the shower until I came out. I had a fixed time to use the shower and toilets. I came out and it was beautiful on deck. As only twelve were allowed on deck at a time, I sat talking to the prisoners, then they would go, and twelve more would come up, and I would talk to them. This would go on till it got dark, then all prisoners had to go back in the hold. I had never questioned whether the rule applied to me or not, so I thought I would try the guards out. I sat looking out on my own, and the security Germans never said a word, so I stayed there till I was tired.

When I came downstairs to the deck the lights were full on. Lights out was 10 p.m., it was only about 9 p.m. When I got to my bunk, Captain Brecon was talking with the other gang of four. When I came on the scene he said, 'John, did they say anything to you about staying on deck?'

'No,' I said.

'Good, keep doing that. You stay after we are gone. Let's see if the Germans say or do anything.'

It was the twenty-third of October. Now and then I would miss my parents, and I would have tears in my eyes. I am very emotional. One of the German security guards was trying to tell me about his family. He had two boys and a girl, and he said he was missing them. He gave me chocolate; anything that I wanted, he would give me.

The twenty-fifth of October was my birthday. After work I did my usual thing, showered and toileted, then I sat on part of No. 4 hatch, talking to some of the prisoners. I had been enquiring whether there were any Cardiff boys on board. There was one from Barry, so I told him where I lived.

'How old are you, son?' he said.

'I am fifteen today,' I said.

It was now getting on for 7 p.m. The shift of prisoners swapped. I was talking to some of the others when a melody from the prisoners in the hold drifted up to the deck. They were humming to a soloist who had a tenor voice, and he was singing, 'I'll Take You Home Again, Kathleen.'

My father very often came home with a little too much drink in him, and he would lark around with my mother by singing 'I'll Take You Home Again, Kathleen', for that was my mother's name.

I started to cry. The other prisoners could see I was distressed, and they wanted to know what had upset me. I told them it was my mother's song and about my father singing it. I also told them it was my birthday, and they began doing everything to try to console me. They went and got the commodore and he came up, and tried his best to pacify me. In the end he asked one of the security guards to take him to the captain, which the guard did.

The captain came back with the commodore carrying a bottle of brandy and a glass. When he came up to me, he said, 'What's troubling you, John?' He was like a father. He gave me a drop of brandy, then said after I had drunk it, 'Go on now to bed.' He said to the commodore, 'Get someone to take him down to the bunk.' An officer prisoner whom I had not seen before took me down to the bunk. All the boys were looking and asking what was the matter with me, but they left me alone. I got into bed and I fell asleep in no time.

I woke up about 1 a.m. The ship had stopped, so I got out of my bunk and went topside. I could see land on the starboard side, and I could hear men talking. I looked over the side, and crewmen were painting like mad.

I came back in. There were no security guards about, but I thought that I would have been seen. Whether or not I was I don't know, but I came back down to the commodore and woke him. I explained what I had seen, and that the ship was at a standstill, just off some coast. I could not see any lights ashore. As it was a moonlit night, there was no reason for the painters to have a light, for it was very bright out on deck.

The commodore asked me to wake Captain Brecon, which I did. I told him the commodore wanted to speak to him, so he got up, and came straight across to where the commodore slept. All the prisoners in the hold, including me, never slept out of trousers; they all slept in some sort of thin trousers. The captain and the commodore got into deep conversation. They asked me some questions. What were they painting?

There seemed to be a red and yellow, I couldn't be sure, but all I could see was whatever colour it was they were painting over it with ship's grey. The commodore said to the captain, 'We must be getting near to where we are bound for.'

The captain said, 'Spain, do you think?'

'I think that's a certainty,' said the commodore. 'Well, there is nothing we can do, so let's go back to sleep.'

In the morning they asked me to try to find where we were and where we might be going. The ship was underway, so other them those who might have woken up during the night, no one would have known that the ship had stopped.

Captain Brecon said to the commodore in my hearing, 'She must have been sailing under the Spanish flag.'

'That's right,' said the commodore.

'If I should ever be released or can get away, I'll put a stop to that,' Captain Brecon said.

I carried on with my work in the morning. Captain Jenks, the German captain, asked me how I was when he saw me around the bridge. 'Very well, thank you,' I said.

'Good,' he said, and carried on. I did the cabins and then helped out in the galley, for that was the place I could learn something. I helped one cook in preparing the dough for making bread, after I had taken the pot of coffee to the steward, so he could see to the officers.

I picked up nothing that day, but I was still having my German lessons, and I had to try hard to make the crewmen think that they were actually teaching me, and that I was doing my best to be a diligent pupil.

My thinking was that, although I was becoming quite good with my German, I must make them think I was a slow learner. If I picked it up the way they wanted me, there would be no chance they would talk in front of me. The cook was the best at teaching. Actually he was dull himself, but he thought he was good, and my German was now much better than his. I ventured to ask him how much longer we would be on the ship. 'I don't know yet,' he said. 'We are stopping somewhere or other, I don't know where.'

After finishing work in the galley (really it wasn't work, but I liked to think it was), I went back to my bunk. The usual number were on the deck, but there was nothing really to see. We had moved out of the sheltered cove and back into deep waters. No one other than the two I had told during the night suspected that we were near land. I was told not to say anything to the prisoners. I looked over to where the committee were, and they were in deep conversation.

Dinner call went out, so I went and helped to bring the prisoners' dinner down. It was a good meal; Captain Jenks made sure the prisoners were properly fed. Three prisoners and I went for the food, which was dished out by the prisoners themselves from communal dishes, and there was never any squabbling about quantities. After dinner the same three and I would take the dishes back, but whereas they went back to the hold, I would stay about the galley, or wander around the decks talking to the Germans.

No one ever said anything to me about this. It was accepted I was going around trying to improve my German, at least that's what they thought. But I could not pick anything up at all. While I was talking to about five Germans in a bunch, as I was talking to two of them, I heard one of the other three mention 'La Coruña'. Now, I had no idea what that meant, but I kept it in mind till I got back to the hatch.

It was stifling in the hole. Fair enough to the Jerries, they opened the hatch a bit more to try to get some air in. I met Captain Brecon as he was just coming out of the hole. I said, 'Can I have a word, sir?'

'Certainly,' he said, turning around and coming back down to the deck.

I told him I had been talking to the Germans, and had heard one of them say 'La Coruña' when he was talking to one of his mates.

Teatime came along, and I had a surprise. After I had helped with the prisoners' tea, as we were eating, the cook came down with the steward and other German personnel. They brought a birthday cake for me. They said they knew my birthday was yesterday, but better late than ever.

The cook who could speak pretty good English had put on the icing 'Happy B— John'. 'I couldn't spell birthday,' he said to everyone listening, and they all laughed. They made me cut the cake, and they started to sing 'Happy Birthday'. I was really excited. I thought it was very good of the steward and the cook, it certainly lifted me.

After tea I went on deck. It was really hot. The sun was shining and there wasn't a breeze at all, it was stifling. While I was looking over the side, my mind just meandering, a couple of the Jerries came up and started to learn a little English, for they all wanted me to teach them. I didn't mind.

La Coruña

Thursday morning, the day after the cake presentation, all the prisoners were told that after 6 p.m. they would not be allowed on deck for a few days. The first mate had some short lengths of planed timber, fixed across the tops of some small drums for anyone that wanted to toilet. They were placed in a cabin in the poop.

There would be sentries outside, so no one would be able to come on deck. The only one allowed out was me. Anyone who wanted to see the captain was to see the commodore, and the captain would come down to see them.

In the galley after doing my chores I was talking to the cook. One of the sailors came in, and was talking about the women in La Coruña. They had been promised half of one day and the other half of the next day for the crew to go ashore. This guy was really excited, and they all forgot about me. I said nothing. It seemed that we would arrive *'früh Morgan früh'* (early tomorrow morning) in La Coruña, Spain.

The Jerries were talking about getting this and that, things that they could not get at home, so I left and no one missed me. I went straight to Captain Brecon, who was talking to Captain Wainright. I told them what I had heard, and he said to Wainright, 'It seems that we are going to be here for a few days.' To me he said, 'Go back up there make out that you want a pee. See if you can find out how long we are going to be here.'

I went back to the galley, and I bumped into the steward. In his very bad English, he asked if I was all right. *'Ja, vielen Dank'* (yes, thank you very much). With that I carried on to the galley. The sailor had gone, leaving just the cooks, and they were talking away. I didn't say anything, but I couldn't really understand them. They were quick, and they had a brogue about their language. They must have been from further east than the others. When they got excited, no one could understand them!

I took the dinner with the other prisoners to the hole. Captain Brecon said, 'Find out what you can. Also, John, I want you to watch the ship going into port, the locks more than ever, to see when full tide is. All the information you can get – if they should want to know what you are doing on deck, say that you have a fever, and you wanted some fresh air.'

I stayed with the cooks all the afternoon, for I had my excuse if anyone would want to know: English lessons. I was helping with the dough for making bread, also the cooking of the tea, in which I was interested, so I stayed there till it was time to take the teas to the hold with the other prisoners. After tea I showered and toileted, and then stayed on deck. No prisoners were allowed on deck now; I was on my own.

I stayed on deck till about 9 p.m. It was dark, but the stars lit up the sky. It was clear. I walked to the galley, hoping that I could see one of the cooks, for I was going to ask for a jam butty. I didn't see anyone around, I was not allowed to go for'ard, so I went back to where I always sat, and no one said a word. It seemed that I was accepted.

I went to bed just after, for I had to get up in the middle of the night. Captain Brecon said, 'I will give you a shout when I think we are nearing the port.' The next thing I was aware of was Captain Brecon shaking me. Everyone else was asleep, so I crept out to where the toilets were in a cabin off the alleyway, and went outside. The two German security guards were sitting on the hatch facing the exit, smoking. They looked at me but said nothing.

I went to where I always sat or leaned on the gunnel. When I sat down it was always on the capstans where the rope is coiled around. I looked out and I could see lights not too far away. I was now more interested, really engrossed, for here I was going into a place I had never heard of. I looked up to the skies.

All the sailors on the ship were now standing to. The ship had stopped and a pilot came on board. The ship carried on into a bay. It was about fifteen minutes till we got to the locks, which were opened for us. Just as we were about to enter, a tug came alongside. The sailors threw a rope to the tug, which the tug's crew caught, and pulled it to the tug. A very thick rope was attached to the thin rope.

The tug tied up and we were slowly taken into the lock. There were quite a few people standing on the quay wall, watching, not shouting or saying anything, just watching. There was no reason to shut the lock gates; we were on even tide to the water in the port.

All the lights of the town seemed to be on the starboard side, and we were being towed to the port side, going through a wide entrance to our berth. We moved into a very big basin. There were quite a lot of ships there, including some German vessels, but there were no port facilities. When came to the spot where we were to drop anchor, which we did, the tug released her ropes and the pilot left. All this took two to three hours.

I was still eager-eyed. A couple of the Jerries, practising their English, said, 'No sleep, Johnny?' I said 'no' in English. They made their way back to their cabins, but I stayed on top for about another ten minutes. I then went straight to Captain Brecon and told him everything that had transpired, estimating the timing of events although I never had a watch. I asked the captain what time it was when I came back down. He told me, and from there I tried to work out the times. Captain Brecon was very pleased. He said, 'Go and get some rest,' and followed me to the bunk.

I was woken in the morning. I had my wash and toilet time on my own. I then went to the galley and helped the German sailors to bring the food down for the prisoners, after I took the dishes on my own back to the galley, where everyone seemed very relaxed.

I did the officers' cabins. It was unbelievable – all three deck officers were in their cabins. One did say *'Guten Tag'* (good morning), but the others just looked. All three walked out, so I got on with the cleaning and making the beds. When I had finished I went to the galley. For some reason I was starving, so cookie made some toast and a cup of coffee, which was always on the stove.

I sat in my usual place, watching everything that was going on. Half of the crew were going ashore after dinner, which was curry and rice, with a piece of sponge with custard after. I really got stuck into my dinner. I now had my appetite back, and the dinner was great. We all had the same, the prisoners and the Jerries.

A tender pulled alongside during the dinner break, and some of the Germans that were not going ashore after dinner took the supplies on board. These supplies were for our ship; the supplies in the hold were for replenishing the U-boats, and any other German vessel that wanted supplies while at sea.

They were taking a lot of fruit aboard. The steward who was checking the supplies threw me a banana and orange, which I greedily snapped up. I sat by the provisions and ate my fruit – it was lovely. I had not tasted a banana for a long time. When I had been to South America I had never bothered, and that went for the orange as well. I was smacking my lips, more or less looking for another orange or banana.

Everything was aboard from the tender, and I gave them a hand to stow the stores in the food cold storage. They had a lot of supplies. This time they had a lot of potatoes, in sacks. We had been having sweet potatoes, and after a while they become sickly. But there again, who were we to grumble? We were the prisoners. When we finished I was given two apples, and I ate those. I have always been a big eater.

The part-crew that was going ashore had gone. The British prisoners were still not allowed on board, and they were lying on their bunks. The tenor was singing and the rest were humming. I could hear them by the cold storage tank, and the singing was wonderful.

Mr Mate came and told them to stop singing, and he was quite rude about it. I suppose they didn't want anyone to know that there were any Englishmen aboard, for across the way about three miles following the coast line there were three British ships in the East Dock. We were in the West Dock, where there were some German and Italian ships.

You should have heard the language they threw back to the first mate. He couldn't speak English, and a lot of the prisoners were shouting 'F— off!' Now, that was really infuriating to the first mate. He was screaming at the prisoners, but they didn't know what he was on about, and they were now laughing at him. Then he was off, threatening them with no food or water. Someone shouted back, 'If you do that, we will sing!'

Some of the prisoners asked me what he had said. 'I don't know, really,' I said. 'He spoke so quickly. With him being bad-tempered, I could only catch that he would stop our food.'

Captain Brecon came up to me then, and said, 'Try to find out when the shore party comes back tonight.'

'As soon as they come aboard I will come back down,' I told him.

Teatime came. I went to the galley. There was nothing for the prisoners. The German helpers were dismissed. The cook who was on duty, who was just learning English, said, 'Nein, nein essen' (no, no meal). He gave me a small dish with food, saying, 'Essen' (to eat). 'Nein,' I said and walked away. If they were stopping the prisoners' food, then I was a prisoner.

I went back to the hatch that we were in. I went straight to the commodore. The prisoners knew something was wrong. 'Where's the grub?' Without answering I got to the commodore. I blurted out, 'He's stopped our grub! I went as usual to the galley, and I was told no grub, but they offered me a plate of food. I told them I didn't want it. None for the prisoners meant none for me.'

The commodore said, 'You must eat, John.'

'No,' I said, 'I will eat when you all eat.'

The commodore got up, walked towards the middle, and shouted for a bit of order. The place went deathly quiet. The commodore stated that, through the singing and the abuse that the first mate received, there would be no food. 'Even John refused a plate of food from the galley.' They all cheered me.

They all lay down on their bunks and started to sing again, the tenor leading the way with 'White Cliffs of Dover'. They carried on singing for about two hours, until the commodore was sent for by Captain Jenks.

On arrival at the captain's cabin, the commodore was invited to a drink. 'Not just yet,' he said, 'I want to know why we have not had tea.'

The captain said, 'I have had a complaint from the first mate about your singing.'

The commodore said, 'What was the matter with it? Were we out of tune?'

The captain said, 'You know what I mean. There is no singing while we are in port, yet your boys broke the rule.'

'We didn't break the rule,' the commodore said, 'it was the way your man treated us. We admitted we were singing, which wasn't very loud, and he came like a bull at the gates to us. If he had come to the top of the hatch and asked us to stop, we would have done so, but, no, he wanted to abuse us, and he has proved that by stopping our food.'

'I cannot sanction any food now,' said the captain, 'for that would cause trouble with my No. 1, so I am sorry there will be no food until tomorrow.'

'That's fair enough,' the commodore said, 'so we will stop singing when breakfast comes tomorrow.'

'Now, sir,' the captain said, 'this is only souring our relations.'

'I am sorry,' the commodore said, 'I will have a word with them, but you know how stubborn they can get.'

As the commodore got up to leave the cabin, Captain Jenks said, 'Won't you have a drink before you go?'

'No, thank you,' the commodore said, and left.

He arrived back at the hatch with his escort. He called everyone's attention, told them the outcome of the meeting, and they resigned themselves to singing again. The time was now 6.30 p.m. and I was really hungry, but I was going to stick with the boys. So I went up on deck and sat where I usually sat. My mind started to wander, and all I could see was trifle, my favourite food. My mother made trifle just for me, for my sisters were not fond of it.

I fell fast asleep where I sat. I said to Mam, 'Can I have some more, please? I heard her say, 'John, you will be sick eating another helping of trifle,' but she dished it out, and I saw it off…

One of the security guards came and woke me up, just as I was having a lump of home-made fruitcake. He offered me a cup of coffee, which I was just about to take when I realised I was one of the prisoners. I was staying with the prisoners, so I declined it.

I sat up on deck till 11 p.m., when the tender that took the Germans to the shore bumped against the side of the boat, which startled me. Looking over I saw the crew coming aboard, so I went below, saying goodnight.

I made my way to Captain Brecon and reported that the rest of the crew was back on board. The captain checked his watch. It was a couple minutes past 11 p.m.

'Sir,' I said to Captain Brecon, 'what is the situation as regards tomorrow? Do I do the officers' cabins, and help in the galley?'

'Yes, you carry on as normal. Later on in the day I am going to ask you to do something for us, so I don't want you to spoil it by refusing to do your normal thing.

'If they offer you something to eat, you must take it. I don't want you following us with our demonstration against them. Now, go to sleep.'

The dimmer light was on. Just before I fell asleep, I noticed that the commodore and the committee were in a deep huddle, talking very quietly.

In the morning I carried on with making the beds and cleaning the cabins. I then went to the galley more or less on the scrounge.

There was no breakfast for the prisoners. Also there was no water to wash or drink. That was the reason why I was in the galley – the Germans treated me well, and really I had no grouse against them. I am British, however, and to my way of thinking I should have been standing with them, but I knew there must be a reason why the British prisoners wanted me to carry on as if nothing was wrong.

Dinner time came, but that was in word only. Still no water or anything to eat, and it was so hot in the hole. Me, I could sit outside, they said nothing to me. I had some toast with some bacon for breakfast, and going to the galley I had some rice and curry for dinner.

But I was anxious for my fellow men, and there was nothing I could do. I managed to get a closed-in tin, something like a cocoa tin, which could be sealed. I cleaned it out, and used it for carrying water. I did that for about three trips before I was stopped by the committee. Captain Wainright said, 'John, you are drawing attention to yourself. You must stop.'

The second part of the German crew had gone ashore after dinner. That was when I had started to take the water down for the prisoners. I was called over to the committee where they were all gathered. 'Sit down, John,' Captain Thomas said.

Then captain Brecon, who really was the boss, said, 'John, listen carefully. We want you to come down to go to bed early than you usually do. Then, about 9 p.m. you will go back up to the deck, asking for a drop of water, saying you think you have a fever coming. We hope one of them will go and get the water. While you draw the attention of the other Jerry, we're going to grab him and then take over the ship – we hope…'

I sat on deck till about 8.30 p.m. I got up, passed the security guards and said 'goodnight' in German to them, for they could not understand English at all. They replied the same. I went down. You could see that everyone was keyed up, for they all looked at me as if I were the Messiah. I went to my bunk and lay down. Captain Wainright said he would tell me when to go.

During the afternoon, while I had been topside, the committee had sorted out who was to be involved in the taking of the ship. All the younger elements of the prisoners were to be involved – no old ones, in case it came to fighting.

If the takeover was successful the men who were to run the ship had also been designated. Timing was of utmost importance, for they had to slew the ship around, then cut the anchor to be going through the locks around 11 p.m.

It all depended on me now. I was told it was time. I went up to the companionway from the hole, where the cabin for the toilets was. The security guards were sitting in the entrance to catch the breeze, for it was still very hot in the hole. I came up with my hand over my head, and said in German, *'Der Durst, das Fieber'* (thirst, temperature, fever).

Takeover

'*Wasser,*' I said. A security guard got up, and moved towards the galley, for just outside the galley was a water tap that the cooks used for cooking; also it was drinking water. I then tried to lure the other guard away from the entrance of the companionway, but he just sat there, so I moved right in front of him, to block his view, still feigning the headache and fever. The prisoners in the hole had to act very quickly.

It was dark outside, for it always got dark around seven thirty, and the prisoners wanted to get to the bridge as soon as possible. In the hole, Captain Powell, a rather young captain, and two other officers were out. They overpowered the guard before he could see them – they really surprised me with their speed.

They bundled the guard down in the hold with a gag over his mouth, there was no noise, for when the other German came back he saw me for only a split second. I was standing in position so that he would see me first, and the prisoners would overpower him.

That's exactly what happened. He came in holding a small jug of water, with a glass. As he stepped over the high step that prevented the water coming into the cabins in the poop section, he looked up and was grabbed by two of the prisoners.

Both guards were relieved of their pistols, and the last one went to join his mate down where the British prisoners were. There were fifteen of them to try to take the ship, including two wireless operators. The men who were designated to take the ship moved up to the top deck. They split; half moved behind Captain Powell and the others behind another officer who was a third mate, whose name I didn't even know.

Both leaders had the pistols that the Germans had had, and the sections of men crept each side of the hatches to the bridge. They went the starboard side, Mr Powell and his crowd to empty the officers' cabins. They had the second and third mates and the steward, who were all asleep. They were all put together in the steward's cabin, with the pistol-packing Powell and one of the other prisoners with him.

Still on the starboard side, the wireless operators and two other officers went looking for the captain, but he had gone ashore with the first mate. This was good for the British prisoners. They went with the wireless operators to their cabin, for the wireless operators slept with their wireless and transmitters in a little cabin on the side. They near enough worked around the clock in two shifts. But here again there was only one officer on duty. The other had gone ashore. The two British wireless operators took over, and to their delight found that it was all British equipment.

On the port side the other section, led by the nameless officer, had the same success as the starboard. They found one engineer in his cabin. The second engineer was in the engine room, so they transferred him to the cabin where the deck officers were kept. The cook and the carpenter were in their own cabins, on the deck under the bridge. They were put together, so the whole party other than the ones looking after the prisoners armed themselves with the pistols they found in the deck officers' cabins, and the captain's.

They had six pistols, and there were ten men. They went down to the crew's quarters in the fo'c's'le and found that there were twelve men there. Half were playing cards, the rest reading or sleeping.

As this was going on, the men who were appointed to run the ship (the party that went down into the engine room) had no bother at all. There were four men down there. They were all gathered around a dynamo. They were taken up and the British took over. They were surprised to find that the ship was originally English, captured in Poland at the outbreak of the war.

They started the engines. The stokers, who were all officers, and the trimmer were hard at it. The ship had plenty of steam, for she was due to go out the next day. They swung her around on her anchor, and, while this was going on, the engineers brought up the heavy hacksaw. The officers on the bow started to cut the anchor while the ship was slewing around.

This had to be done, otherwise the noise of lifting the anchor would have drawn attention to them from the other German ships. It didn't take long, for halfway through the weight opened the cut, and she dropped – it was really so quick. The ship then started to pick up some speed. You couldn't go too fast, for that also would draw attention to yourself. Also, in port, as everyone knows, you have to go at a slow speed.

All the German seamen were kept in the fo'c's'le after the cabins were searched for weapons. There were six rifles and two pistols, all in the security guards' cabin. The cooks were to stay loose, under two guards, to do the cooking. All the officers were put in the ward room, with two guards outside.

The wireless operators were told to use the sets to warn the British that we were trying to break out of La Coruña in the English-captured vessel, *Tri-Mark*. We would make our way to Gibraltar.

Captain Brecon, who was in overall charge, told the security guards watching the Germans in the for'ard part of the ship to bring the captors on deck. He brought some more of the English prisoners to search the cabins. There had been no knives handed in, so he wanted to find the knives that we all know sailors carry. It was still dark outside, other than the stars which made the night bright.

Captain Jenks, going ashore, had to go to the German Legation, so the first mate and the chief engineer had gone with him. The three of them had been together for a very long time and, though the captain gave the orders, they were very close to one another.

They went ashore in the ship's jolly boat for, as the captain said to the mate, one must keep one's hand in and have a little exercise. The working of the oars was very hard, but the captain loved doing it. After visiting the German Legation they had a walk around the town, had a meal, and a wine with their meal. They called it a day about nine thirty and went back to where the jolly boat was, got in it, and started back to the ship.

As they came around to where they thought the *Tri-Mark* was, they were talking away, when the engineer said, 'Where's the ship?' The captain, with his back to the for'ard part of the jolly boat, thought the engineer was kidding. The mate now joined in, saying, 'Where is it?' Captain Jenks said, 'You won't catch me with that one.'

'No,' they said, 'we are not kidding.' The captain had a sly peep, for he was convinced that the two pals were having him on.

When he now saw that there was no ship there, he stopped rowing. Then he looked at the other two in the boat, saying, 'We are in the right area, aren't we?' They both said the same at the same time, 'Yes.' Then, in the distance they could see the boat drawing up to the lock gates.

'Quick!' said the captain. Over to the *Cuxhaven!*' The first mate and the engineer swapped with the captain and started to row as fast as they could. Captain Jenks was shouting, 'Ahoy, *Cuxhaven*!' and he shouted this a couple of times before someone answered. 'I'm coming aboard!' yelled the captain, after shouting his name that of and his ex-ship.

They reached the gangway and sprinted up as quickly as they could. They ran to the cabin of the captain, whose name was Thommson. They startled the captain when they barged into his cabin, for he was miles away reading a war book, and fantasising.

'Quick,' Captain Jenks said to Captain Thommson. He didn't really know him, only having met when they were together with the senior officers getting their orders. 'I have had my boat pinched!' He quickly told the *Cuxhaven* captain about his ship. All the German ships knew that the *Tri-Mark* had English prisoners on her because they could hear them singing. Captain Thommson said, 'Yes, I know.'

'Can you get the lock gates closed? Can you use your wireless? Let's try.' They all ran to the radio shack, where there was a man on duty.

'Quick, can you get to the lock gates?' Captain Thommson said. 'No,' the operator said.

'Get to the Legation,' said the captain. After what seemed an eternity, but in fact was only a couple of minutes, they got through. Captain Jenks told them that the prisoners had captured his ship, the *Tri-Mark*; was there anything that the Legation could do?

'Where are you?' the Legation asked.

'On the *Cuxhaven*.'

'Well, stay there, I'll get back to you in a short time.'

Captain Jenks was really worried, for the English now knew now how the German navy operated, which would be good information for the British. Meanwhile, the Legation had phoned the harbour authorities, explaining about the prisoners taking over the ship. The controlling officer of the authority said he knew nothing about any prisoners being on any German ship, which he said was not allowed. 'Never mind about that,' the Legation officer said (he was of the same standing as a junior ambassador), 'I want that ship stopped.'

The harbour officer looked through the window towards the lock gates, and could see two ships moving out. He had no way knowing who they were, but according to the departure time one was English. A ship from a country that is at war with another country has twenty-four hours to depart before the belligerent country is allowed to leave. This is taken very seriously with regard to warships, but the rule applies just the same to merchantmen.

'Too late,' he told the embassy official, 'they are through the gates.' As he was telling the German this he had a chuckle on his face, for didn't like the Germans. The harbour officer thought that the German captain of the ship would be in hot water over this, but he was glad the prisoners had got away.

The official at the German Legation's next thought was about sinking her with one of the U-boats. He got in touch straight away with the naval attaché, who had gone home, so he phoned him and asked him to come to the office straight away.

Coming to the office the attaché was informed about the situation. He said, 'They have now captured all our code books. There will be hell to pay over this.' He went into his own office where there was a radio receiver and transmitter, and he checked which subs would be near enough. He told the radio operator to get in touch with boat 92, tell the captain the position of the English ship named *Tri-Mark*, and order him to sink her.

This was flashed out. The Legation then phoned the *Cuxhaven*, telling them that everything had been done wherever possible to sort out the matter. Would Captain Jenks please report to the Legation Office to give a full statement in the morning? The rest of the German crew were to be taken on the *Cuxhaven* for the night, then sorted out in the morning.

The tender with the rest of the German crew that had gone ashore, was making its rounds with crews of other ships on her. When it came to discharge the *Tri-Mark* crew, there was no slip. The tender captain was scratching his head. He just couldn't understand where the *Tri-Mark* was. They looked everywhere, but saw no sign of her. They got to the *Cuxhaven*, and a loud speaker informed the *Tri-Mark* crew to come aboard. They were then told what had happened, and they were sick – but not as sick as Captain Jenks.

The *Tri-Mark* was now clear of La Coruña, just outside the territorial waters of Portugal. She was given a course by the British ship *Court Jester*, which was to escort the *Tri-Mark*. Two more escorts were on their way from Gibraltar, which, with a bit of luck, would be with us the next morning.

I now settled in with the galley-only work. I was a little disturbed in my mind, so I went to have a word with the commodore. I saw the commodore sitting talking to two of the officers. The weather was still very warm; but with the hatches wide open, it was very cool on the twin deck.

'Can I have a word, sir?' I asked addressed the commodore.

'Certainly, my boy,' the commodore said. The two officers he was talking to got up and left. 'What is it, John?' the commodore asked.

'I feel very guilty, sir,' I said. 'The Germans trusted me, and I betrayed their trust by doing what I did when we took over the boat.'

'I can understand that, John, but it means that we will be going home, rather than to a prison of war camp. Which would you prefer?'

'I can understand that,' I said, 'but they let me have the run of the boat, and I used it to better our officers.'

'They couldn't have done what they did without you,' the commodore said. 'John, don't worry over it, you did your duty. They won't hold it against you, so I would forget it if I were you.' Looking around the deck, I thought all the officers seemed very relaxed. It was time to put out the lights. They even put the dimmer out so that they could have the hatch opened. There was no breeze at all, it was just a very pleasant night.

I reported to the galley. The other cooks were there, one German who was getting on well with the two British cooks. Because of the rations that had come aboard just before the takeover, we had bacon and eggs for breakfast. There was a lot of cooking: porridge for starters and then bacon and eggs, plenty for all. Everyone was very complimentary about the cooking. Life had now settled down. The new prisoners – the Germans – were let on deck five at a time for about thirty minutes. Then, when the rota had completed, it began again.

A strict eye was kept on them. No talking to the English officers was allowed. They had plenty of walks around the hatches as the English had had when they were prisoners. The German officers were treated the same. They could have a walk around the aft deck around the hatches, but were kept away from the seamen.

The wireless operators, when taking over the ship, had found all the code books in the shack, which was a very good discovery. Captain Brecon now looked after the books, and also kept a tight grip on the ship. He was anxious for the escorts to turn up. Our other ship was with us, and Captain Brecon confided with Mr Thomas and Powell his fears of German U-boats in the area.

Back in La Coruña the German naval attaché was trying to get hold of U-boat 92. He could not at the time get him, for he was under the water, and to broadcast or receive he had to be on top. They were re-equipping all the U-boats with new receivers and transmitters, but 92 still had the old equipment, so they would have to surface. She already had surfaced to get in touch with Submarine HQ at Brest. She had a regular time to contact base, and that had passed.

When she did surface, then the message from La Coruña would be received, but she was at that moment in a bad area. Although it was dark, it would not be safe to surface.

It was 3 a.m. and it was still very dark, and would not be light till around six-thirty, but 92 surfaced for she knew she would be under-water for the day. She dare not come up in daylight, at least not where she was.

When she surfaced the message from La Coruña came through. The captain of the submarine asked approximately when the ship had left the port. 'She left about 10.30 p.m. through the locks, that's all I can tell you,' the Legation naval attaché said to Captain Launch.

Captain Launch whiled away for a couple of minutes trying to determine which course the *Tri-Mark* would take. Talking to his No. 1, he said, 'We know she will try for Gibraltar, but which way? In any case, I don't think we will be able to catch up with her, unless we risk being on top. I don't want to risk my boat that way. We will never make up the time underwater, so what do I do?' he said, looking at No. 1.

'You can try underwater, then they cannot say that you didn't try.'

'But you know yourself, No. 1, there will be no way we will be able to get anywhere near her. All right, we will change course to intercept, and keep our fingers crossed.'

In the captain's cabin on the *Cuxhaven*, Captain Jenks was talking to Captain Thommson. The time was just after 1 a.m. 'Gunter,' Captain Jenks said to Captain Thommson, for they had had a couple of brandies, and were now on first-name terms, 'I cannot face this kangaroo court that will be sitting in judgement against me tomorrow [which really was 'today']. I know you have a revolver – let me do the honourable thing. I would like to go to the toilet, or better still you go to the toilet. Then no blame can be put on your shoulders.'

Captain Thommson agreed to go to the toilet, accepting that his new friend was in trouble, and this really was the only way out. He would have done the same – this is a strict code of honour in the German forces. Although they were in the merchant navy, and this rule should not apply, Captain Jenks knew that this was the only way out. Captain Thommson left the cabin. He had just gone into the officers' toilet when he heard a bang. He ran back to his cabin, with a couple of other officers who had dived out of bed, to witness Captain Jenks's death.

Captain Brecon set a course just outside the Portuguese territorial waters. If there was any danger that they were able to see in time, they could cross the three-mile limit into their waters. The morning was a very calm. Captain Brecon called and got a couple of extra men to keep lookout, but there was no sign of trouble. Although a little more relaxed, he was still trying to think what the Germans had in mind for him.

Captain Launch was trying to get into a favourable position to intercept the merchantmen. He was travelling underwater, about five knots, when he saw two frigates pass him at a distance. Rightly guessing that they were going to escort the merchantmen (though they were a long way from the ships), he said to his No. 1, 'There is no way we will be able to keep up with the escorts, so we will wait here and see what happens.'

After travelling at full speed, the escorts came across the merchant ships at 1 a.m. They signalled the merchant ships how to line up, and they took position either side of them. With a bit of luck we would arrive in two more days' time, for the speed of the merchant ships was seven knots.

We arrived in Gibraltar at 5 a.m. four days after escaping from the Spanish port, and what a relief. As the ship tied to the dock, there were officials waiting to come aboard. The commodore and the organising committee met them, and ushered them down into the ward room, after the German prisoners were escorted off.

Every British officer who had been a prisoner had to go through a panel of officers, stating their name, the name of the ship, when they were sunk, and all the information as regards to when they were taken prisoner, in what capacity they were taken from the U-boat to the merchant ship, and the treatment they received on the ship.

They were all taken then by lorry to a naval barracks where they were given a hearty meal: potatoes, carrots, peas and Yorkshire pudding, with beef, and spotted dick for afters. I thought, *This is my type of dinner!* Then, when I finished mine, being first to do so, I went back for seconds, and I near enough had the same quantity, and still saw it all off.

When we had been in Gib for six days, with the prisoners slowly being taken to England so many to each ship, it was now my turn, with about twenty officers, to go aboard the ship for passage to England. The trip was to take about six days. It wasn't a convoy, it was a fast passenger-type cargo ship, which could do about twenty knots. The U-boats could not match them for speed; the only way they could be sunk was if a sub was in the right position at the right time. We had a destroyer with us, going back for a refit. We arrived back on 21 November, into Bristol, and we were all discharged with a fortnight's leave. I was given twenty-eight days.

When I arrived home my mother and father and sisters were all at the station to welcome me, for I had sent a telegram when we arrived in Bristol telling them when I would be home. After arriving in Bristol we were all escorted to this large empty warehouse where there were about ten tables with officers behind them paying out crews that belonged to different ships. Most sailors stayed with the company they were with, but I chose to leave my company.

I got off the train. My Mam and Dad really embarrassed me with the fuss they made of me when I stepped down. Everyone was looking. Then my sisters did the same, really smothering me with hugs and kisses.

I got home. It was nice to see the dog, and the kitchen. Everything started to come back to me, and I started to have wet eyes. I was overcome with emotion.

Back at the German Legation there was a lot of activity. The day after the British prisoners had taken over the boat, and Captain Jenks had shot himself, they had clamped down on shore leave, they had reorganised their radio system, and they had discharged the naval attaché and replaced him with another. To top it all, U-92 was waiting in the area they thought the ships would pass for five days but never saw anything, so they were frustrated, just wasting time when they could have been better employed elsewhere.

A new directive had gone out: any ship with British prisoners on would not at any time call in to La Coruña. They were to make sure that they had enough fuel and food to carry on. The Legation wanted to know why the first mate and the chief engineer had left the boat to junior rankings. They were reprimanded and taken off to the *Cuxhaven*. All the crew gathered together, and they were flown home, which was breaking international law. The German ship should not have called into La Coruña with any enemy of Germany on board and no hostile is allowed to use transport from a neutral country.

Phase Two

I must be mad. I was determined to go back to sea.

I spent my leave going around with my mates. I never told them what I had been through. I had been advised not to say anything, so I didn't. I just told them where I had been, and what life was like on a ship, which I enjoyed. My parents were against me going back, but I wanted to.

I sat with my father in the house. We were just going around for a drink. I wasn't legally old enough to go into a pub, but my father's attitude was, if I could fight for my country, then I should be allowed to go into a pub. In the house Mam and the girls had gone out to first aid lessons, so that just left the two of us at home. 'Don't go,' he begged me, but I was selfish, I only thought of myself. Although the area round my home had been bombed, I wanted to go back to sea.

He said, 'What is worrying me is whether anything should happen to me. As you know, I am not in the best of health, and now we have the blitzes. I don't think now that we will be invaded, so at least that is one thing that I am delighted with. The girls are good, but they could panic if something went wrong.

'Come on,' he said, 'let's go around the pub. On the way around, John, I want you, if you will, to think over what I have said. You shouldn't go to sea really as you are too young. What, fifteen just gone, aren't you?' he said.

'Yes,' I said. But now I was starting to grow, I knew my father was very proud of me, and he liked me in his company. As we were walking to the pub, he met one of his mates. They were talking away, and this chap was using a lot of foul language relating something. My father pulled him. 'If you don't mind, cut your language,' he asked the chap. I was really embarrassed, for on the ship that's all you hear.

My leave was up on the Tuesday, so I went down the shipping office in Mount Stuart Square. There were a lot of chaps and boys there all looking for a ship. I reported to the desk. The clerk said, 'Would you wait over there? Mr Bellman wants to see you.'

'Who is he?' I asked.

He shut me up straight away with the comment, 'He will shout for you when he is ready.'

I could understand his reaction, for the office was full, and the noise and hum of the place was unbelievable.

I sat among the boys. They were all new boys trying to get a ship. You could see this, for they were all nervous, and all trying to make conversation. When I sat down, one of them said, 'How long have you been coming here?'

'I have only just come,' said I.

This lad said, 'I have been coming here the last fortnight, and I haven't had any luck.'

Before I could say anything, my name was shouted out, so I got up and I followed where the shout came from. The chap who had shouted my name said, 'John Morgan?' I nodded and said yes.

'Come in,' I walked in where there were two other chaps sitting at a table. One of them, pointing to a chair, said, 'Sit down, John,' which I did. 'Now, we know the story when your ship was sunk, but what we want to know about is your time on the U-boat 201.'

I told them that at first I had been delirious. I thought when I came around at first I was in heaven. 'Captain Sturmer put me in his cabin, and the steward who did a few other jobs on the boat was told to look after me. When I came properly to my senses I was terrified, for I don't like being boxed in. The submarine to me is a steel coffin. But the steward, by the name of Heinze, looked after me. Even when we attacked a convoy he consoled me. He said he was as frightened as me, and we gave one another comfort. But I was really frightened when the U-boat was depth charged.'

I told them I was in the captain's cabin all the time I was on the boat. 'I was well looked after, for the captain told me he had a son the same age as me. He could not understand how a boy my age was allowed to be at sea, with a war on.

I told him we could leave school at fourteen, and that it was voluntary until eighteen. It was my choice – my parents were against it. And at eighteen you were conscripted into the forces.

'What we wanted to know was what you heard. We know that you can speak German pretty well, so you must have picked up things that they were saying, especially when attacking convoys.'

'No,' I said, 'I was too ill at first. Also I was not allowed to leave the cabin, unless the steward was with me, and that was only for toileting and showers. Nobody was allowed in the shower room other than the steward. I had a certain time given to me to do the necessary. That was the only time I was allowed to leave the cabin. It was after I started to feel better that I started to learn German.'

'One thing more,' one of the men behind the desk said. 'Will you be going back to sea?'

'Certainly,' I said, 'that is why I came to sign on this morning.' I left them, wondering if Dad had sent them a letter trying to stop me. It seemed very strange that they should want to talk to me.

I went back to the signing-on desk and registered ready for my next ship. There was nothing yet, so I had plenty of time. I sat with the lads I was with. 'Before I went into the office, I was not really honest with you,' I said to the lad I had been talking to earlier. 'I have just signed on, as you must have seen, but I have been to sea. Now I am going back after leave.'

He was all ears. He wanted to know what it was like. I told him that I had been to South America, and was now waiting for another ship. I asked him where he was from.

'Cathedral Road. My name is Tim Ellwood,' he said.

'Mine is John Morgan. I live in Ninian Park Road,' I said. 'How old are you?' I asked.

'Sixteen, just gone.'

'I am fifteen just gone.' It seemed that I was only talking to this lad; no one else seemed interested.

'How long did you wait for a ship?'

'Two weeks,' I said.

'I hope that I don't wait for two weeks,' he said.

'Be patient,' I said, 'it will come. The thing is to be aware – soon as they shout "boy wanted", be up there, consent in hand, and thrust it in his face. Make sure you are the one.'

This went on for a week. Timmy and I were knocking about together. We would go to the shipping office and stay most of the day. We were visiting one another's houses. My father asked Timmy if he had been to sea before. 'No,' Timmy said, 'first time.'

'I have been trying to persuade John not to go back, especially after the last trip, but he is mad. He wants to go back, I want him home. What about your parents?' my father asked him.

'Well, it looks the same. My dad doesn't want me to go to sea, but he won't stand in my way. I am the only boy, like John. I have two sisters younger than me. Dad thinks that I should stay home and look after them.

'He was a collie in Porth, and he had an accident, so he was invalided out. He hasn't worked since. I am not selfish, Mr Morgan,' Timmy said, 'but I want some adventure. I have always dreamt of going to sea, so I want to go.'

'Just like John,' my father said. 'Obviously John has not told you what happened to him on the last trip, so I will leave him tell you. Then you will have a rough idea what you will have to put up with.' With that my father changed the subject, to football.

We were both together down at the shipping office, but whereas I reported to the desk, Timmy could only enquire if there were any boys wanted. There was a ship there for me. I asked the clerk if they wanted any other boys. 'Yes,' he said. I said, 'Can you hang on before you shout it?' With that I called Timmy to me. Although there were a lot at the counter, I got my ship, and Timmy with me.

We were both deck boys, so we had to have a medical. Then Timmy had to get all the necessary papers from the union office. Then we both went to the company that the ship belonged to to sign on. So, after a lot of running around we were told to report to the ship on the Monday morning at seven. It was not yet Friday, and we were both excited, Timmy more than me. I had already been through that. By the time it was four o'clock we were members of the SS *Broadhaven*, 7,000 ton, well deck, general cargo.

On Monday, 8 December 1942, I met Timmy at the lights of Tudor Road and Clare Road. We caught the trolley bus down to the dock gates, to arrive at the ship, which was in the Roath Basin, just inside the docks, at six fifty – plenty of time. When we arrived at the ship, we were met by four other boys, all joining the *Broadhaven*. They were waiting on the quay wall at the foot of the gangplank. They all seemed very nervous.

We joined them. We had all started to give each other our names, when a chap came down the gangplank.

'Joining the ship?' he asked.

We all said, 'Yes.' I was as nervous as the new boys.

'Right, come on deck. Follow me.' We all did. On deck he picked up his board, which he had put on the cleats of the hatch, and asked us all our names. He ticked them off, and designated each name to an area.

'Morgan and Ellwood and Stevens to the for'ard,' he said, pointing to the front of the ship. As he was saying this, two other boys were running their socks off up the gangway. 'Your names?' asked this chap, who was the bosun of the ship, in charge of all deck hands. These two boys gave their names.

We three arrived at the cabin that was for us. Another boy was just behind us. There were two two-tier beds. I said to Timmy, 'I'll take the bottom, you have the top.' The other two, whose names were Terry Stevens and David Allan, had the other two. We were given fifteen minutes to settle in, and were then called on deck, where we were introduced to the ABs, two ABs (able seamen) to one deck boy.

The ABs were Maltese. The two I was with were Ron and Tony and they were very good. After the get-together, we started to take on ships' provisions. We were at it all day. We were not rushed: we had a break for about thirty minutes, then we had dinner, which lasted for ninety minutes, then we had a break around three. All in all it was a good day. We were all excited, even me. None of the other boys had been to sea before, so they were really excited, especially when the bosun told us to be ready to leave on Wednesday.

I said to Timmy, 'What about bringing our kit on the Tuesday?'

'Yes,' he said, 'that's all right, but what if someone steals it during the night – like the dockers and all the people that help to get a ship ready for sea?'

'All right, we will leave it till Wednesday,' I said.

On the way home on the bus the four of us were together. Tim and I got off first; the others, who all lived in Cardiff, were to get off at the terminus and catch their own buses to their destination. After we got off Tim went one way, I went the other. We lived, as the crow flies, about 500 yards apart.

'Can I come down tonight?' Timmy said.

'If you want to,' I said.

'See you later on,' he said as he made his way home.

He called round to the house about 7 p.m. I said, 'I am not going out tonight, do you mind?'

'Not at all,' he said. So we went into the middle room, lit the fire, and he said, 'John, you never did tell me the story about your last trip.'

I said, 'You don't want to hear that.'

'I do,' he said. 'John, I want us to be mates if it is all right with you.'

'Of course,' I said.

'I mean stick together,' he said.

'Yes, I would love that,' I said.

'What about telling me the story of your last trip?' Timmy asked again. I told him the whole story. He just could not believe it. He was very interested in the German submarine. 'Weren't you scared?' he asked.

'Of course I was, but I was too ill at the time,' I said.

Timmy kept asking questions all the time. In the end I said, 'No more, Tim, but there is one thing I insist on. I don't want anyone on the ship to know anything about all this. You are the only one to know. If anyone mentions it, I will know it was you who told them, and our friendship will be finished.'

We carried on talking about ourselves, what school we went to, everything in general. We finished at 10 p.m. We went round and got some chips, then came back to the house, for I had got the girls some. We had some bread and butter, and then Timmy went just after 11 p.m. 'See you in the morning,' I said, 'don't be late.'

Timmy went – he would have been home in five minutes.

We were ready to leave Cardiff on the Wednesday afternoon around 3 p.m. We pulled away from the quay and went into the locks. I was on the fo'c's'le, Timmy was on the wire amidship. We were given a barrage balloon while we were waiting in the lock. We were there about an hour, as another ship came behind us, so that's where the time was taken. We then started to leave the basin of Cardiff, and we were on our way.

The bosun came along to us all, one at a time, to tell us to start throwing the ashes over the side. What a dirty job that was! We would throw a shovel full over the side, and get half a shovel back. It took the four of us just over an hour to clear the decks of the ashes.

The bosun told us tea would be at 4 p.m. but just before the hour for those who were on the first watch. Then it would be fifteen minutes before watches were changed. The new watch would have their grub first, the rest of the crew on the hour. The grub was good. I found that on the ships they like curry and rice a lot; well, I liked it, so it was no bother to me. Timmy was on the very first watch, at 8 p.m. There was no real reason for us to be on watch before that, for we were in the Bristol Channel.

Timmy was allowed to do his watch on deck. He was told to keep his eyes open for German planes sowing mines. I was to go after him. One boy would carry the next four-hour watch, then the other boy would work the deck for a week, then change with one of the other watches, till everyone had their week on deck in rotation.

We were to meet a fast convoy, and go to India with troops. Our ship was army general cargo. We were to meet our ship in the Liverpool Sound. When we got there the next day, the convoy was twenty-two ships, but there were around twelve 'secrets', including a converted aircraft carrier. We left Liverpool on Saturday, 6 December.

The weather was good for a few days, but after the third day Timmy was seasick. I was too, but not half as bad as the other boys. They were all laid up, and the deck's ABs had to stand in for them. On the bridge, I carried on, although I wasn't 100 per cent. When I was on the watch, our duty was to watch for the commodore signals as well as looking out for the enemy.

I had not realised how big the escorts were. There were destroyers and a cruiser with us. We were doing eighteen knots, so we were a fast convoy. This served a few purposes: no submarine would have us, unless she was stationary waiting for us, and that would have to be lucky strike; secondly, if there were any 'hostiles' about in the way of ships, we had a chance. Seeing it was a very long journey, it was imperative to get the army men off, for the grub side of it.

After we had been at sea for eight days, the boys were getting much better, able to carry on with their watches. Once a week we were given a tin of milk, some cocoa, butter and a loaf of bread, which would go hard by the end of the week. We would have the cocoa with a lump of bread and jam in the nights after watch.

We were given quinine tablets, of which we were to have one a day. We had now settled to a routine; all the sick boys were at work. I hadn't had much time to speak to Timmy for one or the other of us was on watch, or asleep when not on watch.

Timmy, after the second week, was on deck. I saw more of Timmy then than all the fortnight before. I asked him how he liked the sea. 'Great,' he said, 'other than when I was seasick.'

I said, 'Don't worry, everyone gets seasick.'

'The crew are great, the officers are great, I really love it, but I don't see you much.'

'When we get into India, when we are tied up, we will be working together. We will have plenty of time together.'

We had found out it was a four-week journey. We had not had any U-boat attacks, which was good. We had three heavy liners with us. I was positive the *Queen Mary* was one of them. I asked one of the ABs if it was one of the *Queens*. 'I think so,' he said, so in other words he didn't know.

Rumours were going around that we would be pulling into Port Elizabeth, South Africa, at the end of a week, for supplies, probably for the troopship. As we would have been at sea at that time about twenty-nine days, we also would need supplies. Although the food was all right, we needed a lot of fresh produce.

We were five days from port, when we were hit by a very bad storm, and the boat was going from port to starboard. I thought at one time, when I was on watch, that we were going to go right over. If ever I was frightened it was then. I was pulled in from the open, and the officer of the watch, who was the first mate at that time (5.30 a.m.) tied a rope around me. He fastened it to one of the hooks that was on the bridge, but I was still kept inside.

We had a full thirty hours of it. None of the boys was allowed to leave his cabin, in case he was washed overboard. I was told to go down into the ward room and rest down there, where I had my food as well. The weather started to ease off after a day and half. I was allowed to go down, and everything began to return to normal.

I saw Timmy. I asked him what he thought of the typhoon. 'Very scary,' he said, 'but I am all right now.'

We were all promised a Christmas dinner and a drink for each man when we arrived in port, for there was no way we could have had such fare during the storm. Also we had no supplies for one. So we had something to look forward to, besides getting into port. How long we would be there for, we didn't know, but having left the area of U-boats we were now in the area of the Japs, and they were worse than the Germans. It was another four days before we sighted land. It was most exciting for the new boys – I had seen it before.

We pulled into Port Elizabeth on the morning of 3 January. We were all in our allotted positions that we had been given in Cardiff. She was taken so far by pilot, then when we got to the basin we were towed in by tugs. Some of the ships went into Cape Town, including the escorts, for it is a vast area for shipping – the docks are enormous. But we and six other boats had to go to Port Elizabeth.

We tied up, and straight away we had lorries with supplies for us on the quay wall. We started to take the supplies aboard just about dinner time, and we were told our Christmas dinner was to be the next day.

By the night we had taken all that we needed in the food line. The first mate was told by the captain we could go ashore the next day after the dinner, but we must all stay together. It was not safe to be on one's own, as there was a lot of violence, especially against the whites, as the South African Coloureds were hostile towards anybody who was not of their own.

We all sat on the deck in the evening after showering, putting fresh clothes on. It was great. Our ABs were telling us stories about their lives, which were very interesting. All of us stayed up till about 11 p.m. then we all split and went to bed.

In the morning we got up at seven-thirty. We were allowed to stay in bed till then. We had breakfast. We then tidied up for a couple of hours, had our morning break, then did nothing till dinner, which was at twelve thirty. As everyone was available, with no one on duty, it was the captain's idea to have it at that time. What a meal – it was a credit to the cook.

We left to go ashore at 3.30 p.m. It was a modern city – the shopping centre was large and spacious. We all had what we called 'channel money', a 'sub', in other words. I drew £5 which was a lot of money. I bought my sisters and mother and father something each. The boys then went into a tavern where we all had a few drinks. I drank gin and bitter lemon. I had only two of those, and I was singing all over the town.

We had no trouble getting back, and we all arrived back by ten, after having a meal in a cafe. We were warned that whenever we went in a place where there were coloureds, we, the whites, would be on one side, the coloureds on the other side – no mixing, this was a strict law. We had no trouble at all. By ten I just wanted to sleep. My pal put me to bed. I don't remember anything that night. But in the morning we were sailing, and I had a real thick head.

Bombay (India)

We left on the morning tide and waited for the rest of the convoy to come from Cape Town. We were outside all the day. It was just getting dark when the convoy we were to join showed on the horizon. As it was passing we all took our places in line. There were a few more ships added to the convoy from when we left Blighty, but our heavy escorts had left us, we had a few less escorts, and the aircraft convertible carrier also left us.

We were to take another nine days getting to India. Where we were going we didn't know. We had a couple of scares on the way. We had fallen back into the routine of the watches. I was back on the bridge watch when there was a panic – it was thought that a hostile plane had been spotted coming from Indonesia. Action stations were called – but it was one of ours that was on patrol.

Three days later, while we were in the Indian Ocean, there was an attack by some Japanese Val bombers. They had come from Sumatra, Indonesia. They came straight at us. It was not our ship but the troop-ships they were after, but they never got anywhere near them. Planes from Africa were on the scene just after the Japs attacked.

They came at us, all six of them, but their aims were bad, and they turned and fled, just as the South African Air Force came on the scene. Our ship never fired in anger, for the troopships were at the front of the convoy, and the planes were nowhere near us, but we were ready. Also it was a good drill for us, for we had to keep the guns supplied with ammunition; I was on No. 3 Lewis guns, supplying them with cans of bullets.

After the stand-down sounded, all the boys remained excited by the action. The first mate was satisfied with the way we had conducted ourselves during the emergency.

We all fell back into our routine, the excitement over for the day. But during the night there was a submarine scare. No ship had yet been attacked, but someone, somewhere thought they saw a periscope. The alarm was given. Although we were not stood down, we all sat around the funnel, for in the nights it is very cold, and the funnel was really warm.

Nine days after leaving Port Elizabeth, we arrived at Bombay. Although harbour facilities were there, there were not enough for all the ships that had come in. Obviously the troopships were first in. While they were unloading we had to wait in the harbour roads. To all of us that had not been outside our own country, it looked a proper shanty town. From where we were on the ship, there seemed to be smoke or a dirty haze over the whole place. One of the firemen said to us as we were looking towards the town, 'Don't dare go out on your own, always go in a bunch. Don't listen to what they say, for they will try to bait you.'

We were outside for two days. Then we were taken in by tug. We tied up. After we had secured the boat, we were allowed to take the hatch covers off. Where we were a typhoon could strike and, if the covers were off, sink the ship.

The time from when we were secured to the hatch covers coming off was four hours. We did not stop for the scheduled tea at six thirty. We carried on in case the Japs bombed us, for we wanted to get away as quick as possible.

The stevedores were on the ship before we had even taken the covers off. We were told that, other than the covers and the sheets, all other equipment was to be taken aft. It was put into the cabins with all the ship's ropes.

We were in Bombay for six days. Each day while the dockers were unloading the ship, we boys took turns outside the areas of the sleeping quarters. We would not move from them, no matter what.

It seems that if there was no onboard security, the dockers would be wandering around the cabins. Past experience had shown that a lot of stuff went missing.

It was 15 January 1943. I will stay this: Bombay was a very dirty place. We only went ashore once. We all stayed together, but we had no enjoyment, and everyone was of the same opinion – let's get back to the ship. So we never left to go ashore again. In the nights, which were quite warm up till a certain time, we would all sit around the fo'c's'le head, just talking. It was here that we started to know the sailors and firemen. As usual, when you get to know people, they are all right.

We left to pick up convoy at 11 p.m. on the fifteenth. We were met, after we had left port, at 2 a.m. They were making up the convoy there. We waited till 7 a.m. then started to move as a convoy.

We were travelling empty to Cape Town to pick up a cargo to bring back to Newcastle. The convoy was breaking up when we arrived at South Africa. Most of the ships were picking up cargoes, but not all were going back to the UK. Some were going around to the Gulf of Aden, to carry on to Egypt and countries around there, with the cargoes they were picking up from Africa.

We stayed in Cape Town four days. We were loaded up with general cargo, and we battened down. We were then ready to move to pick a convoy up just outside Cape Town. We went ashore in Cape Town. It was not much different from Port Elizabeth, but we had our best night there. There was a servicemen's club for the English, and we had a great time. I had another headache in the morning. I said again, no more.

Timmy, by now, seemed to be closer to me now than ever, I suppose because we had been working on deck in the ports. Though he was older than me, he looked to me all the time for decisions. But I really liked him. He was quiet and very obliging, a good mate to have.

The other boys were good as well. Although this was their first trip, they had settled in well. There were no bosses; they suggested something and we would all fall in with it. In other words we had a great group. I was very happy, so were the rest of the boys.

We picked up the convoy, twenty ships with five escorts. We took our position with another ship bound for England. Straight away we ran into bad weather. There was a saying on the ship: if you have bad weather, you will not get attacked by planes or submarines. Although the weather was very bad, we could at least go to sleep when off watch, without worrying about the enemy.

We had it bad for five days. I don't know if we were moving – it didn't seem like it – but the ship was tossed all over the ocean. Some of the boys were sick, though in a small way, and not enough to stop them taking their turn on watches. We were calling into Freetown, Sierra Leone, which from Cape Town was about nine days. That was, if we took one route. The Germans knew what routes we took, so we had a variety of ways there, taking up to two weeks.

No problems. We would be in Freetown the next day. I hadn't had much chance to talk to the boys for, as soon as we were off watch, we were in the bunk. The weather was beautiful, so standing on watch, although tiring, was made more pleasant by shirtsleeve order, with just life jackets on.

Freetown was just a shanty town, with no attractions other than the forces canteen, so there was no point in going ashore. Also we were only there for two days. Half of the ships in the convoy from Cape Town had left the day before. There was talk that they were going to South America. If that sounds like talking out of turn, it didn't matter, for we never left the ship. There were eight of them joining, another six going to the Americas.

We left the next day, with our complement made up to thirty-one ships, with eight escorts. We left at 4 p.m., and we were outside the boom defences by 6 p.m. Freetown, according to the sailors, had the biggest boom defence in the world. The area of Freetown is one large basin.

We were on the trip home now. We expected to reach Newcastle in about twenty-two days, so everyone had now settled down. I was on the deck the following week. On deck it was great; weather permitting, all you did was chip, with a small chipping hammer, the rails or other parts of the ship, then repaint what you had chipped. We had an alert during one night, but came through without any losses, having been at sea three days. In the distance we could hear gunfire. We didn't know exactly where it was coming from. Someone suggested it was the Americas convoy under attack from surface vessels. We did not know.

During the night the gunfire was still there, so it was on the cards that we were not going to get any sleep. The boys on watch were talking away, frightened to sleep and finding it very hard to keep awake. I was all right; I had just started my week of days, so I didn't have to be like them, alert all the time when they were on watches.

A week out we had a U-boat scare. There was an explosion on the other side of the convoy. The sky lit up, then went dark straight away. We saw nothing near us. The alarms had gone. Everyone not on duty took to the funnel where it was warm. After about two hours we were told to stand down.

We had one more scare. No ships were sunk, but plenty of depth charges were going off. We reached the Irish Sea and now there were only two of us. The other must have been making for the South Coast ports, perhaps Southampton. At any rate, she just disappeared. We then ran into bad weather, which lasted for three days. We were to go to Loch Ewe, which is a very big basin similar to Freetown.

We pulled in to there. We took our berth, dropped anchor, but the watches still had to be kept for plane or submarine minelaying. The watch was on deck, where you could smoke if you wanted to.

We left Lock Ewe two days after, with a costal convoy, in which we were the biggest of fourteen ships. We were making our way to Newcastle, where we were to unload. We got there at two in the morning. We were towed by tug upstream to South Shields, where we docked. It was very bright there. They had arc lamps going nearly all the time, but if any Jerry planes came over, they would be put out.

We worked through the night to strip the hatches, and finished at 8 a.m. Then we had breakfast, before cleaning all the ropes, etc, till the decks were cleared by dinner time. Then we showered and dressed in our glad rags, drew some channel money, and went into town.

The dockers were on straight away to unload us, in case Jerry came over. They wanted the ship empty, ready to go back out as soon as possible.

We went into town and we had a few drinks (I had one gin and bitter lemon). I remember we bought some old age pensioners a drink – they thought the world of us. We stayed till throwing-out time (3 p.m.) then we went for tea in a cafe then back to the ship.

We were quitting the ship for leave. It was 18 February, and we hoped to catch the train to South Wales, if we were paid off in time (which we were). It was great going home; everyone was so proud of himself as we got on the train, more or less saying, 'We have just come back from Africa.' We arrived in Cardiff at 7.15 a.m. after stopping off at Crewe. We left the other boys, saying we would all meet in the Kardomah Cafe on the following Monday.

Home for the Brave

It was Friday the nineteenth, and we had to report back on 4 March, so we had just over two weeks' leave. We were all for going back to sea. No one complained. The reason, I suppose, was we had had an uneventful trip. I arrived home unexpectedly, for telegrams were used only by the Government in effect. So there was no way I could have let my parents know that I was back home.

By the time I got in the house, Dad had gone to work. He worked just across the road in the railway sidings as a checker. Although he was in poor health, he still tried to get to work. When I got in the house, Mam made a fuss of me. The girls, my sisters, had gone to work, other than June, who was still in school.

I sat down and I had some toast, two thick slices which I toasted in front of the fire on a fork, and a cup of tea which Mam made, just how I liked it. I gave her the present I had brought from Africa, and I put the girls' presents up in their bed, with their names on them. After having a bath, I put some decent clothes on, then took a walk over to see Dad. I walked into his office. When he saw me he got really excited. We talked for a while, then I left and went back home.

I visited my grandparents, who all lived in Chancery Lane, one set each end, and they made a right fuss of me. By the time I finished with my grandparents it was time for tea. I was sitting down when the girls walked in, for they all near enough came in at the same time. When they saw me they were really excited. Whether it was that I was home, or they were looking for their presents, I wasn't sure. 'No presents this trip,' I said, 'we were never in a place where there were shops. We were in isolated places.'

After tea the girls went to wash and change, and they started to scream, for they found their presents. They came running back down-stairs and started to hug me. I loved my sisters; I think they felt the same.

My father said, 'We will go for a drink after.' But in the evening we had an air raid warning. Although we could hear them, they dropped no bombs, well, not on Cardiff. We went for that drink at 9 p.m. so at least we could have an hour in the pub.

I looked for my mates the next day, which was Saturday. All five of us went to the pictures, as we used to do before I went away, followed by sausage and chips in a cafe in Caroline Street. We were on our way home by nine. Just as we came out of the cafe, the warnings went, but again there were no bombs. We got home, and we all went into our houses, and the all-clear went about 10 p.m. We started to play cards, for we used to do that always on the weekends, when we all had money.

We played till midnight. The boys went home. My mother and father were still up, so we were talking till about 2 a.m. My father never asked me to stop going to sea, for he knew that would be pointless, so we talked about the war, and things in general. I was falling asleep.

I stayed in bed till 11 a.m. Sundays – nobody other than Mam got up early – so I was falling back into the same routine as before I went to sea. When I got up it was very cold outside, but in the kitchen there was a lovely coke and coal fire, and it was warm. The Sunday papers had been delivered, so I sat and read them in the warmth, till dinner time, which was always around 1 p.m.

My mates came around for cards. There was nothing else to do. There were no pubs open, no cinemas, just nothing. This is what we always did, before I went to sea, my mates all being around the same age as me, though I was looked on as the leader.

I lit the fire in the middle room. By the time they came around the room was nice and warm. The next time we played on Sunday it would be someone else's turn to invite us to his house; that was our system.

Monday morning Timmy came down the house. He was down just as I got up, and I could hear Mam asking him if I was like this at sea. Whether I was or not, Timmy would say, 'No.' I came down and greeted him. 'What's the matter, can't you sleep?' I said.

In his sheepish way he replied, 'I didn't know what time we were to meet the boys.'

I got dressed after breakfast and we both left about eleven thirty. We walked into town and went straight to the Kardomah in Queen Street where the other boys already were. We joined them, and then we walked into Woolworth's, where we had dinner. Then we went into a pub and stayed there till just after three, for that was the closing time.

As we said our goodbyes, we agreed to see each other the same time on the following Monday, 2 March. Timmy and I went west, the other two boys went to Roath. I walked Timmy to his house. He insisted that I went in, which I did. I chatted to his mother. She was asking questions all the time about Timmy: was he doing all right? 'Yes,' I said. I could see Timmy was getting embarrassed, so I said, 'I must go now.'

'You must stay,' she said. Really, I didn't want to, but in the end I stayed.

After tea, we went into the front room, the parlour, where he had a record player. Before he went to sea he had collected all the latest records, so I stayed there till about 11 p.m. During the evening his brother and sister came in. He was the oldest, but they were like Timmy, very reserved. His father came in and we had a good talk, but unfortunately he was not like my father: he drank only on the weekend.

The rest of the leave was similar to what I have related. We had warnings but no bombs, which I was delighted with. If we had had bombs that would have started my father off again about staying home. All of us boys had decided to try to stick together on the next ship, so we met down in a cafe in James Street, then went to the shipping office after we had had a cup of tea. We all went to the clerk together. There were plenty of ships, so we were lucky; we stayed together.

All four of us went together to the shipping line's office, where we had to have a medical first. We all passed. We were then asked if we had been to sea before. We all stuck our chests out and said 'yes' in unison. The clerk looked over the top of his glasses. 'What ship were you on?' We all said 'SS *Broadhaven*'. He had one of those wry smiles, as if to say, 'bigheads'.

After we had filled in forms the clerk gave us a form for the next of kin, which we also filled out. Then he signed over, before giving us dock passes and telling us to report to the commercial docks, Newport. He gave us a pass to go there by train. We had to report Thursday at 7 a.m.

We came out of the office and made our way back to the cafe we had been in a few hours earlier. We were delighted that we were all going to be together. Then Terry Stevens said, 'Did you see the look on that clerk's face when we said we had been to sea before? It shook him when we all said the *Broadhaven*.' We were all excited, trying to find out or work out where we might be going. We would probably discover that when sailing down the Channel.

Dave Allan suggested that we all went to the station and found out what time the train left for Newport. So we all left and caught the trolley bus to the city centre. We walked around to the station and enquired what time the train went. The ticket office lady told us that the one we wanted left Cardiff at 6 a.m. That would give us time to get across to the commercial dock.

We all arranged to meet at the station by 5.45 a.m., but, before we went our ways, we decided to have a drink together. So we trooped into the Royal Hotel. We got in there at 1 p.m. and left at 3 p.m. This time Timmy stayed with me.

Mam put him up a meal the same as me. We then stayed in the house. My other mates came in around 6.30 p.m. so we played cards. Before they came, Timmy said, 'I wonder where we are going? I've got a funny feeling.'

'Don't be daft,' I said.

'No, John, I mean it,' he said.

'Too late now,' I said, 'you have signed on.'

'I know,' he said, 'but don't leave me, John, will you?'

'I will try not to but, as you now know, you can be one end of the ship, and I the other end.'

We played till ten thirty, then the boys said they were going. Timmy stayed about ten minutes after. I said, 'Don't worry, we stayed together last time. We will be all right.'

'That's what I like about you, you are confident,' he said.

I saw him to the door. After he had said goodnight to my mother (Dad was in his usual place) he added, 'Can I see you tomorrow?'

'Certainly, if you want to.'

'I'll be around about ten.'

'OK,' I said, 'see you.'

True to his word, Timmy was around at 10 a.m. My mother said, 'He is still in bed, go and wake the lazy devil up.' Timmy came and shook me. 'Come on, you lazy devil,' he said. I got up, and went and had a wash, then dressed.

'Don't you wear pyjamas in bed?'

'What for?' I replied.

'I do,' he said.

'Well, I don't. I like to feel free. Also, when at sea, you sleep in your clothes. So when I am home I sleep in my birthday suit.' Timmy thought that was awful. 'Don't worry about it,' I said. We went downstairs and I made some toast in front of the fire. I asked Timmy if we wanted any, but he declined, saying he had had breakfast. We went into town and did some shopping for when we went back to sea. We decided we would buy things that suited the two of us, for that would save money for other things.

We then went into the cinema. It was a good film, so we decided to see part of it again. We came out about 7 p.m., then made our way home.

Timmy said, 'Come and have tea with us.'

I said, 'Your mother will not want to be messed about getting tea. Also, you know if I came in she would fuss, just like my mother with you.'

But I went in, I said, 'Please don't bother about tea for me.'

However, Timmy said, 'I have meals in his house!' So she fried some of her rations, which really concerned me, for she was putting herself short just to feed me. I stayed after tea till about eleven thirty, talking to his father and mother. They were very nice people, I really liked them.

Timmy at one time went to the bathroom. His father said, 'John, you know, my boy thinks the world of you. Look after him for me, for he looks up to you, although you are a bit young look after him, and yourself.'

When I was going the sirens went. I said, 'I'd better be off. I'll call around in the morning.'

He said, 'About 10 a.m.?'

'All right,' I said as I was going, for the guns were opening up, and I think they were dropping bombs down the docks area. I moved a bit sharpish, and was home in a couple of minutes.

We had no bombs around our way, so we went to bed at 1 a.m. When the all-clear went I was sound asleep. The next thing I remember was Timmy shaking me. 'Come on,' he said, 'it is nearly eleven.'

I eventually got out of bed, and went into the bathroom as I was. When I came back in, Timmy said, 'Aren't you frightened that someone will see you?'

'Not really, for I know they are all out other than Mam, and I can hear her downstairs.'

I got dressed and had my toast, which I really like. I said to Timmy, 'Have some.'

'No, thanks,' he said, but I toasted some for him and gave him a nice cup of tea. I could see he was enjoying it. We went down the local snooker hall till about 4 p.m. Then we both went to our own homes, for we would have to be up early in the morning.

'Don't leave it late in the morning,' I said to Timmy before we departed.

'Listen to him,' he said, 'I can get up early anytime!' With that we went our separate ways.

My father said, 'Coming out for a drink before you go back?'

'All right,' I said, for I had only been with him once, so I didn't want to let him down. So we had tea and another chat, then went out.

To Russia

I was up early in the morning. The whole family was up as well, including my father, for he always liked to stay in bed till the last minute. I must have taken after him. I left the house at 5.30 a.m., having arranged to meet Timmy about 5.40, which would give us twenty minutes to the station, which was only just down the road.

My mother wanted to come down to the station, but I wouldn't hear of it. The girls also wanted to come. 'I am saying my goodbyes here,' I said. I could see Mam was filling up, as was my dad. The girls then started to cry. I said, 'I won't bring you any more presents if you keep on.' So I took my leave of the family. Even I was filling up with tears. I was in the end glad to go.

I met Timmy on the corner. I could see that he had been crying. His eyes were red. I said, 'I had the same problems with my family.' I had my kitbag that my uncle had given me that week. It was an army bag, with his name on it; I thought at least I should have my name on it.

I also had a small case with all my washing kit in, besides other things like underwear. Timmy had the same. You would have thought we were twins or brothers. We had on the same clothes near enough as well. We were talking on our way to the station, more or less to get the tears out of our eyes. In other words, we were trying to put a brave face on.

We met the other boys. There were other men outside or on the station platform. It looked as if they were going to catch the same train as us. When the train came in, they all got on it. There must have been about twenty chaps there.

None got in the compartment that we were in. The train itself looked empty, apart from the lot that got on with us. It took only about twenty minutes to get to Newport, then we all got out and started to walk to the docks. We had to show the pass that had been given to us when we signed on in the shipping office.

The policeman on the gate directed us to the commercial dock where we were to pick up the ship the *Motown*, our ship. After about ten minutes we arrived at the ship. She was a large boat, well decked, about 9,000 tons.

We all went up the gangplank. At the top were two chaps. One was the bosun, and the other was the donkeyman: the bosun in charge of the deckhands, the donkeyman in charge of the firemen and trimmers, and the boilers.

I was in the lead of us four boys with Timmy, Terry and Dave. As we got to the top of the gangway, the bosun would ask your name, then check his list, then direct you to your cabin, in our case in the fo'c's'le point. As I was going through the companionway to the cabin, Timmy was just behind me. When we went into the cabin I bagged the bottom bed, Timmy above, just as on the last ship. Steve and Terry did the same. They were very good pals – in fact we were all close. I could not have wished for better pals to be with under any circumstances. We sat on the bench by the table, and waited.

After about twenty minutes the bosun came in. He introduced himself as Bert Thomas. 'You may call me Bert,' he said. 'I hope that you don't call me any other name. You do your work, and we will get on great with one another. Now, tell me your names, the ones that everyone calls you.' We did so. He asked us if we had been to sea before. We all said 'yes', with our chest out another five inches. 'What ship?'

Steve, being the eldest, said, 'We all were on the SS *Broadhaven*. We all stuck together.'

'That's all right, boys,' Bert said, do your work, we will get on great. One thing I am going to tell you is that, if anyone on the ship tries to interfere with you, you will come to me or the first mate. Is that understood?' We all said yes.

I was still the youngest on the ship, Timmy next, then David, with Steve being the eldest at seventeen. The cabin boys were all around seventeen, although Darren was sixteen. We never bothered with surnames, just Christian names.

The bosun called all the deckhands on deck – that included us as well as the ABs. He paired two ABs to one deck boy. The ABs were all British, which was good, for sometimes on the other ship we had had a job to understand the sailors when they were talking to us.

I was with Ted and Mike. They were between twenty and thirty in age and they looked good chaps. In port our position would be on the fo'c's'le point. We all dispersed and began throwing canvas sheets over tanks and armoured cars. I thought we are going to one of three places: Middle East, Far East or Russia.

I thought, with my luck it will be Russia. By the end of the day, when we were having tea, we all had the same notion in our head: Russia. We had not been told, but we had been told that we would be sailing on the Saturday evening tide.

The bosun told us if we got our work done by Friday evening that we could go home till Saturday 1 p.m. We had a lot of deliveries by lorry: foodstuff, ice and a lot of quinine, with other bottles. The sailors told us to get cracking unloading the lorries. They would carry on tying down. So we and the cabin boys threw ourselves into it, and were finished by Friday dinner.

We helped the sailors on deck after dinner, and were finished at 3 p.m. when we were told that we could go home if we wanted. All us boys, including the cabin and galley boys, washed or showered, which we had to do on deck. I chose to wash and wait till I got home; Timmy would do the same. We arrived home just after 6 p.m. much to the surprise of my family. My father was quick to invite me round the pub, for I had money. It was Friday night, so we would have had his money, but he chose to spend mine! We left at closing time. I said my goodbyes to his mates, and went home.

When I left Timmy on the Friday, I told him I would see him at midday. That would give us plenty of time to get back to the ship. All us boys met outside the station ready for the train to Newport. I had to repeat my performance with my family. I said, 'See when I see you,' and was gone – no looking back.

We all arrived at the ship with plenty of time to spare. The bosun met us and thanked us for being back and on time. 'Change your clothes, and be on deck in thirty minutes' time,' he said. We all sat around smoking till he called us, then we all stayed together and tidied the decks. We had early tea, then the boat was ready for sea. The tugs took us to the locks, where the pilot took over to see us out. Once we were on our way, we had to throw the ashes overboard, which took about three hours.

After that we were put into watches starting on the hour of eight. It was the same system as the *Broadhaven*. As the anchor was being weighed, we had to spray it down, Ted and myself. Mike was in the chain locker. The chute actually run through our cabin, and it makes a right old row – we could hear it on the point, so it must have been deafening if you were in the cabin.

David was on first watch at eight till twelve, with Terry Thorn, an AB. Timmy was on twelve to four with Stan and Trevor. I was on four to eight in the morning, with Ted and Mike. Terry was on deck for a week.

After doing two hours on the bridge on the starboard or port side, according to the weather, you would be relieved to have a smoke and a cocoa, for about ten minutes. Then the man on the wheel would be relieved to go on deck as stand-by while his mate took the wheel, so you have a break.

As we passed Cardiff a little lump came into my throat. We were picking up speed, having found out that we were going to Russia (God help us). There were long faces, for we were dreading this place. To confirm that we were going there, they issued us with long fur coats, thick fur boots, and balaclavas. We had been issued with our foodstuff: bread, jam, butter, tin of milk, cocoa, and tea. These were for snacks after you came off watches. We were to have quinine every day. We could draw 200 or more cigarettes if we were heavy smokers, and tobacco for the pipe smokers. The next week we were to have a tot of rum.

We had now settled into a routine. I was getting on very well with my two ABs. They were very helpful, they liked a joke, and Ted was a scream. He looked after me like a brother. Mike, too, was great. In the night we would play lotto for cigarettes for a couple of hours.

When I went to bed I did was I always did when at sea: left all my clothes on. But I had to get up, for it was really warm in the cabin. This was something I had never experienced on the other ships. It was like a central heating.

In the morning I found out how we had so much heat in the cabins. There were heating pipes from the engine room. Well, I thought, that is good, at least we will not freeze to death. We had a good evening playing lotto. I never won, but it broke the night up. Also I saw for the first time the sailors and firemen mixing. Whether this never happened on the other ship because they were Maltese on deck, and the firemen were British, I don't know. But here they were all British.

I asked Timmy how his two sailors were. 'Great,' he said, so we were all happy.

When on watch our job was to keep our eyes open for the enemy. We were not yet in convoy, but when we joined, it would be important to keep watching the commodore. This was stressed to us. We were shown the flags, and told whatever officer was on watch, whatever flag he told us, we were to put up. The most common flag was the answering pennant.

We pulled into Liverpool Basin at 11.30 a.m. We were to stay there till the next day. A few other ships joined us. During our stay a small whaler came to us, and we had to winch a couple of boxes on board. It was in the evening, on Monday the seventeenth. Just after tea, I was going for a shower, so I asked Timmy (who was off watch) to come with me to the showers, which were in the well of the fo'c's'le on the main deck: showers one side (port), toilets the other. I wanted company my own age. It is wise to have someone with you, just in case. Timmy said, 'Yes, I need a shower,' so we both went into the shower hut.

We were talking away when the door opened. We didn't hear it open, but when it did we both felt the draught, for it was cold. The donkey-man came in, with just a pair of shorts on. He dropped them. While he was doing this, I looked at Timmy and he at me. He was talking to us, but we didn't want to know it. We were full of soap. He just settled himself right in the middle of me and Timmy, rubbing himself against Timmy. I grabbed Timmy by the hand and wrapped the towel around me. Timmy did likewise and bolted out of the hut.

I run straight into the sailor's quarters. Ted was sitting down at the table, drinking tea. He looked up, knew something was wrong, and jumped to his feet. Three or four others did the same.

'What's the trouble?' Ted said, grabbing hold of me, still covered in soap, as was Timmy.

I said, 'The chap in the showers came in, while we were in there, me and Timmy.'

Ted said, 'Who?'

'I don't know, I think he is with the firemen.'

Two of them dived out to the showers. As they did, the donkeyman was coming out, with his shorts on, towel in hand. 'Have you just come out of there?' he was asked.

'Yes,' he said.

'You are not to go in there while the boys are in there, that is an unwritten rule,' Mike said, grabbing him. 'If you ever molest these boys, that's where you will be going.' He pointed to the water. 'Don't ever go near the showers while they are in there, you dirty bastard,' Mike said.

By now we had gone back to our own cabin. A couple of the sailors came in and one said, 'That won't happen again. If he ever touches you, or any of you other boys, just let us know.'

It wasn't to rest there, the bosun, Bert, came into our cabin, asking, 'Who were the boys that were in the showers?'

I had to say I was one, Timmy said he was the other.

'Did the donkeyman touch either of you?' He came straight out with it.

'Well, he didn't touch us as with his hands,' I said, 'he just walked in between Timmy and me, more or less rubbing against Timmy.'

The bosun turned and went back out. I thought that was the end of it. After about fifteen minutes the bosun returned and said, 'Follow me, you two,' pointing to Timmy and me. We got off the bunk, for that's where Timmy and I were sitting. The other two boys, Terry and David, were sitting on the bench at the table, for we only had the one bench.

We followed the bosun to the bridge, where we went into the officer's ward room. The chief engineer was sitting at the table with the captain. Also present were the first mate and the donkeyman. 'Sit down,' the captain said to Timmy and me. The bosun stood just behind us, with everyone else sitting on the opposite side to us.

'I want the truth,' the captain said to Timmy and me, after he had established who we were. I repeated exactly the same account, and swore on the Bible it was the truth. Timmy did the same. They asked the donkeyman if he wished to ask us any questions. He declined – he just held his head in shame.

We were then asked to leave, Timmy, myself and the bosun. We went on the deck by No. 2 hatch. 'What will they do?' Timmy asked.

'Kick him off the ship, if he is guilty. Now get along to your cabin,' the bosun said.

On the way to the cabin, the bosun said, 'We will be having lifeboat drill at 7.30 p.m. It will be dark then, so tell your mates. When the bell rings you are to make your way to the boat stations, where you will all be told what boat you are on.'

At 8 p.m. the bell rang and there was a mad rush to the boat deck. We were all standing around when the second mate started to read names off a sheet of paper on a clipboard. Luckily Timmy and I were together, with our ABs, in the one boat, with Terry and David in the other boat.

After the drill my name was shouted out by the second engineer as we were all making our way to the cabins. I turned around and the officer came up to me and said, 'Remember me?'

'No,' I said, staring at him.

'Remember the *Tri-Mark*?'

'Yes, I certainly do.'

'Well, I was on it, one of the bunch – we really have to thank you.'

'That's all right,' I said.

'No, I mean it,' the officer said. 'I will never forget what you did. Come with me.'

I followed him to the wardroom where all the officers had made their way from the boat stations.

'Gentlemen, may I introduce you to John? I don't know his other name.' All the officers were now looking at one another, wondering why this officer should bring a young boy to the wardroom. I had only left it about an hour ago. 'This is the *Tri-Mark* hero I told you about, on the last voyage.'

They all started to make a fuss of me. The captain said, 'I haven't had chance to look at your papers. How old are you?' I told him. 'You have had an active start to your life,' he said. 'Incidentally, the donkeyman has left the ship, that's all there is to it.'

'Thank you,' I said, then I left the room. I got back to my mates. I told them about the donkeyman. They were delighted he had gone. In order that we would not have any more trouble with him, it was the best thing to do. I went into the sailors and told them the same about the donkeyman. They seemed very relieved now that it was all over.

In the morning we all washed the decks with the hose and the boys with brushes. Then we tidied the ropes till break. Then we all went to be trained to use the machine guns.

We had six naval sailors and three army on board. They were all in the aft sleeping quarters. Above their quarters on a platform was a 4.5 gun, which four of the sailors would man. Two other sailors would be on continuous watch on the guns behind the bridge, the six alternating all the time.

After the morning breaks we were split up on the four gun platforms. I was with my own two sailors as all the other boys were. The idea was that we would bring the ammunition to the machine guns, with my two

ABs manning one platform. The other boys would do the same, only on the platforms on the aft part of the bridge. The Royal Navy would operate those guns, but the boys would supply them with ammunition. The other sailors would bring the shells up from the magazine.

We were not allowed to fire them. The guns were Vickers double-barrelled and double-barrel Hotchkiss. We were shown how to use them in an emergency, but we were not to use them unless told. We stayed at it till dinner time, being shown how to free gun jams, how to reload, everything we needed to know.

After dinner we were to get ready to move. But just before we finished dinner, the bosun came around to the sailors and boys gave them each a thick pair of seaman's stockings to go into the boot. We were all ready now to move out. I was with Ted and Mike on the fo'c's'le point, ready for winching the anchor. Ted was down in the chain locker. The wind started to blow up a bit. I was engrossed in what I was doing, when someone – I believe it was Stan Payne with whom Terry worked – shouted that the barrage balloon was going down. It was really soft. The only thing was to get it down or cut the wire. I heard one of the ABs say that, with it blowing around like it was, it could break the mast on the aft deck.

We were the only ones busy (washing and taking the anchor up), other than the watch that was now back on duty. The rest of the seamen, with the Royal Naval chaps in support, were all by the mast discussing what to do. The first mate came on the scene, and told the bosun to cut the wire. He sent for some wire cutters. 'Everyone clear the deck!' the mate shouted, just as the wire cutters came. He took the cutters, then cut the wire. I could hear the ping as it went through the tackles and was away, into the clouds.

Barrage balloons were used on the ships for coastal work, for that's where you were likely to encounter enemy planes. Well, we had not got one now. I just hoped that it would not be embarrassing for us.

Mike was on the winch, me on the hose, and Ted down in the locker. It was nearly time for tea, so Ted came up. We sat on the hatch, all three of us, Ted said that the donkeyman had indeed been taken off the ship, and they were hoping to get a new chap, but it was cutting things fine. Ted said that was the best thing the captain could do, getting him off the boat.

Then he asked me about the second engineer's comments about me:

was it true what happened on the *Tri-Mark*? Yes, I said, it was true. Mike said, 'You have seen a bit of life for your age. How old are you?'

'I was fifteen last October,' I said.

He said, 'Well, you have already had your share. What made you want to go to sea at your age?'

'I wanted adventure,' I said.

'You have certainly had it,' Ted said.

We were on watch at midnight so after tea, which was at four, I decided to have a few hours' kip. Before I had a lie down I had a swill. David said to me, 'We are pulling into Loch Ewe. We will be there tomorrow night. We are picking up some more ships –' we already had four with us – 'then we are to pick up some more, then go to Iceland.'

It was five thirty before I got on the bunk, and I just dropped off. Next thing I knew the AB on the watch before us gave me a shake. 'Right-o, Johno,' he said. I got up, went and made a cocoa, then went back into the cabin. I had ten minutes before I went on the bridge. I smoked a fag and went on duty.

This was the worst watch of the three, the second mate's watch. He was all right. They didn't talk much to us. They all said near enough the same thing: keep your eyes open. Then they usually went to the other side from where we were standing. We were in the open alongside the machine guns.

There was no excitement during the night. I came off straight on to the bunk and was away. The sequence of times with the watches changed, so now I was back on at 8 a.m. till midday. It was very quiet. I noticed for the first time that we were the biggest of the four ships. We were stacked high with deck cargo, tanks and lorries. They were covered with tarpaulins and were well lashed down.

We had one little bit of excitement in the morning. Terry, who was on days for a week, was told by his mate, Stan, to put the water on for the hose to wash the decks. When you are on a week of days, that is your first job in the mornings – to wash the decks down. Well, Terry went to turn the water on with a key similar to a big ratchet. As he was turning the key, his hand slipped and hit the key off the lug holding the ratchet that turns the water off and on. The key clattered all the way down into the engine room. The engineer of the watch started to scream at Terry, not really knowing who it was. He ran up and, when he saw it was a boy, he went berserk.

It was really lucky that the key didn't fall into the engines, for then there would have been hell to pay, especially if it had damaged the engines. The engineer told Stan and Trevor, in no uncertain manner, that the boy should not have been allowed to operate the key. Even if it didn't do any damage, it could have hit someone on the head, which might have killed them. It upset Terry a lot, for he was a reserved type of boy, a very nice boy, who would do anything for you, always keen to please.

We pulled in to Loch Ewe. It is a very large basin with a big boom defence but, inside the basin, there was no village or town, only a couple of huts for the forces and merchant navy. The watches were kept. I was on watch with my two mates, so someone else had to run the anchor out till tea time, and that was when we pulled in. They kept the watches going but they could walk the decks, instead of being stationary on the bridge.

We were there till tea time the next day. The deck sailors saw to the anchor. As we went through the boom, we were joined by about six escorts. There were eleven merchant ships. Now we were going to Iceland, Hval Fjord, where we were to pick up the rest of the convoy. It was to take us three days to get there. We had no incidents, the weather was lovely, with no wind. It was very peaceful; everybody was relaxed.

It was still very cold, but not cold enough for us to put the very warm fur coats on, nor anything else that was given to us for warmth. We would need them as we got nearer to Russia.

Not on watch, we were all just tidying the ship up. The sailors were touching up the superstructure with paint. We did the cleaning up, chipping the rails and certain parts where we could reach without being off the deck. Although it is a tedious job, it had to be done. We were all working together, having a laugh and telling stories.

We spent three days in the fjord, either waiting for the escorts or waiting for the ships that were coming from America. We were ready to move out at 6 p.m. 28 March 1943. I was the first on watch. Terry had finished his week of days. Timmy was now on deck for the week. The next week I would be on deck. I started watch on deck, then went to the bridge to finish the watch when we began to move off.

It was dark for that far north it gets dark very early. I couldn't see how many ships were in the convoy, or how many escorts. We were second in line on the outside of the square, Iceland side. By the time I came off watch we were well under way. I could just see the ship on the starboard side of us, and just about make sight of the ship in front and directly behind us.

It was a beautiful night. The stars and the moon were clouded over, but there was no wind and we had all been looking forward to this type of weather, for it would help us against the U-boats – that's why it was a beautiful night.

I was asleep in my bunk when the alarm went. Eight Heinkel HE-115 seaplanes came over the convoy. I rushed out to my place on action station. Although my two ABs were off duty, the other ABs took to the machine guns. I ran straight aft to the magazines and collected two drums of bullets for the starboard side of the for'ard part of the bridge. I was not allowed on the bridge, only in emergency. My place would be in the shelter of the first bridge deck, where I would be able to answer the call for more ammo when needed.

As I have explained, we were furthest away from the attack this time. They came in as near to the water as possible, which served them a couple of ways: first, when they came in that low, the guns on the ships would often hit other ships in the convoy. Sometimes they did damage or even killed our own men; second, they would come in waves of four in a line, releasing their torpedoes all at the same time. They were near enough guaranteed to hit one, perhaps two ships. This method was very effective.

This time, however, they missed. We were all jubilant. Also we shot one down. The pilot managed to scramble out. Everyone could see it in the convoy. No one bothered to pick him up. I really felt for him, for he was meeting death in the face.

The next day we had the same again, but this time we lost an ammo ship. It went up in a ball of flame – pretty to watch, but the poor blighters on her never had a chance. Perhaps it was for the best for, if you ended up in the water, your life expectancy would be five minutes, you had no chance in the water, for it was about twenty degrees below. It was cold even on the decks, and we had only just started.

We were all on edge, but we had nothing more. The rest of the day we had nothing; it was the same the next day and the day after.

As we were moving north it was getting colder, and it was light early in the morning and dark early in the evening. It was at 4.35 a.m. that we were attacked again by nine HE-115 torpedoes. They missed, but one of our boats was hit by a torpedo from a U–boat about 8 a.m. We had lost two ships out of a convoy of thirty-four ships, with six destroyers and four corvettes. We had two trawlers to pick up survivors. They were stationed each side of the convoy at the rear. They were not in line; they were available to go to the first ship sunk, but also they were heavily armed. They did good work against subs.

We had also in the convoy three cam ships. They were general cargo ships, but had a ramp on the bows from which Hurricane fighters could be catapulted in an emergency, though after flight they would have to be ditched in the sea.

I didn't know if it was my imagination or what, but Timmy had gone into a shell. He hardly talked. I knew that we were on different watches, but we did see one another for a short while at least. He seemed to have gone into a world of his own. I had a chance on a day we had no alert. It was very peaceful, the weather brilliant, but you could feel it getting colder and colder as went go along. On watch I was using the cold-weather gear that they gave us. It was quite warm with it on.

I collared Timmy when I came off watch. He was now working in the shelter of the cabins, at that moment in the rope locker, so I went to have a word with him. Luckily he was on his own.

'Hello, John,' he said.

'Hello, Tim,' I said straight away. 'Anything wrong?'

'No,' he said.'

'Well, why have you been avoiding me?'

'I haven't,' Timmy said.

'You have,' I said. 'Come on, tell me, is there anything wrong?'

At that moment, Tommy, his AB, came in. 'Hello, John,' he said. 'What's the matter with your mate?'

'I don't know,' I said, 'that's really why I am here.'

Tommy said, 'Have a talk to him, John.' And with that he went back out.

'Come on, I know there is something wrong. Even your mates have seen it.'

'I'm scared,' he said.

'So am I,' I said.

'John, don't leave me, will you?'

I said, 'If you keep avoiding me and your mates, they will all leave you. I am scared stiff, so are all the others – you are not the only one, we are all scared.'

When I left Timmy to go back to our cabin, I fancied he looked a bit better. I thought, *I'd better keep an eye on him.* I went in to the cabins. I saw Ted and Mike talking, so I asked if I could come in. 'Come on in,' Mike said, so I sat down with them, and I said to the two of them: 'About Timmy. He is scared stiff.'

'Yes, I gathered that,' Mike said. 'His mates Tommy and Tom are concerned about him. They were talking to us last night about it.'

'If anything happens,' Ted said, 'without jeopardising your own life, just keep an eye on him. If we are about we will help all we can, as will his own mates.' Ted added, 'He is scared, ain't he?'

'Yes, so am I,' I said as I left.

The rest of the day was undisturbed. It was very warm in the cabins, but when you came out you didn't half feel the cold. Although the sun was out, it was bitter. We had peace that night and the next day. Towards the evening a Condor could be seen flying at the other end of the convoy, but we had no attack. Ted came to me and said, 'John, be on your toes. We will cop it tomorrow.'

We played lotto in the sailor's cabin, us the boys, the firemen and the sailors, for cigarettes. After the play finished I ended up with fifteen cigarettes, each containing hardly any tobacco.

The alarm woke me on the morning 6 April at 5.30 a.m. They were coming at us now. All over the convoy there were Condors, HE-115 float planes and HE-111 bombers. Every ship was shooting. The float planes had released their torpedoes and had not had a hit, but the other planes attacking were more successful.

All our guns were manned. I had my winter clothes on, but I soon took them off. I couldn't run with them on. I just left the boots on. I took two drums of bullets each time – they were awkward besides being heavy. I sheltered in the well of the lower bridge deck I was safe from strafing there. When they shouted 'Ammunition!' I would run up the stairs to the top of the bridge and put them within hands' reach to the users of the guns. I would then immediately go and get another two drums. Each drum had about 100 rounds on each belt.

By standing on the side I could see all the action, but ducked when they were coming in on us. We were getting a lot of fire directed at us from the other ships. Ted, who was on the gun, shouted to me to stay under cover. I know whenever Ted turned the guns on a ship that was running parallel with us, for every time a plane came between them and us, the other ship's gunners would still fire and most of the times they were hitting us.

I heard Ted say, 'I have had enough of this,' and he turned the guns on the other ship. After he got that off his chest he was a little bit better. A plane came in right across the convoy and dropped a bomb alongside No. 1 hatch. The tarpaulin sheets were ripped right off, and the tanks that were tied on the hatch were blown into the gunnel of the ship. They were thrown in between the gunnel and the hatches.

No. 2 hatch was nearly as bad, with some of the vehicles thrown forward into the same position, jammed in between hatch and gunnel.

The ship started to list, and I heard the captain, just above me, talking to the deck officers. He was saying we would have to try to ditch the vehicles over the side. He sent for the army sergeant who was in charge of the naval and army personnel manning the guns.

'How many men have you spare?' he asked the sergeant when he reported. 'Take some of the men that are on the big gun on the aft deck, and put them on the machine guns, for I want the ABs to try to clear the decks.' The army sergeant left the bridge and went and got some of the naval gunners. They followed him to the bridge, where they replaced the sailors. It was at this time one of the Jerries came in and started to strafe us. But the captain could now see how dangerous it was going to be for the men to man the windlass.

The ship was at a fifteen degree angle and the captain was a very anxious man. He didn't know what damage had been done to the cargo in the hold. I was told to stay and carry the ammo for the naval gunners.

All eight ABs, the bosun, the carpenter and No. 1 mate went down to the windlass. The mate said, 'Go and get some wire slings,' and two of the sailors went aft to the rope locker and brought some thick examples.

It was not going to be easy, for they could not get the slings around the equipment, and the slings were very cold on their hands. It was a really good job the decks were not frozen over, but it was still bad.

They got the windlass on numbers 1 and 3 hatches going. No. 2 seemed to be a lot easier than No. 1 to sling, for you could get the slings around them, but it was very hard work, and a few of the men snagged their hands on the wire, which was barbed.

'Take cover!' The captain was on lookout. A plane came firing and dropped its bombs which vibrated the ship again, resulting in the deck cargo moving once more. This time one of the boys was injured. His leg was trapped, and everyone was working frantically to release him. Then we had another plane in to strafe us. This time he caught one of the naval gunners, killing him outright. It was on the opposite side to where I was. I was on the starboard side. The ship was listing on the starboard side, where all the tanks had rolled over.

They took two hours to release the sailor, Stan Payne. By then he was really in a bad way. They put him on a board, stripped him down, and used the windlass to lift him over to the companionway to the bridge, where he was taken into the wardroom. No. 2 hatch had now started to throw the lorries over the side, with two half-tracks. When No. 1 started to lift the tank up, it rose a bit, but the windlass was not heavy enough to lift them up any height.

The top tank was level with the gunnel (the side of the ship used in the well deck) and they managed to topple her. In the meantime the ship had straightened up a bit. It was still, with a list of about eight degrees, which improved the smile on the captain's face.

The ABs managed to get another tank over. The planes had gone back, but it was early in the day yet. The captain stopped the sailors trying to get any more vehicles over the side, calling them to have a break and breakfast. 'That's all right,' he said. So the sailors dropped the windlass masts, tied them down, then had their breakfast. The naval gunners stayed till the sailors had had their meal. Then they were relieved by the watch that was due on. Someone had to take Stan's place, for the time being.

As yet we had had no U-boats that day. The planes came back at 11 a.m., and the sky seemed full of them. I got about six cans of ammo, ready for use where I stood taking cover. The first mate suggested that we do this, for he didn't want us caught out in the open, especially if the guns had run out of ammunition.

I noticed the decks were clouding over with frost. It was now bitterly cold, and the sailors had to keep the frost from jamming the guns. I and the other boys were all in winter gear.

'Here they come!' I heard a voice say. But for the moment we were lucky, for we were the other side of the convoy from the attack. We were nearing the ice field, according to Terry Thorn. We could be shielded from the subs there, but not the planes.

They were attacking us now. Perhaps it was because they could now see the tanks on our ship, or they were just picking any ship, but I thought it was because we had that slight list – plus the visibility of the tanks.

Planes of all descriptions were now attacking the convoy. There are quite a few Junkers 88, one of which we shot down. It was coming at us beam on, and the starboard gunners, on both parts of the bridge, for'ard and aft, had a good view. But it was very dangerous for they were firing at us with their machine guns. I will say this: the sailors, both the naval and the ABs, kept to the guns and it paid off. The plane just about got over the top of us, and then she came down between us and an escort ship. There was some cheering – this was our first kill.

I could not follow the final outcome of the plane, as we were being attacked by another plane. Well, not one – they all seemed to want us. There was plenty of fire power, not just from us but from the other ships, but there seemed so many of them. I was thinking they were bound to hit us and sink us. I was not running to get more ammo. I saw Timmy waiting for his drums to come out of the magazine. 'Warm work, Tim, isn't it?' I said.

'Yes,' he said, and was gone. I had mine and I was gone, for we dare not let the guns dry up of ammo.

The Germans kept at us for over an hour. We had another near miss. A plane came at us at sea level, and she turned into us from the run down the corridor. As she did, she let go her torpedo and started to climb straight away. I think this threw the aim. I heard the mate telling the captain it missed us, having gone in front of our bows a good few feet. A big sigh of relief went up. As he started to go above us, I swear to this day I saw the pilot.

He passed right above us, and what a din. I was really frightened now. I thought this was the end. I was on my own; that made it all the worse, there was nobody there to comfort me. With the row of the plane on top of me, I cowered down in the corner of the structure of the bridge. I covered my head. I was not going to move and I hoped for the best. I was simply petrified. How that plane never got shot down, I don't know. All the men about the bridge said the same.

I was still shaking when I ran to get another couple of drums. It seemed now that everything had quietened down. We could see some of the planes in the distance going home.

We were still in the throes of winter, and the nights were very dark and long. Ted, who was standing by me, said, 'Over there are the ice caps,' pointing to starboard, 'and to port over there is an island, Jan Mayen. We are keeping as near to the ice as we possibly can, for that will protect us from the subs.'

We had no more plane attacks, for it would be dark by the time they could come back. But it was just getting dark around 4 p.m. when there was a loud explosion. One of the ships at the back of the convoy had been torpedoed. We couldn't see anything, only the flash when the torpedo hit the ship. I thought, *The poor sods.*

We had all now reverted to our watches. I was on at 8 p.m. Ted said, 'John, you had better try to get some sleep.' It was dangerous on the decks. They were shimmering like frozen stars at Christmas, beautiful if you could look out through the window and admire it, but I am afraid it wasn't like that. We had to work and keep watch, and try not to let the machinery freeze.

We had tea, hot curry, and believe me it was hot. That did warm us up. I really enjoyed it. The hardest part now was to try to get to your cabin holding your food. We all did it, for we had to. After tea I lay on the bunk. The next thing I knew was being woken up. I was on watch relieving Timmy. Going on the bridge, by God it was cold! I couldn't see anything out on the water. There would be no messages with the lamp, so it was a pointless exercise.

Nothing happened during the night, but on the morning of the eighth, at 8 a.m. A torpedo found one of the tanks alongside us. She lingered for a while before another torpedo sent her down, but luckily the crew had taken to the boats. No one had got wet, and they were picked up about an hour after. We had passed Bear Island, which is right on the edge of the ice fields. At 10 a.m. we lost another ship. I don't know what nationality it was. At the same time, we could see the Condor in the sky at the back of the convoy.

We were now too far out for the planes, so we had to concentrate on the subs. Although a Condor was following, they were not always used as attacking planes. They were mostly used for reconnaissance, for they were easy prey for our gunners, being slow.

We lost two ships inside a space of an hour. One of those hit was full of oil. Someone said she had linseed oil in her. She went down in a flash. I don't know if any of the crew escaped – I hope so. We had run into bad weather. There was a lot of fog about, and the water was boiling, with the wind starting to come up, which with the fog was a blessing. With the weather being bad we felt safe from attack. We had a full day of the fog and wind, so we could all catch up on our sleep, but the fog was icy cold and it was wetting us. Then we left the comfort of the ice fields.

We were in an area where we could be attacked by planes, but very far out, so the possibility seemed remote. I heard the sailors saying so; also I was hoping so.

The weather was still bad, when we began the run-in to Matochkin Straits, which is in Arctic Russia. Not inhabited, it was a shelter for the ships from subs. The planes couldn't get at us in there, it was too far away, so we had the chance to regroup and be off.

The idea of sheltering in the straits seemed good, for we could have a break there. The captain was not thinking like me, however. We had been there only thirty-six hours before we started to move out, to make the dash for Archangel.

We kept very close to land. Although we had plenty of escorts, out formation was different here from out in the deep. We were strung out into two lines; we were on the inside, the last but one. When, well in front of us, one of the ships copped it, by the time we passed she was well down at the bows. There was no sign of life, so I take it the crew must have been picked up. A day's ride from Archangel the weather moderated. It was still getting dark around 4 p.m., so with a bit of luck we would be there on the twelfth.

We were supposed to be going to Murmansk, but that had been bombed out of existence. Also it was still frozen over, so there was no way we could get there. So it was Archangel, up the Kola Isthmus to the Gulf of Archangel. We would be pretty safe from subs once we hit the isthmus, but under constant plane attacks.

We got to Archangel without further loss. Altogether we had lost about seven ships and all the planes that were on the cam ships. I never even saw them launched. I didn't know at the time they had been in the air, but we were discussing it when we dropped anchor in the middle of the Gulf of Archangel.

The ice on the deck and superstructure was really thick, and to move across the ice was now a hard job. But we had to keep the guns free, and the davits for the lifeboats, and things that we were using or needed all the time. We would play steam hoses on the parts to unfreeze them from the ice, then we would try to wrap them up.

We were told not to start taking the sheets off, for it would be a while before they would start unloading us. When they had unloaded us, we were to move up the estuary to load with timber. Unlike our time in, say, Freetown, here we could not do much on the ship when we were in port. So we stayed out of the cold messing about with little painting jobs, in the cabins and engine rooms, with the firemen.

When we dropped anchor, we all went to our cabins. The mate came around and told us that we were to stand our watches, more or less to watch for planes, only in the day. The nights were pretty free of attacks, so we could catch up on our sleep. The officers were very good, they were really easy going. Where we were it got dark around 5 p.m., but it don't stop the Russian dockers; they used arc lamps.

A Real Bleak Hole

The dockers were on the go all the time. They had to be, for there were many ships waiting to be unloaded. We knew that we had to wait our turn. We could not go ashore, for there was nothing there. The Russians didn't want us ashore; they didn't seem to care for anyone other than themselves.

Our first day there was one of the bleakest of my life that far. Timmy and I were sitting at the table. Terry and David went to the galley to bring some cocoa back for us. We had borrowed an enamel jug from the firemen, which saved a lot of trouble. When we finished we would wash it and take it straight back; then we could borrow it again.

Timmy said, 'John, if I ever get back to Cardiff, that's the end. I am packing it in.'

'Well, I'll be honest with you,' I said, 'that's how I feel. This trip has done me.'

'Same here,' Timmy said. 'I don't want to be separated from you,' he added.

I said, 'Let's talk about it when we sign off the ship. We both might be in a different mind then.' At that point Terry came in. David had gone to the toilet. We were all sat on the only bench to the table. David, when he came in, would have to sit on his bunk with Terry.

We talked about the trip, about the naval rating and Stan who had been crushed, and the gunner on the dual purpose guns. We talked about the trip out to India, the climate, how we all enjoyed it, but the rumbling now was this trip. Terry and David came up with the same thoughts Timmy and I had been discussing. They said the same as us; Terry said, 'Dai and I are packing it in when we get home.'

I said, 'Timmy and I were talking about that before you came in.'

'If there was a guarantee that we would go somewhere else, I would stick it,' Terry said, 'but there is no way that I am doing this trip again.' And we all said, 'Nor me.'

We were woken in the morning just before breakfast. About six Heinkel 115 seaplanes, and the same number of Heinkel 111 bombers, were over us. We took our positions for the ammo carrying. All hell was breaking loose around us. For the moment they were not attacking us. They were having a go at the wharf where the big cranes were. We saw two planes go down, but we were not in a position to look all over the place, for we are told to stay under cover all the time except when we were ferrying the ammo.

This attack lasted one hour. They sank one boat going into the quay wall to be tied up for unloading – she had tanks on her. One ship was torpedoed out in the channel. It was still very cold. I think that was more upsetting to us than the bombing and the torpedoing.

We had breakfast as soon as we could see them going away. Three were shot down altogether. After breakfast we carried on messing around, not really working, just keeping out of the biting wind that had started blowing. About midday they came over again. No ships were lost but some were damaged, including ours. We had a near miss from a bomber. It blew the 4.5 gun off its platform, leaving it tilting at a grotesque angle.

We had the rest of the day off after Jerry had gone; no more planes came that day. The sailors began helping the Royal Navy boys to try to put the gun back. We were told to stay in the cabins unless we had another raid.

They got the gun back. They managed it with the windlass – only just, though. They repainted the platform and bolted the gun back down. The gun itself had hardly any damage.

We were averaging two raids a day, except when the weather was bad, when we would have none, so we were praying for bad weather all the time. We had competitions with draughts, lotto and ludo, playing all the time in between the raids. I was knocked out early in ludo. In lotto I was holding my own, and in draughts I was doing well, but I was well beaten towards the quarter finals.

It was now April the second, and we were at last going in for unloading. The tugs were in attendance. We had just started when the planes came again. Now they were really having a go at us. Our gunfire was good, and we had every ship helping out, as well as the shore ack-ack.

As soon as the planes showed up, the tugs let go and beat it – I don't know where, they just vanished. We were left high and dry. We could not use our engines for they were idle, undergoing minor repairs.

The fire from the ships and shore was awesome. Out of six planes that came in, three were shot down. The others dropped their bombs really near to us, but then they chickened out, so we were spared again. However, the bombs threw some splinters in the air, which were very dangerous.

The tugs came back and simply pushed us in to the docks, where we tied up. Immediately the top tanks and lorries on the deck, some of which had been blown into the well of the decks and the gunnel, were wired up and lifted off. Believe it or not, you could feel the ship righting itself.

Stan had died from his injuries. There was no place in Archangel resembling a hospital. They could have taken him further away, but whatever journey he would have undertaken would have killed him. Alan Taylor, one of the ABs trying to free the tanks at sea, caught his hand in the barbs of the wire that was being used to lift the tanks. The hand was now frostbitten, and he was in terrible pain, so he left the ship to go into hospital – but nobody knew where.

The captain asked the English shipping authorities that were stationed there for emergency assistance. We had an emergency – we needed two sailors. We had them within two days. In the two days after we were pushed to the quay wall we had eleven more attacks. A lot of the bombs were near misses, though dangerous because of shell splinters. We found it very awkward being tied up to the wall, for the cranes unloading the ships were in the way when you were firing at planes. You had to try to catch them when came from the behind the cranes. The Jerries were losing a lot of planes, but they were still sinking ships.

The curtains of fire going up made it almost unbelievable that any plane could survive. One plane came down right by us, alongside the quay wall. The pilot must have thought that to survive he would need to get as near the land as possible. Three of the crew got on to the wings of the plane, thinking that someone would rescue them. Instead some Russian soldiers came and shot them. They were only about twelve feet away. I was really disgusted – the airmen had no chance.

The burial of Stan was to be held one afternoon. He was to be buried in the British Cemetery, given by the Russians to the British. We had now opened all hatches. It had been a terrible job. We had to wear thick, woolly mittens. Although they kept our hands warm, they were no good to work in. The dockers were very slow, more so after a raid; the all-clear would go, but you would not see them for about another hour. Then we would have another raid. The day we were to bury our mate, the covers were off. The dockers took longer getting the tanks off the deck, for they had lodged themselves in against the hatch and gunnel.

Not all of us went to the funeral, though all the ABs and us deck boys, with the first and second mates and the captain attended. It was arranged very poorly. The cemetery was not all that far from the ship. They put the coffin on a horse and cart, which I was disgusted with. The cart had not been cleaned. It was a real mess. The man in charge of the horse and cart looked as if he wanted a bath, not a wash. He was dirty, and his clothes were in tatters.

We followed the coffin to the grave, where there was an English priest waiting for us. As the service started, we had another raid, but we managed to bury him. This to me was important, but I thought the Russians should have shown a little more respect, considering that we were risking our lives to get the ships to Russia for them.

The dockers had started in the holes, where they would work twenty-four hours a day, raids permitting. The day after the funeral of Stan, we were attacked again. This time we lost a fireman. He was just coming out of the engine room, when a Heinkel 111 came in low strafing the plane. It happened so fast, we didn't even know that there was an air raid. The fireman was in a terrible mess, for the bullets that hit him were heavy bullets, and he copped three.

There was nothing but gloom and doom on the boat now. After the farce of the funeral the previous day, now we had lost the fireman, whose name was Les O'Brien. There were mumblings, for we had not been given any comfort by the Russians. To work is a hardship, but to be bombed is very demanding.

Timmy had gone back in his shell. He didn't say much, considering he was supposed to be my mate. The other two, Terry and David, were together all the time, but I was one minute with Timmy, the next on my own. It seemed that every minute he was not doing anything, he wanted to lie on his bunk and sleep, leaving me prostrate on my own bunk. Although the other boys were great, I would have liked Tim's company now and then.

By 12 April we were unloaded. Thank goodness – let's get home, I thought, I am very frustrated. I went now more into the seamen's cabin, talking to my two mates, Ted and Mike. I think if it wasn't for them, I would have gone potty. They talked sensibly, and liked a laugh and a joke. That's my temperament.

We were moving to the timber wharf the next day. We had to wait for a tug. When we got there, we were to load straight away from the railway trucks on to the ship, for they could not stockpile the wood on the wharf, otherwise Jerry would set fire to it.

Although the timber was all loose, they left their slings on it and hauled it straight into the hold. Then they pulled their slings out. It ended up in a right mess. There was no time to straighten it. We had to do our best. After two days we were loaded. We had been working during the nights and there was a biting wind. It must have been well below freezing – they were saying about twenty degrees below.

We put the covers on in the morning and had a break. The mate told us to go and get warm. We had planes over, but for some reason they never tried to bomb us. We had to arrange the fireman's funeral. We were not going, only the captain, the chief engineer and the firemen. The mate asked if we wanted to go, but told us he would prefer us to batten down and sheet the hatches.

We did not really have a full load. They had just filled the holes up, in some sort of fashion, and that was it. We sheeted over the hatches. I noticed it was getting lighter and lighter by the day. We finished on the hatches at 6.30 p.m., then had tea immediately. I had a wash and went to bed. I was really tired. I must have led by example, for they all followed, and I bet in our cabin everyone was asleep inside an hour from tea.

We were ready to sail, and to be truthful I could not get home quickly enough, but we were told we now had to wait for a convoy and escorts. We were informed that it should be about a week – another week in this rat hole, I thought. I was getting very despondent now, what with Timmy acting the way he was. The other boys were quite good. We talked a lot, but the thought of another week was the straw that broke the camel's back. We were not doing much during the day. We were asked to carry on with the watches which at least occupied our minds, but we were in sheltered places because of the wind.

Ted came to me while I was on watch, for he and Mike had to do their watch like me. The firemen were rumbling over the funeral arrangements of their mate the previous day. They were going to lodge a complaint to the British Consul, which body we had been seeing quite often. They were also complaining about the hospitality shown by the

Russians to us. They were saying that we should have had our own NAAFI-type entertainment place where we could have a drink and relax. Their gripe was that we were stuck on the boat all the time.

'What's the matter?' said Ted. 'John, you have gone into a shell like your mate. Come on, tell us, what is it?'

'I am all right, but I think Tim is ill. He don't talk to anyone. He goes to bed every opportunity he has, not saying a word to anyone.'

Ted said, 'Where is he now?'

'In bed, as usual,' I said.

'Let's go and wake him up and have a talk to him,' Ted said, getting up and moving to the door with me just behind him.

Going into the boy's cabin, Ted looked at Timmy and turned to the other two boys, Terry and David. Timmy was in deep sleep. Ted asked Terry and David to go into the seamen's cabin. He took them in. All the seamen there looked at the boys. Ted said, 'Let the boys stay in here for a while, for I want to have a word with Tim.'

Tommy Jackson, Timmy's AB, said, 'Anything wrong?'

'No, not really,' said Ted, and with that turned and walked back into the cabin where Timmy was, with me just behind him. He said to me, 'Wake him up, John.'

I gave him a shake. Timmy woke up, and looked at Ted and myself, before asking what the matter was. Ted said, 'Come down here,' pointing to the bench. Timmy got up and jumped down. He had all his clothes on for, as I said before, that is the practice when at sea, or when there is danger about.

Ted came out directly, asking what was troubling him.

'Nothing,' he said.

'Come on, Tim,' I said, 'you don't talk to anyone. You are not eating. All you want to do is sleep.'

Ted said, 'Tell me or I will go to the captain and tell him you are bad.'

'I'm all right,' Tim said, with his voice raised a little. He looked at me and said, 'Why don't you leave me alone?' With that he jumped back into his bunk, turned away and then started to cry.

I went straight to him. 'Tim,' I said, 'what's the matter?'

'I hate it here,' he said.

'I do,' I said. 'I have been bad, I cannot stand the cold. Timmy,' I said, 'don't let me down. I have no one, only you, and you have turned your back on me. I feel that I want to cry. I went and saw Ted. I told him I was under the weather. I hate it here, like you, but don't turn your back on me, Tim.'

Ted went back to his cabin where Terry and David were sitting talking to a couple of the ABs. Ted asked them straight how they felt.

'We both hate it here because of the cold,' said David.

'Well, no one likes it,' said Terry Thorn. 'We are all of the same opinion, what with the way the Russians treat us, it being so cold all the time, the planes all the time, and stuck in the cabins with nowhere to go.'

'How is the youngster next door?' Trevor Jenkins asked.

'I don't know,' said Ted. 'I think mentally he is in a bad way. I don't know if I should tell the captain, or forget it, for if they take him off the ship, that will surely kill him. I don't know what to do.'

They all started to suggest different things, but the answer lay with Timmy. Ted went into the boys' cabin. Only Timmy and I were still there, the others were with the seamen. Ted nodded for me to come out of the cabin. I said, 'Timmy, come on. I'll go and make a cup of cocoa.' I picked the cups up and followed Ted out.

'I will have to see the captain or the mate,' he told me.

'No, Ted, please,' I said. 'That will certainly destroy him, for if they take him off the ship, they will put him in hospital here. You never know what might happen to him.' I said, 'Let me have a word with him first.'

'All right, but I don't think that will do him any good.'

So with that I asked the firemen for a loan of their jug. I went and made the cocoa for the four of us boys.

It was very dangerous walking the decks, for they were full of ice, but I managed to get to the galley and back with the cocoa. I poured Timmy's and mine and took the jug to Terry and David in the seamen's cabin. I asked them to hang on a minute, while I tried to talk to Timmy.

I took the cocoa into our cabin. Timmy was still sobbing. 'Timmy,' I said, 'come on down here. I have made some cocoa for you.' He turned to look to see if I was telling the truth, then he came down. I gave him the cocoa and I said straight away, 'Now look. I went to Ted because I was feeling poorly. What with the cold and you not talking to me, I was really feeling in the dumps, so I went and asked Ted what to do. He saw that I wasn't all right and said, "What's the matter, John?" and his next words were, "You are getting like your mate – come on, snap out of it."

'I asked him to come and cheer you up, but I am going to tell you straight: he wants to tell the captain. If the captain finds out that you are depressed, he will have you put ashore, and God knows when you will get home, for the hospitals here are not like at home.

'What say we start all over again? Let's be together more. People looked on the pair of us and made remarks that we were two mates, always together. But to get back to that you have got to change your ways.'

I went and told Terry and David that we had finished talking, and when they went back into our cabin, I said to Ted, 'Thanks, Ted, I actually feel a lot better myself now. When I came in to you, I was shattered and depressed, but after the little chat, I feel better. So does Timmy.'

We were told that we had to move down to the anchorage ready for the making of the convoy. I was on deck weighing the anchor. Ted was in the anchor locker; Mike and I were on the forecastle, sheltering from the cold. I asked Mike why we had no deck cargo. He said we were taking just enough timber to avoid being too light. If we were empty – what they call 'lightship' – we would be at the mercy of the weather. So timber was ballast.

We remained at the timber wharf for three days after the loading. There was whispering going on that we would be on our way by 22 April, a Thursday. We moved to our allotted position, then dropped anchor. I looked around the anchorage. There must have been about 100 ships, of all shapes and sizes, but a lot of them were still loaded, so they were not in the convoy being made up.

We stayed in the anchorage for another five days. We left on Saturday 24 April. Looking at Timmy you could see the change in him now that we were moving. We were as thick as thieves again. He would come and talk, we had our meals together, and we were always in one another's company.

I was a lot happier now for, when Timmy felt bad, it made me feel bad. Ted told me, three days after he had spoken to us, how much better I was looking, and Timmy. 'I am really glad for you,' he said. As I walked away from Ted (I should have said, when I skated away from Ted) I thought how I really liked him; to me he was great. He was the type of chap you would like around you when things started to get rough.

Bridge watches had resumed. It was David's turn on deck. I was following Timmy. I said to him, 'Timmy, if anything happens, try and make for me, and I will to you.'

The first night was calm. It was light longer in the days, about eighteen hours. The ice was thawing so we made a wider sweep to be as near the ice as possible. That way we would not have the Jerry planes so much, at least, until we started to come down from the ice fields. We expected to be free of air attacks for two thirds of the journey. It would take us seventeen days to get to Iceland.

But we would still have the U-boats to contend with from the start, as soon as we cleared the Kola Inlet. We were going to hug the land as we had done when we came in, but we had lost one ship even then. So we made for the Matochkin Straits, where we could reform to a proper convoy.

We lost one ship coming out of the Inlet. She had run aground, which was simple to do. I was not able to count the ships in the convoy, for we were strung out as far as the eye could see in two lines. The escort was seaward to us but even they were strung out. But we all arrived safe at Matochkin. As we were entering a thick fog came down. You could not see a thing. We were lucky to berth, and the lamp was working overtime trying to let ships know where they were.

We still had to stand our watches. When I came off watch, Timmy came up. 'John,' he said, 'when we were in Archangel, when you and Ted came to see me, I had made myself feel bad worrying about the home journey. It just played on my mind. I was really scared. It was wrong the way I treated you, but I am telling you the truth – I was frightened to come home. I was dreading it, but I do feel a lot better now, thank you, John.'

We arrived in Matochkin Strait on 26 April at 6 p.m. We stayed there till the twenty-eighth, then the fog broke up, and we were able to weigh anchor and move out at 5 p.m. just after tea.

We all came out, twenty-five ships with eight escort vessels, one armed trawler, three corvettes, two sloops and two destroyers. We all formed up. This time we were right in front, next to the commodore. Five lines, five deep, with the escorts all around us, the convoy actually looked very formidable.

Although the ice field had melted down a few miles, they were still big. As we got nearer to the North Pole, it remained very cold. The decks were still dangerous to walk on. We had to keep the guns warmed up, as well as any engine parts that we might have to use. We had no deck cargo, which was a blessing; also, we were not out of the water, thanks to our timber cargo.

By the thirtieth and we had had no incident at all. Other than the ships running aground, we had not lost anybody. At 2.30 p.m. The wind started to blow up. Inside ten minutes we were in a gale. It was the worst weather I had experienced. It came over very dark. The ship was rolling all over the place. Everyone was stood to. The weather was too bad for the U-boats, so at least the captain could concentrate in keeping the ship afloat.

The ship now was rolling from port to starboard, with the gunnel touching the seas. Everyone on watch was taken off the bridge. It was only inside the wheelhouse that you would find anyone. It was pretty full with men. All the deck officers were there, with the captain, and the AB on the wheel. The second officer was giving the AB a hand.

Tea time came and went. We could not get to the galley. In any case the galley was swamped, with no fire going. I didn't know when we would have any hot food. It was now that we really needed it. But a lot of us had about half a loaf of bread, also butter and some jam.

The thing we all needed most was a nice cuppa. We all went in with the sailors, for we were all frightened. We were not the only ones. Even some of the sailors were scared. Being in the bow of the ship, we were tossed from bulkhead to bulkhead. This carried on all night. No one slept; no one wanted to, in any case.

I heard one of the sailors say, 'I hope the cargo don't take the ship down.' When it had been put into the hold, it was not put in tidily, and being loose timber it could end up against the bulkhead, which would take the ship over to a certain degree.

The best place for us to sit was on the bunks. We couldn't do that unless we were invited, however, and no one thought to do that. So we just sat on the benches.

After three days, the gales started to ease off at midday. By about four the wind had dropped right down. But tragedy was to greet us: there were only two of us from the convoy. We had been blown right off course. We all stood our watches, having been told to keep a very sharp eye open for the convoy or U-boats.

The wireless operator was sent for. He was told to use the lamp, and contact the other ship. This he did. The other ship asked what we were going to do. Captain Shields conferred with his officers, and they decided to move as close to the ice fields as possible, for at least they would be protected on the one side.

So the two boats moved near enough into the field. The captain said we would not use the lamp in the dark. He told the cook to get the fires going. We stopped in the field for the night. Although a strict watch was kept, we had no incident. In the morning, first light on the third, we started to move off again. We didn't drop anchor, just in case we had to move quickly; also we didn't want to be stationary in case we were frozen in. We just stopped and started all night. When light came the two ships used the lamps again and agreed on a course to take. We were the leader; they would be just behind.

On Our Own

We were really nervous now. If a U-boat found us we would have no chance; and if we survived the sinking of the ship, we would not last in the water, for it was bitterly cold. In a lifeboat, we would not expect to live more than a day; if we got wet into the lifeboat, we would not survive two hours.

Ted pulled me one side and told me to wrap up. 'Put plenty of clothes on, in case we are torpedoed,' he said. 'You had better tell your mates.' I told all three of them, and they all looked like roly polys. We stayed like this the day through, and the night the same thing, and the next day we carried on the same. It was Thursday, 4 May.

There was one good thing about this ship, the *Motown* – her speed could reach around twelve knots. The other ship could do near enough the same, which was good for us. With the speed pushed a little more, we had a chance to outrun a U-boat. The only way they could catch us with a torpedo was by waiting for us. To do that they would have to be very lucky.

We travelled throughout the day. You would never believe it, it was really tranquil. It was like being on a cruise. You could see the face of everyone on the ship was more radiant than a few days ago, when all had looked drawn and haggard.

We came through the night without any mishap. The next day, about 8 a.m., the change of watches had just taken place when the lookout, Terry, shouted, 'Ship on the starboard bow!' All the men who heard it rushed to have a look. The captain, from his night bunk, rushed to have a look, before one of the officers confirmed that it was an English man-o'-war.

I was looking over the side on the lower deck of the bridge when the second engineer came alongside. 'Hello, John,' he said, 'Good morning,' said I. This was the first time I had seen him since the incident with the donkeyman. 'How do you like this weather?' he said. I told him this would probably be my last trip.

'Why?' he said.

'I just cannot stand this weather. Also, when we came out, it was terrifying, I know someone has got to do it, but I thought the Russians were not helpful at all. There was nowhere to go, just stuck on the ship. It was cold all the time. Even now, in May, it is cold. I would not want to take that chance signing on a new ship, to be on the Russian convoys – no way.'

'I am sorry to hear that. When I saw you in the wardroom, I thought this boy has guts to go through what he has been through, and here he is on another ship.'

As we were talking, the corvette (for that's what it was) was stealing closer to us all the time. 'You have definitely made your mind up then. How old are you?'

'Fifteen and a half,' I said.

'Well, you have been through a lot for that age. I am glad this ship has found us,' said the second engineer.

'So am I.'

By now the ship was really close to us, and the captain shouted through the megaphone, 'Glad to see you. You are the last of the lost sheep.' The corvette took position on the outside of us.

I found out the name of the other ship: SS *Ty Borge*. I believe she was a Norwegian ship. The corvette positioned herself between the two of us, about 400 yards away. It made all of us feel better, at least for a while. We were passing Jan Mayen Island, still hugging the ice. We were coming down for the run into Iceland. Jan Mayen had been on the edge of the ice field when we going, but now she was well away from the ice. That showed it was melting, and the sea was getting warmer. We still wore our winter clothes, for it was not warm enough for them to be discarded. We took orders from the corvette, so we waited for her to tell us when to come down.

When we did come down from the old marker from the ice field, we would be within range of the Jerry planes, as well as the U-boats. Touch wood, we had not had any scares from submarines. Everything was quiet. We were covered in fog again; no wind. It was very hard to keep position, although there were only three of us. It was still dangerous. Late into Saturday, it was still light, and we were making good ground.

Just before it got dark, the fog cleared. About thirty minutes later the corvette dropped a couple of depth charges. We didn't know if there were any subs around, or whether it was to frighten them off, but now we were open to both sides of the ship, we had to be on our mettle.

Sunday at 7.45 a.m. the first of the planes came in at us, six of them, Heinkel 111s. They came in from both sides at the same time, three each side. Although the escort vessel was on one side, it was in a position to change course, where and when necessary.

They planes came just above the waves. The starboard gunners shot one down, and on the port side the corvette shot one down, just after he had released his torpedo. We took one of the torpedoes in No. 1 hole. Although it hit us it made a hell of a bump, but never exploded. The other planes got rid of their torpedoes and went. The chief engineer came and had a look over the side but saw nothing, so we did not know if it had penetrated the bulkhead or not. As the engineer said as he walked away, 'We will soon know.'

The corvette picked up two Germans from the plane they had shot down. The other airman must have got killed. As we were watching this, some of the firemen were saying, 'Leave them there.' I myself thought that was wrong; they are doing their duty, so they are entitled to live. Just before dinner they came back, six again. They used the same tactics, three each side. They came in and dropped their torpedoes, and all six missed. No plane was shot down. 'They will have one more go,' I heard the mate say, for now I had taken my place on the bridge as lookout.

'Here they come!' shouted someone. I had come off watch, the time being nearer to five than four. This time they were Junkers 88 bombers. They were high, but not all that high. There were eight of them. They all peeled off and made a run-in, but they all missed.

We saw smoke coming from one of them as they were going back to base. Whether it got there, none of us knew. We knew that we would not have any more attacks from planes that night. During the night the corvette was running rings around the two ships, dropping depth charges here and there, but we had no attack.

Monday morning they attacked again, with nine planes this time, all Heinkel 111 torpedo planes. They came in using the same tactics, only four abreast this time – the remaining plane was observing and never joined in. The corvette was on the port side, still circling around us, and the four planes coming in on the starboard were no higher than about four feet from the water, the sea being really calm.

They were quite a way off and they looked like something from an epic war film, but this was for real. As they came in they were met with murderous fire from the two ships, and the corvette when she could get in position to fire at them, but she was doing well against the four on the port side.

We could see our hits registering. The planes decided to drop their torpedoes a long way from us, and break right and left of us. But one plane seemed to be touching the water, making straight for us. It had not released its torpedo and it was skimming in towards the bow of the ship.

The sailors on the guns swore that the pilot was dead before the plane buried itself in between No. 1 hole and the sleeping quarters of the crew. There was a terrific explosion. If I had been carrying ammo at the time, I would have been blown over the side, for the vacuum from the explosion was fierce, as it swept down the length of the ship.

I poked my head around the superstructure of the bridge, from where I was cowering. What met my eyes is really impossible to describe. All the gunnel was blown away, and there was a big hole in the side of No. 1 hole, half under the water and half on top. The ship started to list on the bows. Everyone thought she was going to sink.

I was now petrified and shaking. I was still on my own. I looked out to see if there were any more attacks, but could see the planes at a distance going back to base. I looked above me, and I could hear the captain calling the chief engineer to the bridge. When he came almost all the officers were escorting the captain to near enough where the hole was. They were all looking around and passing comments about the hole. I couldn't hear what they saying, but they were having a proper old chinwag. In the meantime the boat was still lowering itself in the water.

Now and again a plank of wood would float out – not much, just a piece now and again. The ship had steadied itself now, and stopped sinking, but the bow was well under the water, and there was no way any of us could get to the cabins to get any of our gear out. We could kiss that goodbye. I heard the captain say to the crowd of officers, 'We will wait and see what happens.'

The ship had stopped sinking, and I asked Ted what was happening – why had it stopped gong under? He seemed to think that the timber in the hold had surfaced to the top under the hatch covers, and that was helping to keep the ship afloat. By now the chief had asked the captain to drop the knots on the ship to about four or five.

The captain called the corvette over, and the captain shouted that he thought that we could make Iceland, as we had only two more nights and days to reach there. We would have to reduce speed. The corvette dropped back and told the other ship what was going on. We were now all crawling along.

We had our meals and we, the four boys, were told to bed in with the cabin boys, which we did. The rest of the crew that had their bunks in the fo'c's'le were told to bunk down in the wardroom.

We were staying afloat. The weather was kind to us, for it was very calm. All that we prayed for was that it would stay like this till we got to Iceland. Late in the afternoon we saw smoke on the horizon. It was another corvette coming to our aid. When she got to us, she took the one side, and our own corvette took the other side. We had no more plane attacks at all.

We had had no casualties during the last attacks, which was brilliant. Ted came up to me and said, 'There you are; it wasn't so bad, was it?'

I said, 'You can't talk me out of packing it in. I have made my mind up.'

I had not had much time to see or talk to the other boys the previous couple of days, for when we were attacked we were either running or taking shelter by our respective guns. We were still doing our watches, and sharing quarters with the cabin boys. Some mattresses had been put on the deck for us to sleep on. That was all right, but it was very cramped. We have only a couple of days to put up with it, so that was not too bad.

No one was allowed to go for'ard, in case of accidents, but looking from the bridge when on watch you could see that hole and the mess. I wondered how we had survived it. We had a very quiet night. We saw a plane just before it got dark, but it was one of ours, a Catalina.

We felt now we were safe, and an air of optimism was on all our faces. With the weather holding good, it was great. We were expecting to be in Iceland the following day, they said in the afternoon. I did not know what was going to happen then. I did not think we would be taking the ship to the UK, so it would be a lift to wherever the ship that took us had to go.

The subject remained: were we going back to sea? Everyone on the ship knew that the four deck boys were leaving the sea. Timmy was talking a bit more. I did not think I would like to have him for a mate any more. He was very moody, and he got me feeling as bad as him. I could never put up with him if he was going to be like that whenever it got tough. No, I thought, when I get home, I am going to think out my future, without being influenced. I am not going to say anything yet to Timmy for he will only sulk again, and I don't want to put up with that, just when the atmosphere is good.

Homeward Bound

We had sighted land. If ever there was land ahead that lifted our hearts, well, Iceland did. Whoever had said we would arrive in the afternoon was right, for we eventually pulled in at 3.15 p.m. We could not drop anchor, for we had no bow – also I don't think we had an anchor – so we were told to go over to the graveyard of ships.

We moved over to where there were seven ships, badly damaged, some with their cargo, some lightship. We were told to tie up against one of the ships. There was no name on the ship, for the plate that was holding the name had been blown off.

After we tied up we had our tea. Then we were told to get our kit ready (a silly statement, for we had none) and to be prepared to leave the ship around 7 p.m. It was quite light so we had no problems, and at seven, or near enough to it, the whaler came and picked us up. The officers stayed, together with the Royal Navy personnel, but the crew was taken ashore. In the whaler it took just over an hour.

We were taken to a YMCA-type building, where there were a lot of merchant navy crews biding their time, waiting for a boat to the UK. We were put into a dormitory where all the crew were together. We boys, all eight of us, stuck together, for now we had got to know the cabin boys they were a good bunch. When we were at sea we were bed-to-work, and we never really saw them – only the cabin boy, Darren Hicks, whom throughout the trip we would meet in the galley. He was great. He was from Cardiff, and we got talking a lot. He said he was packing the sea in. He had the same attitude as me – it was too cold. Although he was working in the galley in the warm, he didn't like it.

I told him I was thinking of finishing with the sea, 'the same problem as you,' I said. I was petrified by the attacks from the planes. Once, now and again, is not so bad, but three or more a day was a mental torment.

All of us boys went out the next day. We were given some money to spend, so I bought some clothes. Back home we would have to use our clothing coupons; here, nothing was on ration, so I kitted myself out. The clothes were very cheap. I wasn't the only one. Timmy asked me to go in the clothes shop with him. That's what gave me the idea of getting clothes.

We met the ABs in the town. They wanted us to have a drink with them. I wanted to, for I thought it was at least a good way to thank Mike and Ted for what they had done for us. We all went in the end. We had a good drink, me with my two gin and bitter lemons and the other boys drinking beer. We stayed there till 10 p.m., then we made our way back to our sleeping quarters, singing on the way. Then we had to shut up, for the other chaps were sleeping there.

We were there for four days, but I never went out again. I just stayed in, playing snooker and table tennis. All the other boys stayed in, for we had spent our money, and there was no way we could get any more. We were told to pack our kit and be ready to move out at nine in the morning. We were put on a cargo-cum-passenger ship. They were going to take half of us, but all the boys went.

We were put into two cabins, the boys four a cabin, where there were four bunks. We were quite comfortable there. The sailors, with the bosun, carpenter and cookie were split into the other cabins. The four cabin and galley boys were therefore alongside us, and we were getting on very well with them, since we had got to know them when we had had to bunk in with them. All of us were mixing in with one another.

Timmy and I were still together, having been more sociable over recent days. It seemed that he had got over his sulks and isolation, and was fitting in with all around him. We were just passengers on the boat, so we had plenty of time to talk or look around.

It was while I was with the sailors, talking to Mike and Ted, that an argument started in the sailor's cabin – nothing to do with Mike or Ted. It really got out of hand. Before we knew, Tommy Houlihan drew his knife and stabbed Trevor Jenkins. Tommy had gone berserk; we were about ten miles outside the harbour in Iceland (Reykjavik). There was no going back. Some of the sailors jumped to restrain Tommy; I jumped up to get out of the way! Ted also leapt up and stood between me and the sailors who were trying to hold Tommy. Ted dived in front to protect me, for Tommy was trying to lash out all the time. One other of the ABs got cut, a bad cut on the arm, before they overpowered him.

They disarmed Tommy and sat him on the bench at the table. I left then when it was safe to, while one of the sailors went for the first mate of the ship. I was soon back in our cabin where the rest of the boys were playing cards. I told them what had happened, and that Trevor Jenkins was badly knifed, lying on the deck. They wouldn't move him, in case they did more damage to Trevor.

Mr Mate came down to the cabins and went into the room where the sailors were. He saw the sailor who was on the floor with a blanket over him, and another under his head. He got down on his knees and looked at him. He told someone to get the steward, and tell him to bring his first aid bag with him.

Inside five minutes the companionway was full of people wanting to know what had happened. The captain was there as well, and he told the second mate to clear everyone out of the area. They took Trevor out, I think to the officers' wardroom. They took Tommy away, tying his arms behind his back and taking him somewhere in the bridge where he was locked in. They then untied his hands; he was only tied so that he could be moved.

Everyone was still talking about it for hours after. I stayed in my cabin with all the rest of the boys, playing cards well into the night. I had lost a few bob. We were like this for three days. We had no incidents with the Germans, so we were otherwise relaxed.

On Leave

We pulled into Birkenhead about 7 p.m. It was still light. In the morning we were all taken to an office. We were taken into a very large room, where we were paid off, presented with travel documents, our money and ration cards, and given leave. We were told to report back at a certain day to the pool office. We all got on the South Wales train, for all of us were from South Wales.

We never saw Trevor again, except from a distance when he was taken off by stretcher and put into an ambulance. We didn't know where they would have taken him, and heard no more about him.

We arrived in Cardiff at 6.30 a.m. Timmy and I walked down the road together, where I left him at the lights. He turned right, I carried on down the road. I would now be home inside five minutes easily. As Timmy and I parted, I said, 'I'll see you,' and that was it.

On the way to the house, I kept thinking about Timmy. Perhaps I had been a bit hard on him, but I felt that he had let me down when we had both needed one another's company, when he had chosen to go into his shell.

I knocked on the door. I was home. At one time I had never thought I would be there again, but there I was. Thelma answered the door. 'John!' she screamed, and threw herself around my neck. Ivy – the next one down, also on her way to work – ran to the door and tried to join in with Thelma, but there was no room for her. Anyway, I gave her a big hug when Thelma let go, as we were walking into the kitchen.

Dad was there with Mam. Mam grabbed hold of me and gave me a big kiss, and the old man grabbed me as if I were the long-lost son – perhaps I was. The girls went off to work.

I said, 'Where's June?'

'In bed,' mother said.

'I'll go and wake her up, I want to see the surprise on her face when she sees me.' I went upstairs into her bedroom and I shook her. 'June, come on!' she closed her eyes as if to go back to sleep.

Then the penny dropped. She jumped up, shouting, 'John!'

'All right, all right,' I said, 'come on, you will be late for school.'

'I'm not going,' she said.

'Oh yes, you are,' I said. 'I'll tell you what – you go to school, I will meet you at dinner time and take you to dinner. How's that?'

'All right,' she said, 'I'll go.'

Dad was just off to work. He worked across the road, so he left dead on time, and then Mam cooked me my favourite bacon and tomatoes, which I always loved to have with plenty of bread and butter.

I gave her my ration card and quite a few bob. I had the sad task of telling the girls I had brought no presents. They would be looking for them as soon as they came home, but this time I had to let them down… unless I went into town. Yes, that's what I will do, I thought: I will have dinner with June, and when she has gone back to school, I will meet Mam and we will go into town. I can buy them something which Mam can decide.

I met my little sister from school, took her to a restaurant, took her back to school, then met Mam in town and went shopping. I had to do it that way as Mam had the clothing coupons. We bought the three of the girls a present each, and that was it. We got home at 4 p.m. and I went and had a lie down.

I woke up. When I looked at the clock it was showing eight thirty. I was half asleep and thinking it was eight thirty in the evening, but it was the next day. So I got up not realising what day it was. I went and had a bath, and got dressed and went down. Mam said, 'What do you want for breakfast?'

'Breakfast?' I said.

'Yes,' she said, 'you were fast asleep so we left you there. You must have been very tired.'

'I was,' I said, and with that I poured a cup of tea out while Mam cooked the breakfast.

As I was eating breakfast I talked with Mam. She told me about the blitzes that Cardiff had had while I was away. It made me smile, the way she carried on about the bombing, as if I had been on Paradise Island. When Dad came in at tea time, he wanted me to go with him to the pub, more or less to show off with me. I said, 'I will see my mates first, then be back at eight.'

'All right, don't be late,' he said, 'for they close at 10 p.m.'

I called round my pals and I told them I was going with my father to the pub. 'You're too young,' Ivor said.

'My father's attitude is, if I can fight for my country, I can have a drink in the pubs.' I didn't know what they were kicking up a fuss for. I knew that I was only fifteen and a half, but I had grown since I joined the merchant navy. I didn't look my age. 'Well, any rate,' I said, 'I promised I would go with him. Why don't you come?'

'No, not yet,' they said.

They were staying in, so I met Dad as arranged. To the Duke of York we went. I knew some of his pals very well. They all started making a fuss, and before you knew it, it was time to go home. We left the pub around 10.30 p.m. and went home. Mam started creating about the old man taking me into a pub. I said, 'Mam!'

'You have done your share, stay home,' she said.

'I love the sea,' I told her, but I am going to be very careful signing on this time. I don't want to go back to Russia. If I can guarantee to get a ship to go anywhere other than Russia I will go.'

'What about your mate that lives around the corner?' asked Dad.

I said, 'We are not as close as we were.'

'Fair enough.' My father did not push for answers so I let it drop there. I told him about the system on the ship, about the two ABs that I had to work with, how good they were. I never mentioned about the donkeyman, but I told him how Ted and Mike looked after me.

We went to bed, and it was great to know I could have a good sleep, unless we had a warning.

The next day I got up around 11 a.m. and then I took a walk around to my grandparents. I visited both pairs. I got home for dinner, then went to the pictures, coming out at 7 p.m., for I stayed to see most of the second-time showing.

My sisters were in and were showing off their new skirts and blouses, for they all had the same. They were going out, but for the little one, who wanted to stay in. I went around to my pals. They never went out much in the week, only at the weekend, so there were two of them at Ticka's house. We played records – he was a fanatic over them – and were talking till 11 p.m. I left to come home, and as I got home the siren went. I stayed with Mam. Dad had just come in, and there was only June there.

Halfway through my leave, I went into town to the market with Mam, and I bumped into Ted, the AB. He was with his brother, who was about my age. I introduced him to my mother, and we talked away for about fifteen minutes. 'I'll see you on the fourth of June, down the shipping office,' said Ted. 'Be there about midday. All the ships will be gone then.'

'All right, I'll do that.'

He bade farewell to Mam. When we had walked away, she said, 'He is a nice fellow, isn't he?'

'Yes,' I said, 'he really looked after me, and I really like him.'

'What about your mate, who lives around the corner. He hasn't been around, has he? Have you seen him since you have been home?'

'No,' I said, 'we haven't had an argument, but I don't want to be bothered with him, so let's leave it like that, Mam.'

There was not much to do, with my mates in work all day. I would only see them in the evenings, and sometimes they would not go out for lack of money, although I always said, 'Come on, let's go to the snooker hall.' Sometimes they came, and I would pay for the tables, which wasn't much; other times they would stay in claiming tiredness. Really, this helped to make my mind up: now I was at the stage of wanting to go back.

My time came up, and I was glad. I went down to the shipping office at about 11.30 a.m. I didn't go in, I waited outside for Ted. I thought Mike might be with him, so I just hung about. Ted came with Mike, and I joined their company, and we all went into the office together.

'No ships, come tomorrow,' the clerk said, so out we came. Ted and Mike said they were going for a drink. I said I was going to the pictures, so I caught the bus into town and went to the Odeon. When I left I said to Mike and Ted, 'What time tomorrow?'

'Same time,' they said.

Nothing the next day. I did the same, only this time I went to the Empire. I met them the next day, Wednesday, the same time. There was a refrigerated boat that wanted ABs and a galley boy, so we dived in for it, for, as Ted said, a refrigerated boat means it is going out to America, or South American countries, or Australia. Anyway, wherever she was going would not be Russia, so we were all for that.

I signed on as a galley boy. I had never done anything like that before. I had my medical and passed. The three of us then went to the shipping company that was employing us, where we were told by the clerk that we would be going out the next week. The ship's name was MS *Topley*, about 12,000 tons. She was all refrigerated. The middle hatch was designated general cargo: this was a small hatch, for a small cargo. 'MS' meant that she was run on oil, which would be smoother for us.

We had all done the necessary paperwork, and were told to report on Friday at the Roath dock, Cardiff, 7 p.m., 8 June. I left the boys, for they were going for another drink. 'See you Friday,' they said.

'OK.' And with that I went home and told my mother. She was very upset. I said, 'Mam, I promise you this will be my last trip. When I come home, I will wrap it.' I told her that we would be sailing the following week. When, I did not know. They would tell us at the last minute, for security reasons.

MS Topley

On the Sunday we went round to Paddy's house and played cards. I left after the afternoon session. I stayed in with my family for the evening, for I had the feeling that we would be sailing the next day. I had already started my duties as a galley boy. It was all right. The cook was a character; we were getting on very well together. Also I liked cooking, particularly as there was always something to eat.

I left with all my kit. Mam insisted on coming down to the dock gates, to see me off. We caught the bus at the end of the road. This bus dropped off at the dock gates. It was a fair walk to the ship across the docks, and seemed more so when you were carrying your kit. I got to the ship and went straight to my cabin. They had put a cabin boy to share my cabin. I didn't mind, as he would be company. He was about the same age as me, and was shy. When I asked him where he came from he told me Stafford Road, top end of Grangetown. In other words he was just around the corner from where I lived.

He had put his kit on my bed. He asked, 'Is that your bunk?'

'Yes,' I said. 'You can have it if you like.'

'No,' he said, 'I will sleep on top.'

When we finished asking all the questions, I moved out to go to the galley. 'Where do I go?' he asked.

I said, 'Follow me,' and I took him to the steward, who was an Indian. I left him with the steward, and I heard the steward telling him his duties.

We sailed at 4 p.m. on the evening tide. It seemed very strange to me, being inside, instead of being on deck. I went outside to watch us going through the locks, then I had to clean the pots and pans. Cook was getting ready for the morning meals. The crew had already had their evening meals before we sailed, so really there was nothing to do, as regards to feeding the men that day. It was a question of getting ready for the next day.

Cook was showing me how to make this and that, and how to cook, which I was very interested in, so I was around him more than necessary. I was entitled to have a break in the afternoon but I wanted to learn how to cook, and stayed with him when he was making bread. I was seeing Ted and Mike more now than when I was working with them. They were two great guys and I really liked them. About 6 p.m. I would be finished in the galley. Terry, the new cabin boy in my cabin, finished at the same time, so we were talking quite a lot. He asked me how many trips I had done. I said this would my fourth.

It was his first. He was a little older than me. We talked for a very long time. I asked him if he had been away before. 'No,' he said, and I could see he was beginning to fill up, so I said, 'What made you come to sea?'

'I wanted adventure, but I never thought about leaving Mam and Dad and my brother, who is younger than me, twelve.'

'Now you have to put your family behind you, for the time being. I was like that when I first went to sea.'

'John, what made you go to sea?'

'I am like you; I wanted adventure, and I had a dead end job as a tea boy on the building site. I thought to myself, John, get out of here, this is no good, the rest of your life pick and shovel. So I finished there and then.

'I went home and said to Mam, "I've finished on the building site, I am going to sea." My parents never once refused me on anything. "If that's what you want, so be it," said Mam, "but I am telling you, John, I don't want you to go." And Dad said, "Don't go to sea, son, wait till you get called up. That will be bad enough." "Dad," I said, "I want away from the life as a navvy, and I would like to go to sea." "You have our blessing, but you must take care." '

Terry asked me to tell him the story of Russia, and my other trips. I said, 'Terry, there must be no way that you will go to Russia. It is terrible. The trip, the cold, the place... You don't go ashore there. Stay away from there.' I then shook him by declaring that this was my last trip. 'I promised my Mam and Dad, who really is not in good health, that this would be my last trip.' I told him of Timmy, whom I had thought at the time was a good friend. 'I fell out with him, for all he did was sulk, going, in Russia, and coming home. He made me feel bad, so we fell out and we drifted apart.'

I told him about Ted and Mike; they had looked after me all the time. I kept quiet about the donkeyman on the Russian trip.

114

I said to Terry, 'I have three sisters, and I love them. Do you smoke?' I asked. 'No,' he said. 'Nor I.' So, I thought, that was a good job. We carried on talking. I turned to him and warned him, 'If anyone tries to interfere with you, let me know.'

'I will,' he said. 'Will anybody try?'

'I don't know,' I said, 'but if they do, tell me.'

There were two other cabin boys, Liam and Ken. I said to Terry, 'We must get to know them. They are probably sitting in their cabin, thinking of home. We should all be together.' I said, 'Come on, let's go and have a chat with them.' So we went next door. They were both lying on their bed-bunks. 'Come on,' I said as I walked in, 'let's talk to one another. My name is John. This is Terry, another cabin boy. Come on, we don't want to be thinking of home.' This was their first trip, and they were both about sixteen. I said, 'Anything you want to know, come and see me.' I told them that this was my fourth trip, 'so I want to break the ice, and help you if I can.' It seemed that my life would be focused on the cabin boys and the bridge.

Really speaking, the steward is my boss. I found that I had more free time than when I was on deck. I determined to use it in learning to cook.

It was after eight and I decided to turn in earlier than usual, so I said to Terry, 'I am going to make a cup of cocoa, and turn in.' We were in the other boy's cabin, and I got up to come out. Terry said, 'I will do the same, as it has been a hectic day. We went to the galley where there was always a boiling kettle of water for the likes of anyone wanting to make tea or cocoa.

While I was in the galley Ted and Mike came in. My face immediately warmed to them. They started to talk. I introduced Terry, and we stayed in there for about forty minutes talking. They asked me how I was doing in the galley. 'All right,' I said. 'I like it – better than being in all the weather of creation.'

'Good,' they said, and we parted.

I had my cocoa and got into bed. I think Terry must have seen my clothing when I got into bed. He started to put pyjamas on. I said, 'What are you doing, putting those on? Terry, pull my blankets back off me.' He was shy. I said, 'Come on.' He did it very slowly. 'What do you see?' I said.

'You've got your trousers on.'

'Exactly,' I said. 'If you get torpedoed you won't have chance to take your pyjamas off. Sleep in your trousers, or nothing.' He got the message, and slept in his trousers.

Terry had led a very sheltered life. He kept asking questions all the time. I was very surprised that his parents let him go to sea. On our first night together, I told him, 'Any time the bell rings it means speed, and it's an emergency. Get to your boat station.'

He said, 'Will you be with me?'

'Yes,' I said, 'if we are working by one another when the bell rings, we will soon know what boat we are in, so we will try and be together.'

We went to sleep then. I looked at him with his head above the blankets. He looked so innocent.

I was woken in the middle of the night. Terry was crying. I got out of bed. I said, 'What's the matter?'

'I miss my mother,' he said.

'Come on, Terry,' I said, 'you are old enough now to be parted from your parents. Come on, don't let the boys next door hear you.'

'Will you stay with me?' he said.

'Sure I will,' I said. He grabbed my arm, and I could sense that he was frightened. 'Come on, Terry, get some sleep. You will feel better in the morning.'

I was up early in the morning, earlier than the cabin boys. I looked at Terry. He was fast asleep. As I was ready to move out, I woke him. 'How are you feeling?'

'All right,' he said.

'Now, concentrate on your job, and I will have breakfast with you, when it's time – that is usually around seven thirty.'

He looked fine now, talking about anything other than his home life. I went out and went to the galley. Wayne – that was the cook's name – was already in there working, getting all the meals ready. We had to do the officers' as well as the men's. We also had six Royal Navy chaps on board and three army chaps.

'How did you sleep?' Wayne asked.

'All right,' I said. 'Don't forget, I am used to it, but the galley is strange to me. I want to learn to cook.' At that moment they all started to come for their breakfasts.

The *Topley* was about five years old. She carried a 4.5 gun on the poop (the aft part of the ship) and four double-barrel machine guns, all

Hotchkiss. There was one double barrel on each corner of the bridge, just behind the stack (funnel) manned by the army and Royal Navy; the other two machine guns were on the front of the bridge manned by the ABs, who are shown how to use them by the naval chaps.

There were four engineers, three mates, the captain, two wireless operators and the steward. The cook and the three cabin boys and galley boy were all in tiny cabins in the section of the bridge. The cook was on his own, and the boys two to a cabin, which consisted of a collapsible table, one double bunk bed and a small wardrobe.

Six firemen and two trimmers were in a large cabin. The donkeyman was in a tiny cabin in front of the firemen's cabin, on the port side of the companionway. The bosun had a tiny cabin opposite the donkeyman's. The six ABs and four deck boys were in the fo'c's'le point, where the chain locker was underneath their cabin, with the chute running through their cabin. This was on the starboard side. The carpenter was in a tiny cabin by No. 3 hold, under the bridge. The crew comprised thirty-eight altogether, that without the army and naval personnel.

I found it very strange working in the galley, as I had been on deck for the previous three trips. Although I saw my two AB friends, I missed the immediate contact of working with them. I always tried to see them to talk to, especially when they came in the galley for hot water, or for the key to the cold tap, which was right outside the galley door. The cold water tap was unlocked for two hours a day. We boys could do our washing in the officer's wash place, and shower there provided we were within the allocated time.

I told Terry and the other two boys about the arrangements for washing. 'Make sure you don't go when the officers want to go.' Also I told them not to go on their own, but to go in pairs. I related the story of the donkeyman on the last trip, when Timmy and I had been in the shower.

I was waiting for the boys to be seasick. That would come in the next day or so. When I was bad on the first trip, that was three days out. We went down the Channel to pick up the convoy. We had found out where we were going: India again, the same calls to Freetown, then on to Cape Town, then on to India. We were loaded with whisky and cigarettes to unload at India, I believed for the British forces.

We picked up a convoy off Ireland. We waited overnight, and the convoy was formed next morning. About 3 p.m. we started to move out.

Our position in the convoy was the outside line from the shore, last but one in the straight line, each ship spaced out about sixty yards from the ship in front, behind, and the ship running on a parallel course. We had as escort six corvettes, one destroyer and two armed trawlers. There were thirty-four ships in the convoy. We travelled at eight knots. Our ship was capable of twelve knots, but we had to conform with the speed of the convoy.

The weather was beautiful, no wind, the water calm. It was like a pleasure cruise. Wayne, the cook, and I were getting on famously. He was going to bake some bread and he asked me if I wanted to help him. 'Of course,' I said, 'I want to learn to be a cook.'

'This is in your own time after tea.'

'Yes, I know, but I want to learn, I don't mind.' We were also getting breakfast ready for the next morning, cooking French fries, or at least half-cooking them, to be finished off in the morning, just before breakfast. I was falling into a good routine with Wayne.

After I finished in the galley, which was about 7 p.m., I went and washed up. Terry was lying on his bunk. 'All right?' I asked.

'Yes, OK,' he said, and he looked cheerful.

'I am going for a wash, then we will see Liam and Ken. We will arrange to have a shower every two days, then we will know when to go.' We went into Liam's cabin and sat on the bunks, two on top, and two on the bottom, and had a good old chinwag. I asked the boys where they were from. Liam said, 'I live in Pentyrch, just outside Cardiff.' Ken said he lived in Ordell Street, Splott.

For the three of them, this was their first trip, and they were really excited. We were all about the same age, but they all looked up to me, for, as I told them, this was my fourth trip. I was the youngest on the boat, Terry was three months older than me, Liam about the same, and Ken about six months older again.

I asked them what they wore in bed. Liam said 'nothing', and Ken said the same. I told them, 'Wear your trousers. Make sure they are dry. Don't wear you working ones unless they are dry.' I explained the same as I had to Terry, and told them about the showers. 'Go to the showers in twos, and always carry or remember where your life jacket is. Always be alert.'

It was about eight thirty when all four of us went for our rations. The boys didn't know what I meant when I said, 'Come on, let's get our rations from the steward.' Ken and Liam smoked, whereas Terry and I didn't. We picked up our bread and milk and cocoa, the milk being condensed. Also we were given our quinine tablets, of which we were to take one a day. We had a pot of jam for a snack after a late watch, if you were hungry.

I began talking to Ted outside the galley, and he told me the boy that they had with them was a proper know-all. 'Mike doesn't like him, for every time we tell him anything he knows it all, and I have gone off him. The other deck boys seem all right, but this lad is a proper bighead.'

'I like the galley, but I miss being on deck, for I liked working with you and Mike,' I said.

We had been at sea three days, and Terry was the first to go down seasick. The next day Liam and Ken were bad, and I was looking after the three of them. The steward gave them tablets, and I wiped them down, every chance I had. Wayne was good. He was very understanding, and let me go to see to them.

About four in the afternoon, tea time, a Jerry plane came over. He did not attack us, but kept a long distance away from the convoy.

Wayne said when I was washing the pots and pans up, 'We will be attacked tonight, so be very careful. Carry your life jacket with you.' On the outside of the convoy were two cam ships, merchant ships with a Hurricane fighter on a ramp. The planes never took off, for really it would have been a pointless exercise. A little breeze was blowing up, and although our ship was well loaded, she was bobbing up and down – I bet the boys who were sick enjoyed it! The deck boys were bad now as well, so the steward had his hands full running between the two lots of boys. We were going to have lifeboat drill, but that had to be postponed because of the boys. Instead, a list went up for everyone to see.

The boys were bad for three days. I looked after them the best I could. I felt really sorry for them. I gave them water when they wanted it. I cleaned the mess they were making, and wiped them down, for they were bathed in sweat. It refreshed them, so it was good for them. By Tuesday they were up and back to work. All three of them thanked me for helping them and keeping them clean.

The escorts caught a U-boat on the surface. As she dived, they dropped some depth charges, but no joy. The rattle of the explosion against the side of the ship startled the boys. At first they were frightened. I told them it was the vibrations on the ship, and they went out to see, but there was nothing to see, only the noise.

After we had been at sea for six days everyone was settling down. I was working long days, for I wanted to learn, and now cookie was letting me cook the curry and rice that we had every dinner time. I would look after the men, and he would look after the officers. All their meals went into dishes, from which the steward would serve them. I was getting good, and really enjoying it.

I realise now why we always had curry. It served two purposes: it kept you warm in the cold (and in the nights it was cold); also for lack of fresh vegetables.

We were well out to sea. The weather was good. We lost our first ship when a tanker went up. The alarm went and we all took our positions on the boat deck. Although there had been no practice, because the boys were all ill, everyone was at their proper stations. We all had our life jackets on and those that were not on duty were there. Most of the seamen and firemen, other than the ones on their shift, were at their allotted places.

The lifeboats were near enough alongside the funnel. While you were there it was quite warm. We started to let flares off, as did the other ships. This was policy now, for it stopped the U-boats coming down the channel between the ships. The subs had had a knack coming down the channel sinking ships left and right of them.

The cabin boys were on the port side, the deck boys on the starboard. Tuesday evening, about twenty minutes after the tanker went up, we lost another right at the back of the convoy. I just hoped that there were not too many casualties. We four boys were sitting on the lip to the funnel, all talking. No one seemed afraid. I suppose we all were, but nobody acted as if they were afraid.

We carried on into the night. There were no more sinkings. We stayed where we were. We were not told to stand down, so we just huddled into one another. The order came at I don't know what time for us to stand down and go back to our bunks.

I was up early in the morning, for I wanted a shower. Terry woke up and asked what time it was. I looked at the clock on the bulkhead, which showed 6 a.m. I told Terry that and he said, 'What are you doing up so early?'

'I am going for a shower.'

He said, 'Can I come?'

'If you want to,' I said.

After the shower it was still early, so I went to the galley and made two cups of cocoa and took them back. Terry said, 'Oh, thanks, I didn't expect this.' We had a little chat, and then it was time for me to go to the galley. The first lot of food had to be ready for seven thirty for the 8 a.m. watch. When I got there, cookie was there. I said, 'I made a cup of cocoa a couple of minutes ago for Terry and me.'

We started to prepare the dishes for the firemen and sailors for them to pick up before they went on watch. They had their own trays, so it was easy enough. As soon as the seven-thirty meals had been served, we started to get the 8 a.m. meals ready, including the captain's. The steward came down to pick the dishes up for the captain's table. He would be gone about seven fifty. We would then concentrate on giving the firemen and the RN and army theirs, which would be put in dishes that two of them would collect. Then the rest had theirs.

Cookie and I had our meals last, for there was always plenty over. I am not greedy, but I do love my food. By being in the galley I could have extras. Cookie showed me how to prepare meat: cooking and boning, and presentation on the table. I asked him if he was married. 'Yes, I have a boy and a girl. I think a lot of them,' he said. 'I love them. When we get home you must come around and visit us. The boy is twelve and the girl nine. I am saving up hard to buy our own house.'

I told him, 'I only live around the corner from you,' and when I told him where, he couldn't believe it.

It was 11 a.m. Cookie and I were having a cup of tea and talking. The dinner was cooking for the eleven-thirty watch when the alarm went. I grabbed my life jacket and ran to see if I could see any of the cabin boys on my way to the lifeboat. I got to my position. The boys had come up the aft end, and they were there. The mate came up to the crowd and said, 'This is a rehearsal, but we want to alter the list. The boys will stay where they are, and the donkeyman and greaser and four firemen with one of the trimmers this side. The rest go over the starboard side.' While he was saying this, the carpenter and three ABs came over to our side.

We had sailors in each boat. The RN and the army boys were to split and come to the two sides. Now we were organised, with sailors and officers to each boat.

We were dismissed just in time to sort the dinners out to the watch.

There was no veg to get ready, no potatoes to peel, for we had passed the last day of that six days ago. The variety of dishes was brilliant. I asked Wayne if he would let me write down the recipes, so that I could make these dishes on another ship or at home.

While we were working, he told me to write down this and that, to make this or that. He was giving me leeway. 'Every couple of days, John, I want you to make this dish.' I was really enjoying it. I was learning from him, and I loved it.

Seven of the ships left us for South America, while the rest of us were going to Freetown first, some to carry on still further. But the ships that left on Friday at 11 a.m. were soon in trouble. By 3 p.m. we could hear gunfire, and it was loud. The next minute we saw two of the ships that had left earlier return to the convoy. The destroyer that was with us went off towards the noise of the gunfire. The commodore signalled 'all to port'. The whole convoy turned sharp to port. It was a nervous time now. We just didn't know what was happening.

Where I was I could not pick up any titbits the way I had done when I was working on deck. I could not even run out to find out, I had to stay put. As lenient as Wayne was, if I started doing that he would soon put me in my place. I didn't want to have any fallouts with him, for I respected him too much.

The next day, Saturday, saw another of the seven ships return. We never knew why, we could only surmise that it was to do with the gunfire. Nothing more happened. It was another four days to Freetown.

We put into Freetown only to pick up water, bananas, coconuts and mangoes. We were there two days, and I was surprised that we didn't take on any fresh vegetables. I did not know why. There must have been about forty ships in Freetown. The place was protected by a big boom defence, stringing right across the mouth of the entrance, which opens into a very large basin.

We were not allowed to go ashore. In any case, I was working all the time, and I was more interested in cooking. Everyone was to stay on the ship. There were no harbour facilities. All ships unloading in Freetown would have barges come alongside, and the natives would unload into the barges. Just outside Freetown was Vichy country, and German submarines were operating from there, a place called Dakar, and we were losing a lot of ships in Freetown. We were going the opposite way, to Cape Town, and hoped we would be able to throw them.

I remembered that, when I was picked up by Captain Sturmer, it was well away from Africa. It was his run, however, so if he were still about, he could be in these waters, as well as the steward, Heinze. I thought they were great – I hoped that they were still about.

It was the second of April and we were in the middle of a right storm. We were lashed for about two days. I thought, when this storm was on us, I hope those boys are not going to be seasick again.

This storm was bad, but there again not as bad as the storms on the Russian run. I told the boys not to venture outside. 'If a wave catches you, you are a goner. There will be no chance of rescue.' Cooking in a storm like this, you had no chance, so we stayed in the galley just boiling water for the men to have tea or cocoa – at least it would be hot. They had their own bread, and they had butter and jam of their own, so they would not starve. Wayne was teaching me to make puddings, and we were having a right old chinwag. I bet I learnt more during the storm than all the rest of the trip. With weather like that, there would be no subs.

In Liam's cabin at night we would play cards, or they got me talking about the Russian trip. We were in one another's cabins all the time when we were not working. We were more relaxed now with each other. I held them in awe, they just wanted me to tell them about Russia.

Cape Town

With no more mishaps or scares we arrived at Cape Town on Friday, 6 April. We docked against the keel wall, and the next day they started to unload us. It took two full days. When we were empty, they started to load us with crates and army equipment, which took another three days. We went to the town on the Sunday. There were plenty of things that you could get as presents. We were told, when we went ashore, not to cause trouble, and always stay in a bunch.

A lot of the firemen and sailors also went ashore, so we all tagged along together – we felt safe with them. We came across a public bar where only whites were allowed. We were all white, so we were all right. We stayed there till 10 p.m. and left to walk back to the docks. We had no real trouble at all, though the coloured children who were still about at this time would spit on us and call us names. We were told to ignore them.

We got on board without any mishaps. We cabin boys decided not to go ashore again, at least there. On the Monday we started to take a lot of fresh veg and meat on board, so now we would be cooking proper dinners, which I loved. The only thing I couldn't get the hang of was the quantities, and how to work them out, but I knew with Wayne's help I would soon learn.

Wayne said to me, 'Tomorrow I am going to be ill. I will come in the galley, and you will do the cooking of the meals for the day. I will act as your boy, cleaning pots and pans, all the jobs that you do, but I will keep an eye on you. I don't want, if possible, to tell you anything. I will clean your veg, and you will do the cooking, so let's see what you are made of. I will tell the steward what I am going to do, more or less, to get his approval.'

I was really excited. The ship was now ready to go out, all loaded up, to go where no one knew. I was going to cook the day's food. The meals from breakfast to tea were all at the same times. As we were in dock there were no watches as such. This was easier for me, but I think I would have been able to cope with it if the meals were split. Breakfast was bacon, beans and scrambled eggs, and porridge, which I made, cooked and dished out with cookie watching, not saying a word. The captain's breakfast was put into tureens. I fussed about so that the presentation of the food would catch the captain's eye.

The ship was ready, all cargo tied down. Only the incidentals were now coming on board. I concentrated on the dinners. I cooked the meat, referring to my notes that Wayne had taught me. He was still not saying anything. He was deliberately talking about other things to distract me, but at the same time watching me. The pudding I prepared was semolina. Up to now everything was all fine, no complaints.

For tea I did curry and rice, and some cake the steward had bought ashore, for the steward is the man who buys the stores for the ship. After tea Wayne said I had done very well. I was a bit cocky over it, just to myself. Although I was as proud as a peacock, I didn't want people to think I was a big head. The steward told the captain what had gone on, but other than the cabin boys, no one else knew. The steward came down and told me, 'The captain said, "Well done" – also to Wayne for teaching me, and having the confidence in me.'

The following Saturday we were on our way out of Cape Town. We cabin boys stood on the rail to watch our leaving the wall. As we pushed out of the harbour itself we went about our work. We had no idea where we were off to. We would know shortly where we were going. We all thought, because there was military equipment on board, we were going somewhere in India, but for obvious reasons they would tell us only when we were at sea.

Having just left Cape Town, we were told that we were bound for Australia. That was a turn up for the book! We would be longer at sea than we had anticipated, making for Freemantle, Western Australia.

That meant that we would be cutting straight across the limits of the Indian Ocean and the Atlantic Ocean. It was known that U-boats operated around that area, as well as Q-boats (armed merchant ships disguised as merchant ships). We were on our own, which to us was a good thing for we could move a lot quicker than in convoy.

We were out of Cape Town three days when we ran into a typhoon, and, boy, this lasted a day. I think we were in the middle of it, so everyone was saying. There were times we thought we were going to sink. If the worst had come to the worst, we would never have made it, for no little boat like a lifeboat would have survived.

We clung on. All the kitchen pans were tossed about the galley, and anything that was loose had the same treatment, thrown all over the place. We were warned not to go outside. We had to stay in the bridge area. All lookouts were called in. It was really very bad. We could not boil water, we were not allowed to light fires, we had to sit it out. We boys played cards, and talked, but the cabin boys had to work. For me there was nothing, so I just sat and talked to anyone that passed the cabin.

The doors on the companionway were shut. This itself was a rarity. All the cabin doors had mosquito mesh doors. No cabin door was closed. The bad weather didn't last long, and we had some wonderful weather after the typhoon. You would never have thought that we had been through such a blow. After ten days we were just three days from Freemantle. The deck cargo was checked, and re-tied down. We arrived at 9.30 p.m. on 24 April. We tied up after being taken in by tugs. The place was really lit up. You would have thought it was Christmas. After tying up, the ship went to sleep, other than the watches on deck, to stop pilfering. Wayne got breakfast ready alone.

Freemantle

We were not waiting for the dockers to come and unload. No one came, anyway. The port was full of ships, so the dockers had no one to send. We didn't mind waiting for them, for that meant that we would be in port longer than anticipated. We went ashore on the Saturday evening, and were amazed to see how wide the streets were. We went into a bar-cum-restaurant and stayed there till we were under the weather. When we left they were still serving drinks, so we never had a clue what time they closed. We found the Aussies in this part of the country great people. They treated us like kings. They couldn't get over the number of boys on the ship. We told them four were on deck, then there were three cabin boys and the galley boy. They thought we were very brave, being so young and going to sea.

They started to unload us on the following Monday. They really got stuck into it, and had us finished within just two days – full days, they worked the nights. The ship was cleaned out ready for the cargo next day, which was sheep and butter to take back to the UK. So we cabin boys decided that we would go out in the evening for a walk around. The four of us strolled through the busy shopping centre and bought some presents. At least I did, for I dared not go back without any presents for the girls, they would kill me. We all borrowed money, which we called 'channel money'. Things there were without coupons, and really reasonable.

We called in the pub/restaurant on the way back. Most of the crew were in there, having a good old sing-song. By the time we left it was about eleven thirty, and they were still open. We had a very good night, really enjoyable. Ted said to me in the pub he had been looking for me, so that the three of us could have a drink together. I said, 'Thanks, Ted, I surely miss you when I am working.' I told him where I had been.

We all made our way back to the ship, singing like hell. Nobody tried to stop us. As we came through the dock gates, the police there were laughing at us, because of the way we were singing. We were all dead tired when we got to the boat. We stopped singing so as not to wake the rest of the crew up, as we neared the boat. It didn't take us long to get to sleep.

We were loaded on the twenty-eighth, around tea time, and were hoping to catch the tide at midday. We left Freemantle at 1 p.m. with tugs in attendance and the pilot on board. When we got to the crossing point outside Freemantle (they call it The Roads) the pilot left us. Now we were on our way home.

The first few days out were wonderful, the weather being very hot. When I finished in the galley I would sunbathe.

Abandon Ship

It seemed everyone that was not on duty was sunbathing. We were doing about thirteen knots. There was no sign of anything, it was as if we were in another world. I was making bread by this time. Wayne treated me as an equal. I could do nearly everything that Wayne could do, and I loved it.

After we had been at sea seven days the weather was still holding good. This day was like any other day but, when it was getting dusk, which was around 9.30 p.m., we were hit by a torpedo, right out of the blue. It struck where the sheep carcases were in the refrigeration. I at that time was talking with Wayne, having a cup of tea. I said, 'What's that?' I had committed a cardinal sin: I didn't have my life jacket with me.

'I think we have been torpedoed,' Wayne said.

I ran to my cabin, which was only about ten feet away. In the companionway, Terry was there. I said, 'Get your life jacket on!' I went next door and the two boys were just coming out. 'We have been torpedoed,' I said. 'Get to the bridge!' While all this was going on, the alarm bell was ringing. When we got outside, it seemed that everyone was at the boat stations bar us.

Ted said, 'I was just coming down to look for you.' The boat was sinking very, very slowly. It was dark and the first mate, who was in charge of our lifeboat, said, 'Everyone here, look to your mate who is supposed to be in the lifeboat, see if he is there.' Besides the first mate, the third mate and the first engineer were in our boat, with some RN and two army chaps. There was plenty of room in the boat when we got in it.

Then the order came. 'Abandon ship!'

Then the lifeboat was slung out. There was no rush. As I said, the ship was sinking slowly, very slowly. It seemed that the torpedo had gone into the refrigeration department, and although she seemed to be sinking, there was a kind of levelling out, and we were holding our own.

As we were milling around the lifeboat, the German submarine came alongside, about 100 feet away. The captain told everyone to get off the ship, as he was going to put another torpedo into her. He then asked for the captain. They said he was still on board somewhere. 'You have ten minutes to get off, and I want the captain!'

'The captain is dead!' the mate shouted out. 'With the first mate – they both got killed with the explosion.'

Although it was dark, we could quite clearly see everything around us. The U-boat was an ocean-going one of the largest type. Mike said, 'Stay by me and Ted. Make sure we are always in your sight.' We all got in the lifeboat.

We boys were told to sit in the bottom of the boat, and not to get in the way as they lowered the boat down. 'Don't forget, I am the second mate,' the first mate said. 'Right, row to the bow of the ship.' The submarine was near enough alongside us, but they never tried to interfere with us.

'Who is in command now?' came from the U-boat.

'I must be!' the first mate shouted back.

'What rank do you hold, over?'

The first mate said, 'The second mate.'

As we waited to get into the lifeboat, I heard the naval chaps talking. 'Let's stay and make a go of her,' one suggested to the senior naval chap of the RN boys on the ship.

The captain came over to us at the same time as the naval chaps were discussing staying on the ship. He said to the second mate, 'Will you go over to the sub if they say they want you? Don't forget, I am dead according to the Germans and the first mate. So it is up to you, for they are doing that all the time now, picking the captains up and taking them back to Germany.'

'I'll go,' the second mate said, 'if they want me. Meantime the naval gunners are getting restless.'

While the captain was with us on the port side, talking to the second mate, the naval chaps came up to the cabin and asked for permission to stay on board, with the object of trying to sink the sub.

'I don't know,' said Captain Howe. 'That means you want to stay on the ship when we have pulled away. What if you miss?' They will sink the ship, then come after us. No, I think you had better get in the lifeboat. That way I know we will be safe.'

The gunner said, 'I know I can hit it – just give us the chance, sir.

The captain was dithering now. He didn't know what to do. He called the first mate and told him what the gunner had said. 'What do you think?' he asked.

The mate replied, 'I would like to see everyone in the lifeboats. Also, you must remember that we have eight boys on the ship, and if the Germans take it into their heads, they will not discriminate between boys and men. No, sir, I would be against it. If they miss, we have all had it. It would be a certainty they would come after us, and that would be the end of us.'

'Everyone in the lifeboats!' said the captain. 'Everyone!'

The German captain's voice came across again. 'Hurry up – and what are you carrying?'

'Sheep and butter!' shouted the second mate, for he had to keep the charade going.

There were twenty-three in one boat, and twenty-five in the other boat. The boys were divided between the two boats, with two cabin and two deck boys in each. Terry was with me, and two deck boys, George and Stan – that's all the names I knew of them. They were good boys, always willing to talk. This was their first trip.

We were put in the middle of the boat, Terry clinging to me asking all sorts of questions. I said, 'Hang on, Terry, I don't know.' I wasn't annoyed, but he never stopped asking things. I didn't know, for this was different from when I was in the boat on my first trip. 'Don't worry, I will stay with you, don't worry.'

The weather was good. With just a gentle breeze. We were now well clear of the ship, and we could see her silhouetted against the background. Both boats were together, and the wireless operators were one in each boat. They told the first mate that they had got a mayday out, for at least about five minutes. So now we were all thinking that it would not be long before being picked up. The sailors had stopped rowing now, and we were all looking at the ship.

The mate said to a couple of the naval chaps in the boat, 'That boat should have sunk by now, and she is still out of the water. She should have sunk by now. What is the hold-up? Jerry has probably taken some of the cargo off her, but they should have been away by now, and the poor *Topley* under the water.' The poor mate was repeating himself.

The first night in the lifeboats was not too bad. It was still warm, and I said, thank you, Lord, for the nice weather. The mate said, 'Open the emergency cupboard and see what rations we have got.' We found that we didn't have much. Seeing that we were still tied up to the captain's lifeboat, the mate said to the captain, 'Somebody has been pilfering the rations.' The captain said to check their rations, and the bosun, who was with the captain, said, 'We are down on our rations. Some thief has taken them.'

I heard the other officer say, 'Let's go back to the ship, if only to go back for some food, in case we are in the boats for a long time.'

There was a wireless operator in our boat (they are like a secret society, you just don't see them). The captain asked him if he had thrown all the books overboard. 'Yes, sir,' he said, 'I put them in the weighted bag.'

'All right, let's go back. Can anyone see the U-boat?' the captain asked. No one could, so he said, 'Let's get on with it.' He told the first mate, who was with the second mate, 'Let's get back.' With the two boats tied together everyone knew what was going on. It was just a case of relaying the message to those that didn't hear it.

Both boats now started to make for the *Topley*, which was still settling in the water very slowly. 'I still don't know why the sub never sank her,' the captain said to anyone who wanted to listen. Someone suggested that perhaps the sub had used her last fish (torpedo) on us and had no more. 'Well, why didn't he shell us? He wanted us off the boat, as if he was going to sink us. Rather strange,' said the captain.

We were near the *Topley* now and the captain told the first and second mates with six men and cookie to go aboard her. They had a terrible job to get up on deck.

If the ship had not settled as she had, I doubt whether we would have got on board. Eventually the men designated to go aboard achieved it, and were soon lost to our sight. The captain, in the other lifeboat, was heard to say, 'Yes, she is slipping away, but very slowly.' He told the third mate to take four men with him and lower the jolly boat and put some rations in it, and some water. 'Go in my cabin and get the guns out. Also take the second engineer and dismantle the machine gun from the port side. Make sure that you get some ammunition. Put that in the jolly boat as well.'

The men did what they were told. The jolly boat, which was on the port side, was brought around to where we were all sitting.

In the Lifeboats

Now all the men were back in the boats, and the jolly boat was well laden with food and water. All three boats were together. One of the sailors had had the sense to bring a few coils of rope, which would probably be very useful. The captain said, 'Let's get clear of the *Topley* and have a look at the situation.' He called a halt about two miles away from the old ship. 'Right, let's see what food and water we have.'

The three boats were all tied together in a little circle. The large lifeboats were given rations for a week, allowing for two meals a day with three cups of water a day. The rest was to be kept in the jolly boat. There were two coils of rope each. Eight pistols and three rifles with ammunition were shared out. Each officer was given a pistol and twenty rounds. The three rifles went one to the bosun, one to the senior AB and one to the senior fireman.

'The second mate will go in the jolly boat,' said the captain, 'with six men: two naval, two firemen and two ABs. All boats will be tied together, and we will cut the ropes if we should run into a storm, but remember you have to try to stay together. Keep the machine guns in the jolly boat.' (The jolly boat does the running around if the ship is in harbour, but not tied to the wall, so that the captain or other officers can get ashore when situations arise.)

'Right, let's be off.' The three boats moved one behind the other, all tied to one another. The masts went up. According to the captain we were making for the French islands or the South African islands. We boys in the port lifeboat, two deck and two cabin, were sitting in the bottom of the boat. Terry and I were together, in between the legs of Ted and Mike.

I heard Mike say to Ted, 'I think there is something wrong with the old man' (at sea a captain is always called 'the old man'). 'Notice he never went back on the *Topley*, he just sat in the lifeboat with the steward. Now, I have never known a captain to stay in the lifeboat if there was a reboarding of the ship. He just sat there giving orders, and that is not like him. Also, you look at him. He has lost his colour, and he is very quiet.'

The captain had given the orders when we left the *Topley*, and had hardly said a word since, and we were only a few feet away from him. I looked at Terry and he sort of looked at me. The two deck boys looked at us, for we were all sitting close together, two facing two, Terry and I, and Stan and Brian. All of us heard what Mike said, but said nothing. The two deck boys were great, they just fell in with us.

Terry asked, 'How long do you think we will be in the boats?'

'Don't worry,' I said, 'the captain will get us there.' Everyone at the moment seemed contented, and everyone was talking. A slight breeze was carrying us.

It was Tuesday and it was very hot. We were having our three cups of water a day (not in the cups we had our tea in, but small tin cups). This hardly quenched your thirst. At first I thought, with all the water we had, why was the captain so mean? Then I remembered when I had been on my own in a lifeboat. When I was picked up by the submarine, water had been a crucial factor.

I was facing the captain. Every now and then when I looked up at him he would grimace, as if in pain. I turned to Mike and Ted and said, 'What does one do if one wants to go to the toilet?'

'Do you want to go?' asked Mike.

'Yes,' I said, 'I am dying to go.'

Mike turned to the first mate and said, 'The boys want to toilet.' The mate shouted this information to the captain.

The captain said, 'Drop the sails and steady the boats. Right, you lads,' he shouted to all the boys, 'jump into the sea and do your business.'

I said to Mike, 'What about our clothes?'

'Take them off,' Mike said.

'All of them?'

'Come on, John,' he said, 'You are not shy, are you?'

'Yes,' I said, 'we all are.'

'Take them off,' Mike said, 'and use your shirt to wipe yourself dry.'

We all stripped off and went into the water. Luckily there were no sharks about. 'In this part of the ocean there are none,' said one of the seamen. As we went in, so did the boys of the captain's boat. Through moving to get in position to go into the water, one of the seamen bumped the captain's leg, and he let out a howl. Now all eight boys were in the water. Our boys of our boat stayed together, and likewise the other boat.

While we were in the water, the steward found out that the captain had broken his leg, a very bad break. Everyone was concerned, especially in the captain's boat. The steward broke one of the bench seats and made splints with the wood, then bandaged it up. We all gave ourselves a good wash down, which is very hard with sea water, but at least it was refreshing. Nobody had soap, so we could not really have a good wash, but it was still refreshing. After toileting we somehow washed the lower part of the body.

I felt really clean now, and I said to Terry, 'I feel great now.' As we were wiping ourselves down, the boat half emptied. Nearly all the crew in the boat did what we did and dived in. After everyone was back on board, we had something to eat.

It was a good job that we went into the water, for if that sailor had not bumped the captain's leg, he would not have said anything, at least not before we got to some proper authorities. At least it was now in splints. One of the sailors used his sheath knife to make the splints, by cutting one of the bench seats. The pieces he cut off, he whittled down to the splints. That would have to do. We were glad that the food had been shared out between the three boats for, as Mike said, if we lost the jolly boat, we would be in trouble.

It was cooling off now in the nights. Whether that was because we were moving to the west, we did not know, but in the day it was still very hot. Wednesday was another hot day. It was really murder. It was so hot you wanted to drink all the time. Fair enough to the captain, he did let us have an extra cup of water, but that only tickled our throats. No sooner did you drink it, you were looking for another one.

The captain was more or less laid out in the bow of the boat, and the steward was with him now all the time.

The whisper going around was that, when the captain abandoned the *Topley*, being the last man off, he got off on the starboard lifeboat, which was his station. The U-boat, being on the port side, would not be able to see him. In that way he could fox the U-boat captain. The lifeboat had already been lowered on to the water. The steward and the captain had come down the rope ladder, which had been thrown over the side when the order came to abandon the ship.

As they descended the ladder, the steward first and then the captain, there was a straight swell. The lifeboat drifted about two feet away from the *Topley*, just as the captain was putting his foot on the gunnel (gunnel is the topside of the boat). His foot slipped because of the swell, and it went between the lifeboat and the *Topley*. The lifeboat came back against his leg, crushing and breaking it.

Although one or two of the occupants of the lifeboat saw it, not much notice was taken of the incident. Although he let out a yell, because of the noise about with the ship being abandoned, no one heard – or, if they did, no notice was taken. The captain then told one of the ABs to go on the *Topley*, and cut the rope ladder, and dive into the water to get back on the lifeboat.

It was getting dark now. The time was approximately 9 p.m. We were on the course set by the captain. It started to blow up a bit, so the captain said, 'Drop the sails.' The three boats dropped their sails, but we were still being carried along, by the water, which now was getting choppy. If it got any worse we would have to cut the ropes, for if one wave caught one boat one way, another wave might catch another boat in a different direction, and that would cause a catastrophe.

The boat to suffer worst was the jolly boat. There were seven men in it, and already it was bouncing about. The captain was beginning to worry about them. If it stayed like this, that would not be too bad, but he was contemplating bringing them back on one of the lifeboats. As the night progressed, the weather was getting worse. 'Cut the ropes!' the captain ordered. They were cut immediately. Each boat was now on its own. The captain shouted, 'Try and stay together!'

The second mate, who was in charge of the jolly boat, at about 2 a.m. told all six of his crew to tie themselves together, and tie themselves to the boat. Our lives now depended on one another, and working to keep afloat. To make things worse, we had lost contact with the other boats. We were in trouble.

When the captain in Lifeboat 1 shouted to the other boats cut the ropes, there was sense in the order, for now the storm was life-threatening. With the boats being tied to one another, No. 2 lifeboat was nearly upended. The boat showed it was free, for she was much easier to handle, but it was still very hard, for the waves now were tremendous.

We had to go through the night with this storm. In daylight things always seem better than at night, for you cannot see things in the night. The boys were told to sit in the well of the boat. If it wasn't so serious at the time it would have looked comical. We were nearly into one another's pockets. This was happening in both boats.

'Remember,' I said to the boys in a whisper, 'we are in good hands. The sailors will look after us.' Other than the captain telling the crew what to do, and those working to keep us afloat, the rest were all sitting like us in the well of the boat.

All through the day we were like this. We did not know where the other boats were. As we hit the top of a wave, we would be on the lookout for the other boats, but there was no sign of them. We went into the next night. There was no let up with the storm until about four in the afternoon. Then the wind and turmoil gradually dropped.

When it was safe to sit on the seats the captain told us to get up. We were all soaked to the skin, but we never complained. The sailors had saved us, and we all knew it. The captain said, 'Let's have something to eat, Mr Steward.' He was in charge of rations, so he gave us all a little extra bread and a little meat, and our cup of water in turn. 'Get the brandy out,' the captain said, and the steward produced a bottle, giving the ABs a tot. After the men had had theirs, he gave each one of the boys in the boat a little tot – small in comparison to what the men had, but there were no complaints.

At 9 p.m. the weather was as it had been before the storm. It was dark, but you could see the stars, which gently lit the sky up. It was a little cold, for all our clothes were soaking wet. We had to keep them on, but if the weather was good the next day, we would strip off at least to our trousers, and the sun would soon dry our clothing.

The captain was now in a lot of pain from his leg. The steward was giving him a lot of tablets to try to kill the pain. As soon as the tablets wore off he was in agony, as you could see by his face, for he was grimacing nearly all the time.

The captain asked the third mate to use the sextant. When he put it to his face, he found that it was broken. One of the arms that make the sextant was twisted, as if something heavy had fallen on it, so it was useless. 'I don't know what we are going to do now,' the captain said, talking to the third mate. 'I don't know where we are. I have no idea where the storm took us, not a clue. I just don't know where the storm has taken us,' he continued, repeating himself. Our intended course was to go around the African coast. We had been at sea now ten days so really we should have been around St Helena – or that is where we would have been if the weather been all right.

'Put the mast back up,' the captain told the third mate, 'and get someone who is fit to try to climb to the highest point of the mast. Tell him to have a good search around for the other boats. Be careful,' he said, 'we have got company.' A school of sharks was following us. We were all more scared now than before.

'Nothing in sight!' shouted the AB on lookout.

'Will you get up every now and again?' the captain asked the AB. (I think his name was Lomas – I really didn't have much to do with him.)

'Yes, sir,' he replied to the captain's request.

Liam, who was in the captain's boat with Ken, asked one of the sailors about getting picked up. 'Don't worry,' the AB said, 'we have plenty of food and water. We'll get picked up, don't worry.' It was Saturday. We had been at sea two weeks, but in the lifeboat about ten days. It was a good job the captain had had the presence of mind to go back to the *Topley*, and take some food on. The day was really warm, which made us all the more thirsty. It was unbearable at times. There was no sign of the other boats, and now it was a worry.

The captain was now having his leg seen to more than before. The poor man was in a lot of pain, but you never heard a word from him. The steward was very worried over the captain, for he had a high temperature. The steward kept bathing his face to keep him cool, and was fussing around him all the time.

A lot of the crew in the boat wanted to go to the toilet, but with the sharks following us there was not much chance of that. Everyone wanted to wash, to freshen up, for no one had been to the toilet or had a swill since the storm started. The ABs and the RN chaps all volunteered to scale the mast looking for the other boats, but were scaling the mast about every hour shouting, 'Nothing in sight.' We had a meal and we didn't know what it was, dinner or tea. We had lost track of the time.

The next day was another scorcher. We dried all our clothes. There had been no sign of the sharks for the past twenty-four hours, so we were able to cleanse ourselves. A lot of the seamen were now coming out in sores, and they were itching. One of the sailors tried the sea for a bath and toilet, and nothing happened, then another one did the same. It didn't take long for nearly everyone to go in, including the four boys.

The steward looking after the captain was a worried man, and through that he had seemed to age. He had not said a word, nor had the captain in the past twenty-four hours. We all suspected the worst – all the morphine had gone, and now there was nothing to kill the pain. Everyone in the boat was glancing all the time at the skipper, praying that he would come around. Captain Howe was a very considerate man. Everyone on the *Topley* respected him, for he was a real charmer.

We all had faith in the third mate, but he seemed a bit young to be in charge of a boatload of seamen. 'Get the flares ready,' said the third mate, and the bosun went into the locker under the seat, and pulled two out. They were soaking wet from the storm. 'Put them to dry.' So they were laid out by the bosun, who was in charge of them. He said to one of the ABs, 'They may look dry eventually, but I think they will be wet inside.'

We were now into Monday, and as everyone was waking up, long faces could be seen. Someone behind us said, 'I think he is gone.' I looked at the captain and he was resting in peace. Believe it or not, he looked a very young man. His age was about fifty.

We were very upset. We four boys started to cry. To see the skipper dead, was too much for us, and not just the boys. Some of the ABs who were a couple of years older than us were also crying. It was a really sad day. The third mate said a little service over him. The steward by now was in a terrible state. The skipper's body was laid on the water. We had nothing to put his body in, so it was gently lowered into the water, having been smartened up by the steward, until it disappeared.

We kept thinking about the skipper all day. We could not get him out of our minds. Liam said to Ken, 'We won't be far behind him.'

'That's silly,' one of the ABs said, 'you are young, boys, you have your life in front of you.'

'Don't worry, we will get out of this,' one of the RN boys said. 'Come on, you boys, face reality. The captain was injured, and in a lot of pain. Besides breaking his leg, he had a heart attack during the night, and he died peacefully. He was a very brave man.'

The third mate got hold of the crew in the lifeboat and stressed that we had got to keep going if only for the young boys – 'So let's all pull together.' He added, 'You all must be alert to any conditions that may arise. Keep scanning the horizon for our boats, and hoping that we may come across some other ship.'

We had no idea where the other boats were. Every time we went on top of the waves, everyone on the seats would be scanning the waters for the other boats. 'Put the mast up,' the mate ordered, at least if they are around here, they will see us.'

I am a very proud person as regards to being clean, but, through not washing in unsalted water, my body was really itching. Washing in the sea was cracking my skin, and the sun was making it all the worse. To go to the toilet was very embarrassing. I was getting over being shy, but Terry was terrible. I had a terrible job to convince him that by him being so stubborn, he was drawing attention to himself. In the end I succeeded and he began to get used to it.

The deck boys were like Terry, but in the end all three of them, Terry, Brian and Stan, would strip off as if they had been doing this all their lives.

I was talking to Mike and Ted a lot, and the same old question came up: will we ever be picked up? 'Don't worry,' Ted said. Mike came in and said, 'We are now in the shipping lanes. We will soon be picked up.'

'What about the other boats?' I asked Ted.

'Well, they should be around us.'

'I hope so,' I said. 'I would not want anything to happen to them.'

Cookie was sitting more to the bow. He was unofficially in charge of the food and water. 'Are you all right?' he asked me.

'Yes,' I said.

'And your mate?'

'Yes, we are both all right.'

Through it being hot, with the sun blasting down on us, we were further apart than when the storm had been upon us, but still close together. We were all on about the sores. 'Keep your shirt on,' the mate advised us. I said to Terry, 'This is definitely my last trip.'

'Yes, and me,' Terry said. 'Don't leave me,' Terry said.

'Don't worry, I won't.'

We were now talking about going over for a toilet and wash, but the sores were worrying me – the salt water would play havoc with them. However, nature was calling. I said to Mike, 'I want to go to the toilet,' and he relayed the information to the mate, who was sitting on the tiller. The mate said straight away, 'They can't – there is a school of sharks following us.'

This was hard for us, badly for we wanted to go. 'Try to hang on,' Ted and the first mate said.

Our chests were showing the sores that were on them. Wayne, the cook, said to Mike, look in the cupboards under the seats to see if there is any ointment in there.' Ted looked in the three cupboards on the starboard side; there was no first aid kit. 'Look the other side,' cookie said. There was nothing in the cupboards. 'Check the port lockers.' Yes, there was a first aid kit. On opening it, cookie saw a small jar of cream for sores. 'Well, I am sorry, there will not be enough for everyone.'

'Give it to the boys,' someone said.

'There will not be enough even for the boys.'

'Well, spread it out,' someone else shouted.

'Mike,' I said, 'will it be possible for someone to hold me over the side, one on each arm, with me straddled with my feet on the gunnel?' I had now got to the point where I must forsake my pride and embarrassment to do my toilet.

'I suppose so,' Mike said. 'I will ask the mate.' The mate reluctantly gave the OK.

I would not let anyone other than Mike and Ted hold me, having overcome my embarrassment only for Ted and Mike. I dropped my trousers and went to the gunnel. I climbed on to the bench seat, and Mike and Ted held me facing them and allowed me to toilet. 'You other boys look for the sharks,' said Ted. 'If they come too close, yell out.' Although I was well out of the water, we still had to be careful.

When I came back on board, Terry said, 'I want to go.' He dropped his pants and did the same as me. I washed my backside with a handkerchief that I had in my pocket. I felt really refreshed, after giving my face a swill by splashing water on my face.

Ted and Mike were great. They held the other two boys, Stan and Brian, and all four of us were refreshed, thanks to them. Cookie then smeared a little ointment on our skins, all four of us. He told us to put our lifejackets on, to protect our bodies from the sun. I sat back down in the well of the boat alongside Terry, and my mind went back to the first time I had been in the lifeboat on my own, after the other man had died. That was sixteen days into my first trip, and now we are getting near to that point on this one, so it was getting very worrying.

I was praying silently, when the boys were asleep, to be rescued. They were sleeping a lot now, and I was following suit. There was nothing to see. No one bothered to talk now, for we had been in the boat too long. We heard the monotonous drone of the AB on lookout – 'Nothing to report' – every hour. All sense of time had gone. It was only when we got our rations that we knew whether it was dinner or tea. We knew breakfast by the day dawning.

We had another fine day. I said to Terry, 'Please God we won't have another storm like the last. Even in the Russian convoys we never had waves as big as those.' When in daylight I had seen the size of them, they were like mountains above you. You would look up, and then see yourself going to the top, then being dropped into a trough, then back up again. Each time your inner thoughts would tell you this was going to be your last.

It was great to know that we had survived it, and I prayed that we would not have another like that. The mate was now worried, for we still could not see the other boats. We were lost, and he openly said it. 'I have no sextant, no compass, nothing. We have got nothing. I pray that we will see the other boats.' We had our tea: water and dry bread, which was dry through being in the sealers.

After tea it warmed up a little. Now it was getting dark. It started to rain. In the warm countries – down the Indian Ocean or wherever we were when it rained it certainly came down. In five minutes we were all soaking wet. Now it was going to get cold, so we had another miserable night to look forward to, but at least we were still alive.

'Sharks about!' someone shouted. I thought that the last school had gone. Everyone seemed to be awake when the cry went out, and all started to look for the fish. We all seemed to spot them at the same time, on the starboard side. It looked a biggish school. Now we were all keeping perfectly still, for we didn't want to end up in the water.

One of the ABs asked the mate where he thought we were. 'No idea,' he said. 'Don't worry, we have plenty food and water. Come on, keep your heads up. The lookout, whose name was Wain, got to the highest point of the mast that he could manage without spilling everyone in the lifeboats out. 'Nothing in sight,' was the cry. I think all heads dropped a little. 'Let's have some luck in the morning,' someone said, and every-one murmured approval.

The night just dragged on. We were all falling asleep in dribs and drabs, only for a few seconds. The wireless operator and the tillerman were designated lookouts. It was a wonderful night now, calm after that rain shower. The wind dropped. Daylight came and we had breakfast. The mate came and sat with us. He said, 'Don't worry, boys, we will not be all that long now. We got an SOS out so we know someone will be looking for us. Just keep your chins up.

'I will say that you are the best lot of boys that have served with me.

You have been excellent – no griping, you have been marvellous.' Poor old Wain was still jumping up and down, trying to see if there was anyone about. 'Like that man Wain,' continued the mate, 'no moaning, just tries his best. And I can say that for all of you.'

'I haven't seen any of the sharks today,' said one of the firemen.

'No, I think they are gone,' said one of the RN chaps. 'I am going in to have a s— anyway,' he said, so he peeled off his clothes. In he went. 'It's nice and warm,' was the first thing he said. After about ten minutes he came back into the boat. 'That's better,' he said. Another naval gunner went in.

One of the other naval gunners went in, and immediately the mate shouted out, 'Only two at a time! The rest of you keep a sharp lookout.' It was the boys' turn, and one of them, Stan, went in with his trousers on. You should have heard the ribbing he had. You would have thought that we were in a cosy cafe, with all the banter. Everyone had a wash and toilet, and we were all feeling refreshed. I said to Terry, 'See what I mean, Stan has drawn attention to himself, and the crew will now look for him every time he wants to toilet.'

To look at the mate you could see he was a confident man. He didn't say much, but you could see his attitude, supremely assured. He was sitting by cookie, and he said, 'I have kept a 100 per cent boat, through all the wind and storms, and I intend to finish as I started.' But he was in for a surprise. In fact everyone was.

One of the firemen, by the name of Dodds, throughout the day had been dipping an empty bean tin in the sea. This tin was kept for bailing water from the boat. Fireman Dodds had been drinking a lot of the seawater. No one noticed, as now we were at the stage where everybody was head down, either sleeping or fantasising. We four boys were all close together, still in the well of the boat. It was more comfortable there; also we were under the control of Ted and Mike.

AB Sitwell, who thought himself an intellectual, asked the mate where he thought we were. 'No idea,' the mate said, so the AB said to him, 'Well, according to the sun rising we are going on a westerly course.'

'Yes, that's right,' said the mate. 'I might as well tell you, I have known this since the storm, but I didn't want to say anything, in case you started to panic.'

'In other words,' the AB said, 'South America.'

'That's right. The storm blew us well off course. Probably the other boats are with us somewhere or the other.'

Suddenly, fireman Dodds, hallucinating, stood up in the boat. He looked really awful, disorientated. He was shouting and cursing. It was all rubbish. No one knew what he was on about. He jumped into the sea, still shouting, then he was gone. He had taken his life jacket off. The poor man, I was really upset over it.

The mate said, 'Don't drink the sea water. We have three cups of water a day. You have got to try to accommodate that. I know it is hot. We are now coming to the situation where we have to strictly ration the water. We are well into May. We have been in the lifeboats more than ten days. Come on, the mate said, 'We can do another ten days, if you put your mind to it. That's if we have to. It's no good sulking. Talk to one another, that will help all of us.

'That will take your mind off the lifeboat. We are still better off than a lot of boys who were torpedoed. They were in the boats with no water or food for days. At least we have water and food.'

The days were blistering from the sun, and now we boys were feeling it. We were suffering from cracked skin, and the salt water was getting into the cracks. There was nothing we could do, only try and cover up the infected area. All our bums were sore from sitting down all the time, and we were all fidgeting and moaning. It wouldn't have been so bad if we could only stretch our legs or lie down.

Some of the naval gunners, who were a fine lot, were doing their best to comfort us. Other than that you would not knew they were there. It just shows what discipline does for you. A couple of them came and sat with the boys, telling us stories, some of which were really funny, and would make anyone laugh.

By Saturday a great breeze was blowing, having started about two days earlier. The canvas, though now a little tatty, was still doing sterling work. It was moving us along at a great pace. Palmer was the man on watch; he had just relieved one of the naval chaps. Well into the afternoon he became excited, swearing that he saw land. The mate jumped up and looked to where Palmer was pointing. All he could see at that moment of time was a haze.

Palmer was sure that he had seen land. Although no one questioned it, the haze was making sighting bad. Palmer was trying to convince everyone willing to be persuaded. One of the naval chaps got up, his name being Smithy. He looked out to where Palmer indicated, and said, 'Yes, there is land,' in a matter-of-fact way.

The mate got up and looked out over the bows of the lifeboat again. 'Yes,' he said, 'I think there is land there,' and murmured to himself, 'though I've no idea where we are.'

Now in the boat everyone was excited, especially us boys. Everyone wanted to work to get the boat in. The mate said, 'I only want the people who have been working in the lifeboat to work to get the boat in.' In other words he didn't want overenthusiasm – we were doing very well with the sail.

By the time we got to the land it was getting dark. The mate reaffirmed his authority. No one was to wander off when we reached land. 'Drop the sail,' he ordered, as the boat ground to a halt on a shale beach. 'We will go ashore, but stay at the water's edge.'

Everyone was now really excited. I said to the boys, 'At least we can stretch out and sleep properly.' We all piled out of the boat as soon as it touched the beach, and most of us just collapsed, through our legs giving way, for we had not straightened them for fourteen or fifteen days.

Ted came over and asked what the matter was. 'Crawl ashore, lie on your backs, legs in the air. Do a cycling motion – they will come back.' And that's what we did.

Jolly Boat

The jolly boat was the last in a line of three, being a small boat. When the wind started to rise, Pengelley said to the other six men in the boat – Horton, Arlott, ABs Leek and Owen, RN Harvey, and Turk, firemen – 'I think we are going to have a rough night.' Being the second mate, in charge, he had every confidence in the men in the boat, and knew they had every confidence in him. He relied on the six of them, knowing that the two firemen were big strong chaps, their knowledge of the sea first class.

Pengelley heard the order to cut the ropes. Now the waves were beginning to grow in size, and he was worried, for these boats were not for this type of weather. He thought it was a good job the food had been distributed to the other boats before this lot started.

The waves were getting fierce, and it was taking a lot to handle the boat. All had their life jackets on. The loose stores in the well of the boat were helping to steady the boat, but the violence of the sea was awesome. They would be up on top of a big wave, with the channel in front about twenty feet, and they would be looking down the gulley, all frightened to death. There was no way this boat would survive this. At least three times they thought they were going to capsize. But they just managed to hold her. They had lost the other boats, and now knew that they were in trouble, for if they were upended they had had it.

They were being showered with heavy sprays, knowing one heavy wave could mean they were goners. It was worst at night when they could not see anything. At around 8 a.m., they were all dead tired trying to keep afloat. A big, heavy wave came, took them and ripped them apart. They were all flung in the water. Luckily they all ended up together. But after about an hour they lost Arlott, and about another hour later lost Smithy of the RN. Thrown all over the ocean, they grew smaller and smaller in number. Turk was the last, about three hours after the capsize.

No. 2 lifeboat had been about twelve feet away, but the voices of the sailors in the water had been lost in the screaming wind.

Paradise Island

Getting out of the boat was hard, for we could not stand. Our legs were wobbly. 'Take your time!' someone shouted to us, so we joined shoulders and walked a little way supporting one another. Gradually we got our legs going. We walked about 100 yards, all of us in the boat were using the same method. We boys were delighted. We stuck together until we could balance. We walked a few times back and forth, and that was all we could manage. We then sat on a large rock, talking. The third mate gave the tea out, same as usual, but this time it was most enjoyable. After having the regulation drink of water, we were overtaken by sleep. At least, we boys were.

Next morning after breakfast the engineer and the third mate, with the bosun and fourth engineer, split the survivors up into foraging parties: three parties of three, AB, one fireman and one RN. The rest were to stay put. The foragers were given till 1 p.m. 'No matter where you are, you will turn around and come back when the sun is right above you,' instructed the engineer. 'One man's to be in charge, and I am plumping for the naval gunners.' Each one was given a revolver in case of trouble. 'This weapon is to defend yourselves,' the engineer continued, 'not for any other purpose. Understood?' The three leaders said, 'Yes, sir.'

The three parties turned. One went south, one north, and the other to the east through the woods. 'We will light fires on the beach,' said the third mate. 'I think we have some tea that we took off the ship when we went back.' He asked one of us to go and look into the sealers. We all went for something to do. We found the tea. It was a small sack, enough to make about 100 cups, so we got the fire going well. Then found that the only utensil we had to boil the water was the cask that was holding our drinking water. It was useless to boil water in, as it was made of wood.

Everyone's face dropped. There was nothing that anyone could do, only go scrounging along the beach. We were forbidden to leave this part. We noticed that the engineer, the third mate and the wireless operator were in deep conversation. Then two men were selected to go along the beach, with the third mate with a revolver. They were going along the beach to see what they could find, also to see if there are any footprints telling them the other boats had beached.

By one o'clock no one had yet returned. The beach party returned first. They had found nothing, and they had looked to see if there were any boats hidden. By one-thirty the other parties had returned. The south party had come across some wild bananas and coconuts. Also there were some wild hogs – the west party had come across the same, seeing some wild animals roaming about. The north party had seen some sort of life that had been on the beach, but it looked like old footprints with no shoes. 'That wouldn't be any of our party,' said the third mate. 'For starters they would be wearing shoes. Also, if they had landed on that beach, where was their boat?' Also they had come across some sweet potatoes – at least, they thought that was what they were. They all brought some samples of their finds back (though not the hogs and wild animals). 'Tomorrow we will go deeper,' said the first engineer.

We had dinner, a little different from before. We had bread, which was now really hard, bananas and coconuts. They had brought back eight coconuts, which was one between four. It was a change; nobody moaned.

In the morning the first engineer called everyone to a meeting and he spelt it out. The boys would start at all times on the beach scrounging. Two parties would go out, with six men to a party. The reason for the bigger parties was to bring what foodstuff they could muster, excluding things that needed cooking, as we had nothing to cook in. 'You will work on a different angle from yesterday's,' said the engineer, 'one south, one north. The rest will stay on the beach, pull the lifeboat up the beach and hide it. The foraging parties are to leave at eight, to be back by two. Look at the sun for your time.'

We boys were a lot happier now. The night had been good. We all sat around a big fire, talking and laughing. It was like the Scouts' campfire, which brought some memories. Liam told the other boys about the scouts he had been in, before he came to sea. The third mate noticed the change in the men, but more so the boys, for he had been worried about us, when we were in the boat.

At eight o'clock the two parties left the camp. We helped with the lifeboat, pulling it from the water. We looked for stout branches, trimmed them, and rolled the lifeboats on them up the beach. It was very hard work, for we were weak, and it took it out of us, but we managed after about four hours. The beach was about 100 feet to the trees. We were shattered and we all stretched out. Most of us fell asleep, until we were awakened by the return party – and with them they had some of the men from the missing Lifeboat 2!

There were three of them: ABs Peter and Philip, and RN Stan. Everyone was excited, for at least we had Lifeboat 2 on land. The jolly boat was now the worry – did they make it or not?

The other party, which was led by wireless operator Jerry, came back in with berries, which were very tasty but, as the third mate said, 'If you eat them, you will have the runs.' They also brought some more bananas and coconuts.

The three members of Lifeboat 2 said to the leaders, 'We are up the mountain. Where we are we can see everybody around. We saw your party a long way off, but were not sure who you were. Before it gets dark, why not move with us to the other party?'

We told them the captain had died, and that one of the men had been drinking seawater, and had gone berserk, and thrown himself into the sea.

They decided that with the light still in their favour we should join the others up the mountain, so we packed what we had and all moved off. It took three hours to get to the other party. It was the mountain climbing that took it out of us. When the first mate saw us, he was delighted. 'Now we are lacking one boat,' he said. 'Let's hope they are all right.'

Cookie made the newcomers feel at home. He shared what they had, which was similar to what the third mate's party had. Everyone was asking questions, really excited. 'Tomorrow we will sort ourselves out,' the first mate said, for now he was in charge of the whole party. The engineers were only in charge if there was no senior deck officer about. All the boys were together, all making a fuss with one another, and all wanting to tell their own story, which really was no different from any other chap's.

When things started to quieten down, one of the firemen asked the first mate where he thought we were. 'I don't know,' he replied truthfully. The mate said, 'All I can tell you is that we had a change of orders when we left Australia. We were to make our way to Mauritius. We were told at the last minute to call there for new orders.'

After the mate finished the wireless officer said, 'If we were calling in there we might have been told to make our way through the Mediterranean Sea, which would have saved a week of our time.'

It was now discovered that the first engineer was ill, and he was looking it. A bed was made in one of the caves on top of the mountain. The mate said, 'I don't want to see you up till you are feeling better.' The steward was looking after him, so we all know he was in good hands.

The mate called everyone other than the sick engineer to a meeting. 'We will not lie about,' he said, 'Starting with the boys: the galley boy and his mate the cabin boy will help the cook, and if any other help is wanted, two deck boys will help. The rest of the boys will collect wood for the fire, and keep the camp clean. Six men with the third mate will go out in one of the lifeboats and go to one island at a time, looking for the jolly boat. You will take rations for three days; you must come back by dinner time of the third day.

'The bosun will take a party of five. All these will be named in a minute. The army sergeant will take five men; the second engineer will take five men. Now, let's pair you off. The third mate will take three ABs and three firemen. The bosun will take carpenter, donkeyman and the two trimmers and the radio man. The sergeant will take three RN and two army. The second engineer will take his mate, the third engineer, and the other radio chappy, and the two oilers. You will have a rifle each. The shore parties and the boat party will have two revolvers.

'The guns are only to be used in anger. While you are out, some of the camp will play Indians and make some bows and arrows. They will be used for getting our meat.'

Before the shore parties left they were instructed to kill a couple of hogs or whatever animals they found that were eatable. 'Bring a load of sweet potatoes, for we can roast them by the fire, and cook the animals over a spit. I want you shore parties back by 6 p.m., no later.' They all moved off, and the camp seemed empty. The boys went for the wood, and the mate posted four men as guards, about 300 yards from camp.

I was delighted to be back with Wayne cooking. It did not matter what we were to cook, it was better than doing nothing. I could not wait to cook the hogs over the fire, and Wayne was trying to think what meals he could give the men, for they were fed up with dry bread and water. Terry fetched getting wood for the fires, and some of the wood was put into the caves to keep dry, in case we had another storm.

The mate was looking through his binoculars. Where he was standing he could see right around the island, and he could see other islands around this one. It looked as though the next island going west was a larger one than ours.

The camp was more shipshape now. Terry said, 'All us boys are going to sleep in one of the caves. We are getting branches to put on the floor for us to lie on for beds.'

'That's great,' we all agreed.

As I was sitting down with boys, Terry said, 'You can speak German, can't you?'

'In a fashion,' I said.

'Where did you learn it?'

'Well, for starters I pick things up very easy, no matter what it is. I don't forget it.' I didn't want to relate too much about when I was in the U-boat, so I said that in school I was always top with my marks.

It was the same as the cooking. Wayne would only have to show me once and I would have it. Also I loved cooking. 'Let me ask you all not to let on that I speak German,' I said. 'I am a wanted person with the Germans, and if ever they found out who I was, it would be very hard for me. So please forget what I have said.'

The mate continued searching with his glasses for any signs of the jolly boat. He was also looking to see if there was any smoke about, for the boat would be wherever the smoke was.

He noticed the mountains were quite bare in places. The trees from the water's edge had thinned out. He went to sit with the first engineer, who did not seem to be any better. No one knew what the trouble was, but he was losing weight, which was now obvious. We were all losing weight, but that was through lack of food. This man was weak and did not want anything to eat. He just wanted to sleep.

There was no way we could get a meal ready for the chaps when they came in. We could only have what is in the camp. If they brought hogs and potatoes that would be a godsend. So we just sat around talking. I noticed that Terry and I were very close. We were always looking for one another's company, as well as that of the other boys. We all got on well together.

The first party came back, bringing a stag. It was a big one, a beauty, plenty for everyone. Wayne shouted for me. I went over. 'Do you want to give me a hand cleaning it out and cutting it up?' There was no way you would be able to put that on a spit, for it was much too big. So it was decided that we would have two spits and cook double. They also brought mangoes, yams, and sweet potatoes – plenty of them. So now we would be able to have a good meal.

Just as we got organised, I said to Wayne, 'I cannot stand killing animals.' Terry, who was with me, said, 'I will give you a hand, cookie.' Although the stag had been killed out in the fields, I just could not touch it as it was. 'I will do something else,' I said, and with that I began putting the potatoes around the edge of the fire. It would be two hours before the meat was cooked, so we had plenty of time on our hands. We didn't want a big fire in the dark, so we knew that it would be done before it got dark. We got two fires going for the roasting. Each man would get two fair-sized potatoes. Sweet potatoes are larger than our type of potatoes, a lot larger, so two would be ample.

The other party came back in. They brought near enough the same as the first party, but no stag, no meat at all. For now we were well stocked with food. The last party came in, and they brought a hog, besides the potatoes. No one had used their rifles, and the mate seemed very pleased. In the day they had made half a dozen bows with about six arrows to each bow. They would be preferable to guns for shooting animals, for we had to keep the ammunition.

We had tea and it went down a treat. The steward tried to give the engineer some meat, but he would not eat. Otherwise the men were well contented now, and relaxed. They were talking about where they had been.

The next day the mate sent them out again, but with instructions to see if they could find the jolly boat. 'Don't bring any meat back,' he instructed, 'for in this weather it will go off. Seeing that there is plenty about, we can get a day before, for the next day. At the moment we have enough.' The three parties went out again to look for the other boat. 'I want you back before it gets dark,' the mate said.

The engineer was worse now, and it looked as if he would not last. The steward was with him all the time.

The mate looked through the glasses again. He was convinced that we were on a chain of islands, with the furthest island as a point, and another four in pairs. The bosun and his men made for the island alongside our island on the west side. They got to the shore and walked as far as they could, looking for things that we could cook in, as well as looking for the boat, but really speaking there was no way the boat would end up there. They found nothing.

The sergeant and his men visited the other islands. To the north they had to cut their way through thick undergrowth. They found plenty of foodstuffs, which they collected. They also found a type of jerrycan, which they brought back, and some mangoes. The second engineer and his party went to a point we had passed to land where we did, to the south. They found nothing of the boat, and nothing to cook in. They all made it back around 7 p.m. with the stuff that they had gathered. The jerrycan would be very useful. We cut the top off with the sailors' knives off, and we had something to cook in. The mate decided there and then to make a cup of tea, to which everyone agreed.

'Any idea of the names of these islands?' the steward asked the mate.

'No idea at all,' he said, 'but I get a sneaky feeling that they are French islands.'

The mate asked the sergeant if he could find his way to where the forest was. 'Yes, it is not far from here as the crow flies.'

'I want you to go out tomorrow and take the boys with you,' said the mate. 'Collect all the ferns you can carry. I want to use them as beds. Also I want to use quite a few making an SOS on the beach.'

We were all right for water. There was a stream just by us. The water was very cold even in this climate, and it tasted good. There was also a lake, formed by the water running down the mountain. The mountain was not very high – about 3,000 feet above sea level – but very steep in places. When we climbed it the first time, it took it out of us, for we had been sitting in the boat for some time. The lake was about halfway up, in a little valley. There was an outlet from which the water ran down to the sea.

The mate said he had no objections to anyone wanting to go for a swim, so the lake was handy for washing. Really, we were set up for life if we wanted, but no one did. The engineer was now in a critical condition. We were trying to keep quiet, but Wayne said to me, 'I don't think he will make it through the night.'

The third mate returned at about 11 a.m. having found some utensils. At least we could now cook. They reported that there was no sign of the other boat. They had scoured the next island going north, and found plenty of game and food, and fruit. The mate told them to rest up. We would next try the furthest island. 'This is the side we landed,' said the third mate. 'It would be this side, if any, that they would land.'

The mate now had all the boys cleaning the utensils with sand, for he wanted to use them as soon as possible.

He called a meeting after tea. He spelt it out about the other boat. 'We have given them plenty of time, and no trace of them can be seen. Let's have a two-minute silence for the second mate, Mr Pengelley, and his crew.'

When the two minutes were up, the mate said, 'The boat will go out in two days' time, with a fresh crew. Mr Third Mate, will you take the boat out again?'

'Certainly,' he said, and the same crew volunteered.

'Right, that settles that,' the mate said. 'Sergeant, I want you to take your men out. We want some meat. Also look for a plant with very big leaves, like a rhubarb plant. I want the leaves to act as plates. I want security on the camp – two men on each path that leads up or down either side of the mountain. I know I have said this before, but we don't know yet who is on these islands. Tomorrow the second engineer and his party will go out get some ferns and put them down on the beach in an SOS. Make them big enough for any plane to see them, and make sure that they do not blow away – anchor them down. Then bring a load up here for the beds.

'The bosun will take the boys down to the beach and search the beach properly. All the boys can go down, and you can have a swim there, but you must be here at 5 p.m. Cookie, let your boys go with the rest, and the tension that is within them can be released. You will see the fern party – you can help if the second engineer wants, otherwise do your own thing, but search the shoreline properly.'

As soon as it was light the next morning, Thursday, the third mate and his crew left to go over to the other island. The last thing the mate said before they went was, 'Be back tomorrow night at six at the latest.' The other parties all left by 9 a.m., and the boys left at the same time. The camp was empty other than about twelve men. The steward was still with the engineer, who was no better. He took a drink now and again. One of the reasons that the mate sent the boys out of the lamp was that there would be no row.

I said to Terry as we were going down to the beach, 'I don't know, it seems very strange that the mate has not put people at vantage points to look out for ships, for us to be rescued. I thought that he would have at least three lookouts at different points around the island, with a big fire to act as a beacon. Once the fire has got a good hold, dampen it with wet leaves, which would be at hand all the time to make smoke.

'Let's ask the bosun when we are down on the beach, and perhaps we could influence the mate to set up the observation points.' We arrived at the beach, and we went in about fifty feet into the wooded area and had a good look around. We found nothing, only our lifeboat, which we had put there a few days earlier. They must have used the other lifeboat to go around the island. It was really warming up. The other beach party with the ferns had not arrived yet, so all we boys went to the end of the beach and stripped off to get a tan all over. We had a tan to our belt, but nothing down below.

Terry was alongside me. He said, 'John, we have got no clothes, for all our clothes are rags. We've got no underwear. I am embarrassed for I have always worn shorts underneath. We've got no socks, our trousers are in pieces, our shirts are also tattered – much more of this and we will have nothing to put on. I am really sick of this now,' Terry said.

'I am too,' I said. 'The quicker we get rescued the better.' There was never any doubt that we would be rescued.

We all fell asleep, and were awakened by the second engineer and his party. The bosun and some of the men helped to put the palm leaves down, and then they all sat down. I did not see Mike or Ted much as they were working, in my opinion more than the others, to try to get us rescued. They were out on their own, as security guards, foraging, doing everything. The third mate had left early that morning to search around the west island. I hoped they would find the jolly boat, for I hated to think that they were dead.

The mate decided that in the morning the second engineer would take the other boat out and scour the other island at the point the most northerly. He would take the bosun and eight men, making ten in all. We knew that this would take a few days. The mate decided that the ABs would go with him, and the RN sailors, to make up the number.

The new party was to be off at first light. They were to take some meat, and ship's biscuits and some fruit. They had plenty of water, so they would be about five days out. They would take longer to reach this island, for they had to start off by travelling alongside the length of our island then the other island, going down the length of that, till they came to the apex island. This island was like a star to the other islands.

The mate named this excursion Boat 2.

During the night the first engineer died, to everyone's dismay. He passed away at 2 a.m. The mate decided with the steward that they would bury him at sea. They had some old canvas down in Lifeboat 2. As they had no sewing kit, the best course of action was to rope him in securely.

The steward said this was the way he would want to go. The second engineer with the bosun and the rest of the designated crew would bury him about four miles out, provided that it was still calm.

There was a small service with the third engineer reading the gospel. He recited from memory, for there was no Bible on the island. After the service the men going out in the boat made a crude stretcher. They carried him down to the beach, put him on the boat and rowed out to sea. They laid his body in the ripped canvas, said a few words, and he sank after his body was put on the water. There were a lot of wet eyes as they pulled away.

Coming back towards the beach after the funeral, Mike and Ted did the tiller work. They came close to the beach but continued moving along our island. The current was strong but after about three hours they got to the other island. In the boat were one rifle and two revolvers. They went up the island to see what they could find – looking for the jolly boat was the priority.

They split up, five in a party. Ted went in one party with the bosun, while Mike went with the engineer. They went west and south and they arranged to meet in the evening at 8 p.m. They found that the game and food were plentiful, but saw no boat and found no utensils. When both parties got back they had with a meal on the rocks enclosing the bay. 'We will go on to the next island tomorrow,' said the engineer, for he was in charge of the party. They all got behind the rocks and slept. It was cold, for there was nothing to cover them.

The first mate was worried, the third mate had been gone for three days now, and there was no sign of them. He was worried that something might have happened to them, although the sea had been calm. He had not passed his thoughts to the rest of the camp, as he didn't want to worry us over it. But by tea time there was still no sign of them, so, when everyone other than the security was together, he told them that he was worried over the third mate's boat, as it was well overdue. The bosun and his boat would not be back for a few days yet, so he could not go and look for them.

'In the morning,' he said, 'as soon as you have had breakfast, I want all the men to go out to the four points of the island to see if they can see anything. The boys will stay in the camp, with the cook. You can cook the meats ready for tea tomorrow,' he said to Wayne, 'and make a good tea for them when they come back.'

At 7 a.m. the party split up into twos. 'There will be fourteen men searching,' said the mate. 'Be careful. Look before you commit yourselves. Right, be off. Be back by tea time. I will go with the two army chaps.' He pointed out the paths that each squad would search. 'Don't forget, right down to the water.'

Cookie started to organise the boys into parties, one party of two boys to bring water, one party of two boys to clean camp, and two boys to get firewood. I and Terry were to help him. It seemed very strange. The camp was very quiet, and inwardly everyone was worried for the third mate and his party. Tea time came along and no one had returned. Then about 7 p.m., two parties came in together. 'Nothing,' they declared. Then the mate's party came in; they too had nothing to say. The other three parties told the same story: no sign of the men or any wreckage.

That night, which was the Saturday, it started to blow up again. Before we could do anything the skies emptied down. It was terrible. The rain soaked us before we could get into the caves. It was warm, which was a good thing, and we sheltered in the three caves that were there. All the boys were together. The laughter had gone from their faces. I think everyone wanted to be home. I know I was. I thought, *If I ever get out of this, this will be my last trip, no more.*

Terry, who was sitting by me as always, said, 'What are you thinking of?'

'Home,' I said. 'I wish I had never come back to sea. My dad was always on at me to pack it in. I kept saying, "This is my last trip." I said that on my second trip, and now I am saying this on my fourth trip. But this time I mean it. Terry, don't say anything, but I am really homesick. When everything was all right it was great, but I cannot put up with this.'

'I am here,' Terry said. 'I feel like you do. I will not go back to sea. This is my last. We will be out of here in no time,' he said.

'I hope so,' I said. 'Come on, let's mix with the boys. It will take your mind off things.'

After about three days the rain stopped. The sun was out straight away, warming the place up. We had plenty of dry wood, so we brought it out and got the fires going.

While we were concentrating on the food, two firemen began fighting with knives. The mate dived in between them, and stopped them. Forcefully, he said, 'As if I haven't got enough worries, without you two. Get the steward,' he said to Liam, who happened to be right by the mate.

Liam went sharply to the steward, who was in the cave. 'The mate wants you,' he said to the steward, and out he came. 'I want these two logged,' the mate said, 'and when we get home, they will be reported.'

I was trying to be busy with cookie. Terry was on the spit cooking the meat. I was sorting big green leaves, for we were cooking them as cabbage, and they were not bad. The only thing that we missed was salt. Cookie was experimenting with sea water, and was getting the water for cooking down to a fine art, mixing ordinary water to dilute the salt water.

The steward walked around and gave everyone a quinine tablet. 'I can only give you one a week,' he said. We all thanked him. He was a very quiet chap. He often thought of the captain and the engineer, for he had been with them for years, and both had now gone.

We supplemented our food with fish. We had five in the fishing party, until one of the RN chaps broke his leg. He was down fishing at the side of the bay, where there are large rocks. Jumping from one rock to another, he slipped and broke his leg. The party he was with, put on some splints that they made, and roped his leg by thinning the rope to make it like strings. The rope was brought every day down to the beach, in case it came in useful.

Liam and Ken were with us all the time. They were helping cookie, for they were two great boys, and always willing. Being with us, they got a little extra in the way of rations, and any titbits that were going. Cookie liked them – actually he liked all of us. The deck boys kept more to themselves, but we mixed as often as possible, especially in the nights. We all slept together. The nights were getting a little colder, and we had nothing that we could cover ourselves up with, so by being together we got a little warmth.

We had a smashing tea laid on: stag meat, potatoes and cabbage. For gravy, we had the juice from the fruit, which was delicious. Everyone complimented the cook for his ingenious gravy. Don't forget, we had only the one utensil. Cookie suggested that we boiled the potatoes first, then cooked the cabbage after, and it was a great idea.

By Sunday the mate was very worried. He sent out pairs to go to high points and search for the third mate and his party. The mate was considering going out in the boat when it returned with the bosun. I must keep the engineers and the wireless chappies here, he thought, in case something happens to me, for you have to have a leader. I must try to sort something out.

On the Tuesday the boat with the bosun was sighted. Everyone, near enough, went down to meet it. As the boat landed, the shore party took charge of the boat while the occupants got out and stretched their legs. They gathered around the mate, and reported nothing to declare, no sign of the jolly boat, and that the apex island was the same as the rest, with plenty of foodstuff and meat.

The mate said to the boys in the boat, 'I regret to say we have not seen the third mate and his party since before you went. I am worried. I just don't know what to do. Let's get back to the camp, and if anyone can come up with an idea, let's hear it.'

Nobody came up with anything, so the mate said, 'I want five people to cross over to that island. I want you to go over the top of the island so you can see in all directions. This means whoever goes in the next boat will have to go right around our island and cut across to this island.' He pointed to show which one. 'I want a different crew, so that you can have a rest. The one in charge will be the sergeant. He will take four men, two RN and two ABs. Right, that's all for now. Go and get some rest. Have your tea first, and get to bed. I want to see the army sergeant, and get Duke and Tom, the ABs, and Smithy and Turk of the RN.'

They came and gathered around the mate. He told them to go in the morning to the island he pointed to. 'Do you think five of you will be enough?'

'Yes,' said the sergeant.

'Go over the top and see what you can find. Be very careful, for we

159

have lost one boatload already, and I don't want to lose any more. Leave early in the morning. That's all, and good luck.'

Next morning, after a fruit breakfast and water, the five set off for the other island. We had not searched this island, though we had been to all the rest. We thought the boat with the third mate had gone around this, and something had happened. 'I want to know,' the mate said. 'I expect you back in three days. Be careful.'

It was 4 p.m. when they landed on the island. They hid the boat and cut inland to go up the hillock. It was not as steep as 'our' island. Looking here, there and everywhere, they started to go gradually up the incline. They had walked about a mile up this hill when one of the boys said, 'Look, we are walking on a track – there are footprints here.' So they stopped. They could see the tracks going upwards all the time, so they followed them. Then the ground got hard.

They took cover. Although the vegetation was sparse they had places to conceal themselves. They looked around but saw nothing. The prints were gone now, it being a stony area. They climbed the rest of the way, being very observant now, until they came across two paths, one going east, and the other going west down a big drop to the floor. But the most startling thing was that this was a German base.

'I want a man either side of the paths going down – in case the Germans are up and about here – to give us the wire if they are coming,' said the sergeant. There were bushes on top of the high rock face. It was a sheer drop of about 200 feet. In the harbour-type basin were two U-boats and a cargo ship of about 8,000 tons. The base itself consisted of two large diesel storage tanks and a jetty to take the U-boats. They could not see immediately below. They had to watch that they were not seen. There appeared to be a barracks; also there was a stockade, with guards.

They could not see a lot of what was down there. The sergeant said, 'Come on, let's get out of here.' They got the two boys who were watching the paths, and made a very quiet withdrawal. To be honest, the sergeant could not get back quickly enough.

The third mate, when he left, went around the island until he was in position to cross to the other island. It took him about four hours for the tide was really bad. He got over, and the men decided to have a look around the beach. They went about three quarters up the mountain and decided to come back down to the beach, where they made camp for the night. It was rather cold in the night, for there was a wind blowing from the sea. Next day they decided to go around the island in the boat. The third mate thought there would be no way for the jolly boat to be on the south side of the island, but he would have a look in case.

Rowing around the island they passed a type of lagoon, and thought nothing of it. They just passed it, looking for signs of the jolly boat. They went past the lagoon's entrance, not knowing it was a German base, for if you looked from the sea you saw nothing. Then a motor launch came up to them, full of Germans. They were shocked. They were made to turn around and row to the entrance, going into this harbour.

They rowed to the bank, where they were told to go, and were ordered out of the boat. They were lined up and taken into a type of canteen, where they were told to sit. Being in charge of the boat, the third mate said to the men, 'Don't say anything. We have been sunk and in the boat for two weeks. We have nothing in the boat to incriminate us, like food.'

The Germans asked who was in charge. 'I am,' said the third mate.

'Come here,' said a German, in perfect English. The mate got up and went to him. The German asked where the boat had come from. The mate told him, 'We were torpedoed a couple of weeks ago.' He was vague about the length of time because he didn't want them to suspect that the British had been on the island for a longer time. He was asked the name of the ship, from which port it had left, the tonnage, what it was carrying, where it had been making for, and the U-boat's number. This he said he didn't know.

'Are there any more of you?'

'No, none,' he said.

'Where are the rest of your crew?'

'That's we want to know. That is why we were looking for them, when you stopped us. We were in a bad storm a couple of days ago, and I thought perhaps their boat had overturned, or washed up around here.'

'Where is your camp?'

'Well, we have no camp as such. We are on the beach on that island there.' He pointed. The mate was told to sit with the others. As he went, the German called for one of the RN chaps, Whitley.

Whitley was asked the same questions. He gave near enough the same answers. Then it was the turn of one of the firemen, Edwards. He said pretty much the same. Meanwhile the third mate told those out of earshot of the guard, 'This is all that is left of the crew, and we are on that island, on the beach behind us.'

Hamman, the German officer, had gone through six of us and decided that enough was enough. All the ones he had spoken to had given the same sort of answers. He went out and left the prisoners with just the guard. They were in there for about three hours. Nobody came in all that time. An officer then came in. He said in German, 'Essen' (to have a meal). 'Yes, please,' the third mate replied. After about thirty minutes some Germans came in carrying trays. One of them spoke but no one answered, for no one could speak German.

The food was bangers and mash and it was very nice. They all enjoyed it and said thank you. Whether the Germans understood, nobody knew. After another hour sitting in the mess hut, they were told by Hamman to follow another German, and he led across the yard, to a big double door. They walked in to be confronted by a crowd of British personnel, prisoners of the Germans. They were shocked to see so many men there. They all gathered around wanting to know who the newcomers were, what ship they were from, firing all sorts of questions.

They answered all the questions they were asked. Now it was their turn to ask questions. They asked what the others were doing there. 'We were all taken prisoner when our ships were torpedoed,' said one. 'They are going to take us back to Germany when they are ready, we don't know when, but here it is cosy. We have a good meal once a day, and there is plenty of fruit here, so we are doing nicely. They don't bother us. They leave us to our own thing.'

It was now Saturday. A small boat with armed Germans in left the island fortress and searched the island behind their island. They left around 3 p.m. and went around the south side, where it was open to the sea. They beached their boat on the sandy beach next to the one where the *Topley* crew had landed. They decided to stay there the night. They had iron rations, for they had known that they would not be going back that night. They would have to search the island, and they would want light hours. They were not allowed to light fires in case there was someone on the island.

They were awake at dawn, and were on their way inside thirty minutes. As they crossed from south-east to west, they could see smoke, about two miles away. Treating it with caution, they proceeded slowly towards the smoke. They caught sight of the camp from about 400 yards away. They saw the cook and a boy preparing the breakfast meal. As they moved slowly nearer, they saw other boys around. Then, as they got nearer, they saw the men.

Now Sergeant Hauser was undecided, for he didn't know how many there were. Also he didn't know how many weapons they had. He had nine men, beside himself, all fully armed. He called his second in command to discuss the situation. The second in command was for taking the camp. 'Right then, take five men around the other side, in case some of them make a break for it,' said the sergeant.

Sergeant Hauser didn't know how long it would take to get to the side he wanted the five men to go, but he allowed two hours for them to get there. 'I will be going in then,' he told the second in command, Karl.

The British security that was halfway down the hill heard movements from their hideaway. Thinking it was the relief, Short, an AB, was just going to shout, when Young, another AB, saw that they were Germans. He put his hand over Short's mouth to stop him saying anything. They watched the four Germans go by. 'What shall we do?' Short said.

'There is no way we can warn the camp without being seen,' said Young. 'If we could get one of their guns, it wouldn't be so bad, but there is no chance. 'Let's try and get behind one of them at least,' said Short. Young said, 'right, let's try.'

They came out of their hiding place, but soon gave up. There would be no way they could attack one of them, for the woods were sparse, and they would be seen a mile off. 'Well, let's try,' Young said, with desperation creeping in. They wanted to do something, so they decided to drop down lower down the mountain and come around from the north. They managed to get round the Germans, all well and good.

German Camp

He volunteered that some of the boys had gone about ten days ago, and they hadn't been seen since, they must have drowned. The two security boys that were captured, Short and Young, were brought forward with the other German. They had fallen for the five card trick, as the Germans were getting ready to storm the camp, one of them dropped out to go to the toilet, and it was as he was coming back to join his mates, he caught the two of us behind the backs of his mates, he surprised them and kept them where they were, till the camp was captured.

We were all mesmerised. We just looked. The German who was asking the questions said, 'Spricht Deutsch?' (Speak German?). Everywhere I looked everyone was shaking their heads, including me now. Those who were still on the floor received the indication to stand through the soldier lifting the muzzle of his rifle up and down. The Germans then put all the boys in a bunch with a couple of the other crew. One of the soldiers was told to ask us who was in charge, which he did in broken English.

'I am,' said Mr Quick.

'How many?' asked the soldier, indicating the bunch of us there.

The second engineer said, 'All here,' circling his hand around us.

'I want the caves checked again,' the German told his men, so two went into each cave. The Jerries searched around, but they didn't have any lights, and there were a lot of dark corners, in which our men were hiding. Having had a quick check when we were about to leave, I knew that there were four missing. Looking around the crew, I could see also that they had not found the other security guard ABs, Gerry and Paul. They were on the far side, away from the beach. I hoped that they would not get caught. That would make six, plus the mate's party.

That left fourteen altogether free. How many revolvers we had, I didn't know, but I thought it was about eight.

We were marched down to the beach in two parties. This took about three hours. We were first on the beach, and we were put in the boat as the first party. All the boys were in this party. Six of the Germans escorted us, and they left four on the beach with the other party. I heard one of the Jerries say to his mate, 'They aren't going anywhere.' It was hard for me to ignore that remark, and I had to look away.

We arrived at the German camp. We were all very surprised to see the size of it, especially the large buildings that were well hidden in the rock and jungle. A cargo ship and a U-boat were there. We were delivered to the German camp, and put into the mess room. We could tell it was a mess room by the cruet sets on the tables. We were given a hot meal with some hot coffee, and it was very nice – bangers and mash, with bread and butter. We were like prize dogs. Everyone there was gawking at us. We were surprised to see the German ships and submarines, and as we were eating another U-boat came in.

The Enemy Below

I was really intrigued by the U-boats, for I was wondering if Captain Sturmer was still about, but I dared not ask, as they might tie me in with the *Tri-Mark* incident. Also I dared not speak German. It would be handy to know what they are going to do to us, and handy for the officers to know what was going on. I therefore didn't want to advertise that I spoke German.

The second engineer, Mr Quick, sent word around quietly that we were the last of the crew of the *Topley*. The others in the other lifeboat had not been seen since the storm. If everyone kept to that story, at least we would have a chance. You never knew what might happen for us if the others were still free.

The Germans were now talking to us one by one (not the boys yet, just the men). They tried tricking the men to say things that they didn't want to say. They said to one of the men, 'That chap that was in here a minute ago said you all landed on the island.'

'That is right – what was left of us.' He then told this German, Hamman, that nine of our party had gone out to look for utensils to cook in, and that we never saw them again.

Each man went in, and they all near enough said the same thing. Then they called one of the boys in, deck boy Radford. He said the same as everyone else. When he came out, one of the guards said to another guard, 'When the other boatload comes in, I think that will be the lot.' Hearing this I told Mr Quick what I had heard.

Mr Quick softly said, 'How do you know that?'

'I heard the guards talking.'

'Do you understand German?'

'Yes, but please keep it quiet. I don't want anyone to know.'

'The ship will be ready to leave in approximately three days' time, for the blacksmith has to make a special part that goes in the propeller shaft. This will take a few more days. I have got to know,' said the commandant, 'for our subs will have to know well in advance, so the ship will have an easy passage.'

The other boatload of prisoners had come in now. We were in an adjoining room to the mess hall. We could hear them coming in, but we were not allowed to contact them. They were given a meal. Then, after the Germans picked one out at a time and asked them questions – and their answers must have been the same as ours – we were all put together then taken out to the stockade.

The commandant said, 'What day is it?'

'Sunday,' said the second in command, who was the first officer, Schultz.

'Tell them that I want that ship repaired and on its way by Wednesday.'

All the *Topley* crew that had been caught had been interrogated. To begin with, they were put with all the other prisoners on the ship, but it broke down and they were all brought back ashore. Then they were imprisoned with the third mate's crew that went missing, so they were all together and soon saw each other.

The third mate came over with the lifeboat men that had gone with him, looking around for the first mate. Coming up to Mr Quick he asked where the first mate was. 'We don't know,' Mr Quick told the third mate, Mr Dodds.

'How did you caught?' Mr Dodds asked.

'We were surprised early in the morning, 16 June. They took half of us on that day to here, and the rest the next day. They got round our security guards, fired into the air, and we all were taken prisoner.' He didn't want to tell the third mate that there were still five left on the island, for the less that was known, the better. The captured men and boys were told not to speak of these men.

Mr Quick was frightened to say too much, for there were a lot of prisoners there, and he did not know if one of them was a plant. He merely answered questions, not always giving the right answers. He quickly turned the conversation around to Mr Dodds, asking how he had been caught.

'Bloody stupid of me,' he said. 'We rowed right in front of them. They saw us and sent an armed boat after us. When they caught us, they towed us in.'

'Who gave our camp away?' Mr Quick asked next.

'I didn't. Nobody did – as far as I know. We made out we had been at sea since we were torpedoed.'

'Well, they found us too easily,' said the second engineer. 'I told all the *Topley* crew to stick together, and say nothing other than the name of the ship and that we lost some of the crew when the storm blew up. If asked how many were on the boat, say you don't know. You were too busy with your own work. Say nothing.'

All of us boys were together. We were put with the other boys who had been captured before us. I was with Terry, Liam and Ken. We were always together, and Terry and I were now very close. He was a comfort to me, and he was always there for me. I was very surprised to see the size of the stockade. The other boys told us that they were loaded once on the ship, but when it started to move out it broke down. They were unloaded again. I noted a strange flag painted on the side of the ship. 'Swedish,' someone said.

'That's not allowed,' someone else said.

'Go and tell the commodore,' one of the boys said. 'What can he do about it? Nothing.'

The food was good and there was plenty of it. Also there was plenty of fruit here to which you could help yourself, provided you behaved yourself. According to the guards, we would be on our way on Wednesday. On Monday the captain of the freighter had his birthday. The officers of the ship, and the submarine and army officers, attended his party in the wardroom. It was a lovely cool night outside, but in the stockade it was very warm. We could hear the Germans singing. It reminded a few of us of the singing in South Africa.

About 2 a.m. we in the stockade heard rifle fire, and automatic fire from a Spandau, with a lot of shouting going on. This lasted for over an hour, with the whole camp lighting up. The firing was here there and everywhere. It would quieten down, then start up again. Then it stopped.

We never knew who it was. As before, we kept our thoughts to ourselves. I said to Terry, 'I am waiting for the doors to bust open any minute now, and for us all to be rescued.' But now it was getting light, the firing had stopped. I knew our chances had gone, and I felt sick.

Terry said, 'You never know' – and with that the doors flew open, and a bloody big kraut stood in the middle of the doorway, and shouted in German, 'We have beaten them!'

Someone in the crowd asked who. The Jerry started to laugh. Then he shut the doors of the stockade.

There was a big buzz going on around the prisoners. Everyone was trying to find out what the German was on about. We started to think that the last prisoners that came in would know, and this carried on till dinnertime. Then the doors opened and six of the *Topley* crew walked in, four RN chaps and two firemen. As they came in, they saw us as we saw them. We all made for each other. Mr Dodds asked where the first mate was. 'He was killed with four others,' came the reply. 'We lost five trying to rescue you, but we gave a good account of ourselves. We took seven Germans out.

'As we were getting out of the boat with the Germans, the first mate, who had the glasses, was counting us off the boat. So were the other members of the crew that were watching. He said to one of the RN chaps by the name of Tony, "How many did you make?" They both came up with the same number: twenty-six. They would look for the others the next day. There was nothing that they could do, but, I said, "As soon as the others come in, we will go over and get the others to come with us. We will take what we want and dispense with the camp."

'We watched the camp all night. The German boat left first thing in the morning. We counted a couple of extra guards. Now the wait was to see how many were captured. In the meantime the mate stayed with Tony, and sent Jeff, an AB, down to the two that were looking after the lifeboat. You could get in a position to see the German boat pass the island from a hillock near the beach.

'They were to watch for the German boat to pass back to their camp with the rest of the *Topley* crew, then we would go over and fetch the rest of the crew that Jerry never caught. The rest of the squad, still with the mate, were searching around for the paths down to the German camp, so they could watch without being surprised. When they were going to attack the German camp, they wanted to know the exact layout. The mate thought that it would be better for him to observe, while the remainder of the crew gathered to him.

'He was also thinking what plan of action to take, and how to use the men. This was really awkward, for there were not enough firearms to go around. But he had to make an effort to rescue his crew. He wanted to see first how many men there was left, then he would make his plans.

'Ted and Mike were the two left on the beach. They got the boat out after it was confirmed that the Germans had gone back with the rest of the prisoners. The mate had sent two down to Ted and Mike to go over to the British camp. It didn't take them that long to get to the British camp, where they immediately saw the four that ran in the cave. One of them had gone looking for the two security chaps, who were still in hiding, for they were frightened that someone might have said that they were about.

'All six were now together. They now joined the four that had sent for them. Mike asked one of them what had happened. We were a little restless, for we were wondering why we had not been relieved at the time we should have been. They decided to go and find out, and were on their way to the camp, when they heard gunfire. Only a couple of rounds were fired, which was enough to warn us. They crept as near to the camp as they dared. They watched the Germans search the caves. They saw the injured RN chap come out, and Short and Young being brought in by the Germans. They then watched the crew being bundled together into two groups, and marched down to the beach. This was not the beach that we landed on, but a smaller one. We then went back to where we had been on watch, frightened to go into the camp, even though the Jerries had gone. We just wanted to think.

'We thought that now we were on our own. We didn't know that anyone had escaped the Germans. We thought that you were all caught, and we sat there trying to think what to do. It was really worrying. Then you showed up – what a relief, thank God.

'Taking with us what we needed, we made our way to the beach, brought the boat out from the hiding place, and rowed across to the island the mate was on, above the Germans. We got to the mate just as it was getting dark. It was pitch dark when the mate called us all together, and spelt out what he wanted to do. The only ones who did not participate were the two chaps on the pathways down to the Jerry camp, keeping watch. This was Monday night.

'They all agreed to try to free their pals, as the mate said, better sooner than later. They nevertheless decided to wait and try on Tuesday evening. Then, after thinking, the mate changed his mind for a number of reasons. The ship could be ready to sail the next day, if they acted sooner, the men would not be able to dwell on the forthcoming action, so they would not worry about it; also the mate was trying not to let anyone down, for if the boat should go, he would feel responsible.

' "I have changed my mind," said the mate. "Leaving it till Tuesday would have made a lot of you nervous, so we are going tonight around midnight. Also the boat might sail out tomorrow, and with it all our mates. Get as much rest as you can, other than the security." The party was split into two, one each path.

'They started off at 11 p.m. and got to the perimeter at 1.30 a.m. Not knowing exactly the time, for no one had a watch, he told everyone that both parties should make the bottom of the paths near enough together. "First look for cigarette-smoking guards." We had between us six revolvers, three each party. The PO (petty officer) took the other party. They thought that the Germans would be smoking or having a break, for in their minds they had nothing to worry about.

'The PO's party was facing the ship about 200 yards away from the pathway. They studied form, and thought it was clear, they could see a machine gun on the bridge, but no one near it. It was there for the prisoners when they board the ship. The PO told one of his men to try to get across, up the gangway, and attempt to get the machine gun. "Creep around the office building, to the corner of the building ready for the run across the open space to the gangway on the aft end of the ship." They steadied themselves ready for the dash. "Right," said the PO, and two of them with revolvers in hand dashed to the gangway. A wide-awake guard saw them and fired. It missed whoever he aimed for, but they still ran to the ship. The PO and the rest of the men his side made for the stockade, with only one pistol between them. They made a dash to the big doors, but were stopped in their tracks. They came under heavy fire, and they withdrew straight away. "It's hopeless," the PO said, taking cover. The two that raced to the ship got to the gangway. The captain of the ship came out and said, "What's going on?" One of the men with a revolver, in a million-to-one shot, aimed at the voice, and caught the captain, who fell dead on the deck.

'The two who were just running up the gangway were cut down, dead. While all this was going on the mate's party had crept down to the end of the path, where there was a hut, and tanks holding diesel. The firing from the other end of the camp, alerted the guards at this end. As the mate run to open the valves of the tanks, he was cut down. Ted and Mike tried to get to the hut, for they knew it was an ammunition storage shed, but they were cut down. The mate himself opened up on the shed. There was a terrific explosion, and the whole place lit up, but the tanks never caught fire. After about forty minutes under increasing fire, the rest gave in, for they had nothing to fight with.

'Out of thirteen men, five were killed, including the mate, Mike and Ted. Three were injured. Those who survived were taken into the German mess hall, and were interrogated till about 11 a.m. They were given a meal, and then taken over to the stockade. The injured were taken to the medical hut. We saw them the next day coming on the ship.

The Germans were now satisfied that they had the lot of us.

Prisoners' Ship

The Germans were furious with us over the shooting and the ammunition shed, for that was where they kept the shells and torpedoes and all small arms ammunition.

The German casualties were seven dead and seven wounded, mostly those who were caught in the explosion. Two were badly hurt. The death of the captain of the ship was a loss to the Germans.

The rest of the crew had come into the stockade after being captured. I was looking for Ted and Mike. When I couldn't see them, I thought that they had not been captured. But when I asked where the rest of the crew were, 'Dead,' was the answer. 'Ted and Mike?' Yes, I was told, we had lost five men, that included Mike and Ted. I started to cry, for they were my strength and I doted on them. Terry tried to console me. We sat in the corner where all the boys congregated, both crying.

Wayne was looking out for Terry and me, for he thought Terry a nice boy, and had taken to him like me. He found us both and tried to console us, for he knew how much I worshipped Ted and Mike. That was really the reason he came over when he heard that the two ABs were killed, for normally the men didn't go where the boys were. It was like being out of bounds.

Still grieving badly, I remained in a shell of my own, with Terry always trying to comfort me. Wayne went to the senior British officer of the camp and asked him if he would ask the Germans for some medicine for me. Before the shooting, the relationship with the Germans had been good, so the British officer had no reason to refuse the request from Wayne.

The British officer was Commodore Thomas, a very placid man. When he asked the German guard officer, he was flatly refused. He came back to Wayne and told him the Germans would have nothing to do with the request.

'But he is only a boy,' Wayne said.

'I am sorry, he will not listen.'

The German ship was ready for the prisoners. They would be loaded, today, Wednesday as the old captain had required. The Germans had promoted the first deck officer, by the name Krammar, and the new first officer was Launch. At 9 a.m. on the Wednesday they asked our ten senior captains or officers if they would like to go to the funeral of their mates, who were to be buried after the Germans. They said they would like that, also that they would like to go to the German funerals, saying that the Germans had been good to them. So they were allowed to go to the two lots of burials. The fallen were buried one by another, German and British, and the ceremony was conducted very well.

Ship Bensmark

It was midday when the loading of the prisoners took place. They were all put in No. 4 hole, in which there were three-tier bunks, with wooden stairs going down into the hole. The bunks were very close to one another, but there were still not enough for the men. When I saw that we were being trapped in the hole, I panicked. With the U-boat when I was captured I hated it, for I suffer from claustrophobia. I was whimpering away all the time, and clutching to Terry. Terry was sleeping up close to me, mostly with his arms across my chest.

The name of the ship was *Bensmark*. She went out at 6 p.m. There were now no British personnel on the island, only the dead. Nine Germans remained there. They were going on leave, having been out there for two years. There was to be another ship coming there in the near future, with replacement personnel and stores as well as to replenish the submarines.

The ship Bensmark was a captured Norwegian ship. It had been in the port of Hamburg when the Germans invaded Norway, so she was seized as a prize of war. The crew were told either to work for the Germans, with German officers, or be interned. All but five of them said they didn't want to work for the Germans. The five who stayed had big families to support. The crew other than the five were replaced by Germans.

The German captain who took over the *Bensmark*, Captain Otto Dorf, was a very nice person, very firm but understanding. He treated everyone on his ship as equal – he was from the old school. The other officers were of poor quality: arrogant, proper Nazis. The five Norwegians comprised two in the engine room north, greasers, and three ABs. They kept much to themselves. It was the money they were after. They were reliable and good friends to one another, though they didn't have much time for the Germans.

When the ship had been seized, she had been put into dry dock and converted. The first two holds were for oil, No. 3 hold was refrigerated, and No. 4 hold for general cargo. Altogether she was in dock for twelve weeks. When the alterations were finished, she was painted, and the barnacles were scraped off. By the time she was ready for sea, she was like a new ship.

Midway through July 1940 she was loaded up with oil, frozen products and general cargo. She left Hamburg and made her way to the North Sea, where she changed her flag. She was now Swedish. The Channel was more or less in German hands, for this was after Dunkirk. By hugging the coast, and being Swedish, the *Bensmark* presented no problem from the English point of view.

She had a hatch behind the bridge and in front of the funnel for her own storage of coal. During the early part of the war, when the Germans overran different countries, all ships captured that were in good shape would be converted, the *Bensmark* being the second such ship. There were no guns mounted on them, but they carried guns to be used when necessary. These were all double-barrel machine guns, in the stores under the bridge. The Germans had quite a number of ships that they took over as prize ships during the war. The *Bensmark* had sleeping quarters in the fo'c's'le head for the AB and firemen, with the trimmers. There were quarters in the aft end for passengers, such as the soldiers. The ship was about four years old, about 10,000 tons, with a speed about twelve knots. There were four deck officers with four engineers.

Being a Norwegian ship originally, she was under an agent. She operated in the Mediterranean, bringing cargoes from Spain to Germany, where she would be loaded to take a cargo back home to Norway. Other than the five Norwegians who stayed on the boat, the rest of the crew were interned in a prisoner of war camp.

The new captain of the *Bensmark* was once the first mate, Mr Krammar, who took over after the tragic death of Captain Dorf. The bosun took over as third mate, for everyone stepped up a rank.

The last British Prisoners aboard were the boys, myself and Terry the last of all. As we were escorted to No. 4 hold, I had a terrible feeling of fright and didn't want to go into the hold. I resisted entry. The German soldier escorting us pushed me and Terry into the hold. I was shouting, and trying to get back on deck.

A British officer on the stairs to the hatch came up and took hold of Terry and me and brought us down into the hold. I was resisting very vehemently, and it took another British officer to grab me, and carry me down, with Terry also shouting he didn't want to go down there. The

British prisoners were now shouting at the Germans to leave the boys on deck, but the hatches were closed on our entry.

There was one light in the hold. It was really grim, damp and over-crowded. The bunks were just slats that you lay on, and it was more or less two to a bunk, sometimes three. Wayne, hearing the commotion, saw me being manhandled down the wooden stairs, and he made his way to all the *Topley* boys and told us to follow him. It seemed that each British ship's crew had its own space, which was really a good thing.

As we arrived with our own ship, a couple of the crew asked if we were all right. It was decided there and then that Terry, Liam, Ken and I would all sleep together in the bottom bunk, with the deck boys two to a bunk on top of us. It kept all the boys together from the *Topley*, which was a good thing. It would have been then that Ted and Mike would have been really appreciated, but there was no use trying to think what they would have done if they had been around. In fairness to Wayne, he had been brilliant.

Hell Ship Bensmark

We all felt the ship moving. We were now trapped in the hold, and it was stifling. We were on our way – where, no one knew. We had been told when we were in the stockade that we were going to Germany, but for the moment the ship was going very slowly, probably to manoeuvre out of the bay. A few of the seamen were asking for water, including the boys. The commodore was telling everyone to be patient. There was drum in the corner of the hold; when it was used the smell was unbearable. Although we had yet to experience it, it was telling us that, when everyone started to use it, we would have a terrible smell in the hold with no let out, for they had sealed us in.

The commodore called for order. He wanted to have a committee to negotiate with the captain, regarding the complaints that were bound to emerge. Already there were rumblings. 'There will be four more officers with me, so I want them elected now,' he said. It was decided that Captain Oliver Brecon, First Mate Allsopp, Captain Chilvers and Captain Webb were to be our spokesmen. 'All complaints will be dealt with by us first,' said the commodore, 'and if there is a chance it will be acted on, the complaint will be put to Captain Krammar.'

We moved out at 6 p.m., so we believed. The Germans had taken all our valuables – from the men, as the boys had nothing in the first place – so we could only guess the time by our meals. The commodore asked if there were any stewards there. Five men put their hands up. 'Well, I want one of you to take notes.'

'We cannot do that for we have no paper,' came the reply so that was knocked on the head.

'Well, you can go as tellers, whenever there is a vote. Will the elected personnel stand up and give your names. Only your names, we don't want to know your ship's name, for security reasons. Now, I want everyone to note who the committee is. I think the first thing we must do is consider the welfare of the boys. We must try and get them out, or in a better position. These boys should not be down here with us.' Altogether there were fifteen boys, and the oldest being eighteen, and the youngest being me. We should not have been put in with the men.

The commodore continued, 'Let's see if we can get them somewhere else. Also if we can get the toilets emptied twice a day, for with the heat down here, and that smell, we will all be dying of cholera. We cannot do anything about the food yet, for we haven't had any, through the ship leaving. We can understand the problems.

'So tomorrow we will see what we can achieve as regards food and fresh air.' The commodore, when he was speaking, stood on the stairs. The four committee members came and stood by him as they were elected. There was only one light, hanging on a long lead from the hatch. The bulb was of very poor quality, giving a little light. With this bulb being in the middle of the hold, it was casting a lot of dark shadows. As the bunks were three tiers high, it was only the top bunk that was getting any light, and the shadows were thrown around the hole through the height of the bunks. Towards the bulkhead around the hole, it was pitch black.

Now this did not help the boys, for they were near enough in pitch blackness. This was frightening me, and some of the other boys, I was sobbing all the time. Terry found it very hard to console me. He was gripping me, as if his life depended on it, and muttering in my ear all the time.

All the boys were falling asleep now. We all took it to be night. The ship was moving fast in the water. We could tell because we had the propeller shaft running right through the hold, and the vibration was terrific. Eventually the hole went quiet, but the sobbing of some of the boys was keeping others awake. All seamen, when they have been going to sea for a long time, awaken around times of the watches. You could hear certain individuals asking what time it was, but no one had a watch. Even if they had, they probably would not be able to see it.

The *Topley* crew were together, talking a lot to one another – also to the boys, for they didn't want the boys to think that they were left out of anything. Wayne was great; he involved the boys all the time. They were talking now about the islands. The time was about 5 a.m., a really funny time to talk about the islands. It seemed that someone had come up with the answer to the question of where the islands were situated. They were a group of islands between Prince Edward and Gough Islands. These are well off the African coast. I don't think these Islands belonged to any one country. I shouldn't think so, for the Germans would not have been allowed to build the port as they did.

We had been at sea now twenty-four hours, and the weather was very heavy. In the hole, it was hard to breathe, and a lot of the chaps were getting very disorientated. About evening they started to cry for water. We had not seen a German since we had been battened down. We had had nothing to eat. The stink from the drum was nauseating, and the men were vomiting all over the place. It was about 6 p.m. when the hatches were opened, about four of them, in the area of the steps down into the hold. The air was sweet and beautiful.

The German officer on top of the steps came down two of them, and you could see his face grimacing from the smell. He said, 'Appoint yourself a leader,' to which the commodore said, 'We already have.' He also told the German that we had appointed altogether five officers to represent the prisoners. 'All right,' said the German officer, whose name was Heinze Brunagger. He was now second mate, having been promoted after the death of the original Captain Dorf. 'Be ready to come on deck. I must have your word that you will not misuse our trust.'

During the break, while we were waiting to be summoned to the bridge, the tea was brought to the hatch – big dixies of soup (well, that's what they called it) and a lump of bread, nothing like we were used to. The soup was a piece of potato and a very small piece of meat, the rest was water, and coloured to make it look like soup. It did help for five minutes to quench the thirst. After we all finished we were still hungry and thirsty, we hauled the dixies to the top, where a German soldier on duty guarding us picked them up.

After an hour the officers were called for. They were shown into the wardroom, where the captain, Mr Krammar, was seated at the end of the table. The officers walked in and took their position around the captain, waiting to be invited to sit down. Mr Krammar started to spell out what he wanted in regards to discipline of the prisoners, with the officers standing around him. 'You will have one meal a day. You will have, according to the water situation, two cups a day. You will not be allowed on deck. We will open the hatches for about an hour a day for fresh air.'

Captain Krammar made the point that any disturbances on the ship would be met 'with discipline that you Britishers have never heard of.'

The commodore interrupted the captain, and quoted the Geneva Convention to him. 'I am not interested,' he snapped back at the commodore. 'For the sake of your prisoners' welfare I suggest that you obey the rules that are laid down by me.

'There will be no noise at any time, no singing, no banging the bulkheads. In other words I don't want to know that you are there.' Captain Krammar could speak perfect English. He had been in England for five years before the war, working for an instrument firm.

Back to reality. The commodore interrupted the captain and stressed that there were about fifteen boys down in the hole. Some of them were suffering from claustrophobia, and one was crying all night. He felt he was trapped, for he liked to see the sky. 'Could you, the captain, find a place for the boys, if I guarantee that they will behave? Perhaps do menial jobs on the deck?

'Captain, we have a couple of men who were injured, and they are not receiving the medical treatment that they should. Could you see that these men receive attention to their wounds, as down in the hold they could get an infection in their wounds without the proper treatment?'

'There will be no concessions to anyone at all,' Captain Krammar got up and walked out.

The commodore turned and walked out, and the rest followed him. They were really disgusted by the way that they had been treated. Captain Oliver Brecon said, 'I can see we are going to have one hell of a trip.'

The commodore said, 'I want you four to remember what was said in there, and what goes on on this boat. Whoever survives to the end of the war, make sure that man gets his comeuppance.'

They arrived back at the hatch to No. 4 hold, where a guard was standing. One of the German seamen opened the hatch, and the five seamen re-entered the hold. They called the prisoners to order, and spelt out what the captain had told them, explaining that the boys were to stay where they were in the hold.

Through the hatch covers being off, there was light in the hold. The officers noted that there was a twin deck just a couple of feet away from the stairs. When they got to the bottom, they looked up, and could see the twin deck was on the starboard side. 'What if we were to make a little bridge from the stairs to the twin deck, and put the boys only up there?' asked one officer. 'They could if necessary take their bunk beds with them. We want a couple of stout pieces of wood to go from the stairs to the twin deck, to walk across. Right, let's get some of the men to check the linings of the hold. Seeing it is a general cargo hold, it should be lined.'

They got some of the men to check the linings and any loose ones to pull them off. They had ten pieces, so they used six of them, in pairs three across, one on top of another to make it stronger. The width was five inches, and the thickness one inch. They got all the boys together and told them to carry the bunks. The commodore then thought better of it, and asked for some men to carry the bunks across to the twin deck.

Most ships have a twin deck, which is always in the No. 4 hole. The reasons are that the twin deck carries special cargoes, which never amount to much, and that there is always a companionway from the twin deck, usually to the aft cabins, which houses the ropes, paints and other things for the maintenance of the ship. There is a steel door that is always closed to stop the weather getting in.

There were plenty of volunteers to take the bunks all the way. The boys would have struggled with them. When they were all across, the boys could now be a little more comfortable. No men were allowed on the twin deck, only Wayne, for they looked on him as a father figure. I was now more controlled, until the covers went back on. I started to scream, and Terry and a couple of the officers had to grab me and restrain me. I was up the stairs hitting the hatch covers, and in a very bad way.

There was a crewman with a soldier on the deck. Hearing me, this crewman opened the hatch and screamed at me. Terry and the British officers were trying to hold him back. The commodore said to all men, after getting their attention, 'I am sorry, men, we did our best. My advice to you all is that we don't give that pug a chance to have a go at us. So, if we conform to the rules that he has laid down, that will be to our benefit. I hope,' he added very quietly.

We had our meal, which this time was very hot. We still had a lump of bread, but the soup was a fine liquid. We used it as water to drink rather than as a soup, for the holes were still very hot. Two men were very ill. They had been brought to the twin deck, for it was a little cooler. The RN chap who broke his leg was also in a very bad way, yet there was nothing that could be done for any of them.

The committee decided to have another go at the captain, so they shouted to the guard. The guard called his NCO and told him of the request. This NCO went and saw his officer, who went to see the captain, and the captain turned the officer down flat. 'I have no time for their little complaints,' he said.

The boys were very quiet now. They had no clothes on, for they had none. They had around them a torn old shirt to hide their modesty. Nearly all the prisoners were in the same situation. They had not washed for three days. It was early Saturday morning, and the drum was filled, to overflowing, spilling on the deck. The men whose bunks were near were trying to push into the middle. The stench was terrible. The committee now decided that enough was enough. They started to thump the hatch covers, and everyone began shouting and screaming. This went on for three hours. All of a sudden the hatch covers came off. The captain was there. He had an automatic in his hand which he had just taken off the guard. He screamed into the hole, and then fired a burst into the crowd in the hold.

'I warned you,' he yelled at the hole, then told the crew members who had opened the hatch to cover up again. Three men were hit and killed. Two were injured. Furthermore, the *Topley* crewman that had been injured trying to rescue us at the stockade soon died. Around the time as the captain sprayed the hole, he got an infection in his wound. Seeing there was no treatment available, he just died. Everyone in the hold was very upset now, losing men unnecessarily. There were a lot of rumblings going on.

A storm was blowing up. We could tell very easily. Every time the ship reared up the propeller, being out of the water would race, until it came back into the water. Through the ship being light, it was tossed all over the ocean. In the evenings it was getting colder, so we knew we must be moving out of the warm areas, like India or Africa. No one knew where we were, but we did know now that in the nights it was getting very cold. Although the hole was stifling in the day, at night it was the reverse.

We had had no tea, and it looked as though we would not have any. Everyone seemed to be losing weight. We were toileting in the corner behind some big wooden boxes, but the men down below were suffering. The ship's tossing about was washing the decks with the excrement, and now the smell was all over the hole.

The commodore was taken ill. He was a fine man for his age. He had been called back to sea when war broke out. He was sixty-three then and was now near sixty-seven, and the strain of the past couple of months had been too much for him. They had put him up on the twin deck with the other injured, and those who had died, all laid out away from the boys, but it was bad enough.

Captain Oliver Brecon had taken over. The committee agreed that they would not shout for the captain. The attitude of the men was that if they got hold of him they would delight in killing him. The boys had been very quiet for a last day now, for now we had come into Sunday. Realising that screaming and shouting was not going to do any good, I wanted to be able to concentrate on what the Germans were doing, for they were talking the other side of the steel doors from the twin deck.

I asked Wayne when he came to see us to ask Captain Oliver Brecon if he would come and have a talk to me, as there was something I wanted to tell him. About an hour after I spoke to Wayne, they both came over, and I asked to speak to the captain confidentially.

'What is it, my boy?' Captain Brecon said.

'Let's go over here,' I replied. 'I want Wayne and Terry to be with me.' All four of us moved to a secluded spot.

I asked Captain Brecon, 'Have you ever heard of the ship *Tri-Mark*?'

The captain thought for a minute, then said, 'Yes, wasn't that the ship that British prisoners captured?'

'Yes, that's it.'

'What has that got to do with you?'

'Well, I was the instigator of the British prisoners taking the ship.' Then I told him the story, about the lifeboat, the U-boat, and the transfer to a German ship, the *Tri-Mark*.

'How old are you?' Captain Oliver Brecon asked.

'I will be sixteen in a couple of months' time,' I replied.

'Well, how is this going to help us?' the captain asked.

'For one, I speak German, and understand it.'

'Where did you learn to speak German?'

'On the ship and the submarine. They taught me, and I am very quick at learning and picking up things.'

I then said to the captain, 'I think this is the reason for Captain Krammar acting the way he is, over the *Tri-Mark*. One other thing, captain, and you, Wayne and Terry – not a word of this must be repeated, for obvious reasons. I would be a dead duck if he found out,' I said, referring to the captain Krammar.

'I will listen to all the conversations that go on with the guard and crew members. I might be able to pick something up.

'I will come and see you every day,' said the captain, 'then you can report to me, without drawing attention to us meeting like this.'

When Captain Brecon went he was confronted by one Mr Horsey, a captain in his own right.

'Have you looked to see if there is an inspection cover on the drive shaft?' asked Horsey.

'No, we would not be able to see it,' Captain Brecon said. 'It's very dark over that side of the ship, but we will have a good look.'

After an extensive search they drew a blank. As one of the engineers said, it would probably be in hold No. 3, just the other side of the bulkhead.

The storm, after two days, had stopped. We had had no food for the past thirty-six hours, and everyone was thirsty. Also the deck was awash with excrement, and people were being sick with the fumes from it. At six thirty in the evening I heard the German guard tell some of the officers to take the drum out and clean it. They put the hose down the hold and cleaned out, giving us another drum.

We had no food that night again. Most of the men soaked themselves with the water from the hose. Although it was sea water, it was refreshing. The bodies were taken out. Captain Brecon asked if it was possible to see the captain. Permission was granted, and he and the other three went to the captain's wardroom. They complained about the one drum, about the deck with the spillage, and about the sick ones. They said they were frightened that cholera would come into the hole. Would it be possible to leave the hatch opened for a few hours a day?

'No,' the captain said. 'I have given in with the drums, and cleaned your pigsty out.'

It was late Sunday night. The storm having petered out, most of the prisoners were settled in for the night. They knew now when it was night and when it was day. I listened to the Germans and confided with the boys the goings on. We settled for the night. All the boys were tight against me when they slept. For a start there was not a lot of room there. But this was also to keep my thoughts away from the claustrophobia.

Terry would always put his arm across my chest. Also it was getting cold, so we couched into one another to keep warm.

It was 28 June we believed. We could not wash. I wash my backside every time I use the toilet; well, I had not been able to do that. Through not washing our bodies generally, we were all smelling.

We had lost another prisoner. Now Captain Brecon reckoned that this captain had gone too far. He asked the guard for a meeting to talk to the captain, and also to have the dead sailor removed and buried. When the others had died, they would not allow any of us to attend the burial ceremony. Captain Oliver Brecon thought that they were just thrown overboard. He was allowed to go and see the captain with the others of the committee. They had placed the dead sailor alongside the hatch, while the officers went to the wardroom.

They complained to the captain about the number of men dying and that nothing was being done by the captain to try to save the lives of the men. 'If that's all you've got to complain about, you are wasting my time,' the captain said and got up and walked out, leaving the four officers standing there speechless. When they got to the hold, the dead sailor was nowhere to be seen. Captain Brecon asked the German guard where the dead sailor was. The guard made out he could not understand English. 'They have thrown him over the side,' said one of the officers.

Captain Brecon was furious. He turned on his heels and stormed back to the bridge. The German guards, who were always on the deck, stopped him by using their rifle to club him. The other officers rebelled over this. They were clubbed and manhandled to the hatch, where they were put on the stairs. The other officers came and took them down.

After the rumpus of the morning with the committee, the captain did not give us any food that day. Also he kept the hatches on with no air in the holes whatsoever, tragically the commodore passed away. Everyone was incensed. They started to bang the bulkheads with anything that came to hand. The committee was trying hard to control the men, and once again, Captain Brecon asked to speak to the captain, telling the guard that the commodore was *kaput*, that is, dead.

Wayne was with all the boys on the twin deck, trying hard to give us confidence, keeping us thinking about different subjects all the time, but we kept moaning about the drinking water. Having none we were thirsty all the time. With the hole very hot, it was something that would not go away. Really, it was a little cooler up here on the twin deck than in the hole. Now all the men had lost the will to live or fight.

By Tuesday the smell was really unbearable. The drums were full. The saying going round the hole was, 'If he doesn't feed us then we will have nothing to get rid of.' In other words we would not need a toilet, for we would have nothing in us. There were now three men ill, and a lot of rumblings going on.

Although we had had grub on the island, it was never enough. We could always make it up with fruit. Too much was not good for you, for that could go right through you without the proper staple food. We thought it was about midday. The sailors, who were a hard crew, started to create about the hole. The banging on the bulkheads was like a drum. The ship being empty, the sound was carrying. Captain Brecon and the committee were being completely ignored. The protest went on for about two hours. Then the hatch flew open, revealing Captain Krammar with the German guard's automatic in his hands.

At first the prisoners thought that they had won the day. When the covers came off, they started to cheer. But they were rudely shaken. This time the captain fired the gun in the air. It went dead quiet. Krammar said, 'I warn you. The next time it will be in the hole again.' He gave the gun back to the guard and stormed away. The covers were put back on, but before they actually covered right up, Captain Oliver Brecon shouted to the German captain for permission to talk to him. 'Just you,' was the reply, and Captain Oliver Brecon got out. The guard was going to cover the hatch up. Captain Brecon stopped him, and said, 'Leave it open.' The guard left it open, though he didn't know what Captain Brecon was on about.

Captain Krammar stayed where he was, and shouted to Captain Brecon, 'Tell your men to be quiet!'

Captain Brecon said, 'There are dead men down there,' pointing to the hole. 'Commodore Thomas is also dead.' Captain Brecon was arguing with Krammar, deliberately to keep the hole open. He said that the bodies were decomposing, and that it was a disgrace that an officer of the German navy should treat prisoners as he had done. Also it was against the Geneva Convention. 'What you have done is against all principles of the human being.'

'Mr Brecon, please leave,' said the captain. In a way, it was a complete waste of time, but through Brecon's standing up to the German, the boys were having some fresh air.

Captain Brecon cut him short when he said, 'I sincerely hope that you will never be taken prisoner. I know you will never be treated the way you have these boys.'

When Captain Brecon went back into the hole it smelt a lot better. Also the toilet drums had been cleaned out and washed in the sea. There were bore holes, and ropes were put through them. After the drums were roughly emptied, they had to be scraped out with a type of scoop, as no one would be able to lift the drums when they were even half full.

The boys did this job. Although it was nauseating we did it without complaining, and all mucked in together. After the drums were washed out, the boys threw some water on their bodies in an attempt to wash. They were ushered back into the hole, and the hatches were replaced. About two hours after that, we had something to eat and drink. The same food came all the time. We noted the weather was not so hot. Whether this was to do with where we were, we just didn't know.

Everyone now seemed a little calmer, although we had lost another chap during the argument between our captain and the German captain. The saying in the hole was now, 'By the time we get to Germany, the ship will be empty. There will be no one alive to testify against this German Captain.' Liam don't say much, being a very quiet lad, but he remarked, 'I wonder if this treatment is intentional, for now we are losing men like flies.'

Touch wood the boys seemed to be holding up well. I was a lot better, but still detested the covering of the hold. I kept on saying, 'This is a steel coffin.' The boys were trying to pass it off, and talk about something else. 'There is one good thing,' one of the boys said, 'we will not be sunk by a U-boat.' Everyone had a smirk on his face. Not knowing the time, we all slipped into dreamland, Terry doing his normal thing of putting his arm across me, in case I woke up with claustrophobia.

On Thursday, I was one of the first to wake up, as usual. The other boys were waking gradually. Terry and I went to the ablutions together. One stopped other people while one went, then we would swap around. You could not clean yourself after emptying your bowels.

I had never thought I could take someone like Terry to be with me at such moments. I had really liked Mike and Ted. They were good, and always went out of their way to look after me. They had really been my protectors, and I loved them and worshipped them, so I really missed them. Terry would not leave my side, always comforting me, putting himself out for me, no matter what.

British Ships

I think if I had not made friends with Terry, I probably would have grieved. I would have lost my marbles. Terry was there for me. He pulled me through a very rough period, and I idolised him, for when we were in the hole with the covers on, he comforted me. If I ever came out of this, I knew Terry would be first, second and third in my life.

Another great person in my eyes was Wayne. He was great to all the boys, a proper father figure. I promised that, if ever I got out of this alive, I would pay him a visit. I would also like to keep in contact with his family, for, if they were like Wayne, he would have a very good family. I felt I would love to see his children, and wife.

I was daydreaming as usual. All us boys were sitting in a type of circle. There were fifteen of us. Everyone had a mate who was always with them, sitting next to him or, if they went to toilet, they would stand guard, while one went. They were a very supportive group to one another. The hole was like a cage of monkeys, all talking at once. The person who died two days ago was still with us. With the heat, his body was decomposing, and the smell was bad. What with that and the general smell in the hole, it was terrible to bear.

There were five chaps very ill. Each day brought more up to the twin deck, for up there it was a little quieter and cooler. For the moment we boys had not been affected, but I did not think it would be long, what with the inadequate food and water, the humid conditions and the smell. In talking, we had all come to the conclusion that cholera would strike us next.

Twelve had died either through illness, killed outright through gunshot, or from wounds a couple of days after they were shot.

I was hungry. So was everyone else. The topics of our conversations were grub and water.

The time was, we thought, about 10 a.m. We worked that out from the changing of the guard, which we had got to recognise as occurring every two hours. Suddenly we heard a gunshot. The hole went deathly quiet.

Everyone stopped talking. We could hear feet running on the deck above. Ordinarily we would have never heard them, but we did this time. The next thing was that the ship stopped – the shaft for the propeller stopped – and now we were all excited. Rescue, we thought. Captain Brecon had a quick talk to his committee, then made his way to the twin deck.

He came over to the boys. While he was doing this the other committee chaps came up on the twin deck. 'John, come here,' he asked. I went to him. 'I want you to keep your ears open, and try to find out, when the Germans are talking, what's going on. I will stay up here with you. As the Jerries talk, you let me know what is going on.'

Captain Oliver Brecon now addressed the hole, commanding utter silence. 'We wait about thirty minutes. Then, and when I say, I want everyone to sing "Rule Britannia", as loud as you can.' The reason for the thirty minutes was to allow for the whaler to come from the war-ship, so they would be able to hear us.

Excitement was terrific now. Everyone was sure it was rescue. Captain Brecon asked everyone to be quiet, for he wanted me to hear what was being said. Two Germans were talking and they were commenting on what was going on. I was now relating what they were talking about, and all the boys were listening to what I was saying. They were getting very excited. I told them that there were seven battleships, for that is what the Germans were saying. It was, as Captain Brecon said later, a squadron of cruisers, with destroyers.

The morning watches had changed. The routine was the same as any other day. Everyone got on with their work. The soldier on duty at the hatch of the prisoners had taken over for his two hours. There was no strict discipline, for the soldiers were allowed to smoke and talk with whoever wanted to talk with them. The soldiers were going on leave, after being on the island for well over a year. There were nine of them, and their sleeping quarters were in the aft part of the ship.

The soldiers' cabins were just two, very comfortable, enough to take the nine of them. There was one cabin each side of the companionway. Next to the starboard cabin was another short companionway that led to the bulkhead doors to hold No. 4, which was locked with two handles locking into lugs. This was the twin deck entrance. Next to the soldiers' cabins were the paint locker and the rope and canvas locker. At the other side of the soldiers' locker was a very small locker, for what purpose no one knew.

The mid-morning shift had relieved the soldier on the hole. He was sitting on the hatch covers where the prisoners were underneath, just smoking and daydreaming, probably of his home. His family had not seen him for eighteen months, not knowing where he was, for he was not allowed to say.

He was awakened from his fantasy when the big gun echoed from across the waters. Looking over the gunnel on the port side he could see a number of warships, about six or seven he thought of different sizes. One ship had fired the shot across the bows of the *Bensmark*, while Captain Krammar was in his own cabin, looking at some confidential papers.

Captain Krammar rushed out with the papers still in his hand, shouting, 'What was that?' although really he knew it was gunfire. Looking across the water on the port side, he could see a few warships on the horizon. One of them, a destroyer, was making for the *Bensmark*. 'Stop ship!' Captain Krammar shouted to the bridge. The ship slowed to a halt, it was 10.45 a.m. when the first shot was fired. This destroyer was making fast to the bows of the *Bensmark*.

A lamp started flicking from the destroyer as it was making fast speed to the *Bensmark*. The flicking light asked, 'What ship are you, and port of call?' That's easy, thought Krammar, if that's all they want. 'Ship *Bensmark*, port of call La Coruña, Spain,' his radioman flashed back.

The destroyer received the message and passed it on to the cruiser in attendance, in fact there were three cruisers and four destroyers, known as L squadron. The cruiser answered back by telling the destroyer to put a boarding party on her to check for contraband. Although the cruiser could see that she was light ship, they were just checking her out.

Cruiser squadron L was five days out from Cape Town, South Africa, in search of Q ships (armed merchant ships). It was also looking for blockade runners, and supply ships for U-boats. It had been out for fifteen days on patrol, and found nothing, so it went back to Cape Town for some supplies.

As the squadron set out again it was a very fine day, visibility excellent. On the radar screen a blip appeared at 9.45 a.m. Captain Tomlinson, the squadron commander, ordered an alteration to the course to investigate. At ten forty-five smoke suggested it was a cargo ship of some kind. Could be a Q ship, thought the captain, on his second trip out from Cape Town.

'Put a shot across her bow,' he ordered the gunnery officer, and at the same time ordered one of the destroyers to cut across her bow. The shot was delivered at 10.50 a.m. The destroyer had made her turn and was on her way. The merchant ship (for that's what it looked like) was high out of the water. It could be a trap, but she would have no chance against the might of the seven ships.

The destroyer sent a signal asking what ship she was, and her port of call. The *Bensmark* identified herself as such and said she was bound for La Coruña. The message was transferred to the squadron commander, who in turn ordered the destroyer to board her and search for contraband. The destroyer came close to the *Bensmark*, eyeing her.

On the run in he kept watch on the starboard side of the *Bensmark*, leaving the starboard side to the destroyer *Ascid*. The destroyer put her whaler on the water, with ten naval personnel, armed to the teeth, with an officer on board. A signal from Captain Tomlinson, on the flagship cruiser, said, 'Make sure you take a signalman.' The officer told the man who brought the message to get his mobile kit and to accompany him. At midday they were ready to go aboard the *Bensmark*.

The destroyer ended up about 500 feet from the *Bensmark*. The captain of the *Ascid*, Captain Trigg, used the megaphone and asked for cargo, or scrambling nets, or a rope ladder, to be put over the side. On the way across, in the whaler, they could hear singing. They stopped, for they could not believe their ears. It sounded as if it was coming from No. 4 hold. Now, with the motor stopped, they could hear 'Rule Britannia'.

'Send to the flagship, "British prisoners on board",' said Captain Trigg. They started the motor again, and still no rope ladder or nets came from over the side. The officer who was near the ship in the whaler said, 'Please put a ladder over the side.' The ship was very near the *Bensmark*. The officer shouted again, and with that the ship started to move forward. The officer was screaming at the ship to stop, but to no avail. It was now picking up speed, and the whaler was being left behind. She started to follow the *Bensmark*, with the officer still shouting, until he got near enough to see the bridge.

He ordered the captain to stop the ship. The captain ordered abandon ship. They all made for the boat decks, lowered and got into the lifeboats, ignoring the pleas of the naval officer.

Rescued

The British prisoners were very quiet. I was relaying what was said above me, including the news that the warship had arrived. I didn't hear the number of the ship, but I heard the German on deck say the whaler was only a few metres away. He told me that the captain had told the crew to make sure the hatches were battened down properly. 'The little boat is about 300 metres away,' he said, 'Sing; sing loud!'

I said to Captain Brecon, 'What does he mean?'

'Sing as loud as you can!' Captain Brecon instructed the prisoners, and said to me, 'He wants us to let the Britishers know that we are in the hold.'

They all started to sing 'Rule Britannia', and they sang for all their worth. The light in the hold was one bulb. It was more or less parallel with the twin deck in the middle of the hole. Those at the bottom were in semi-darkness, but those on the twin deck were a little better. As I was relating what the Germans were saying, I froze. My face showed fright, and I started to shake.

Wayne asked me, 'What is it?'

'They are sealing the hold up.'

We could hear hammering, which was probably wedges being hammered into the cleats. I said, 'This is a steel coffin, we are trapped, there is no way out!' I was now really distraught. I was shaking and screaming. The other boys started to scream and shout, 'Let me out!'

Wayne, Captain Brecon and a few of the other men did their best to get us out, but we were sealed in. The hold started to sing again. Everyone was encouraging everyone else to sing, but that was not in the boys' thinking.

The ship had now started to move again. You could hear the propeller shaft vibrating as it started to move. Also water was pouring in from the casement of the propeller shaft. Those who had been singing one moment, were now making for the stairway the Germans had made for the prisoners on the island, screaming their heads off.

There was no way out, only the proper way. All channels of escape had been explored a long time ago. I heard the 'abandon ship' order being given out. I told Captain Brecon, in a scream, that the Germans were abandoning the ship. The water by now had started to cover the floor. The stairway had broken down with too much weight on it.

Those that were on the stairs when it collapsed fell back into the hole that was awash with water. With the poor light you could not see properly. The poor souls were panicking, and it would not be long before the same happened to us. A few of the boys were already panicking on the twin deck while the level-headed ones were doing their damndest to stop the panic. The captain and the other officers were trying to calm things down. The men who had been on the stairs when it collapsed were now trying to get back to the twin deck. Now it looked like every man for himself.

The whaler had caught up to the bridge, and its crew heard the captain of the cargo ship shout, 'Abandon ship!' The lifeboats were lowered, and the crew were hastily getting in. The whaler was by now near enough alongside, but was obstructed from getting to the ropes that lowered the boats. Although the ship was still high out of the water, you could now see she was being scuttled. She was still moving slowly, and the German captain was making out he didn't know what the officer of the whaler was on about.

The squadron commander, Captain Tomlinson, sent his other destroyers to assist the one at the cargo ship. He had read the situation that the boat was being scuttled. He already knew there were English prisoners on board, for the destroyer sent to board the *Bensmark*, had signalled the information back to him. He ordered the other destroyers to get to the cargo ship and rescue the prisoners immediately – never mind anything else, get those prisoners out.

The other destroyers were soon at the scene. They could not find a way to board the *Bensmark*, for the Germans had cut the ropes and there was no way to board her. Things were now getting desperate. When the other destroyers came up they were frightened to come too close, in case there was a collision. If that happened, the other ships would be concentrating on rescuing their own naval personnel, and there would be a panic.

What they decided was that the destroyer *Thunder* would go around to the starboard side, and come on top of the *Bensmark* so that a couple of naval chaps could jump aboard. The Germans had now pulled away, well away from the *Bensmark*. They just waited to be rescued, sitting watching the rescue attempts.

Captain Krammar said to his second officer, 'I am hoping by scuttling the *Bensmark* all traces of the Britishers will be in the boat at the bottom of the ocean. This had to be done, for after shooting them in the hole I am a condemned man. This way I have a chance, as long as everyone keeps their mouth shut. You tell them in your boat, in case we get separated.'

They lowered their boats and pulled wide of the *Bensmark*, which was still moving slowly. They pulled about a mile away in the opposite direction from the way the *Bensmark* was moving, while the Britishers were doing their best to board her.

They could hear the prisoners screaming, and making a terrible row. Both lifeboats were now together and tied up to one another. Mr Krammar laid the law down about collaborating with the enemy – in other words he went out of his way to terrify the crew, threatening what would happen when they got back home. They could see now that the *Bensmark* had stopped. Also they could see some men on board. Captain Krammar said, 'Is everyone here? Anyone missing?'

The five Norwegians who had served on the *Bensmark* before the Germans had seized her in Hamburg, had taken steps to stay on board to release the Britishers. They had talked among themselves long before the ship was to be abandoned, and the two greasers said they would hide in the engine room if they thought the Germans would scuttle.

As the Germans had abandoned ship, the three ABs and two greasers, as well as one German soldier, had immediately hidden themselves. The greasers hid in the boiler room amid the coal, and they watched the first, and second engineers open the scuttling valves, after starting the engines slowly, so that the ship would move forward. That in itself would hamper any rescue from the sea.

The German engineers opened four valves. They were talking a long time, until satisfied that the job was done properly. The water was now rushing in. It had already caused blowouts in the boilers and fires that were soon consumed by water. Stig and Ole were biding their time waiting for the Germans to vacate the engine room. It was lucky that the bunkers were full with coal, for it was that which saved them from the Germans.

As soon as the engineers left, the greasers dived in the water at different valves. The water was now about eight feet high. They turned three valves off, but found the water had moved stuff on top of the fourth valve, and they could not shift it. They had, however, stopped the inrush of water, and it would give them a little bit more time. The two Norwegians did very well considering that, through the water rising, the lights had gone out, and they had to feel their way in the dark, diving into the water with a lot of flotsam impending them. Also they had to work either side of the ship, two valves to port and two to starboard. They shook hands in the darkened engineroom, and wished each other luck, satisfied with the job of work they had done.

They went up on deck. The effort Ole had put into the valves (especially the one that was blocked) had taken it out of him. He was glad that Stig was with him, for he came over queer. But when he got up on top, the air stimulated him, and he felt a lot better. When they saw the panic at the stern of the boat, they rushed to help the other three Norwegians, Olaf, Larson and Gunn – also Fredrick, the German soldier, who didn't like what the German captain had done, and was doing, to the British prisoners.

Fredrick didn't want to be tarred with the same brush. He was the German who had been telling me what was going on. When I was on the twin deck, I would listen to the German talking to Larson on the deck, knowing now that there was someone who could speak German. He would talk loudly so I could pick everything up, when he was talking to the Norwegian.

They now realised that they had to get a heavy hammer. The hammers were in the rope locker, close by in the aft end. Fredrick ran and got another hammer. While they were trying to get the wedges out, Fredrick attempted to hit the handles out of their lugs on the steel door in the companionway to the twin deck. As he was busy there, the five Norwegians were desperately hitting the wedges out. While three of them were doing this, the other two went to the rope locker, and brought all types of rope and tied the ends on to the capstan. When the hatch was opened, the ropes would be in place to throw down into the hold. At the same time the German, Fredrick, brought the rope ladder that was in the rope locker, and had it ready for the twin deck.

Banging away at the arms under the cleats (lugs), he could hear the panic the other side of the door. He got one arm released, and as this happened the hatch covers were off. The tarpaulins were rolled back, and the ropes were thrown down to the men. There were eight ropes, all tied ready for use. Now the German, Fredrick, was nearly overcome by exhaustion, and one of the Norwegians, Olaf, came and took over. The door was free. The sight for the Norwegians was unbelievable. Naked boys ran out, all terribly thin. The German and the Norwegian who had worked together on the door now ran in and put the rope ladder down into the hold, tying the ends on to massive rings attached to the bulkheads.

Two of the other Norwegians fetched a cargo sling and dropped the net from the twin deck hold. The water was now about ten foot deep in the hold. There were quite a few non-swimmers. They were standing on the bunks. A few of the Norwegians went down into the hold with Fredrick the German and helped the non-swimmers to the cargo nets, and saved them. The prisoners were throwing themselves off the cargo ship. There were British Naval whalers and other little boats. All the boats that these ships were carrying were being used.

The *Bensmark* was sinking fast now. The Norwegians and Fredrick came up and saw all the bodies all over the ocean, or so it appeared. Terry had hold of me, knowing that I was not a good swimmer. Just before we jumped in, I said to Terry, 'Don't leave me, will you?'

'I won't,' Terry said. Although we were top side, there were still a lot to come up. The Norwegians and Fredrick were throwing light ropes to those that could get hold of them, and they were pulled up. The Norwegians were cursing the Germans, for the hole was stinking – they could not believe the smell that was coming up from the hole. Olaf said to his compatriots and Fredrick, 'Come on, it is time to go.' The water was now nearly to the deck outside the hold, and there were still men trapped in the hold. But it was too late; there was nothing anyone could do.

When the Norwegians came out on the deck with Fredrick, the screams were awful. The water was gushing into the hole from the decks, and you had to get off now otherwise you would be taken down with the suction, and it still could be too late. The Norwegians and Fredrick jumped into the water. Really speaking they could have walked into the water, for it was now touch and go. They swam for their lives away from the *Bensmark*.

The *Thunder* had tried to get in alongside the *Bensmark*, but could not manoeuvre into the cargo ship, and decided to move around to the starboard side. This obviously took time. As the cargo ship was still moving this made it very hard to get alongside. The captain, whose name was Joyce, could now see that the cargo ship was foundering. The situation had changed. There would be no way to get alongside the *Bensmark*. The destroyer might be dragged down with her, for he could see that it would not be long. So he moved to the stern, then stopped, for now he could see all the prisoners fighting for their lives.

'Launch the whalers and the small boats and rafts – anything that will pick people up – and get those poor souls out of the water,' he ordered. He was frantic and he was chasing his crew to do more, although they were doing their best. All the *Ascid* boats were picking people up. They had nets over the side, and everyone was working hard.

Terry and I had now jumped into the sea, Terry clutching my arm. We were swimming away from the *Bensmark*. I was a hindrance to Terry with my swimming, but we made our way across to a whaler that was picking up the prisoners. Terry thought we were going to make it. All of a sudden a big seaman prisoner barged into Terry and me. The chap was about fourteen stone, a big lad, and he was another who could not swim properly. He was floundering, and he hit us.

Wayne had now got to one of the boats. He knew I was a poor swimmer, but thought the distance we would have to swim was achievable. This chap somehow got between Terry and me, and he almost knocked me out. I was sinking under the water. Wayne dived back into the water looking for me. Also one of the RN chaps on the nets saw what happened, and he dived in. He had a better view than Wayne, and went to where he had last seen me.

Dizzy, and with my head under water, I thought, I'm going. Then he saw Mike and Ted, and they were signalling to me to come with them. They had their arms outstretched, beckoning me to join them. I now had my hand outstretched, trying to grasp Ted's and Mike's hands. They were saying, 'Come with us, we will all be together.' I was clawing my way, saying, 'Wait for me, I have been looking for you. Hang on, I'll be with you now.'

This naval chap had seen me get bumped and noticed that I never responded. He grabbed me and pulled me to the whaler, where I was hauled on board. In the meantime Terry was shouting out, and working himself into a terrible state, for he had lost me. A naval chap, who was soaking wet, shouted, 'Here, son!' Terry looked towards him, not knowing what he meant. The sailor grabbed him. 'I lost my mate!' Terry screamed out. 'Here he is.' Face down, I was being pumped of water.

They turned me on my back with my head on the side. One of the naval chaps started to push up and down on my chest for a few moments. The chap got up and said, 'Sorry.' Terry started to cry and got down on his knees, and hugged me. 'Don't leave me!' he kept crying out. Wayne had now arrived after looking for me. He was on his knees, watching Terry hugging and holding me, when he noticed my eyes flicker. 'He's alive!' Wayne screamed out. The chap who was giving me artificial respiration turned and got down, pulling Terry off me, and started again on my chest.

I opened my eyes. Terry was kissing me, and crying. I said, 'Where did Mike and Ted go?' I was trying to look around for them. 'Where are they?'

Wayne said, 'They are gone.'

'I saw them just now,' I said and Wayne played along with me, saying they would be back in a minute, they had gone to see someone.

Terry got back down and hugged me. 'Don't leave me, will you?' Terry said.

The sea was full of bodies, all desperately trying to swim away from the ship, for they knew the suction would take them, if they did not get away. They were all struggling as a result of being weak, through lack of grub. But they were desperate men, and they were doing their damnedest to get away.

The destroyers, all four of them, had their boats in the water, trying to pick up all the men out of the sea. The weakened men just could not help themselves to get into the small boats or whalers. The RN chaps worked their socks off helping everyone. The one with all the boys in, including myself and Terry and Wayne, was now being taken to the destroyer *Echo*, whose Captain was Brockway. While most of the boys climbed the scrambling net, they took me on a stretcher on a sling. Terry would not leave me. When they got on deck, however, they began to take me away, leaving Terry on deck. 'I am going with him,' said Terry, moving and grabbing my arm. The captain was watching, and shouted to the first aid man, 'Let him go with his mate.'

We were taken into a small ward. I was immediately put into bed. Terry would not let go, so they put a bed alongside me. They stripped us and gave us a bed bath. The orderlies made remarks about how thin we were, like skeletons. The doctor then came and examined us both. He was shocked to see our bodies. 'They will need some building up,' he said, and with that some of the other boys were brought in.

They were all put to bed, stripped off like Terry and me. We were now in a dressing gown in bed. The other boys were now going to have a bed bath. The first one was stripped of his mouldy old torn shirt. All of them were like that in the hole. The other boys started to laugh, but in reality no one was truly laughing, for no one had washed since leaving the stockade, and they all stank.

Outside in the water, there seemed to be a never-ending stream of men trying to swim. The little boats were picking them up as quickly as they could. In between the little boats would go to their mother ship, unload, and go back for more. The sailors handling the little boats were really exhausted, but they fought the fatigue to rescue all they could. At exactly at twenty minutes to five, the *Bensmark* slipped beneath the water, taking with her about twenty men trapped in the hold. The full amount had not been established yet, for the survivors were on different destroyers, and there were still a lot in the water.

It was just getting dark when the destroyers signalled that all living survivors were on board, including five Norwegians and one German army personnel. Captain Brockway of the destroyer *Ascid* signalled, 'Shall I pick up German survivors?'

'No, take your station, end of message.'

The four destroyers were now overcrowded. They were told to keep station for the night, and in the morning the cruisers would take some of the passengers. The very sick were to stay on the destroyers.

The battle squadron circled around all the night in a big arc, and arrived back to where the *Bensmark* had sunk the day before. The Germans in the lifeboats were at the time not to be seen, they had drifted. After breakfast all the survivors were transferred to the cruisers, other than the very sick. Wayne was to leave us, but all the boys were to stay on the *Echo*. It would be for only a few days that Wayne would be away. Wayne, to all us boys was a very special person. He had time for every one of us boys, but we all knew his favourites were Terry and me. This was only because we worked with him. He was a special sort of man. We were all given a small meal, which was all we could have managed after being starved.

The Norwegians and Fredrick were taken with Captain Brecon to the squadron commander of the group. He made representations to the captain of the cruiser, Captain Tomlinson, explaining what they had done for the prisoners, saving all our lives. They were put into a cabin on their own, and they were treated the same as us Britishers. Everyone was allowed a shower and shave if they wanted. We had not washed or showered since we were on the islands. Everyone was given clean clothes, then a small meal. It would have been very unwise to overfeed them, for they had to be brought along slowly to solids.

At around 10 a.m. the destroyer *Ascid* went to pick up some of the German crew. When it hoved to, Captain Trigg, over the loudspeaker, told the ABs, carpenter and bosun to row over to the destroyer and come aboard. As the Germans came up the scrambling nets, they were lined up, and searched. One pistol and four knives were taken from them. They were taken down by the marines to the cells and locked up. When that was done, the *Ascid* moved off.

Inside another hour the destroyer *Ice* moved up and, over the loud-speaker, asked for the firemen and trimmers. They came aboard and were searched. Nothing was found. There were no greasers, as the Norwegians were the greasers on the *Bensmark*. They were taken down by the marines to the cells. Then, the destroyer *Thunder* came up about 2 p.m. and wanted the German soldiers to come aboard. Before they came aboard, they were told that if they were caught with a weapon, they would be put back into the lifeboat.

During all the transactions, Captain Krammar was doing all the translations. The soldiers left, then the engineers were next. They were all searched as they came on deck. The deck officer and the captain were last. They were told to stand outside the wardroom on the deck till they were called. With a double sentry from the marines, they were kept there for five hours without a drink of water. The marines were relieved every hour.

During these operations with the Germans, Squadron Captain Tomlinson asked if there was a Captain Oliver Brecon on any one of the ships. He wanted him and his committee of five to be brought to the command ship. After a few hours, all five of the delegation officers from the German ship *Bensmark* were brought to the cruiser, the command ship. They were given comfortable quarters. The name of the command ship was *Mango*. The squadron was now on its way back to Cape Town, where all the rescued British sailors would be hospitalised.

Hospitalised

Next morning the delegation of five was invited to the wardroom, where Captain Commander Tomlinson was to chair the meeting, with a secretary taking notes, and the second in command. First things first, Captain Tomlinson enquired how many prisoners were on the *Bensmark*. He was told there were 318 from the island and that three more were picked up when we had been at sea a couple of days. Fifteen of the prisoners were boys. Captain Tomlinson asked Captain Brecon to break down the times from when they left the islands.

When Captain Brecon finished, the committee all left after the commander said, 'That will do for now. We have picked up 254 survivors,' but Captain Brecon cut in and told the commander that we had already lost thirteen who had died before the rescue.

'I cannot tell you where the islands were,' Captain Brecon said before leaving. 'We were taken by U-boats over a long period of time. The best people to ask are the last prisoners that were captured on the islands. They would probably know. The third mate was the first to be brought in, with about nine others. Then a couple of days after they were brought in, the rest of the crew was found on another island, and they were captured, other than the thirteen or so who made a rescue attempt that which failed, in which they lost about five men.

'The last ones to come into the stockade were the ones that came by their own lifeboats, for they were blown towards the islands. They would have more idea than us, for they were on the islands a couple of weeks before capture.'

The day after we were rescued, all the boys were in the sick ward. Terry was as ever close to me. After being cleaned up and having a small meal of solids, we went off to sleep, Terry with his arm across my chest, as if holding me, the same as every night on the *Bensmark*.

Late in the evening of the first day on the destroyer, Captain Brockway and the duty officer paid a visit to the sick bay. Walking around they came across the two beds together, where we two pals were fast asleep.

Frowning, he said, 'This is not to be sanctioned, two beds together.' The doctor who was in attendance said that he had given permission for the beds to be together, for the two boys would not be parted.

Mr Brockway looked down on them, commenting that they were like two little dolls. He was asking himself how children like them could be allowed to go to sea. 'Leave the beds together,' he said, for they actually looked contented and at ease. All the other boys were asleep. They looked a lot bigger than the two he had just seen. As he walked away, his eyes were filling up. He thought, *What type of hell have these boys been through?* As Captain Brockway left he said to the doctor, 'Look after them, won't you?' The doctor confirmed that he would.

Most of the prisoners, after having a shower and a meal, were feeling a lot better. They had been told they could walk the decks, but not to impede the crew. There were still some prisoners who were poorly, and the medical staff on the British warships cared for them, cleaned them and comforted them.

The warships had now finished picking everyone up. The flotsam milling about was tremendous. The bodies of a couple of the prisoners who were trapped in the hole were floating around, and it was really disconcerting.

With the ship now back in formation with the rest of the squadron, Captain Brockway could hear the boys laughing and joking around. He was delighted now that they were recovering, and the older boys and bigger boys were mixing with all who had been prisoners. The men came up to Terry and me, and they laughed and joked with us. They made a right fuss of me, for they knew I had been translating what the German was saying, and they were happy that they had all come out of it well.

Ken and Liam were around the bed a lot, for they had been with Terry and me on the *Topley*. We were all talking about when we got home. We were finishing with the sea.

We eventually arrived at Cape Town. All the walking patients were taken off first into waiting ambulances and whisked away to the hospitals that were on stand-by to receive us. When our turn came to move out (we were the last on the ship), Captain Brockway came up to all of us boys, and wished everyone the very best of luck. Then we were taken out to the waiting ambulances. After about an hour, we arrived at the Cape Town Infirmary. Terry and two other boys who were in the stockade before we arrived were taken together to this hospital.

All four of us were put into a little ward. Straight away we were all given a bed bath, then put into clean pyjamas, and then we had tea. It was around 6 p.m. As soon as I had tea, I wanted to sleep. Terry had his bed put alongside my bed, which was strictly against the rules, but they waived the rules for us, and we both fell asleep, needless to say with Terry's arm across me.

We were woken early in the morning. We were all washed in bed. Our two new mates were coming in and talking. They were all a couple of years older than me and, I think Terry. By now I was looking forward to my birthday, wondering where I would be when it came along, 25 October.

We had a good breakfast, still not too much as we had to be weaned on small meals getting to larger ones each day. About 10.30 a.m. a couple of chaps in uniforms came in with clipboards in their hands, with official-looking papers on them. They sat down alongside Terry and me, and started to ask all sorts of questions, first to Terry. They began with the day he signed on, and where he lived. 'In Upper Grangetown,' said Terry, which was down the road from where I lived. In the opposite direction from Timmy. I thought, I wonder where Timmy is now. Then, after a while, the men finished with Terry. Staying where they were, they started to ask me questions, talking across Terry. We were told not to get out of bed, so we just lay on the beds.

They asked me all sorts of questions, including my date of birth. When I told them, Terry's ears cocked up. 'Ah, your birthday is in a few months' time.' When they finished, they asked me a funny question: 'Where did you learn your German? You are not sixteen yet, but you speak German very well, so we have been told. You were the one that the German soldier was talking to when the ship was abandoned.' I told them the whole story.

Then the officers asked how old I was when I first went to sea. 'Just gone fourteen,' I said.

'You were small, weren't you?'

'Yes,' I said, but I had two good mates who were a lot older than me and they looked after me.' Where were they now, the question was asked. 'They were killed trying to rescue us on the islands when we were taken prisoner.'

With that, the two officers got up and said, 'Look after yourselves.'

Turning to the rest of the boys, they said, 'And that goes for you to.' Then they were gone.

Each day now we were getting stronger and feeling a lot better. Wayne stopped by, bringing us all sweets and chocolates. It must have set him back a few bob.

Wayne stayed with us for about two hours, and made a right fuss of all in our ward. When he was going he turned and said, 'I will call in again, just before I leave Cape Town.' I called him to me, and I thanked him for what he had done for me, and what he had done for the boys on that hell ship.

He left with his eyes full, 'Look after yourselves!' he shouted to everyone.

They interviewed the third mate from the *Topley*, for he could be the one to throw light on where the islands were. No one else seemed to know. The third mate described the journey from Freemantle. 'About two days from Freemantle we were advised to go to Mauritius to pick up new orders. On the fourth we were torpedoed by a U-boat, although he did give us time to get into the boats. The German captain asked us what we were carrying. We told him, and then took to the boats and left.'

He told the full story, including the unsuccessful search for survivors from the missing jolly boat. He told them how the search had led to the discovery of the German base.

'Weren't we surprised! It was a well-positioned camp, with all the mod cons. Oil storage was camouflaged, there were deep-water inlets to take a merchant ship, also submarines at that time there were two.' They asked the third mate if he was willing to help to find the islands. 'Certainly,' if we can rescue them, I am all for it,' the third mate said. One of the three officers who were interviewing the third mate said, 'We never thought of that; that throws a different picture on the situation. We will be in touch when we are ready, but this must be kept quiet.'

A hospital ship came into Cape Town, and most of the survivors from the island were taken on board. Although most of them could walk, they were all undernourished, so they were taken by ambulances. Left behind were the delegate of five officers that had run the prisoners on the *Bensmark*, the third mate, and Terry and me. We were kept in hospital. All our other pals had gone on the hospital ship. They said that we were too ill to go, and that we would have to stay a while longer. Wayne came in just before they sailed. Terry and I were near to tears, for we were being left behind. Wayne's coming in made it all the worse. But he did bring the pair of us a lot of goodies. He hugged the two of us, and he went. We were really upset.

He gave me and Terry his address and made us promise that we would go down to see him. We both promised that we would. He lived in Grangetown, the lower end. We did find out after a while that there were other survivors still in the hospital. We both thought that they had all gone on the hospital ship. The Norwegians were in barracks in Cape Town, waiting for clearance, for they wanted to join our Merchant Navy. They surprised us about ten days after the hospital ship had gone by visiting us. They brought some goodies in and were great. We thanked them for our lives, and they made a right fuss over us.

The German soldier was in the same barracks as the Norwegians, but was not allowed out. He was kept separate from everyone, except the Norwegians. But where the Norwegians were allowed out, the poor German soldier was not.

They kept Terry with me deliberately. He could have gone on the hospital ship but declined the offer. I didn't know anything about this, until the authorities told me. They thought it was better for me if Terry stayed. I was still ill, and Terry was really great to me. I loved him for it. Without him it would have taken longer to get better.

The German crew of the *Bensmark* were all taken to prison, which was a very harsh place. It was an island prison in the bay of Cape Town, something similar to Alcatraz in America. I was told that they were in a prison where they would be roughly treated, but within the rules of the Geneva Convention. In all honesty they didn't deserve to be treated well. As far as we were concerned, the harsher the better.

I learnt after a while that, after the La Coruña episode, the Germans were very strict on their ships. No enemy prisoners were allowed to roam the decks of their ships. Probably that was the reason Captain Krammar would not let the boys on deck. But there again there was no reason for him to treat us the way he did.

A week after the officers had asked Terry and me about the islands, they came back. It was the day before my birthday. Well, surprise, surprise, they brought some new clothes for Terry and me, for a birthday present. I was really pleased that Terry had the same as me. After all the presents were given out, they sat down and went right through my history from the time I joined the MN.

The officers seemed satisfied and left.

The next day the hospital baked a cake with sixteen candles on it. It really got to me, but Terry was comforting. He would not let me cry, for that's what I wanted to do. I was thinking of home, my mother and father, with my sisters. I was really choked, but Terry was his old self, reassuring me all the time.

We came out of hospital on 29 October. I was feeling a lot better. The hospital discharged us to the care of the British Consul's home, in Cape Town. We were being kept handy now, awaiting the trail of the Germans, which would not be for a few weeks yet. We were allowed to do our own thing, and soon found out where the Norwegians were.

We went down there after getting permission from Mr Pride, who was the consul in Cape Town, to see the Norwegians to thank them for everything. Fredrick, the German soldier, was in ordinary slacks and shirt, basking in the sun. We talked to all of them, and even had dinner in the barracks. We stayed with them till about 4 p.m. then made our way back to the consulate.

A preliminary hearing took place on 26 November. We were given fresh clean clothes and money for our pockets, and were taken to the court-room. There we met Captain Oliver Brecon, with the other officers that had formed the committee. The consul was there with his wife, whose hospitality we had received, and they had been great to us since we had come out of hospital. Their names were Joan and Charles Pride. The consul was with us all the time, whenever we had official functions. Sometimes his wife would come. She always introduced us as her two boys, for she treated us like sons. In fact she had two boys back in England in the forces.

Mr Pride told us that, when we were called up, we should just say what we saw, without anything additional. 'Just speak the truth.'

The hearing went on for three days. We were not called up on the first day. Captain Krammar was there with his officers. They were not called to the stand, they just sat and listened through the interpreter. I was called the next day, and I was asked to report what I heard from the soldier from above. The soldier was not allowed in court, for fear of reprisals.

I told them in German, for I was asked to speak German. I think the reason was so that they would witness my knowledge of German, and know I was not lying about what I heard. I told them everything, including the time when we heard the wedges being driven home, and how I had started to panic.

The Norwegians were brought to court the next day, which was the third day. They testified to what had already been said – there was no cover-up. The court sat till 7 p.m. and adjourned the proceedings till after the war. The prisoners were to be kept in the prison they were already in till after the end of hostilities.

I asked Mr Pride why it was put off to the end of the war. He told me, 'They have a lot of our men as prisoners and, if we gave them the punishment that they are entitled to, nobody knows what the Germans will do. We might hang them, which they deserve. All the evidence that has been given, and records of all the court proceedings, will be kept in the British Embassy till the war ends. The reason for the evidence to be heard now is in case the key witnesses meet with unforeseen accidents during the war.

'Well, John and Terry, this will be the end for you here. Arrangements will be made for you to go home in a couple of days' time, so enjoy yourselves while you can.'

The third mate, Mr Dobbs, was at the hearing, but was not involved with regard to the discipline of the prisoners on the *Bensmark*. He went to the hearing believing, as did a few of us, that the case would be closed and punishment meted out. The third mate made it his business to come and talk with us. He wanted to know if we were both better, and he came each day we were there. He told us on the last day that we would not see him again, as he was going out with the squadron to try to find the islands. 'Checking the maps, I think it could be the Crozet Islands, which belong to France anyway. We are moving out in the next day or so, so I will bid you both all the best.' We shook hands, and he was gone.

About three days later, Mr Dobbs went with two senior naval officers on a Sunderland flying boat. They are very big craft, carrying a crew of nine, and they can be out four hours. They were used mostly for U-boat hunting. 'I have never been in a plane,' Mr Dobbs told Captain Brecon, who was staying in Cape Town for the time being. 'We are making for Gough Island, which we are going to use as a base, from where we will check all the surrounding islands.'

The Islands

As soon as the plane was serviced and cameras were put aboard, it left and started towards Bouvet, a small Norwegian territory, about 1,000 miles from Cape Town. They found nothing. The next day they went alongside the area that had been covered the day before: nothing. They continued this for a week, Africa side of Gough, not missing a mile. Each day they began from where they had left off.

They were now getting cheesed off. All they could see was water. They were more or less finished, having covered everything from the Atlantic Ocean, when they hit the French Islands of Crozet. They had been deserted a long time ago by the French. As the plane came to the islands it climbed to a very high altitude, and cut the engines so that it could glide across from the north towards the south east. They took a lot of photographs.

They believed they were not observed, for they were high. Gliding down the arc that they took, it would have been impossible for the Germans to hear or see them. When they got back Mr Dobbs was excited to get the pictures developed. Behold – there were the islands! They were French islands, so the British could not ask anything about the islands, as the French were sympathisers with the Germans.

The reconnaissance party went back to Cape Town the next day delighted that they had found out where the islands were. They had seen no trace of Germans there. Knowing that the camp was on the west side, well concealed, they had no worries. The military took over now, and they started straight away to make all the arrangements. They asked Mr Dobbs about the first mate's effort to rescue the men in the stockade, consulting him on all matters concerning the island, seeing that he was the one that went looking for the jolly boat.

Terry and I were given the very best of welcomes from Mr and Mrs Pride. I would go as far to say that they treated us better than they would with their own children. We behaved ourselves. We were swimming in the pool nearly every day. Now you could see the improvement in our bodies. We were putting on weight, and our bodies were becoming more tanned and physically improved. I could swim now. Terry had encouraged me. I was not as good as him, but I was a very much-improved swimmer. We would swim, then laze by the pool. The servants were great to us. There are four of them. We got on very well, laughing and talking with them all day, and never wanting for anything. Mrs Pride told the servants to look after us, and they did. You could see the servants idolised the Prides. They had their own quarters; they did what they liked within reason, and the Prides looked after them.

Life is Wonderful

Mr Pride had to go up country for a couple of days, and wanted us to go with him, to see what life was like in the country. We travelled about 300 miles away from Cape Town, and were away for two days. Mrs Pride was all for us going with her husband. She was heard to say to some of their friends, 'Charles is like a kid with the boys. He loves them.'

It seemed that a British subject was in trouble in a place called Mosselbaai, which was on the coast. He was accused of the rape of a black woman. For a white to go with a black woman was itself against the law. This person was in serious trouble. We went swimming on the beach. We had a security guard with us, for Mr Pride was to be away for a time. We had a meal laid on, and had a great day out. We stayed the night, together with Mr Pride, in the residence of the governor of the province. They sat talking all the night, while we sat outside talking to the servants, who were very good to us. We left about 2 p.m., and arrived back at the consulate at 8 p.m.

We had a shower and then put fresh clothes on, then had dinner. It was a new way of life there, and we were both enjoying it. When we got up the next day, which was Saturday, I said to Terry, 'I am going to write a letter home.' He said, 'I will as well, for we have had no contact with home since we left on the *Topley*.' So, after breakfast, I asked Mrs Pride if she had writing paper.

Terry and I went with Mr Pride to watch a football match. The names of the teams escape me, but at the time they seemed funny names. The game itself was a good one.

By Christmas the Prides were doing their best to try to keep us there. We did not mind, although we would rather have been home with our parents. I missed them, and Terry said the same, but we kept this to ourselves for we didn't want to offend the Prides. The Prides won the day, for we were told that we were going home on 30 December, so we had that to look forward to.

We had a marvellous Christmas. It was right what people were saying about the Prides – they had been so happy since we came into their lives. There were plentiful presents for Terry and me, including a nice watch each, with our names on the back. We had clothes and two pairs of shoes each, with our names on the back. Terry and I, with tears in our eyes, went up to the Prides and kissed them and hugged them for what they had done for us. You could see how happy they were, with tears rolling down their faces. We were not the only ones who had nice presents. The servants, all four of them, and the chauffeur had very desirable presents, and I thought what a wonderful couple the Prides were. The only disappointing thing was that we could not give them anything, only our love, which we meant.

On Boxing Day we all went to the big regatta that was held in the bay. While we were there, Mr Pride pointed out the prison the Germans were in, but we were not interested. We enjoyed the regatta, and after the events had finished we went out in the boss's boat. So ended a great day, and Christmas.

It was on my mind that we would be leaving soon. As much as I loved it there, and the Prides, I was now really homesick, and wanted to see my own family.

In a barracks well outside Cape Town, a composite force of South Americans, British and Indians were assembled, and were put into training in conditions that they would most likely meet on the islands. Mr Dobbs was with them. They were put through their paces all together, including a demolition party, and signals, and navy personnel.

The plan was for the cruiser force that rescued the *Bensmark* survivors to escort two landing crafts, borrowed from the Americans in the Far East, with small dinghies on the decks for the assault force to go ashore. After studying the photos that were taken, it was decided that the main force would use the routes that the first mate had used.

There would be a small party on the island that the *Topley* crew had been on until the Germans captured them. They were to make smoke, for the Germans to see. The idea was to draw the Germans to the camp that the *Topley* crew used, capture the investigating Germans, and take their helmets. Donning the helmets, our party would move back to the German base, with their helmets just showing over the gunnel of the boat.

The main party would take the same journey as the first mate took,

213

using both paths, left and right. If by chance there were some Germans on watch, they would be dealt with by the scouts in front of the main party, when the time was ripe to attack, which was scheduled for just before dusk.

The warships, after discharging the task force, would proceed north around the uppermost islands and come down on the western side, which would be blind to the Germans.

The attack force would arrive at least thirty-six hours from the time of assault, take their positions in their own time, and be ready when it got dusk around 8 p.m. Then they would proceed to their individual targets and secure them. The boat party dressed in German helmets should at that time be just about to come in. They would make for the wireless shack and destroy it. Each prong would have three attack parties, one to destroy the German barracks, two to safeguard the prisoners.

The boat party, after destroying the wireless shack, would help in anything they saw that needed their attention. They wanted the HQ left intact, in order to get hold of their papers. 'As soon as you have done your particular jobs, I want the HQ protected,' said the colonel. 'You will leave the prisoners where they are, till all hostilities have ceased. The assault force will be 400 strong. As from now no one will leave the camp. Mr Dobbs, you will be made comfortable on the ship, and I must stress that this operation will be kept quiet.

'The name of the operation will be Force 27, in honour of the twenty-seven men who lost their lives on the islands. That's all, gentlemen. I will keep you posted. The military commander will be Colonel Watkins, and the second in command Major Allsopp.'

By the end of December we were looking forward to going home. Terry and I decided to go and say our goodbyes to the Norwegians and the German soldier. We took a few goodies in for them, for they had no money to spend. The German solider, Fredrick, was very pleased. He was a young fellow, and very polite. He told us why he had revolted against what his countrymen did. 'I am a Christian,' he said, 'and my family is. What they did was wrong.'

We spent about two hours with him and the Norwegians, and then called into the hospital to see if any of the *Bensmark* prisoners were still in there. They had all gone home. So we left and, as we did, we bumped into Mr Dobbs, the third mate. We asked him if they had found the islands. 'Yes,' he said, 'but that is all I can say.' He asked us when we were going home. 'On the thirtieth of December,' we both said. 'We are looking forward to going,' I said, 'but in all honesty we love it here, though we are a little homesick.'

On 1 January 1943 everyone was warned to stand by at midday. It was confirmed at 1700 hours (5 p.m.) the two LCT (Landing Craft Transport) were being loaded with troops, and a small cargo boat would also carry troops. They left at 0200 hours and they picked the cruiser squadron up outside the basin of Cape Town. It was to take five days to arrive. They would be there at around 0100 hours provided that the weather was good.

It turned out to be very good. The soldiers were discharged quickly and efficiently at the designated place. Then the ships, the small cargo boat and the warships, went to the top of the islands, to the north, well away from prying eyes. They were to stay there till 7 January and be in position for the attack to start at dusk. They would leave their berth at 1000 hours.

The landing crafts would be in hiding at the northern island the opposite end from where the fleet was. The decoy would be put ashore on the old *Topley* sanctuary where the crew would light a fire, with the rest of the troops on Island B, the middle island, where no Germans went.

Everything went well. The Germans fell for the fire ruse and sent a boat, with four Jerries in, in proper battle order. They were captured as soon as they put their feet on the shore. The replacements went in with German helmets on, and five with their hands on their heads to impersonate prisoners. Their guns and grenades were in the well of the boat.

Their hands went on their heads as they turned the rock that was jutting out, which would make them blind to the Germans, until they came to move into the harbour itself. The third mate was with the party above the camp, where there were two pathways to the bottom, one leading to the offices by the stockade, the other to the tanks and ammunition shed.

A message flashed to the next island brought a boatload of troops, fifteen in all. They put the four German prisoners into the largest of the three boats that were there, and they were then taken back to the main party on the middle island, with an escort of eight men.

By the time dusk came, everyone was in position. Surprisingly there were no Germans about on the two pathways down. The destroyers were by now making their way to the entrance. They were to arrive about an hour after the action had started. Their job was to block the channel, or entrance, to make sure that no U-boat would try to get out.

Since the *Topley* boys had been captured on their island, the Germans had been sending a pair of sentries to the bluff on top of their camp, with a wireless. They would arrive at about eight o'clock, and come down just before it got dusk. Although they were watched by the assault party, the Germans suspected that there were no enemy soldiers about.

Although they had seen smoke earlier on they thought that their job was done. So they made their way down, shadowed by two of the assault party, until they went into their barracks, where the two scouts were waiting for the main party to come down and join them.

Right on time the assault went in, just as it was getting dusk. The Germans had switched their lights on, although they were poor lights, merely casting shadows about the place. The boat came in as the assault party by the tanks came down. They took the sentry out at the tanks. Someone shouted to the boat, thinking they were Germans. No answer came from the boat. Now there was firing going on at both ends of the camp. The boat party landed. The Germans that were there were very surprised. They were trapped. They gave in. The firing around the diesel tanks was very light. The reason was that the German soldiers looking after the tanks were mainly in their billet. They were cut off. There was no way that they could get down to the tanks and the ammunition shed. All Germans that side of the tanks and water and ammunition were taken.

The other party around the admin building was in complete control. The Germans in the billet were trapped and the firefight was useless. The Germans gave in. There was a cargo boat and one submarine in the port. They were sunk deliberately so as to block the channel so nothing could get in or out. In the stockade there were twelve prisoners. A couple of Germans tried very hard to get to them before the assault troops could. They were cut down.

It was all over by midnight. The Command HQ of the Germans was checked out, and a lot of very useful information was discovered. The

German prisoners were the commandant, the captain of the cargo ship and U-boat, four army officers, the crews of the sub and cargo ship, and sixty-eight soldiers and maintenance personnel.

The boat party that was to take the wireless shack out did so without any fuss, the two operators being taken by surprise. The amount of useful information was tremendous. The cargo ship was found to be unloading barrels of oil and other items, supplying the U-boats and the garrison. These boats were loading up in South American countries, and supplying the Germans. In this way they were beating the British blockade.

The force was there for three days, trying to trap any subs that were due in. One was expected in two days' time. The Royal Navy would be waiting for them.

Delay

On the 28 December Terry and I were swimming and lying about the pool. Mr Pride was there, sitting under a parasol reading and writing. Mrs Pride was sitting in a lounger by us. We lay on the grass. 'I am sorry, boys,' Mr Pride said during the little break he would take now and again to talk with us. 'I know you were due to go on 30 December, but I have to go over to London, to the Home Office, on the 4 January. I thought that I would be able to look after you to make sure you were on the right planes. It only means that you would be a couple of days late. I should say now that this is only a provisional date, but I will let you know as soon as possible.'

Terry and I looked at one another, and thought it was great. We wanted to go, and we didn't want to go, for it was so good there. 'I am glad you are stopping a little big longer,' Mrs Pride said. 'It will also help you to build yourself up.' I knew that I had lost a lot of weight. My legs when we first came there were pitifully thin. But I was building my frame back up, and the same was true of Terry.

I said to Mrs Pride, 'We have been with you about two months now. We were really not in a fine state of mind when we came, and we were oh-so-thin, the pair of us, but thanks to you and the boss, we have put weight on. We are happy and we both love you and the boss. Thank you.'

'Let's change the subject,' said the boss, so we asked him if we could go to see the Norwegians before we went, also the German. 'Yes, I will take you in on the Monday. I want to make arrangements for my trip to London. I can see about you while I am in the office. I am not pushing you out, but I expect you want to get home to your own families. We will be extremely sorry to see you go, for we love you, and you have made a difference to our lives. We will be sorry when you go.'

I asked Mr Pride if our letters had gone. 'Yes,' he said, 'they went in the diplomatic bag two days ago.' I then asked him a very strange question, which to me was very important. 'We know the army and navy have gone after the Germans on the island. We know that they will take prisoners, and we know that they will be brought back here. What about our friend, the German soldier who helped to save us? He cannot go back with his own lot. What will happen?'

'We have never thought about that,' said Mr Pride. 'You are right. What can we do to help that boy? He was a young soldier, about twenty. We would not like to see him get into trouble with his own kind, for if they thought that he helped us, they would kill him. Leave it with me. I will have a talk with the military. If you see him tomorrow, say nothing about the assault on the islands, for he would worry.'

The boss left Terry and me at the pool, and went inside with his wife. I thought we had upset them, for they did not want us to go. While they were away, I said, 'Terry, thanks for everything you done for me, for I know I was gone. I saw Mike and Ted beckoning me to them. I have not said this before, but they said that I was on my way out. I can honestly say they were down in the water about eight feet away, saying, "Come on, John, we have been waiting for you," with their hands beckoning me to them.'

'Yes, I know,' Terry said. 'You were with me one moment, then you were gone.' He told me the full story of my rescue from drowning.

I said to Terry, 'I idolise you. I want you to be my best friend for life.'

'That goes for me, too,' Terry said. 'I want to stay with you all the time.' We agreed that we would stick together, and one would not go without the other. We sealed it by cutting our hands and clasping them together. Then Terry said, 'We are blood brothers now.' We hugged one another.

We were not to go out on our own. If we wanted to go anywhere, we had to have a security guard from the consul. The one we had was a big chap, and he was very good, but it was very rare that we went out. It was so good to stay in. We had all the comforts that we would want.

We went down to see the Norwegians when Mrs Pride was visiting the hospital. We left her while she went in. We went down to the barracks that the Norwegians were in. The German soldier, Fredrick, was there as well. We were told by the Norwegians that they were going to work on British ships, and they were moving out the next day. It was lucky we had gone that day. The Norwegians were very excited. They were joining a ship in Cape Town, and had to be on board by 7 a.m. The German soldier would be on his own, but was told they were going to send him to Canada, for there were a lot of German prisoners over there. That would be better than staying there on his own. I felt very sorry for him, for he did a lot for the British prisoners, besides giving me the information on ship.

There were none of the island prisoners in the hospital there now. They had all gone home except for two more that had died. It was empty of our friends. We waited down in the reception area, for there was no point in us going around the hospital. We knew no one there. But Mrs Pride made it her business to try to talk with everyone. Needless to say, we were in there a long time.

'I am sorry, boys,' she said as soon as she saw us.

Mr Pride went away again for three days. We therefore had had another postponement. We were now going on the eighth, my mother's birthday. I said that to Terry. The trouble now was that a lot of paperwork was necessary. In Spain, where we had to go to change planes, they were stricter. Mr Pride had to get us passports, and a lot of other paperwork had to be done.

On our own, I said to Terry, 'I want to get home now. I miss my parents.'

'So do I,' Terry said, 'but we will miss it here. I still want to go home.'

I said to Terry, 'This is my lot, I am not going to sea again.'

'I guessed that, the way you have been dropping hints,' said Terry. 'I am not going, either,' he said.

I said to him, 'You don't have to stay home because I am finishing.'

'I am not. After the way we were treated and all that, I would not go back again.'

I said, 'You would if I was, wouldn't you?'

'No,' he said. 'I decided I would not go again when we were in the lifeboats, when we got torpedoed.'

'What we going to do when we get home?' he asked.

'Well, first I know now that I am growing and putting weight back on. If I get to the required size and weight, I will go in the army.'

'So will I,' Terry said. 'Anyway, let's get home first and after a spell we can decide what to do.'

On 6 January Mr Pride came into our bedroom about 6 p.m. He had not long come in from work. 'A few ships have just come in,' he said. 'They have been to what you call the Paradise Islands. They have about 100 Germans on board. They stormed the islands, meeting very little opposition. They destroyed the base, sunk a U-boat and a cargo ship, and took all their crews into captivity. There are about 150 altogether.'

I then asked Mr Pride again about the German soldier that helped to save us on the *Bensmark*. 'We know the Norwegians have now gone to work on British ships, but this poor German will be on his own.'

'No, not now,' Mr Pride said, 'he is going to Canada, and he has been told to say that he was captured at sea, on the *Bensmark*. He has to say that, for he might somewhere, sometime meet another German who will say that he is a traitor. So it will be better for him to say he was captured on the *Bensmark*, and nothing else.'

We were getting very excited now, we are going on 8 January. The Prides had bought us cases for our clothes, and we would pack the next day.

Going Home

I wished that I could stay there with Mrs Pride – she was a lovely woman – but it would be impractical. I was desperate to get home now. I wanted to see my father and mother and sisters. I worshipped my father. 'Wait till you meet him,' I said to Terry. 'You will like him.'

Terry was watching me. He asked, 'What are you thinking of, John?'

'Home,' I said, 'my parents. I love them, and now I just want to get back to them. What about you? You don't say much about your parents.'

'I love my parents,' said Terry. 'I have a smaller brother, whom I love, and my sister who is a year younger then me. We were always fighting and arguing. My dad is good, but he never involves himself like my mother. He is a very quiet man, a good man. I love him like I love my mother.'

I then said, 'I miss Mike and Ted. They really looked after me, more so on the Russian convoy. They would not let anyone mess about with me, they were great. I know you looked after me, and that I am grateful for. I love you just the same as the others.'

On 7 January our cases were packed, with all the clothes that the Prides had bought us. They bought exactly the same for both of us. They said we were rationed in Blighty and everything had coupons, so that's why we were given clothes now. We had a big party. There were quite a lot of people there. Most of them we had never seen before, but they made a right fuss of the both of us. We each had a small glass of champagne, just for the toasts. I could see the Prides were now really cut up, but they put on a very brave face.

It was about 2 a.m. when the guests started to leave. Now we were very tired, but we had really enjoyed the party. 'John, can I come around your house when we are home?' asked Terry.

'Of course you can, and I will come around your house. We will stay together when we are home, and go everywhere together.'

'Yes, we will do that. Come on, let's get to sleep.'

I said, 'Goodnight, Terry, see you in the morning.' It was morning – 2.30 a.m. 'What am I talking about? See you,' I said.

We were in bed when Mr Pride came in. He said, 'I went to the office today, to pick up some papers and our travel documents. 'Our flight is at 2.45 p.m. so we will leave here at 12.30 p.m. That will give us plenty of time to get to the Airport.'

We got up at nine, showered and dressed and came down and had breakfast with Mrs Pride. The boss had gone back out again, 'But he won't be long,' said Mrs Pride. Terry and I opened our hearts to her, and we both went and kissed her, with wet eyes.

Hello, Mam and Dad

The chauffeur put our cases in the consulate's car. Everything we had came from Mr and Mrs Pride. The crunch time came. Mrs Pride turned to us, and said, 'I cannot come to the airport, so I will say my goodbyes here.' She came to me, crying. When I kissed her, she held my hand, and she put some notes of money in my hand. 'No,' I said, and we were all crying. 'Take them,' she said, and she did the same with Terry.

'We don't want them,' we both said.

'You will be on the plane a while,' she said. 'When you get to Spain, and when you get home, you will need the money.'

We were still holding on to her, the pair of us, and the chauffeur said, 'Come on, boys, we will miss the plane.'

'My address is there,' said Mrs Pride. 'Promise me that you will write, now promise.'

'I will,' Terry and I both said. 'We will write,' I said. 'We both promise, and thank you again.'

'If you want to come back here after the war, you come. I will pay for the two of you. Now, don't forget.'

As we got into the car she would not let us go, and the chauffeur had to part us. We had arranged through a phone call that Mr Pride would meet us at the airport. As we drove away, Sam, the chauffeur, said of Mrs Pride, 'She is a wonderful lady,' to which we both agreed. 'She is very kind to my family, and I would do anything for her and the boss.'

We arrived at the airport. The boss was waiting for us.

'Hello, boys,' he said. 'I expect you are excited, at last on your way home.'

We both said, near enough at the same time, 'Not really.'

'Excited to get home, yes,' I said, 'but not leaving your home.'

'I can see that both of you have been crying, and I expect my wife was crying as well – probably started you boys off.' We did not answer of him. We went through to register in, and then passed through the gate to the waiting area. We had about an hour's wait.

When it was time to board the plane, Mr Pride said, 'Don't look back, boys.' Going aboard, we were shown our seats – we were travelling first class, for Mr Pride's rank demanded that. We were made very comfortable, fussed over from the time we boarded till we touched down in Madrid. It took us seven hours in the air. This was the first time Terry and I had ever flown, and it was exciting. I really loved it, and regretted it when we landed. The boss said, 'Now stick with me, do not wander.'

We now had to wait for a plane to Britain. It would have to go to Southern Ireland first, for the danger to neutral countries was always imminent.

We boarded the plane to Bristol at 6 p.m. It was a ninety minute journey. We had waited three hours for a plane, even from Dublin, for the war was affecting everything. Once again we flew first class, and were fussed over. We were now on the last lap for home. We were both looking out of the windows and we would swear that we could see Cardiff. We hadn't yet crossed the Irish Sea, but we were willing ourselves to think that.

We landed at 7.45 p.m. The boss insisted that he put us on the train to Cardiff. We had a taxi from the airport to Eastville Station. The boss found that there was a train at 8.30 p.m., which we caught and boarded. We got on the train, and then stepped off to thank the boss for everything that he had done, and his wife. We both did something that we were not ashamed of: we kissed him on the cheek, and we started to show tears again. 'Come on, you are men now,' he said, and you could see that he was tearful.

The train moved out. As he walked with the speed of the train, the boss threw two envelopes into the carriage. 'My address is on there. Don't forget to write.' Those were the last words we heard, for the train was now picking up speed. We waved, the pair of us, till he was out of sight.

There was a chap about forty years old in the compartment and two old people, man and wife. The forty-year-old said, 'Evacuees, are you? Going home?' for he could see that we had medium-sized cases with us. Terry and I looked at one another and said yes.

'How long have you been away?'

'About six months,' Terry said.

'Oh, not long.'

'Long enough,' we both chirped back. The old people spoke now. They asked us if we were going to Cardiff. We both answered yes, we were from Cardiff. The old couple said, 'We live by Roath Park. We have been to see our daughter in Barnstaple. We stayed a couple of weeks, but now we are both glad to be going back to our own house.'

The other chap got off at Newport, and we were both glad, for we thought that he was nosy. Terry asked why he wasn't in the forces. The old couple heard us. 'Perhaps he is unfit,' said the woman.

I said, 'He looks fit enough to me.'

'You cannot always tell by looks,' the old man said.

We started to pull away from Newport. The excitement was now showing on our faces. It was obvious to the old couple. 'I see you are glad to be home,' the man said. We never answered him, just talking between ourselves. I looked at Terry and thought, if it wasn't for him, I would not be here now. To me he is a great mate.

We arrived at Cardiff General Station and said goodbyes to the old couple. We decided to walk to our homes, for we both lived five minutes' walk from the station. Terry lived the other side of the railway line to me. If there had been a bridge crossing the lines, we would be two minutes from one another, but we had to walk around.

We walked down Tudor Road. We came to the lights. One turning was to Grangetown, which Terry would take. First turning right, he would be coming to Jubilee Street, then Stafford Road where he lived. I was to carry on up Ninian Park Road, the top end. We said our good-byes at the lights. I said to Terry, 'Thanks for everything,' and he said the same to me. He turned. I said, 'Don't forget, ten thirty in the morning,' for we had arranged that he would come to our house first, and the next day I would go to his house.

I carried on down Ninian Park Road. It was dark, being about 10 p.m. I had a watch wrapped in a cloth, in my pocket. My chest was sticking out a mile – it was a good job it was dark. I hurried the last 100 yards, got outside the front door and knocked. My oldest sister opened the door. Because it was dark (for no lights were to be shown), my sister had a job to distinguish who it was. I said nothing. Then, all of a sudden, she screamed out in a sort of frantic yell.

My dad ran out, thinking that my sister was being attacked. When he saw me, he grabbed me in a bear hug – and he was a big man! I was pulled through the door by my dad. You could feel the warmth in the house. My mother came and met me in the passage. She was kissing me all the time and I wasn't even in the kitchen yet. My sisters would not let me go. They too were kissing me all the time. I was now getting embarrassed. I got into the kitchen, in the light, and Mam would not let me go.

My mother said, 'Where have you been? Hang on, let's get you something to eat and a nice cup of tea.' Mam cooked bacon, eggs and tomatoes – lovely. I got stuck into it. When I had finished, Mam sat down. They were all waiting for me to start telling them of my exploits. But before I could start, Mam said, 'You have lost a lot of weight.'

'I know,' I said.

'We thought you were dead, for your money stopped from the merchant navy. We were told that you were missing, but here you are.'

'No more,' my father said. Then there was a knock on the door. My middle sister went to the front door. I just about heard a voice say, 'Does John Morgan live here?' I thought, *That was Terry's voice! No, it can't be, I just left him*. But it was.

My sister came in and said, 'There is someone to see you.' I thought before I went to the door, who knows I am home? It couldn't be Terry. I reached the door, opening it, for my sister had just left it ajar. There was Terry. He burst into tears. 'What's wrong?' I said, noticing that he still had his case with him. I brought him into the middle room. 'What's wrong, Terry?' I said. I had one awful job to understand him. He was in a terrible state.

I called my mother and father. They came into the middle room asking what the trouble was. Terry was still crying, really badly. I told my mother and father that Terry had been with me on the ship, and that he had saved my life. By this time Mam was comforting Terry, with his head on her shoulders. 'Come on, let's go into the kitchen,' Dad said. 'It's a lot warmer in there than in here.'

I said to Terry after we got into the kitchen, 'Hang on a minute.'

My father said, 'You girls, go to both Nanna's –' for they both lived in the same street – 'and tell them John is home. Then come straight back.' The girls put their clothes on and went out.

My mother asked Terry if he had eaten, 'I don't want anything,' he said.

I said, 'He has not eaten, for he has still got his case with him.' My mother cooked the same as I had, and Terry did eat it. He enjoyed it, that I could see. My mother said, 'What's wrong, my son?'

'My mother and father have been killed by a land mine that

demolished our entire street, killing forty-four people. I went into a corner shop were my mother got her groceries, and the man said, "I thought you were dead, got killed with your family. It was terrible, everyone from your family was killed, and we thought that you were as well, for we could not recognise some of the people." I have no one now,' Terry said, and he started to cry again.

'Come on, Terry,' I said, 'you can stay with me, can't he, Mam?'

My father said, 'Of course he can.'

I said to Terry, 'Have a wash – that will make you feel better. I will take your case upstairs to my bedroom.'

'That's right,' said Mam. 'I will go and make the bed, for it has not been used since you were home last time. You will have to sleep together, until we get sorted out,' said Mam. 'We had a bad blitz in June, just after you went to sea, and that was the last blitz that we had – on 12 June 1942.'

'We have had nothing at all since then,' my father said. Mam left to make the bed. As I was going to speak to Dad, Terry went into shock. He collapsed on the floor. Dad picked him up, and shouted for Mam straight away. She had just finished the bed, and was tidying the room. She came diving downstairs when Dad called. Terry was just staring, with no life in him. 'Take him upstairs,' Mam said.

Dad said, 'I will carry him,' for really there was no way I would have been able to carry him. In the meantime Mam had got some draught medicine she had used before.

Dad put him on the bed, and was just going to take his clothes off. I said to Dad, 'I will take his clothes off and put him to bed.' So Dad went out. 'If you want a hand, let me know,' he said, and with that the girls came home.

Mam brought the medicine upstairs and gave it to Terry and she closed his eyes, for he just kept staring and I was upset and panicking. 'Dad!' I shouted. 'Can we have that talk tomorrow?'

'Certainly, of course.'

'I am staying up with Terry.'

Whatever that medicine was, it had quietened him down, so I didn't get into bed, I just lay along side of him. I held his hand, murmuring, 'Come on, Terry, come on.' I fell asleep. I woke up in the middle of the night, for I was cold. I put the top blanket over me, and it was a lot warmer.

At 7.30 a.m. Mam came into the room and asked how he was. 'He has not said anything?' I said.

'Don't worry,' Mam said.

'But I can't help it. This boy saved my life, and I am not moving from here.' Dad came in. He decided that he wasn't going to work. 'Are you all right, son?' he asked me.

I got up and grabbed my father, and started to cry. 'Don't let him go, Dad, will you?' He was holding me tight.

'No, we won't,' he said. 'Come on down and have some breakfast.'

'No, I am staying with Terry.'

Mam brought breakfast for me. I had it upstairs in the bedroom. Terry was still in shock. Mam said at 9 a.m. I am going down to the hospital, City Lodge, to see the doctor. Mam had worked there for eight years, and had packed it in only recently, so she went to see the doctor that she knew. He wanted to come to the house, for we lived just around the corner from the hospital. He brought some tablets and a bottle of medicine with him. He examined Terry and said, 'He will be all right. He has had a terrible shock. He should be all right tomorrow.'

Dad did not go to work that day. In the afternoon he came upstairs and sat with me and Terry, although Terry never knew. Dad wanted to know what had happened at sea. I told him, including the part Terry had played. 'Dad,' I said. 'I love him. He looked after me all the time on that hell ship, and he saved me. He would not let me go, unless he was with me.' I said to Dad that, when I had been home the last time, Mam had met Mike in the Market. 'I will say, the two of them, Mike and Ted, they looked after me until they got killed.'

I also related how when I was drowning Mike and Ted were calling me to them. I told Dad the whole story of my rescue from near drowning.

'Dad, I have finished with the sea, and Terry has. This was agreed on the way home, before Terry knew what tragedy lay in front of him. Terry stuck by me, and I will not leave him go. If it came to a decision by you and Mam, and the answer was no, I would walk out with Terry.'

'Now, none of that,' Dad said. 'You know that we will stick by whatever you do, and we will treat Terry like you, like our son.'

'Thanks, Dad,' I said, and got up and hugged him.

I sat with Terry, and I was nodding off. My youngest sister knocked on the door. The older two had gone to work. I said, 'Come in,' and she came in and ran straight into my arms. She would not let me go. She had not said a word yet. 'Come on,' I said.

'I love you,' she said.

'I love you too,' I said.

'I miss you.'

'Come on,' I said. Anyway, I am staying home now, and Terry is going to stay with us, so you will have another brother.' She kissed me again and went out downstairs. I had sandwiches for dinner, and Mam cooked a veg tea. She put one for Terry, and said, 'When he wakes up, I will give it to him.'

I stayed with Terry that night as well, just lying on the bed with all my clothes on. Mam and Dad walked in about 9.30 p.m., wanting to know if there was anything that they could do. Mam gave Terry his medicine, although he didn't know he was having it, and I fell asleep. I woke up about 1 a.m., Terry was still out, and I went back to sleep.

In the morning I got the envelope that Mr Pride had thrown into the compartment. There was £20 in there, which was a lot of money. I gave it to Mam. She didn't want to take it. I insisted – she took it in the end. I told her where it had come from. Dad already knew the story.

Dad had gone back to work now, and I was lying on the bed, and I fell asleep. Terry came round and saw me where I was. He put his arm across me, and he fell back to sleep. Mam came in about an hour after, and saw Terry had come to. Remembering what I said about him putting his arm across me, she smiled and went back downstairs.

Dad came in from work. Mam said, 'Go upstairs very quietly and look into the boys' room.' We had not moved from when Mam was upstairs. Tea was ready, another cooked veg dinner. This time the older girls came upstairs and made a fuss of me and Terry. They were up there about thirty minutes. Mam shouted to them that their dinner would get cold. She brought mine and Terry's upstairs. He was looking a lot better now.

I said, 'Do you want a bath or a wash?'

'I will have a bath,' he said, so I went and ran one, then called him in. I went downstairs to talk to the family. My grandparents came round. 'Where is our new grandson?' they enquired. 'Having a bath,' I said. 'Where have you been?' – they kept shooting all types of questions at me. They had thought I was dead, for when Mam said the allowance I had left her had stopped, that was a bad sign. They assumed I was dead until they received the letter I sent from the Prides', which arrived just a couple of days before we started to travel home.

Terry shouted for me. I went upstairs to him. He was shy. He wanted me to take him downstairs to meet the family. I wanted him to get to know everyone, including the girls, so I brought him down, and he looked entirely different, very clean and smart. I introduced him to the girls and both grannies. He was now more relaxed, and we had some sandwiches and a cup of tea. Then we went upstairs to talk.

I said, 'Terry—'

He said, 'Before you say anything, will you come with me down to where I used to live?'

'Certainly,' I said, 'you know I will.'

'I want to find out what happened.'

I said, 'Terry, there is a home here for you. You are welcome to stay as long as you want.'

'John, I would love to stay with you. I will have a talk with your mother and father as soon as they are on their own, but you will have to come with me.'

'You know I will,' I said.

'We will go down, John, tomorrow. I want to find out where my family is buried. My mother's brother lived two doors away. I need to know if he got killed.'

'Terry, don't upset yourself. We will go and find out, but don't get uptight about it. Also,' I said, 'after we have done the necessary down your street, we will have to go to the Merchant Navy Office, and tell them we are finished. Is that what you want, Terry?' I said.

'You want to finish – you are packing it in, aren't you?'

'Yes, I said.'

'Well, I am, I am not leaving you.'

I said to my dad, 'Whenever I go to sleep, Terry always puts his arm across my chest. He's done that right from the off. When we were taken on that hell ship, I was screaming. I didn't want to be trapped in the steel coffin, for the hatches were closed, and it was dark, and, Dad, I was frightened. Terry always put his arm over me to comfort me. I love him for that. He was simply great. He is just a little older than me, but you would never get a better mate than Terry.'

Dad was going for a pint. He did that every night that I can remember. 'John, are you coming out for a pint?' he asked.

I heard my mother say, 'Leave them alone. Anyway they are too young.'

My father said, 'If they are old enough to fight for their country, they are old enough to drink and go in a pub.'

I said to Terry, 'Do you want to go round the pub with Dad?'

'Up to you,' Terry said.

I shouted down to Dad, 'No, we will come out tomorrow night,' for we were both still tired, though we were getting over the bad times.

Terry said to me, 'Did you open the envelope Mr Pride gave us?'

'Yes,' I said, 'this morning when you were having a bath. There was twenty pounds in it.'

Terry opened his, and the same was in there. 'I am giving this to your mother.'

'Our mother,' I said. 'Start accepting that. My mother and father are now your mother and father. Then we will be a lot happier. By addressing them as Mr and Mrs Morgan, you will be like a stranger with us. No, Terry, Mam and Dad. If you like, when Dad comes in from the pub, we will have a talk.'

'All right, I would love that, for I want to know what is going to happen to me.'

'Nothing,' I said, 'while you are with me, nothing.'

All the girls had gone to bed, and we were talking with Mam, when Dad came in. After he had taken his coat off and sat down, Terry said, 'Can I speak to you, Mr Morgan?'

'Just a minute,' Dad said, 'do not call me Mr Morgan, nor my wife Mrs Morgan. Just like John – Mam and Dad. What did you want to speak to me about?'

'Well, it's about me staying here,' Terry said.

Dad tried to make it easy for him, and said to him, 'We are treating you the same as John. You are, as far as we are concerned, our son, and you will be treated as such.'

Terry got up and said, 'Thank you,' and kissed Mam, and shook Dad's hand. 'I won't let you down,' he said.

'We know that. We love you for what you did for John. Right, let's have no more of this. You call us the same as John does, and you do what you like, like John.'

We then told Mam and Dad that we were finishing with the sea. 'We are going down to the shipping office in the morning to resign from the sea, as well as other things. I have had enough,' I said, 'The last trip was hell.' Now that was the first time I swore in the house.

'I am very glad over that,' Dad said.

We went to bed. Terry was a different boy altogether. He slept against the wall, with me on the outside, for the bed was in the corner of the room. Terry got in, and said, 'John, I love it here, and I love your family.'

'I told you at sea that they were great,' I said. 'If you ever have a problem and you want some advice, Dad will listen and help you. You be happy, that's all we want. We will have to write to the Prides to thank them, and for the money.'

'Mam, we are going to Sattford Road, and then down to the shipping office.'

'Why are we going to the shipping?' Terry asked.

'Well,' I said, 'they are going to know that we are finishing with the sea. Then they have to give us identity cards, then ration cards, then the money that is due to us.'

We walked down Ninian Park Road when we left the house about 11 a.m. We were talking and we did not realise that we were now in Terry's street, outside where his house once stood. Terry started to cry, 'Let it go, don't be ashamed,' I said. 'Get if off your chest.' We stood a very long time there. Probably Terry was thinking of the times when he was with his Mam and Dad and brother.

We started to move away. Terry said, 'I want to go round to the next street. There is a friend of my father's there. Perhaps he can shed some light on what happened.' We walked two streets to where this man lived, a Mr Thorn, who had been a long-time friend of Terry's father. We knocked on the door, and a lady answered. Terry was just going to ask for Mr Thorn, but the lady recognised him before he could say a word.

'Terry Radley!' she said with a startled expression. 'We all thought that you were dead!' She said, 'Come on in.' Terry introduced her to me. I shook her hand, then she said, 'Let me make us all a cup of tea, then we can have a talk.' She told us of the night of the blitz. 'I think it was around the twelfth of June, I am not sure of the date. It started with a warning, about half past midnight. Nobody bothered, for we had been having warnings nearly every night. This night was no exception.

Nobody bothered to get out of bed. And before you knew it, the next street was down. The poor souls never had a chance,' she said.

'Everyone was digging for two days. Every person they got out was dead, including your family. We thought that you were with them. We were all searching for you, until they told us to stop. As there were no more bodies there, we thought that you must have been blown to bits. Even your grave has your name on the stone, for all your family was put in the one plot.'

'Where have they been buried?' Terry asked her.

'Cathays cemetery,' Mrs Thorn said. 'I don't know where, but you can ask the attendant on the gate, he will tell you. There were so many being buried, we just didn't know which was which.'

Terry thanked her for all the information, and thanked her once again as we left. It was now dinner time. We caught the trolley down to the docks, for there were many cafes there. When we got off the bus, we went straight into a cafe and ordered pie and chips.

We stayed there till 2 p.m., and then went around to the shipping office. We told the clerk that we had finished with the sea. 'What are your names?' he asked. We gave them. He then went and checked some papers. He came back and said, 'John Morgan from Ninian Park Road.

'That's me,' I said.

'Ah, wait a minute,' he said, and he vanished. We waited for about twenty minutes. When he came back, he said, 'First the both of you have to go to the shipping company that employed you, as there is some money that is owed you there. And your name?' he said, nodding to Terry.

'Terry Radley.'

'Yes and you,' he said. 'Before you go, Mr Chamberlain wants to see you, John Morgan. Go to the second door on the right.'

We went to the door. I knocked, and a voice said, 'Enter.' As we entered, Terry was told to wait outside. Terry turned and left the room and I followed him. 'Where are you going?' the voice said. 'I want John Morgan.'

'That's me,' I said, 'but if you want me, I want Terry with me.'

Terry said, 'No, just you.'

'Either you come in with me or I don't come in at all.'

Mr Chamberlain got up and came around to the front of the deck, towards the door. 'Hang on a minute,' he said. We both stopped. 'Come in,' he said. We both walked back in. I turned to this Mr Chamberlain. 'Whatever you want to say or ask, you can in front of my brother,' I said.

'Sit down, the pair of you. We want to know the full story of the *Tri-Mark*, he said. I repeated the story as it had happened. Terry had heard bits and pieces, but not the full story. He was goggle-eyed listening, but said nothing.

'I have to have your story,' said Mr Chamberlain, 'it has to go to London. We just missed you before your last trip. What was your last trip like?' We both related this. Now he was goggle-eyed.

'I cannot believe that people as young as you two, could go through what you have been through,' he said. 'More so you, John, for you had a bad experience with the *Tri-Mark*.'

We were in there just over an hour. As we came out, Terry said, 'You never told me the full story. No wonder you are frightened of being caged in. I would be in a submarine.'

'Come on, Terry, let's forget it,' I said. 'Don't say anything to Mam and Dad, will you?'

'Not if you don't want me to, I won't.'

'Come on.' I said, 'Let's get up to the shipping company that employed us. I don't want to come down here tomorrow, I want it all wrapped up today.'

We dived round to the company office. We told the receptionist who we were, also asking for the pay that was due to us. She said, 'Please sit down,' which we did, and we started to talk. Terry said, 'I like your father, he is very easy-going. I know I am going to love it here.'

The receptionist came back out after a fairly long spell. I was getting very impatient. At last we were called into the office and given an envelope each, after we declared our names. We signed for the envelopes which held our money. 'There is a statement of what you have earned,' said the official. 'You understand that the day you were torpedoed your pay stopped.'

'No, I didn't know that,' I said. 'You are telling me all that we have been through was for fun, not money? With our lives on the line all the time? I think this is disgusting.'

He said nothing as he gave us our employment cards. 'I have been told that you have now finished with the sea. You have to re-register at the Labour Exchange. Also you must change your identity cards at City Hall.'

I more or less snatched the documents from him, and turned and walked out. 'Come on, Terry,' I said, and he followed me. 'I didn't know any of that,' I said, still fuming.

It was now time to go home. We caught the trolley bus to Ninian Park Road. Terry said as we were sitting on the bus, 'You lost your wing there, didn't you, John?'

'Yes, I did. To think of all we went through, and we never got paid at all, not a nickel.'

I was surprised that Dad did not invite us to the pub that night, for he always liked my company, and now Terry's. I later found out that he wanted to see Vince, his mate, a very good friend of the family. He was asking Vince if there was any work for the pair of us down at the Forestry Commission, where he was the manager. If there was any work there we would have it, for Vince and Dad had been mates for years. Dad wanted to ask him privately, so if he said no, well, that was it.

We had a long talk with Mam, and I could see that Terry was much relaxed. We went to bed about 9 p.m., for I was shattered.

When we were in bed, Terry said, 'I am going to the cemetery tomorrow.'

I said, 'We are going, not you.'

'All right, John,' he said.

'Come on, Terry, I want to be part of your life as well as you be part of mine – no secrets.' He asked how was it that we had a proper bath-room, with a bath, toilet, and washbasin. I told him that, after the first blitz on Cardiff, the family that owned the house sold up and went. They were loaded. They had the shop in front, which was a grocer's shop, and two horses in the stable, and two carts in the back, so really speaking we were very lucky.

'I'll say you were lucky!' Terry said. 'We had a sink bath once a week, in the kitchen. My mother would go out, and me and my little brother would bath, with my father sitting in the kitchen to warm the water. When one got out, the other used the other's water, just pepped up with hot water.'

'I am glad that we sorted the money out,' I said. 'Now, when we start work, how will we work out the money?'

'Don't worry, Terry, wait for it to come.'

We had a couple of bob now. We opened the envelopes from the shipping company and found that we had £23 each, so we were loaded. We had given Mam hers, and we kept the rest. 'We are going to the cemetery in the morning,' I said, 'and calling back into the city hall for our identity cards. If Dad asks us to go to the pub, we will go, all right?'

'Yes, OK,' said Terry.

We got up early in the morning, after a good night's sleep, for we were both tired. We had breakfast and went to the market and bought some flowers for the graves. I bought the same as Terry. We caught the bus. Terry asked the attendant at the lodge where his family were. The chap gave him the number of the plot, which we both made a note of, just in case one lost it.

We followed his directions. The plot was a good way from the gate. We arrived there, and it was sunken down, it looked awful. Terry started to cry. 'Let it go, Terry,' I said. 'Get it out.' I consoled him the best I could. We were both wrapped in one another's arms. We stood by the grave for a while. I said to Terry, 'Give me a pound.' He gave me a note. I put in the same, and I said, 'Come with me.' He followed me as I went over to where some gravediggers were working.

'Could you do me a favour?' There were three of them. I held the notes for them to see. 'Could you put a bit of earth on that grave over there,' I said, giving them the number, 'and build it up? We have been away, and now find that this has happened to our family.'

'If you wait a minute, we will do it now,' one said. We waited and they made a very good job of it. We were both satisfied, and we gave them the money, and they were pleased. We put the flowers on the grave. One of the workmen came over with a large flowerpot. We put the flowers in and it did really look nice. I was very pleased, especially for Terry, who looked a lot better now than when we first arrived.

Looking for Work

'Dad, there are a lot of things I haven't told you, but when I do it will be in dribs and drabs.' Terry had gone to wash, and there was no one else in the kitchen. 'Dad,' I said, 'you must realise, I would not be here now if it wasn't for Terry. I owe him a lot, besides my life. I have become very close to him, and he to me.'

'You know I have said that he can stay, if it makes you happy and Terry is happy,' said Dad. 'I am proud of the two of you. Neither will be treated differently from the other.'

'Thank you, Dad,' I said. 'Give us a shout when you are ready.'

'We won't have to worry about bombing now,' Dad said, 'they have not been over for a long time.'

I went upstairs to the bedroom. Terry was sitting on the bed. He had been crying. I said, 'What is the matter? Why are you crying?'

'Your family,' he said, 'they have taken me in. I am with my best pal, and I am crying for I am happy again.'

I changed the subject, 'You must call them Dad and Mam. Anyway, Dad is going to give us a shout when he is ready.'

He shouted for us. We came downstairs and went out straight away. As we were walking down towards the pub, the Duke of York, we bumped into Mam and my youngest sister, June. Mam said, 'I hope you are not taking them drinking.'

I said, 'Only a pint, Mam.'

'You should be ashamed of yourself,' she said to Dad.

I winked at Terry – she always gave him a rollicking. Every time he took me to the pub, she would get on his back. But he never took a blind bit of notice.

On the way to the pub I bumped into one of the mates, I had knocked about with before I went to sea. 'I didn't know that you were home. I'll call around tomorrow,' he said as he left us.

At the pub, Terry said, 'Surely we are too small.'

'Don't worry, I said, 'the landlord is a good friend of the old man.' As we walked in, all my father's friends made a right fuss of me. When I introduced Terry they took to him and treated him the same way.

Dad's close mate, Vince, came in. He knew me well. I told him about Terry, and he took to him straight away. Dad bought his friend a pint. Before Vince sat down, he asked Terry and me to go outside with him for a moment. We both followed him. He said, 'There is a job down the yard for the two of you, if you want it. 'Yes, please,' we both said. 'Well, report at seven thirty down the yard.' I knew where his yard was. 'We will be there,' I said. 'Monday, don't forget.'

We went back in and sat with Dad, they were playing nine-card don. Vince sat with us, and we had a good evening. The boys were taking the mickey and trying to wind us up but, knowing them as I did, I said to Terry, 'Take no notice,' and it was great. We had only two pints, but we paid our turn. We had a very pleasant evening. As we came home, Dad said, 'Did you get the jobs?'

'Dad,' I said, 'you know quite well we had the jobs. You fixed it up for us. I guessed that when Vince called us outside. Thanks, Dad.'

For the first time, Terry called Dad 'Dad': 'Thanks, Dad.'

The next day was Thursday. When June came home from school, I said, 'How would you like us to take you to a cafe for dinner tomorrow? We will pick you up at school dinner time, and we will go to Kardomah and you can have what you like.' She was really excited over this.

Terry said, 'You think a lot of her.'

'I do with all the girls,' I said.

The next night my mates called, all five of them. We went into the middle room and I introduced Terry to them, and told them he was my adopted brother. They liked him, and he liked the boys. They left about 10 p.m. We went to bed, Terry still with his left arm over me and his face close to mine. We woke up at about nine and we talked in bed for a while. We were taking June to dinner, so we got to the school, in plenty of time.

We had a nice dinner. Terry said, 'I want to go half.' I didn't argue, and I said to June, 'Thank your brother, he went half of the money.' So she kissed him and me, and then we took her back to school. You should have seen Terry's face. He was full of beans over what June had done. I told Terry I wanted to go into town and get the girls their presents, for I always tried to bring something home. If I didn't bring anything I paid Mam, and she used the coupons and bought whatever she thought they might want.

We had been home eight days now. I was really looking forward to starting work.

When we went to bed that night, I said to Terry, 'Did you see the papers?'

'No,' he said.

'Well, they are bringing a law saying half of the recruits that get called up will have to go down the mines. I am not going down there,' I said. 'If your registration number is for the mines, that's where you go. Never mind if you want to go in the forces, it will be the mines. I am not going down the mines.'

Next day we each wrote a letter to the Prides. Terry told them about his family and that he was staying with me, and that we were starting work on Monday at a timber camp. He told them that we were looking forward to it. We thanked them again for what they did for us, also for the money, and we both said we would come and see them at the end of the war.

On Friday and Wednesday nights my mates went to Army Cadets, so Terry and I decided that we would join, next Wednesday, at Kitchener Road School, just around the corner.

My mates had been around more regularly now that I was home. They told me it was law, that you must join some cadet force. I told them we had decided to join on the Wednesday.

We all went out on Saturday to the pictures and then to a cafe for fish or pie and chips, getting home about 11 p.m. We sat and talked with Dad for a while. Mam always went to bed early, so we talked well into the night, and could my father talk!

We had been home for about six weeks now. We were into March. We asked Vince for some wood to make a cross. He did better than that – he had one made for us, in mahogany, and it was expertly crafted. 'Bring the names and I will get it done for you,' he said. When it was finished it was beautiful. 'Seeing that we work Saturday till 4 p.m.,' he said, 'take half day Monday and go to the cemetery.' We both thanked him, and on the Monday we did just that.

The grave was nice and tidy. We saw the workmen that had tidied it in the first place. I said to Terry, 'Give me a pound, and I'll put one,' I said. 'Come on, you give them this couple of pounds, and they will always keep the grave tidy for us.' They said they would – they already had been doing it, so we knew that they would continue.

We came home and we had tea, and went round with Dad, just for two pints. We had the usual banter with his mates. When Vince came in, he asked if everything was all right. We both thanked him. We watched the cards, and put up with the banter, and took it all in good fun.

We joined the cadets on the Wednesday. There was a large crowd there. No one knew our past, not even my mates. We were accepted in the company, and we both enjoyed it. Terry and I were every happy. We were together all the time. I knew he gave in to me all the time, rather than arguing. He just wanted to show that he thought a lot of me. He appreciated what I had done with the grave, and that in itself made him happy. I think by then he was getting over the loss of his family, and was very pleased by the cross that had been made for them.

I had not been in the cadets long and they made a lance corporal. I think this was because the gang that I was with all respected me. I was like a leader to them, and I think for that reason I was made up.

We were earning good money at work. Terry and I paid Mam the same money. He was calling Mam and Dad by those names, and he was very happy with us.

It was soon 'double summertime', so it was around midnight before it got dark. This was for the farmers, so they could get their work done. We were both doing well at work, and Vince had told Dad that we were two good workers, and he was more than satisfied with us. Dad told Mam, and she let on to us.

Looking for the Army

We were in bed one night when I said to Terry, 'I don't want to get caught with the mines. I am thinking about the army.'

'Don't leave me,' Terry said.

'I am not. I am thinking for the two of us.'

When you are seventeen you had to register, and Terry was about due for that. I would not be for another six months. We had to think of something. I could register with him, saying that we were twins. I hadn't got my birth certificate – that was lost with the bombing of my house – so I could send away and get a new one. 'I will ask Mam where to send for it,' I said to Terry. 'You can get a temporary one from Cardiff, the Births and Deaths office, so that is what I will do. Then, if we can alter the dates of our births, that's what we will do. Then we can volunteer for the army. That way we will miss the mines. Great I said, 'I don't want to leave you.'

Terry went to sleep, his arm automatically coming straight across my chest.

Next day, before we went to work, Terry asked Mam about the birth certificate. She told him to go to the office. She said, 'I will come with you, take an afternoon off from work one day next week, and we will go in together.' I then asked Mam for my birth certificate. She went upstairs and brought a box down with all the important papers in, and she found mine.

I said to Terry, 'We will not be able to work it this way. My birth certificate will give me away.'

'What are you on about?' my mother said.

I then told her how everyone must register when they are sixteen, and explained that when the time came, so many would be for the forces, and so many for the mines. 'I just cannot go down the mines, Mam. I will kill myself rather than go down the mines, so Terry and I have hatched a scheme. I think first of all we must say that we have lost our certificates.'

'I won't be a party to this,' my mother said. I said, 'You haven't got to be. Just down where the office is, you go shopping. We will meet you in Marks and Spencer's, at the cafe.'

We decided to go on the Tuesday. We both rehearsed what we were going to say, deciding to say that we were twins. From what we had been told, the forces would not separate blood brothers, especially twins.

We went in on the Tuesday and asked for new birth certificates. We were asked our names, and we both said the same surname, with our own Christian names. We told the official that we had lost the originals through an incendiary bomb dropping on our house and setting it on fire. Funnily enough he never asked where or when. We gave our birth as the same day. 'Who's the oldest?' he asked.

I pointed to Terry, and he said, 'I am.' Good job we got it right; we could have pointed to one another, then the game would have been up.

We had settled down now, and were both happy in work. Vince was great to us. He treated us like his own. But we did not take advantage. We worked hard, and did what we were told.

When we came home from work on 17 April, we found that the daily papers had a full story about Terry and me, all about the *Bensmark*, even including photographs. I asked who had done this. We found out the next day after some phoning (although the public at this time were asked not to tie the phone lines up). It was all due to Mr Pride – he thought we were entitled to a little publicity. The phone box was outside the door. We were inundated with calls, and it was really embarrassing. I said to Terry, 'I just hope that they do not connect us with the story.' When my father read about it, he had the two of us together and asked why we had never told him. I said, 'Dad, remember, I told you I will tell you in dribs and drabs. I didn't want to be reminded about it. I told you the most important thing and that was about Terry.'

'I think you should have told me,' he said. 'What about the other trips? I never pushed you to tell me anything, but I think, as I am your father, I am entitled to know what my boys have been up to.'

'Dad, Terry and I have decided to be twins, for we want to go in the army.' I said about the mines. 'I am scared about being trapped.' Now I thought I had better come clean and tell him everything, including that I could speak German through being on a U-boat. He was shocked about the *Tri-Mark*.

He was completely stunned. 'John, you have not played the game with me.'

'Dad,' I said, 'I love you, and there was no way I wanted to worry or hurt you and Mam.'

'I cannot believe it,' he said. 'You and Terry must have been through hell.'

'Yes, we have and, as I told you, not once, about six times, if it wasn't for Terry I would not be here.' I could see Terry was reddening up. 'No, that's the truth, and as I said before, I love him for what he did.

'Dad, I want to ask you to ask Mam to adopt Terry. I want him as a proper brother, and he wants it. That way we will not be cheating when we go in the army. Dad, also I want parental permission for Terry and me, in separate letters, to join the army. We will not be going for a while, for Terry will be seventeen soon, and I have to be the same age as him. I won't be till October. We are going as soon as you give permission to the recruiting office, and we want to go when Terry is about seventeen and seven months.'

'All right,' Dad said, 'I am going to lose you again, and now I am losing two of you. I can understand that you don't want to go down the mines. As far as I am concerned, the pair of you have done your share in this man's war. I will give the consent with my blessing.'

Terry asked Vince for permission to have the following Thursday afternoon off, so that we could enlist into the army. We knew we would not be in for another couple of months. Vince said, 'Haven't you boys done enough already?' He had been shocked to see the paper with the story, and he was upset a little for us boys wanting to go in the army, for now he loved the two of us.

Dad started the proceedings for the adoption in May. When Terry was upstairs, I said to my dad, 'It is Terry's birthday on the twenty-eighth. Would it be possible to have a bash without telling him before the day?' I asked Mam when she was going to town to go into Samuel the jewellers and get a gold bracelet with 'Terry' inscribed on it. I gave her £50, a lot of money in those days. It cost £45, and the inscription of his name £1.

I told Terry that Dad had started the process of adoption. He was really delighted. 'Mam was going to buy two single beds,' I said, 'but she said "Seeing that you are going in the army, I won't bother." ' We had another one in the family: Thelma was courting. He looked a nice lad. He was around the house all the time, and I wound him up terribly, and my sister. 'You cannot come in our bed,' I said, 'as it's full.' His name was Tony, and he reddened up. Sometimes they wanted to go in the middle room, and I said to him in front of Dad, 'No snogging.' Thelma said, 'Talk to him, Dad, what do you want him to say?'

Soon the kitchen was empty. Terry was having a bath, June was in her friend's house across the road, Thelma and Ivy were out with their boys. (Ivy was courting but would not bring her boy home, for she said I showed her up.) Dad said, 'We have booked the Duke upstairs. We will say nothing about it.'

Before 28 May I was promoted again, to a full corporal. The commanding officer said he could not believe how quickly I picked things up. Now I was taking a lot more responsibility, and getting on well with all the boys. In bed one night I said to Terry, 'I know I have been pushy but, Terry, I am going to go in the army. Now, I am not forcing you. If you don't want to go, that will be all right with me.'

'John, I am not leaving you,' he said. 'If you go I go. Whatever you do I will do with you.'

Terry's birthday was on the Saturday, which meant we could lie in on the Sunday. He had a lot of cards from the girls and the family, and he was choked. We went off to work and the boss said, 'It's your birthday, Terry, isn't it? Go on, have a half day on me.' So we both shot off. When we got home, Terry told Dad about Vince. 'How did he know it was my birthday?' Terry asked.

'I don't know,' I said, 'I never told him.' Dad had, but made out he didn't know.

Everyone gave Terry presents – the girls, the grannies, and a joint present from Mam and Dad. 'And we are going to the Duke to celebrate tonight,' Dad said. I gave him my present, the gold bracelet. He started to cry, and run upstairs, I went after him. 'What's up?' I asked.

He said, 'You saw it. Everyone was giving me presents.'

I said, 'Yes, I know, that's what we always do.'

He grabbed me and hugged me. 'Thanks, John, for the bracelet.'

I said, 'Cut it out,' but he was emotionally upset. He settled down after, and we talked about everything and anything. We stayed in the bedroom and we both lay on the bed, until Mam came into the room to tell us tea was on the table.

We had tea, bathed and dressed, and walked around the Duke. Terry said, 'Where is Mam?'

'Around her mother's,' I said.

'I thought she would have liked to come around for a birthday drink.'

'She doesn't drink,' I said.

The Duke seemed a bit empty, very quiet, for usually it filled up about eight in the evenings. We walked in the bar, and Terry said, 'Three pints, please.'

'Do me a favour,' said McDougall, the landlord of the Duke and a very good friend of Dad's.

'What is it?' we both asked.

'Could you take these chairs up into the big room?' said McDougall. 'We had a party last night down here, and I have had no chance to put the chairs back.'

We took a chair each, Terry in front. 'In there,' I said. He opened the door. It was dark. Although it was light outside, the blackout blinds were down. 'Terry, put the light on,' I said. He fumbled for the switch and put it down and the light came on. As it did, everyone sang 'Happy Birthday' to Terry. It was packed, including Mam and the grannies, and the girls with their boys. My mates from the cadets were there, and most of the bar were upstairs. But you had to be a member of the bar downstairs – no strangers gatecrashing. Dad came up with Vince and his wife. They gave a wonderful present to Terry and me. 'This is for my two best workers,' he said.

The presents were a ring each with our initials, TM and JM. We both thanked Vince and his wife. We thought they were wonderful. They asked Terry to make a speech. He couldn't, he was too full up. I had to get hold of him to stop him crying. We had a great night, and a selected few came back to the house after. McDougall brought a few bottles around, Vince brought a few, and there was already plenty in the house, which Dad had been stockpiling for a few weeks. The festivities went on well into the night, and we boys were dead beat and went to bed while the party was still on. Both of us were well drunk. We had one hell of a job to get into bed. We were laughing, and we both struggled to undress. Eventually we got in bed, still with some of our clothes on.

In June we went to the recruiting office and officially volunteered for the army. The official looked at us, and asked how old we were. 'We are twins,' I said, 'and we were seventeen a couple of days ago.'

'You will be called for a medical in about five months' time. You have to be seventeen and a half now. You will hear from us.' With that we came out feeling very pleased with ourselves.

Mam and Dad were called up in front of the adoption board. Terry had to be there, and I was there with him. We asked our boss for time off on the Monday, for that was the day that everything for the adoption was to be dealt with. They asked Dad and Mam a lot of questions, which took over an hour. Then they asked Terry if he was willing. He had to explain that his proper mother and father, and all his family, had been killed. And after deliberating they called us back in, and they granted Mam and Dad custody of Terry.

'I am really excited,' he said when we came out, and you could see it – we were all excited. We went down to the pub that night, and Vince came up and shook Terry's hand. 'You are with a good family,' he told Terry, and Terry said, 'I know, I love them.'

We had a good evening. Vince was a great chap, and his wife. We had taken to them as they had taken to us. He called round the house often to see Dad. They love going up the woods rabbiting and duck shooting. We went with them at times, usually Saturday evenings and Sundays. There would be about six of us, their other mates coming with us.

We had had our papers to go for a medical, reporting to St John's School on Wednesday, 25 July. We were both nervous. It was packed there. I was kidding myself that I had grown up since I had left the merchant navy. I thought that I had recovered from the trauma of the *Bensmark*. I was really frightened that I would fail, and Terry would pass. It would be the end of me; I would not be able to face people again, I would kill myself.

Passed for the Army

'Let's wait and see,' Terry said. Now he could see I was in a bad way. I was worrying myself sick. 'John,' Terry said, and he gripped hold of me. We were being stared at by nearly everyone in the classroom we were using as a changing room. 'Come on, John,' said Terry, 'think of my birthday bash, the good time that we had.' A chap walked into the room. He said, 'Strip right off and put your trousers back on, then hold them. When you are called, come to the first desk where a medical officer will see you. As we were changing Terry heard someone say, 'Boy scouts are being called up as well,' to the chap next to him. He knew I had heard it too. 'Take no notice,' Terry said.

We were now sitting in just our trousers. Terry tried his best to distract me from the forthcoming ordeal. Half of the classroom had been called in, when they shouted, 'Terry Morgan! Terry said, 'Now, I will be just in front of you. Come on, smile,' he said, 'it won't be that bad.' Terry went to the first of five desks. When he went they called me. I went in, and the doctor checked my chest and body. Then I moved to the next man.

Terry was still in front me. I followed him to a man who checked my privates and my rear. He put the instrument with which he checked my limbs on me, then he checked my privates again. 'How old are you?' he asked.

I had already rehearsed what I was going to say, I had my date down to a fine art: 'Seventeen years and five months.'

He looked at my privates again and said, 'When were you born?'

I was ready for him. He said, 'You've got no pubic airs around your privates. Are you sure you are gone seventeen?'

'Yes, sir,' I said. I told him that my father was the same. 'It is something to do with my genes, the same as my dad.'

'Is that your brother in front of you?'

'Yes, sir,' I said.

'Well, he is fully matured in his privates.'

'Well, that how it is. One of us had a throwback.'

'Well, I suppose I can let you go,' he said.

'Thank you, sir,' I said. He wasn't daft.

We then went to the eyes, then the ears, nose and throat, then the final one to pass. He went through all the examination papers. He looked very hard at me. Terry was standing on the side. I was sure the doctor could see him, knowing that we were twins, one being a little bigger than the other. I was frightened to look at Terry, for I could see by the smile on his face that he had passed. The doctor went through my papers again. He said, 'Drop your trousers.' I dropped them, and now I was sweating. I knew I was going to pass. He used a pen to move my penis over to one side, looked very closely at my skin, then my ball bag, then said, 'Get dressed.' I pulled my trousers up. He wrote the paper out and gave it to me. I couldn't move. There was a long line waiting to go through the final examiner; I just stood there looking at the paper. Terry grabbed me, and then I could see that I had passed.

We got dressed. I was really excited, bubbling all over. 'There you are,' Terry said, 'all that moping around for nothing. What was all the fuss about?'

'I have no hairs, that's what was holding the line up.'

'I never noticed,' Terry said.

'Well, let's put it this way – you have more than me.' I told Terry how the doctor had quizzed me about it.

We had passed; that was the important thing. I was really chuffed that we are going together. 'I would not have gone down the mines,' I said.

'I know,' Terry said.

'Now we are going into the army,' I said. 'Let's go in Marks and have a cup of tea. Then we will go home and give them the good news. Dad will not like it, for he dotes on us, you must see that,' I said to Terry.

'Yes, I have noticed,' Terry said.

'Also Mam will not like it. She will play hell with me, both for going into the army and for taking you.'

'You are not taking me – I would not go without you. I think Mam knows that.'

'What would you have done, if I had failed?'

'I don't know,' Terry said. 'What would you have done, John?'

'I would have killed myself, for I can't live without you, as simple as that, and I would have done the same if I had passed and you didn't.'

'I would have joined you.'

We got home at dinner time. Mam was there. 'How did you get on?' she asked.

'We both passed,' we said together.

'Good,' she said, 'There was a chap who knocked the door for you,' Mam said.

'Who was it?'

'I don't know, I told him you were gone for a medical for the army. He said he was from the Royal Navy.'

I said to Mam, 'He can't have me, it's too late,' winking at Terry.

'He is coming down tonight.'

'Well, he had better come another night, it's cadet night.'

By the time it was time to go to cadets, he had not come and we didn't wait for him.

Every time we had cadets, I got my oldest sister to clean my boots and Brasso my belt, and Terry got our middle sister Ivy to do the same. We paid them sixpence for the chores. At cadets, I completely forgot this chap, until halfway through the evening a naval officer in his full uniform with a lot of gold braid on his sleeve came into the hall where we held the cadets.

He approached the officer of the cadets, Major Jones, and asked for permission to speak to me. I was called out to talk to the officer. As I walked to him, I called Terry out, and I turned to Major Jones and said, 'With your permission, sir.' Terry and I walked to the officer, who said, 'I want John Morgan.'

'That's me,' I said. 'What you have to say, I am afraid that you will have to say in front of Terry,' whom I introduced.

'All right,' the officer said. 'I am Commander Keane,' he said to Terry and me. We had moved to a classroom where we could talk in private. 'We are still very intrigued in what happened on the *Tri-Mark*. I know it will take a long time to tell us. We have most of the story, but there are a lot of gaps we must fill in. Can you have tomorrow off from work?'

'Yes,' I said, 'as long as you ask the boss.'

'We will go down to your works in the morning. What time does the boss get there?'

'Nine,' I said.

'Right,' he said, 'we will get there just after. I will pick you up. Where does the lad live?' he asked, pointing to Terry.

'His name is Terry,' I said. 'Where I go, he goes, and he is living with me. You will understand this when we sit down and talk.'

'I will pick you up at 9.15 a.m. at your house,' he said to the pair of us, as he got up to leave. Terry and I saluted him as he went, and he saluted back. I think I noticed a wry smile on his face as he turned and went.

We left the cadets. There was a big buzz going around – a top naval officer there! It was nearly nine thirty. We were a little late, but the excitement of the night had kept them all back. We all trooped round to Ma Doodies, who ran the local chippy. She had always made fishcakes but, through the war, she only made them for our gang of five now and then. She was a lovely lady. She always looked after us, as we never at any time gave her any trouble.

When we got home, Mam said, 'That bloke was here, the naval bloke, but Dad spoke to him.'

'Yes,' I said, 'we saw him around the school. He wants us to take a day off from work. I don't mind. He said he would take us to work, and see the boss, about nine fifteen.'

We went to bed. We did not stay up all that late now that we were working. But we were both wide awake still with the excitement of passing for the army.

The officer was true to his word. He took us down in his staff car to the works. His driver was a petty officer, and he was great. When the officer went to see the boss, he was telling us yarns, and he had us in stitches. We got out of the car when the officer returned for us.

The boss was with the officer. We followed him into his office. The naval officer explained, and apologised for us being late. 'It was my doing,' he said to the boss.

'That's all right,' said the boss. 'They are good boys.' The boss looked at us and smiled; we got on well with him.

We were taken to the Royal Navy recruiting offices, where we were ushered into a large office and brought a cup of tea each. Then a few more officers came in and sat around with a secretary. The officer that had brought us there came in. He first asked if we had any objection to the other people being in the room, which we didn't. Then he introduced all three of them to us.

'John, and you, Terry, we would like the full story of your time on the *Bensmark*, from the time you were torpedoed on the *Topley* till you were rescued, including the rescue.' I told them everything with Terry's help.

We had dinner, for which we were taken to a restaurant by the recruiting officer. We had a very good meal. Then, at about 2 p.m., we started again filling in gaps. I insisted on telling them how my close relationship with Terry had come about. I said, 'Now he is a Morgan. My parents adopted him, and we all love him, me more than anyone, for he saved my life. So you can see why I insist that Terry be with me all the time. After all he is my brother.'

When I finished about Terry, the officer said, 'Tell me what your part was with the *Tri-Mark*.'

'Nothing really,' I said.

'Come on, John, we know different.'

'Well, all I did was to translate what the Germans were saying, for they never knew I could speak German.' When I had just about finished, the officer holding the enquiry pressed a bell. In walked Captain Brecon, the escape officer on the *Tri-Mark*. He came rushing to me – he wasn't under the jurisdiction of the Royal Navy, that's why he made a move to me. He hugged me and was even kissing me.

We both sat down, and I started to cry. Terry grabbed my arm. 'Come on,' he said. They were all trying to console me. We had a break for ten minutes, so I could compose myself. Captain Brecon was full of praise for me, and said, 'It was John Morgan who helped us to take over the ship. We certainly had to thank John. He made it all very easy, what with his speaking German, and not being frightened of them. He relayed everything we wanted to know, and he even helped in distracting the guards, to allow us up out of the hole.'

When it was all finished they thanked me. Captain Brecon said, 'John, we know that you were fond of the commodore. Well, he died about six months after we got home.' Captain Brecon said, 'I see your exploits were in the *South Wales Echo*. You had very good publicity, you and your friend.' I told Captain Brecon about Terry, that he had lost all his family through the blitz and was officially adopted as a Morgan, and all my family loved him.

'I heard that you have finished with the sea,' the commander said. 'Yes, Terry and I are going into the army.' I told them I had done four trips, including one to Russia. 'We are going to publish the story in the national newspapers,' he said, 'to get more volunteers for the Royal Navy and merchant navy. Do you mind?'

'Not really,' I said, 'but I have to be very careful, for I cheated to get in the army. If you print my date of birth, I will be doomed. I would rather that you don't print my or my brother's date of birth, or about Terry being my brother through adoption. I cannot see us getting in the army if this part of the story leaks out.'

Everyone around the table looked at one another. The commander said, 'Don't you think that you have done enough?' I explained that we could be sent down the mines, 'and I cannot stand being shut in. That was my trouble on the *Bensmark*. That is why Terry and I are great pals. He comforted me on the *Bensmark*, and I won't forget it. We both want to go in the army, so please don't spoil it for us.'

Just before the meeting wound up, which was at 4 p.m., after a long day, Captain Brecon got up and presented us each with a watch. 'This is from the *Tri-Mark*, a big thank you from the boys.' Then he took us out to tea, but first to the market to get the watches inscribed. My watch was 'To John from the *Tri-Mark*', and on the other he just had put 'To Terry'. It seemed that Captain Brecon had been trying to get hold of me for the past twelve months. The watches were from a pool of money donated by all the prisoners from the *Tri-Mark* for me. We then went for a wonderful tea, before escorting Captain Brecon to the railway station. He gave us his home address, and made us promise that we would pay him a visit within the next four months. 'I am going to hold you to that,' he said, and we shook hands. He put a white fiver, crumpled up, in my hand, money that was left over.

Terry and I had £5 each. We waved to him as the train pulled out, and we said we would go over.

Terry said as we were walking home, 'I am going to the cemetery on Sunday.

'Not on your own,' I said. I told you before, we, I will fall in with everything you do.'

Life is Wonderful

Commander Keane had assured us we would not have our age disclosed, and Terry and I had our photos taken in different poses. We went back to work the next day, and the boss was delighted that we had been recognised for what we had done when we were at sea. We were on good money with him. There were ten others working down on the lumber camp, and it was very hard work. He still paid us for all the time we had been losing. We both appreciated that, and he got a good day's work out of us. We were never late, and we did not mess about. We talked to the others, but we were always in our own company.

Sunday came. We went to the cemetery after dinner, for on Sunday mornings, there were no buses running. In the afternoon it was a full service, so we caught the Cathays bus, and walked down to the gates from the bus stop. On the corner of Whitchurch Road, whom should we see but Liam? He made a right fuss of us. He had packed the sea in along with Ken, whom he had seen once or twice. He told us he was working in Guest Keens and Nettlefolds. 'Money is all right,' he said, 'but I miss the boys like you two.'

Terry said, 'We are going into the cemetery,' and Liam said he would tag along. He read the stone, but I don't think anything connected in his mind. We laid the flowers on the grave, which was kept very tidy. I was pleased, so was Terry. After a little while, when Terry had had his couple of minutes with his thoughts, we walked out. We left Liam on the understanding that he would pay us a visit.

'I saw your photos in the *South Wales Echo*,' he said, 'and your story. It was good. I told my Mam and Dad that you were with me on that hell ship, and they were really excited over it.'

I said, 'Keep your eyes open, for there will be another piece in the dailies.' He walked to the bus. We shook hands and parted. 'Don't forget, call down,' I said, 'and you better make it sharp, for we are going in the army soon.

I said to Mam, when only Terry and I were with her, 'Dad's birthday is at the end of August, isn't it?'

'Yes,' she said.

'What about us giving him a surprise, like we did with Terry – what do you say?' I asked.

'Great, I would love it.' So we started to make plans. We were going to cadet camp in a week's time, so we would have to move a bit sharpish and start to get some drinks in. So all three of us decided to ask McDougall to come after he shut, for we knew he would have a few bottles on him. Terry and I would see McDougall early the next night and arrange a bash upstairs, like the one Terry had.

We got Vince to say that it was his wife's birthday, for we knew that Dad wouldn't let Vince down. We told Vince that, as we were on stop fortnight from work, we would call around and see him when we came back from camp. McDougall fell in with everything, for he was a good pal of Dad's. We bought the drinks for the house around Mac's place and had a hell of a job to sneak them in the house. We borrowed a bike with a carrier to get them home. Then we had to hide them from Dad's prying eyes, shoving them under our bed.

We went to camp. We were there only for a week. All my pals were with us, and we had a great time. We went into Porthcawl a few times, but really speaking there was plenty to do in the evenings. I was a full corporal and I didn't really like it. About halfway through the week in camp, I handed my stripes in. They asked me why. 'I am not one for giving orders,' I said, without telling them I just didn't want to boss Terry about. They could see I was serious. All the boys were begging me not to do it. I said, 'It won't make much difference, for Terry and I will be in the army soon.'

We had glorious weather down there, and we all had a good tan on. I was really happy. I was with all my mates. I liked the training we were doing, even the map reading. Everything was exciting. Well, the saying goes, when you are enjoying yourself all good things must come to an end.

25 August came we were all excited. We gave Dad his presents in the morning. We bought him fifty Player's in a pack each, Terry and I, and a double-barrel Boss shotgun. He was over the moon with the gun, and you could see he was a little full up, so we hugged him and shook hands. He went off to work. We were not starting back till Monday.

Terry suggested that we went to the cemetery after breakfast. I agreed. There was nothing more that we could do for the party, that was all in Mam's and the girls' hands. We told Mam that we would be back at dinner time. We bought some flowers outside the cemetery. The grave was very neat, and I was just as pleased as Terry. We came home after about forty minutes at the grave, and we went up into our bedroom and we just talked. We asked Mam if there was anything that she wanted us to do. 'No,' she said, 'I am going around Nan's.'

She took June's clothes with her, for she was to come with Nan Gilligan round to the Duke. They had to be there by 8 p.m., for we and Dad would be leaving about that time, and we didn't want to bump into them. As Mam was going round (according to her) to see her mother, no one thought anything of it. We came into the pub, finding it half empty. Bar staff had been employed for the night, so McDougall and his wife could have a night off. Vince came down just as we got the drinks. 'Come on,' he said, 'we want to start to party,' so we trooped off, Dad first, then Vince, Terry and me.

The lights were on this time and, as Dad walked into the room, they all started to sing 'Happy Birthday' He was gobsmacked. He turned to Terry and me and said, 'This is your doing!' Vince acted as master of ceremonies, and gave a little speech. My five mates were there, and all Dad's mates. We had a great evening, and I was done for. I was drunk, as was Terry. We still had the drinks in our house that we had to bring down from under the bed. Luckily for us, Thelma and Tony came back with us – in other words they brought us home.

Thelma poured black coffee down us. We were all right, but I didn't have any more to drink, only lemonade. The party lasted till two in the morning, and Mam had to put Dad to bed. Tony helped us to bed. We made a lot of noise trying to undress. Dad shouted, 'Are you all right?'

'Yes,' we shouted together, but continued making a row.

Tony was staying at our house. He was to sleep on the settee in the middle room when everyone had gone. We eventually got in bed, and fell asleep.

Next morning I woke at nine. It was Sunday. I looked at Terry; he was still fast asleep. I had a bowl alongside me – Mam must have put it there for the two of us. Well, we never used it, and I took it down when I got up. My mother asked if I was all right. Terry was still fast asleep. I said, 'He's out to the world.' Mam was the only one up beside me, and she made a nice cup of tea. I said, 'Seeing Terry in bed fast asleep as he is, you would not have thought he had done what he did for me. He comforted me all the time in that hell ship. He kept with me when we dived off the ship. Terry would not leave me.' With that I started to cry. Mam came over to try to console me. I was really bad now, crying like a baby, and Mam was worried. She had never seen me like this I was uncontrollable, and Mam had to call Dad down. He came rushing down, wanting to know what the trouble was.

I went into a trauma. I was just staring. Mam said to Dad, 'Take him up into our bed, and I will go down to the City Lodge,' as there was no phone in the house. There was one just outside, but she decided to go down to the City Lodge, where she knew a couple of doctors from when she had worked there. She explained about her son. The doctor gave her a bottle of draught, a strong liquid, not used generally. Dad took me upstairs. I was just limp. He put me to bed, and I fell fast asleep when Mam brought the liquid up to me and made me take it. 'Let him rest,' she said to Dad.

The girls were just about coming downstairs, and heard a commotion, and wanted know what all the noise was about. Terry got up, and when Mam said I was bad and in her bed, he went and sat on the bed with me. Now all the house was awake. Tony stayed in the room not to get in the way. Thelma made tea. Mam wanted Terry to come down and have a cup of tea, but he would not. Mam said, 'There is breakfast on the table.'

'I don't want any,' he said. 'Now, come on, Terry.'

'No, I don't want any,' he said. 'I am staying with John.' He just didn't want to leave me, and he made that quite clear to Mam.

I woke up. I saw I was in Mam's bed. I said to her when she came up, 'Mam, I want to go back to bed in my room.'

Terry said, 'I will take him back.' He put me to bed, and sat in the chair by my head. Mam brought two cups of tea up, but I had fallen asleep again. It was because of the medicine I had taken, which made me very drowsy. Mam said, 'Come on down,' to Terry, but he would not listen. 'No, I'm staying with him if you don't mind,' he said to Mam.

Mam cooked dinner, a little late, with the girls giving her a hand. 'What's the matter with John?' they wanted to know. 'The trouble with John,' said Mam, 'is he bottled everything up. With all the business at the meeting, everything was brought back again. They just will not let him forget. I wish they would leave him alone.' Mam brought the dinners up for Terry and me. I was still fast asleep. Terry said, 'I'll have mine with John, that will encourage him to eat.' Dad looked in, then said, 'You are back at work tomorrow from the holidays. Are you going?'

'Not if John is like this,' Terry said. 'I am staying with him.'

'Well, I'd better let the boss know,' Dad said, 'I will pop around his house tonight.'

I woke up at seven thirty. Thelma walked in. 'I came to see how you are doing,' she said. I asked where Tony was. 'Downstairs,' Thelma said, Terry was still on the chair. 'Terry, you must have something to eat.'

'I will in a minute,' he replied.

Mam then brought a couple of sandwiches up. 'I will keep the dinners for tomorrow,' she said. With the sandwiches she brought some trifle, for that was one of my favourite dishes. Terry now loved it too. 'How are you feeling now?'

'All right, Mam,' I said.

'Come on, eat the sandwiches,' Mam said to the two of us. 'Come on, Terry, you have got to eat as well, otherwise I will have you bad as well.'

Mam went downstairs, and after a couple of minutes she brought some tea to drink. 'Here,' she said. 'I know you both want some tea.' She put the cups down on the dressing table that we had by the bed. 'Now, I want to see the plates empty when I come back.' As she went back out she said, 'A couple of your mates called round. I told them that you were ill and in bed. I think they thought they were going to come in and play cards. I told them that you were not well at all.'

We ate the sandwiches and trifle. Mam turned on me and said, 'You are not getting out of bed for work tomorrow. Your father has gone to tell your boss that you are ill.'

'I will not be going,' Terry said very firmly. 'I am staying with John.' Mam never said a word. Terry looked at me; I was fast asleep again. Mam had given me another droop of medicine, and I was out to the world.

I took three days to get over my illness. When I got up, there was no ay I was going to cadets. Vince came the day I got up. There was a big fire in the middle room. I was there, still in my pyjamas, Terry as always with me. We were playing records when Vince came. He brought some fruit, and he sat talking to us two boys. He told us that he didn't want to see us before next Monday. Dad knew that we loved Vince. He said to

Vince afterwards, 'Those boys idolise you, and I think your coming around made them better.' Terry would not go to Cadets without me.

We stayed the rest of the week at home, and both went back to work on the Monday. The boss welcomed us back. We carried on as per normal. At the end of the week, we both went to the cemetery. Each time before we came away I would walk off so Terry could have a few moments with his family. He would have a little weep, and when he came up to me, I would hug him. 'Come on, Ter,' I said, 'let it go.' By the time we got to the gate, he would be very composed.

That night we played cards with the boys in the middle room. Thelma was moaning that we had had the room all week, it was her turn, she told Mam. I said, 'Mam, she only wants to snog in there.'

'Leave her alone,' Mam said. We went to bed after playing cards. I said to Terry, 'Thanks for staying with me.'

'Forget it,' he said. I was now back to square one. I felt great. I had put on a bit of weight, and perhaps an inch in height. I wanted to grow as much as I could.

'John, I love your family,' said Terry. 'I still can't get over the way you all brought me presents. I will treasure your present all my life.'

'Forgot it,' I said. 'Come on, let's get some sleep.' Over came his arm and off to sleep we went.

On Monday, 23 September it rained all day. We still worked out in it. We had oilskins and put a good day's work in. Vince was not amused with the conduct of a few, who moaned all the time. When we were at work, we treated Vince as our boss, and we gave him that respect. We only spoke to him when he told us to do something, and I know he appreciated that.

I said to Terry, coming home from work, 'I am going to write to the Prides, and a letter to Captain Brecon telling him that we will be over on 6 October. I will tell him we will be on the 12 p.m. train. Terry, what was the name of the English Captain on the *Bensmark*, who did all the looking after us?'

'The spokesman? His name was Brecon,' Terry said.

'I thought it was,' I said. 'Do you know that there are two Captain Brecons? One we saw the other week, Captain George Brecon, whom we have just written to, and there was a Captain Oliver Brecon on the *Bensmark*. Now, what a coincidence. I wonder if they are related. I will ask him when we go over there to Bristol.'

We both wrote to the Prides, and gave details of everything that had happened to us since we left. Terry put that he was now a Morgan. We told the Prides we had passed for the army, and were waiting to be called up. We said that we would be out in South Africa as soon as the war finished, and were hoping to stay out there and live and work, 'with your help'. We both signed our own letters, 'Love you, and thanks for everything.'

Sunday, 6 October came. We had arranged to visit Captain Brecon of the *Tri-Mark* that day. Although we said we would be on the 12 o'clock train, there was no 12 o'clock. The nearest was the ten thirty from Cardiff, so that was the one we caught. Captain Brecon, being the organiser he was, had checked the trains. He was at the station waiting for us. With him was a young girl about fourteen and a boy about our age. As we got off the train, he ran up and made a terrible fuss of us – more so with me, for I was involved with him on the *Tri-Mark*, but he did not leave my brother out. He introduced his son and daughter to us. Then we had a steady walk to his house, which was in the reserved area of Temple Meads, only a stone's throw from the station. We were given lunch as they call it – we called it dinner – and we sat talking all the afternoon with his very pleasant wife, and his two children. We had a light tea, and then had to say our goodbyes, for our train was at 6 p.m., and if we missed that we would have to wait till 10.15 p.m. We were escorted to the station by the full family. Captain Brecon was very excited – he just could not do enough for us. We told him it would be a little awkward for us to visit again, for we would probably be in the army. We were waiting for our papers.

Captain Brecon was no relation to the captain Brecon on the *Bensmark*. He didn't even know him. The man we visited had retired from active service, and just helped where and when necessary. As the train came in, we boarded into a compartment containing three people. The captain's parting words were, 'I hope my boy turns out half as good as you were.'

I looked at Terry. I said, 'What does he mean?'

'He just thinks the world of you, that's all.'

We waved our goodbyes and the train left the station. 'Don't forget to write,' were the last words we heard. We signalled that we heard him, then sat down. We sat next to one another and talked quietly between ourselves.

We had our cooked dinner when we got home. Dad had gone to the club. As we were eating, Terry said to Mam, 'We were given a cooked dinner. This dinner is three times as big. They were very dainty dinners, but we ate them.'

On Monday, the next day, we went to work. Late in the day the boss asked us if we would stay on for an hour. We both agreed to. We got home about 7 p.m. having finished at six thirty.

Where we sat for our meals there was a brown envelope for each of us. We both opened the envelopes together. These were our calling papers, with a five-shilling postal order – our first day's pay. We had to report to Whitchurch Barracks by 4 p.m. on 24 October.

My mates had earlier called around, but we had only just come in. So we told them that we would not be going to the cinema as we always did on the Monday. We decided that we would stay in, now that we knew that we were going into the army. You could see from Mam's face, and Dad's, that they didn't want us to go. 'You have only just come home,' said Mam, 'now I am losing you again. Now it's the two of you. It's not fair.' Mam was near to tears, and I went over to console her. Terry did the same. 'They will be all right,' Dad said. 'They will have one another for company. They both know how to look after themselves.

In the Army

We went into the middle room. It was quite comfortable in there. We didn't have to light the fire as it was quite warm. We put the record player on, and we started to talk about where we might go, and what we might train for. Everything was confusing our minds. I said to Terry, 'I am worried.'

'Why, what's the matter?' Terry said.

'Well, you know when we had the medical they said I had no pubic hairs?'

'I know.'

'I haven't even now. I am frightened they might turn me down, and they will keep you. I will kill myself, if that happens.'

'Don't be silly,' Terry said. 'I'll look after you. Let's see what happens.'

'But you don't realise, I have a small ding-dong, and when they see me when I have to show myself again, they will turn me down.'

'Let's get everything right,' Terry said. 'To change the subject: date of birth. I'm the oldest by two hours. We've got our names right now so we won't worry about that. We've got our addresses right as well. Anything else?'

'No, I don't think so.'

Terry said, 'Don't worry, our kid.'

'I won't,' I said, 'as long as you are with me. We will give our notices in tomorrow, and finish at the end of the week. I think Vince will understand. We will go to the cemetery on Sunday, and then get ready for the big day.' We both resigned from the cadets on the Friday. They wanted us to finish on the following Wednesday. 'No,' I said, 'it will be Friday, as we have a lot to do.' I said to Terry, 'Let's invite Vince and Dad for the evening with us before we go in. We will pay for the rounds. That will show our appreciation to Vince, and it will make Dad proud of us.'

We asked the boss if we could finish that Friday. 'Also,' I said, 'we would like you and Dad to come and have a drink with us on the

Wednesday before we go in. Also Terry and I would like to thank you, and your wife, for all that you have done for us.' The boss said, 'You can finish on the Thursday, for that is when the week starts, and also Thursday is pay day.'

We sat in the house on the Wednesday a week before we went in. There were only Mam and Dad and Terry, so I said, 'As you know, my birthday is on the twenty-fifth, the day after we join the army. Well, after this birthday, I want my birthday to be recognised on the same date as Terry's, so that wherever we go and people ask us our date of birth, mine is the same as Terry's. Would you accept that?' I asked Mam and Dad. They both looked at one another, then they said yes. 'I want to hold my birthday do this year on the twenty-third, on the Wednesday. We have asked Vince if he will have a drink with us, and he has said yes. I don't want a big party, just you, Dad and Mam.'

'I am not going around the pubs,' she said.

'Well, you, Dad, and Vince, no one else, for Terry and I want to pay for the drinks for you and Vince.'

We went into work on the Thursday, our last day. All the workers made a fuss of us, and we promised that we would pop down now and again.

Vince every week brought the pay packets to the individual out in the yard. He gave us our money around noon, and then said, 'You can go now. I will see you round your house or at the pub.' I said to Terry on the way home, 'We will wash and change, go into town, and buy the odds and ends that we need.' When we got home, Mam was surprised. 'What's the matter?' she asked. 'We got the sack for messing about,' I said.

'What did you do?' she asked.

'Well,' I said, 'Terry wouldn't do a certain job, and when he asked me, I wouldn't do it.'

'Your father will go mad over this!'

'Don't worry, Mam,' Terry said. 'He's having you on. No, he gave us our money and said we can go.' And here's the best: we had not opened our packets so we did there and then, for we still gave Mam her money, and we found an extra £5 note in the packets for the two of us.

I gave Mam her wages and Terry did the same. We gave her one of the fivers from the pair of us, so I owed Terry £2 10/-. Also, as I said to Terry, we had our first day's pay from the army, so we got to cash it. We went out with Dad on the Thursday night. The boys called round – they were going down to the snooker hall. Dad liked our company. He was a very proud man when he had the pair of us round him. Vince was at the pub as usual, and we all sat around. Then Vince started to wind us up, but we laughed and watched the card game. I knew I could now play it. I had watched Dad often enough, so I said to Terry, 'Game for putting a knock on?' We went on, and we played quite well. They all started to have a go at us. We didn't win the game, but we enjoyed it. We played for a pint a corner, so we had to cough up.

We didn't go to cadets on the Friday as we had finished. Instead we sat up in our bedroom, talking. I said to Terry, 'I am not taking any of my treasures in the army.' We both had very expensive watches, and there was a story attached to each one, as with my ring, and Terry's gold bracelet and ring. 'If you should take them off for a second they will be gone. Also, if we are captured by the enemy, they will take all our jewellery.'

On Saturday night we went with my mates to the pictures, seven of us. Coming home we went to the cafe we always went in when we went to the pictures, where we had pie and chips, and we got home about 11 p.m. Dad, as always, was home by then, so we talked for about an hour. 'I want you boys to listen,' he said. 'We have had a very tough time with you, John more so than Terry, what with the ships that you have been on. What I am saying to you two boys is, be very careful. You are my life, I love you both, and your mother. She is breaking her heart now, because you are leaving us again. So please be careful and come back. Don't take silly chances.'

We had a letter from the Prides on the Saturday from South Africa. They said they missed us both. Mrs Pride was looking forward to our visit after the war, hoping that we would come out. They said they would find us work.

I read the letter out to Mam. Terry read his out as well, they were identical. I looked at Mam, and said, 'Don't worry, when I come out of the army I will stay home, that's a promise.'

The next day all the Sunday papers were carrying our photos and story on the front pages. We raced through the two papers we had to see if there was anything about our dates of birth or how old we were. True to Commander Keane's word there was nothing about our age at all, only that we were very young to have gone through what we had been through. It was a very good write-up, taking most of the front page. The photos of the two of us were very good. But would we be remembered on Thursday? Would they recognise us from the photos?

I asked Ivy, when she was going to the shop, to get another two papers, so that I could keep the articles. Also I wanted to send Mr Pride one, for I knew he had been the instigator of publication in the *Echo*.

We asked Mam if we could have dinner early, as we wanted to go to the cemetery, but we were inundated with knocks on the front door. People we knew were coming around, so in the end I was glad to go to the cemetery away from it all. The grave was still very tidy we took some daffodil bulbs and planted them ready for next year. We had quite a few bulbs; we got them cheap, for they were out of season. Come next March there would be quite a few flowers on the grave.

I said to Terry, 'If you want to say something, carry on, I'll understand.'

'Don't be daft,' he said. 'Well, if you are not going to say anything, I will.' I bowed my head and thanked Mr and Mrs Radley for their son, had now come into the Morgan household. 'I love him,' I said very quietly. Terry now decided that he would say something out of respect. I walked away. When he finished, he said, 'Why did you walk away?'

'Well, I thought it right – you might have wanted to tell them something.'

'Thanks, John,' he said, hugging me.

We got back home about 3 p.m. We sat in the middle room and talked. I said, 'I would like to go into town tomorrow. I think I will take June to dinner, I know she would like that. Then, after, you and I are going to Jerome's to have our photos taken. I would want one of you in my wallet. Also I think Mam and Dad would like one of us, for the last time I had my photo taken I was in school.'

'That's a good idea,' Terry said. When we were having tea, Terry suggested to June that we took her to dinner at the cafe we had been to before. 'Oh, yes, please!' June said. She went straight over to Terry and kissed him before sitting down. You should have seen his face, red as a beetroot. I said to her, 'What about my kiss?' She came to me and gave me a big kiss. Thelma's boyfriend was having tea with us. I said, 'You cannot go in the middle room, as Terry and I have some letters to write.'

Thelma said, 'Oh, Mam, he is doing this deliberately.'

I said, 'You only want to snog in there.'

'Tell him, Mam,' she said.

Mam said, 'Leave her alone.' Tony's face was red as well.

'All right, this time we will let them snog in the room,' I said. 'We will write upstairs, Ter.'

We went upstairs, having told the boys that we would not be playing cards, as we had to go and see the rest of the family before we went in the army. We both wrote to the Prides. I said, 'I don't know if I told you in the last letter, but Terry is now my brother,' and I bracketed it by saying, 'I love him.' I said that we were going in the army on that Thursday, and that we were both excited. I then related the big write-up we both had in the Sunday papers. 'I am sending a copy for you,' and I said, 'Could you please let the servants see it. Thank you once again, will keep in touch. Love, John.'

We both near enough finished on the same time. Terry put them in envelopes while I carried on writing to Captain Brecon. We finished then went downstairs. June and Mam were there, so we sat talking. Tony and Thelma were in the room. As I passed the door, I said, 'I'm coming in, no snogging.' Mam said, 'Leave them alone.' Ivy was court- ing the rest of Cardiff I thought. She was never in, and always with a new boy. We really didn't see much of her. We sat talking to Mam and she kept on – 'You two be careful,' she kept saying. We waited up for Dad, for we both liked talking to him.

Wednesday came. We walked to the Duke with Dad. You could see how proud he was. We walked in, and the boys in the bar shouted, 'Here come the conquering heroes!' My father gave them a nasty look, and they soon shut up. Vince came about five minutes later and sat by us. Terry got the drinks in. We decided, seeing that we were not much in the line of drinking, just to have two, perhaps three, no more. We put a knock on for cards, and when we got on, we were knocked off. So we talked with Dad and Vince, and before we knew it, it was time to go. McDougall wished us all the best. 'We will be back and forth, before we go abroad,' Terry said, and all the boys wished us luck.

We walked home. Vince came with us, and came in. There were a couple of bottles still in the house. Mam played hell with Vince and Dad, but they knew her, and took no notice. Terry and I had shandies. At twelve, I said, 'I am off.' Terry and I shook hands with Vince, and he wished us all the best. 'Don't forget to come and see us,' he said. 'We will,' we promised, and we were gone. We slept like logs, no talking, Terry as always crouched into me, his arm across my chest.

We got up and had baths one after another. We dressed in our tidy clothes, went down and had our breakfast, and packed our cases, the ones the Prides gave us. They were just under medium in size, so we packed what we wanted. We did not put pyjamas in, for the boys would laugh at us. We decided to catch the bus for Whitchurch Road. They ran all the time, so we thought 2 p.m. would do us right. As we sat talking to Mam, you could see she didn't want us to go. Dinner time came and we had a sandwich and a cuppa before leaving to catch the bus. Mam hugged and kissed us. We left without turning around, and caught the bus to Maindy Barracks.

On the bus Terry said to me, 'John, we have not collected the photo we had taken in Jerome's. I have still got the receipt in my wallet.'

'Keep it safe,' I said, 'and we will collect them when we can get a day away from the barracks.'

We arrived just outside the driveway to the barrack gates, which were just across the road from the cemetery. We arrived at the gates at 15.15 hours (all times for us would now be army times) and walked into the guardroom. The corporal of the guard was heard to say, 'They are calling the Scouts up now, we must be desperate.'

We gave our names as John and Terry Morgan and presented our call-up papers. The corporal said, 'Over there to the admin block,' pointing the way. We felt very conspicuous, really small. We went into the building, where there were tables with NCOs sitting behind them, about six of them. There were about thirty civilians, called up like us, sitting against the other wall. We were called to one table, and the corporal asked Terry his name and then his address, his date of birth. I must remember 28 May, I reminded myself. Terry was asked his religion, and his next of kin, for which he put Mam down.

He was filling his AB64, Soldier's Service and Pay Book. He was asked what work he had done and what insurance firm. All that finished, he was given his AB64 and then told to sit against the wall with the others. I was next. I went up in front of the table as Terry had done. The officer asked me the same questions as he had asked Terry. The corporal asked if we were twins. 'Yes,' I said. 'Oh,' he said, then he finished my book and I went and sat with Terry across the hall.

1600 hours came and everybody was called to stand, to take the oath.

Then we had our injections, first the TAB, then the TET. Then we were weighed and our height was taken, both figures being entered in our AB64. When all that was finished we had to go into a large room, where we were told to take all our clothes off, and put our trousers back on, till the doctor came and examined us. I was really nervous now. Terry said, 'Just brazen it out, don't think about it.'

The doctor came in with a sergeant. The sergeant said, 'As we come along the line, just drop your trousers. We call this FFI – free from infection. Throughout your army career, you will have a lot of FFIs, so you will know what we mean.' We were in the middle row, towards the end. Terry was before me and, when the doctor came to him, Terry dropped his pants. I was next. I dropped mine. The doctor looked at what I had, then looked me in the face. He didn't say anything, but carried on, saying, 'Turn around and bend down,' which I found most embarrassing.

It was well gone 1700 hours, and I was feeling a lot better now that was all over with. We had to congregate outside, where we were formed into a squad and marched behind the big buildings alongside the parade ground, to some Nissen huts. We were split up between two huts. Terry and I were still together and we were right in the middle of the hut. We plonked our cases on the beds, which were typical army cots: three biscuits, three blankets and a straw pillow. I was talking to Terry (as yet we had not spoken to anyone else) when a big goon came up. 'Titch,' he said to me, 'F— off down the end!' He dumped his case on my bed. I said, 'This is my bed, and I am staying here.' Everyone in the hut witnessed it, and did nothing.

He grabbed hold of me, I lashed out at him, and he hit me with his fist. With that Terry lashed out at him. 'You squirt!' he said, as he hit Terry in the face. Terry went down and caught his head on the corner of the spring bed. He lay motionless. I got up and lashed out at the goon but missed him.

I dived on Terry, shouting, 'Terry, are you all right?' He did not answer me for a couple of seconds. By now a few of the brave ones had come over. I told the goon to get down the bottom. 'I am staying here, shift me if you can.' I went for him again, but I was no match for him. While this was going on, a passing sergeant heard the commotion. He was standing in the doorway when Terry was laid out. He walked down just as the goon was lashing out at me again. The goon never saw him, for the brave ones blocked his view of the sergeant.

'Attention!' the sergeant barked out. I was groggy and Terry was still on the floor. Everyone else jumped to attention. The sergeant turned to one of the men nearest him. 'Go down to the guardroom and tell the guard commander I want two men as escort. Say Sergeant Hillard sent you.' The chap more or less ran, but he was told not to run, for that was against army discipline. He was back in a matter of minutes with two armed soldiers.

While the chap had gone to the guardroom, the sergeant sent another chap to the medical room to get the doctor. He came about the same time as the escort. While this was going on the sergeant looked at Terry and me but did not say anything. He did not say anything to the goon either.

'Everyone, sit on your beds!' he commanded. The goon picked his case up to go back down to the bed he had vacated. 'Leave it there!' the sergeant commanded.

The doctor and the escort had arrived. Sergeant Hillard turned to the escort, and then to the goon. 'I am placing you under arrest. Your name?' The sergeant made a note of it. 'Take him. Tell the guard commander I will be down now to file a complaint.' Terry was put on a stretcher and carried across to sick bay. I walked alongside him with the doctor and the sergeant. They put Terry into bed, and I stood right by him. The doctor said, 'He will be all right. You come with me into the surgery.'

'I want to stay with my brother, sir,' I said. 'He will be all right,' the doctor said.

'If you don't mind, sir, I want to stay with him,' I said. 'We are twins.'

'Very well, but I want to have a look at those bruises.' The sergeant then took our names and numbers. We had to check by getting our AB64s out. The sergeant noted that we were twins. 'All right,' he said, 'Stay where you are. I will see the doctor,' which he did. He came back and said, 'It is all right, you can stay with your brother.'

Then he asked what had happened. I said, 'A misunderstanding.'

'Come on, that's not good enough,' he said. 'I want to know what happened, why Hartnell attacked you. I will find out, you can be assured of that, but I rather it came from you.'

'It is as I said, sergeant, a misunderstanding.'

I sat with Terry. He was awake now and he said he was all right. They brought our tea in. It was like swill. We smelt it and left it, we just could not eat it now. At about 1930 hours I started to feel groggy. I was sitting holding Terry's hand and I passed out. About two minutes later, Terry did the same. It was the needle we had had when we came into the admin block.

The orderly corporal who had to be on duty, because there was someone in the sick bay, came down to see if Terry was all right. He was told to get a bed and put it alongside Terry, but we were out to the world. He knew what the trouble was: the TET injections. So he put me into the bed by Terry. He took my civvies off, and Terry's were taken off. Both of us were in noddy land. Sergeant Hillard came over and said to the corporal, 'Look after them, they are special.'

We both woke up at midnight. The corporal was still on duty. He had to stay there in case something went wrong. He heard us talking, and he got us a cup of sweet tea each. After we drank our tea, we both fell back to sleep.

We were woken when reveille sounded at 0630 hours. Our first morning in the army and both of us were in sick bay! We had a wash. Our cases were over in the hut, so the duty orderly (a different person from the corporal) allowed us to wash in the clinic. Then we had breakfast at 0730. This was quite good, so we felt a lot better, but we were still feeling the bruises. Terry was recovering. The knock could have been more serious. We were discharged at 0900 hours after the doctor had been. The sergeant who had taken us to the medical centre picked us up and took us back to the Nissen hut. All our new mates were waiting for us. Now we could go and get our army clothes and everything that gets issued to new recruits. Terry and I had to go on CO parade at 1000 hours, with that goon. We picked up our uniforms. There was nothing to match our size, but that went for everybody. We had to stay in our civvies to go to CO parade. Others went to the tailors to get them altered, which was to take all morning.

Sergeant Hillard had been in the army for the past ten years. He was great chap. He took to us – you could see it a mile off. He picked us up and took us to the commanding officer. There were two other officers there as well. We waited outside the door. The goon was there under escort. There were also a couple of other soldiers with different NCOs waiting to go in. We were taken in first, with the goon, Hartnell. The charges were read out by the RSM (Regimental Sergeant Major) whose name was Black.

The CO asked Terry and me what had happened. 'How did you get that black eye?' Terry was asked.

'I fell and hit my head on the corner of the bed, sir.'

'And you?' he said to me, 'you have a thick, cut lip. How did you manage that?'

'An accident, sir.'

'Yes, I know, how did you get it?'

'I slipped on the floor, and caught my face on the side of the locker, sir.'

'I want these two boys brought back to me at 1500 hours today.'

We were taken out with Sergeant Hillard – we were not marched out, we were dismissed, as if we were out for a walk. Hartnell was kept in, and the sergeant had to go back in, once we were outside, while the charge was read: bullying, assault and physical assault. The sergeant stated what he had seen. 'I heard a disturbance as I was passing between huts seven and eight. I had been designated those huts to train them as 3 Platoon. I stood in the door. A gathering of personnel were watching this man strike T Morgan, who went to defend his brother, J Morgan, who was no match for this man.'

Hartnell was sent to Colchester Army Prison for fifteen months with the CO's words ringing in his ears: 'We don't want bullies in this regiment. Dismiss!'

We collected our kit, all of it, on Friday after the CO's meeting. The sergeant had us all outside, lined up. He told us everyone had to learn standing orders, which would be on the noticeboard every night. There would be a question and answer on the board. 'Each individual must read them, because you will be asked the question, and some one else will be asked the answer.'

It was time for dinner, for which we went to the mess hall for the first time. We sat with our new mates. The dinner wasn't all that bad. We ate it, and the sweet was good. After dinner everyone had to clean his kit. We all cleaned our kits while sitting on our beds. We were in denims, our dress uniforms being with the tailors. Sergeant Hillard came in and shouted for the Morgan brothers. We got up and went to him. He adjusted our tam-type hats properly on our heads, saying nothing, only, 'You have to look smart for the CO.' We marched over to the CO's office. On the way, the sergeant said, 'Where did you learn to march like that?'

'In the cadets,' we said.

'Very good.' At the CO's office the sergeant knocked on the door, and we were called in. The CO said, 'that's all right, sergeant,' and dismissed him. 'Sit down,' we were told.

'My name is Price. I saw you this morning and I thought that you two boys were a little small. I checked your records and find that you volunteered. What age are you?'

'Seventeen and a half, sir,' Terry answered.

'Who is the oldest?'

'I am, sir,' Terry answered again.

'Is there anything that you want to tell me?'

'No, sir.' We didn't know what he meant. It could have been something to do with the goon. I have seen your faces somewhere, and for the life of me I don't know where.

'What work did you do before you came in the army?'

'We both worked together down in the lumber camp at the bottom of Leckwith Hill,' Terry answered. I had not said a word yet, and I was hoping that it stayed that way. The CO changed the subject and asked us how we were feeling. 'All right now, sir, both of us.'

'Well, you look after yourselves. Any problems like last night, you come and see me.'

We went back to our Nissen hut and carried on cleaning our kit. The boys in the hut asked what had happened. We told them it was a misunderstanding. They were all saying different things, and that we should have told the truth. I said to Terry, quietly, 'They can talk – not one of them came and helped us.'

'We will keep to ourselves,' Terry said.

I said to Terry, 'If Dad knew about this, he would come and smash that bully. He would create hell up here.'

'Let's forget it,' Terry said.

On Saturday we were still cleaning our kit. At least we had some experience through being in the cadets, although the girls had cleaned our boots and belts. We still knew how to do it: burn the toecap and heels and tarnish with a toothbrush or tablespoon, then spit and polish. Gradually it will really shine. A lot of the boys were coming over to watch and take pointers, but in all honesty we were not interested in them. Our concern was for one another.

We looked at the company noticeboard. Company orders were there with our names on them. We had to be outside company office at 0900 hours on Monday for four weeks' physical training at Hendon. Although it was Saturday, we were not allowed out without a hat. They had taken them off us when we received our kit, so we were stuck in the barracks all over the weekend.

In the Army (Hendon)

We went over to the NAAFI in the evening. A couple of the boys came to speak to us. We answered whatever they asked, but we just wanted to keep to ourselves, for to me they seemed a gutless lot. On Monday, while we were outside the company office, our sergeant came up to us. 'Just do your training up there. Don't get involved in anything.' There were twelve others besides us going to Hendon. The intention was to build us up. We got on the three-ton truck that was taking us, sat ourselves down on the bench seats, and we were on our way. It was about an hour before someone spoke. They were all nervous. When they spoke they said silly little things. They brought us into their conversations and we responded. But we were as nervous as them.

We were at the new camp by 1300 hours. It was more like an open-air place, with long wooden huts and plenty of grassland around. It looked pleasant. We were shown our quarters. There were boys from other regiments, all new. Altogether we had thirty-six in the hut. We were taken to the mess hall. The food was a diet-type fare. We did nothing in the afternoon, just sat about on our beds. We were fourth from the end. We were still bed-by-bed together, which I was glad, for I had plenty confidence when Terry was with me. We began cleaning our kit. One of the know-alls said, 'What are you doing that for? It's just gym kit all the time.'

Terry chipped in and said, 'What happens when you rejoin the regiment?'

'Oh, aye,' said this chap.

We sat talking in a group. We carried on with our kit, till about 2000 hours. I said to Terry, 'Let's go over the NAAFI, where we can get something proper to eat. The tea was yet again just diet food, and I was starving. Also I wanted some paper and envelopes to write home. We went, but the food there was no different. We didn't bother. We just got the writing paper and envelopes. We went back and wrote the one letter between us. I wrote the first half, and Terry wrote the second half. It wasn't much, only to let the family know we were in Hendon.

The boys were gathering around our beds. They seemed all right. One or two of the boys that had come up from Cardiff opened their mouths about the fight. We brushed it off as much as we could. Those who were from other parts of the country asked where we were from. 'Cardiff,' we said.

'Yes, I know,' said one, 'your regiment is from Cardiff.'

'Yes, and so are we,' I told him.

The next day we were up earlier than at our training camp, at 0545 hours. We took a run after washing and doing the beds, then had breakfast. Then we had to clean the dormitory. Next we were in the field doing exercises. This was followed by swimming, at which I was pretty poor. Terry gave me confidence. He thought I was mediocre, but he said, 'There we a lot worse swimmers than you.' As we progressed I began really enjoying swimming lessons. After swimming that first morning we were then taken into the gym and onto the bars to stretch us. Afterwards we had a break, then it was out in the fields doing running and exercises. Then dinner – we knew what we were going to have, for all the meals were diet meals.

In the afternoon we went for a hike, then, when we came back, some more press-ups in the fields. This was the pattern nearly every day. Sometimes we would have something different, such as tree climbing, and hikes with full kit. It was great, or at least most of us were enjoying it, and the instructors, firm and fair, were meticulous in organising workouts. I think we all liked them. We didn't do any military training at all, just the physical training.

At the end of three weeks and four days, we were weighed and our height was taken. I had gained two-and-a-half inches, and Terry the same. I had put on a stone and Terry the same. I think everyone near enough put on the same amount of weight. I said to Terry, quietly, 'I know I have put weight on, for I think my thighs are developing.

'Give us a look,' he said. I showed him my thighs and he said, 'Yes, you are right. My thighs are really taking shape too, and they are like steel.' We both felt really good.

We had put some colour on through being outdoors. This training had been entirely different from pounding the decks of a ship. This was a new life to us, and we were enjoying it. We were taken back to Cardiff about 1030 hours, and got back to Whitchurch Barracks about 1445 hours on the Friday. We were told to put our kits on the beds. We could go home till 2359 hours Sunday. This we did.

Back home and we knocked on the door, although we both had keys. I wanted to get the girls going. June answered the door, and shouted, 'The boys are home!' She kissed Terry and me. When Mam saw us she was delighted – the rest of the family were all at work. She hugged and kissed me and Terry the same. When Dad came in he was overjoyed to see the pair of us. 'We must celebrate,' he said. 'We must go and see McDougall.' Terry and I looked at one another.

'I know it was your birthday a few weeks ago,' Mam said, 'but we did as you asked – no cards to the camp. So here are your cards and your presents. I had honestly forgotten all about my birthday. I received casual clothes from the girls, and I noticed a card from Thelma and Tony. I'll have her, I thought, when she comes in. I had a shirt from Mam and Dad (don't forget all clothes were on ration).

Terry came up and gave me a beautiful ring. I thought, *That must have cost him a pretty penny*. I hugged him, and nearly started to cry. 'Thanks, Ter,' I said. (He told me in bed later that Mam went and got it. She had made two journeys into town to get it, for she said she had seen the ring that would suit me, but thought it was too dear. I said to him, 'I have not changed one bit with you, and I will always be there for you.' He said the same, and we hugged one another.

We had tea. The girls came in, and Tony was with Thelma. It seemed that he now come down for tea after picking Thelma up from work. I said to her, 'Who is this chap Tony on my card? I didn't know that he was staying here. Now, if you had put "the snogger" on the card, I would have known.'

'Tell him, Dad!' Thelma said. 'What about?' asking Dad. 'Snogging.' I didn't say anything for I didn't want to push it too much. But Tony was red as a beetroot. He was a nice lad, older than Terry and me. He was serving his time as an electrician, that was why he was not in the army. He was very quiet lad.

Next I started to torment Ivy about her boys, and she said the same as Thelma, 'Talk to him, Dad.' I said, 'What you want to talk about, Dad?' He took no notice. I said to Terry, 'Let's go upstairs, for we can't have the middle room, as there will be some snogging going on later on.' Terry and I went upstairs. I flopped on the bed, as did Terry, only this time, we were just on top.

We came downstairs at 1900 hours, and started to talk to Dad. We told him all about the training. He said, 'I can see it – you have both put on weight and you have both shot up. You look great, the two of you. Did they teach you to box there?' We looked at one another. 'I know,' he said, 'I was told two young boys, twins, were involved in a punch-up, and that you both ended up at the medical centre. I was told all about it, and I was going to go up there, but your mother stopped me.'

'Don't ever do that, Dad,' we both said at the same time. 'We are the ones that will have to live with it,' I said. We can take care of ourselves.'

'Yes, you are right, your mother said the same thing. But this chap was a lot bigger than the pair of you, and it should have been stopped.'

'Yes, Dad, let's forget it. We have, haven't we, Ter?'

'Yes,' said Terry.

We both went upstairs and one after another had a wash. Dad was near enough ready. I said to Terry, 'I know we both agreed to leave our valuables home, but I am taking my watch, the one from Captain Brecon. When we finish training, I will leave it at home. There no point in the two of us taking our watches, but in training I think it is important. I also noticed that I have some pubic hairs coming. Terry could see that I was in discomfort a lot, adjusting myself all the time. 'Don't worry,' Terry said, 'Everyone goes through that stage sometime or the other.'

Dad shouted for us, and we came downstairs. Mam called, 'Not too many!' As we strolled round to the Duke, you could see Dad was proud as Punch walking with us. As we went in McDougall glanced up while pulling a pint, and said, 'Here come the warriors.' Everyone made a fuss of us. If we had drunk what everyone wanted to buy us, we would never have woken up again. Vince walked in and bought us a pint. He had heard about the bully, and we said he had been put away for it. No more was said about it. Vince said we looked great, and kidding us he said the work had dropped down a bit. We had a great night. By the time we went home, we were a little the worse for the drinks. McDougall was pleased that we boys were all right, for he was good to us, and we really liked him. He would very often give us free drinks. When we wanted to pay, he would not hear of it.

When we got home, the girls had just come in. They always tried to get in before Dad got home, as he always played hell if they were out late. The girls had getting in before Dad down to a tea, and they would immediately dive upstairs to bed. But this time they were caught. Dad started to shout at them. 'Dad,' I said, 'they stayed late to see us, for if they had gone to bed, we would not have seen them. We had only saw June when we came home, for the girls had not come in from work. When they did, we were lying on the bed asleep, and they were out again when we went downstairs. I said to the girls, 'I am glad you came in late, for we would not have seen you. Are you both working tomorrow?'

'Yes,' they said. Dad turned round and said, 'Sheltering them again.'

The pair of us stayed up talking to Dad. He never mentioned the fight again. When we went to bed, I said, 'I wonder who told him about the fight? I am glad he never came up there, for we would have never lived it down.'

In the Army (Whitchurch)

We went back on the Sunday night. We got back a little early, so that we could sort our bed and kit out. We were with a different set of lads, for the lot we joined up with were now two weeks from finishing the recruit training, when they would be going to another camp for advance training. We had a new set of lads who would go with us into a new lot of training.

We were shown into a Nissen hut. There were quite a few boys in there already. It seemed the boys returning from Hendon were now making up this new squad. We were glad to have new mates, for the others had done nothing for us. I think someone should have stood up to the bully. Terry and I we were the smallest boys there, which everyone could see. The new boys were nervous and would not talk to one another. There were no bullies here.

Everyone got on with his own thing. They had come in on the Thursday and were already kitted out. In the night on the Sunday we went back, you could hear them crying, or at least whimpering. I would have thought they would have done that on the first night, not the Sunday night. Perhaps they had been doing that for the last few nights.

We got up on reveille, washed and toileted, then made our beds. Some were still in bed when we were called out for inspection, showing a clean rifle. We had had the presence of mind to read the noticeboard. On it was, 'Rifles will be cleaned and polished.' The late ones had a hell of a rollicking. Some of them had not washed or shaved. We had time to start cleaning the Nissen hut. Breakfast was at 0745 hours. When we came back, we finished off the cleaning and put on our best battledress, which had already been altered.

We were all lined up on the square while all the squads were accounted for. The commanding officer took the parade. It was as if you were a spectator – enjoyable to watch. After the parade was dismissed, we were kept on for drill lessons. When you were drilling, every action required from you would be shouted. 'One, two, three, one!' After drill we changed into fatigues, went to the NAAFI, then after twenty minutes were back on parade. We learnt how to use the rifle, being shown the parts and names. The Bren gun was dealt with a step at a time.

Our squad sergeant went by the name of Prince. He and Corporal White were good. They knew their stuff, and were always prepared to listen. We were given current affairs lessons. The first one we had was about bullying. Whether this lesson had always been scheduled, or whether it was because of what had happened, I don't know, but they related that a bully had just been given fifteen months in Colchester! Nothing more was said about it, but those that had come on the Hendon course knew all about it.

Terry and I enjoyed the training. We had become disciplined through being at sea. The other boys found it very hard to acclimatise themselves to it. The NCO liked a joke. They had dry senses of humour that we related well to.

They had taken our caps off us at the weekend, so no one could go out. Then they called us outside, and said that we could go home for the weekend, giving us our caps back. We jumped at it and took our caps. Then Terry asked if the other boys were going. They said, 'No, only you two, because you are twins.' I thought, *Bullshit!* 'No, thanks,' Terry said before me. 'If they cannot go, we don't go.'

'But you have been given special permission from the CO himself.'

'No, thanks,' we both said. 'Permission to rejoin our hut.' This was granted, so we went back. We said nothing to the hut, we stayed in just like them.

The six weeks went by, and we passed out, with just one little hiccup during the rifle and weapon training. I boobed on something – I cannot recall what it was all about – and Sergeant Prince said, 'After tea, come to my billet, and I will give you a pass to get home, to get you away from me.' I had been giving him stick, so he was giving me light banter. I told Terry what I was going to do. 'He might not take it as you mean it,' said Terry. 'Come on, we will have a laugh.'

'You are terrible for winding people up.'

So, after tea, we went to the sergeant's billet. I knocked on the door. 'Come in,' someone shouted. There were about seven NCOs there. 'Yes, Morgan, what do you want?'

'You forgot, sarge,' I said, you told me to come to your billet and you would give me a pass to go home,' and before he could say anything, 'also one for my brother.' Well, the uproar in the billet was tremendous.

I was dismissed – they could see it was all in fun. I thought, in future they will be very careful what they say to recruits. We were on our way out when Sergeant Hillard called us back. Standing up and going to his locker, he pulled out a paper with photos of Terry and me. 'Is this you?' I looked at it, and tried to study it, then I gave it to Terry. I was shaking slightly. The sergeant said, 'Don't be nervous.'

'What do you think?' I said to Terry.

'Nothing like us.'

'Come on, we know it is you.'

'Without being rude, if that is so, why are you asking us?'

Everyone's eyes were on us. I said to Terry, 'That boy does look a little like you, but you are a lot older than him.'

'No, that is not us,' Terry said. 'Come on,' the sergeant said in a kind of gruff voice, but in a fatherly way, 'it is you.'

I looked at Terry and we both said, 'You are mistaken.' Looking again at the photos, I said, 'This boy here is a very young lad.'

'Why did you bring your brother in the first place?' asked the sergeant.

'Because we do nothing separately. We are always together,' I said.

'All right, go on,' he said, and we came out of there. Terry had a go at me for larking about. 'Come on, Ter,' I said. 'You have got to have a laugh.'

'That wasn't a laugh.'

'Come on, let's forget about it. 'I am sorry,' I said to Ter, 'it will not happen again.'

When we had gone, Sergeant Hillard said, 'It is those two boys, I'll bet my wages on it.' They all looked at the photo and all agreed it was us, but they also agreed that they would not say anything to anyone about it.

Terry said, 'John, I know you likes a joke, but don't bring attention to yourself. Otherwise we will be both out of the army.'

'I promise,' I said to Terry. 'Come on, let's get our kit done, then go over the NAAFI.

We were soon in our last week. We went over to the administration block where we were going to have a mental and written exam, to see what we were good for – whether we stayed in the Welsh Regiment, or went into the Tanks or the REMEs or Royal Engineers, whatever. The two of us were kept together. We did the putting the square peg in a square hole, and all the other tests we had to do, then the theory side of things.

In the Army (Brecon)

Well, no more about the slip-up. The next day it was on the noticeboard that we are posted to Brecon, for advanced training.

First we were going on a long weekend leave. We packed our smaller things in the small pack, which is used when you are in action. We left the barracks at 1400 hours. As we were walking to the bus stop, Terry said, 'While we are here, I would like to go to the grave.'

'By all means,' I said. We bought some flowers just outside the cemetery and went to the grave. It was immaculate. The workers were about 200 yards away. We put the fresh flowers on the grave, I said my little piece, and Terry said his; he was wet-eyed, and I wasn't far from it. On the way out we went to see the workers. Terry had the two pounds we always gave them, £1 each, and we asked them, now that we were in the army, they would they look after the graves, for we would not be able to get there all the time. They promised that they would, and I believed them.

We were moving to Brecon on the Monday. We were now into November. The news from France was that we were still advancing. Although there was heavy fighting, we were doing well.

We got home about tea time. Being on holidays, Dad was delighted to see us, and Mam. They made a right fuss of us. The girls were not home from work yet, nor June from school. When Thelma came in she brought Tony with her. Thelma made a fuss of us, and kissed me, then the same to Terry. Tony was always nervous when he saw us. I said to Terry, 'That's it, we can't have the middle room tonight, for there is going to be some snogging going on in there.' Now Tony had gone red. Thelma said, 'Tell him, Mam.'

'What is she going to tell me?' I said.

Terry said, 'When will tea be ready, Mam?'

'In thirty minutes,' Mam said.

'Come on, John, let's go upstairs.'

'Where we going tonight?' Dad said.

'Where we going, Ter?' I said.

He said, 'The pictures, or the snooker hall, or around Mac's?'

'Going around Mac's, Dad,' I said. 'You know quite well I am.'

'Well, you might have company,' Terry said. 'Stop encouraging them to go drinking,' Mam said.

Dad said, 'I haven't said a word,' and I chipped in and said, 'But you wanted us to say that, Dad, didn't you?'

'Go on, hang me,' he said jokingly.

We went upstairs, had a wash, and went into our bedroom, talking till Mam shouted for us. Ivy came in with June, and they all kissed us. I said to Tony, 'Does Thelma kiss like that?'

'Shut up, you,' she said, and Mam said, 'Leave her alone.' Dad never said anything when I tormented the girls, but really I loved them.

We were now all sitting down to tea. I said to Tony, 'Don't spill anything on the table cloth, as it has to go on my bed as a sheet.'

Thelma went potty,' Dad, speak to him!'

'Leave them alone, son, he said.

'All right,' I said, 'but wait till you start drinking.'

'He's not going drinking,' Thelma said.

'But he will when we go back. Dad will say, "Fancy a pint, son?" '

'He's not going or doing that,' she said.

'All right, I rest my case.'

After tea, Terry and I went upstairs to have a lie down. Before we dropped off, he said, 'You don't half torment Thelma.'

'I love her,' I said to Terry, 'and I want to get Tony going.'

'Leave them alone,' Terry said.

'All right, I will.'

The next thing I heard was Dad shouting, 'Are you asleep?'

'Yes!' I shouted, and we came down and went round the Duke. We had the usual fuss made of us. Vince came in. He sat with us, and we talked all night. We did not play cards this night, we just talked. McDougall was talking to Dad and Vince. 'I bet they are cooking up something,' I said to Terry.

We went straight to bed when we got in. I was really tired. We talked for a while. I said this to Terry: 'If anything happens to you in the army, such as getting killed, I will be right with you. I will kill myself, I mean it, Terry,' I said.

'Don't be silly, John.'

'I am not silly,' I said, snapping back at him.

'I didn't mean it that way.'

'Terry, don't let's argue. I love you, and that's it. What I said I will do.'

'I love you, John,' and I will do the same. Let's never get parted. We will not be divided.' We went off to sleep.

We were due back on the Sunday around 1900 hours. That day, Ivy was out with her boyfriend, Brian, Dad had gone to have a lie down (which he did every Sunday), Thelma was in the middle room, and Terry was with me talking to Mam. 'Mam,' I said, 'I don't want anyone sleeping in our bed.' I was thinking that Tony might use it. 'I don't want them in the bedroom at all. There are a lot of valuables in there, and I don't want them taken.' Terry gave Ivy a receipt to pick up some photos that Terry and I had taken in Jerome's. 'Will you ask Ivy, or whoever goes in to town, to pick them up for us?' I asked Mam.

After tea, Thelma and Tony went back into the middle room. As we were going, I knocked, on the door. 'I am going now, sis,' I said, and, I kissed her. I shook hands with Tony. I said, 'Come on, Terry, 'say goodbye,' and he did the same. We boarded the three-tonner that was parked outside, one of two, and we were off. We left Whitchurch Barracks with mixed feelings. None of our NCOs were coming with us, so we would be starting fresh with new NCOs up at Sennybridge, for we had just found out where we were really going now: on advance training to Brecon.

Sennybridge is about five miles from Brecon. It's a mixed camp, Welsh Regiment and Welsh Fusiliers. We were going to do a lot of exercises, which I liked. I had never been to Brecon, nor had Terry, so it was a novelty. It took about three hours to get there. We were mixing with the other boys; it seems they liked our company. 'I wonder what the sergeant will be like,' someone said. 'Look around and see for yourself,' a voice said. It was our sergeant. 'You can let me know when you have finished your training,' he said.

He told us where the messroom was and where the NAAFI was. 'At 1400 hours I want you outside this hut in fatigue order, for Bren gun firing on the range. By the way, my name is Morgan. I and Corporal Evans, who will assist me, will be with you throughout.'

We had dinner. Dinners were all the same in the army, no matter what camp you were in. The first day we joined we turned it away, for we thought it was pigswill. We were now eating it, and enjoying it. After dinner we lined up under the supervision of Sergeant Moorland. Peter was his first name. We then marched with Corporal Evans to the range. We did slow firing at 100 yards, then 200, then 300, then 400 then 500 yards. I thought it was great, and so did my brother.

We were up there till 1600 hours, then we were marched back. In our hut, while we were out, a duty rota had been pinned to the noticeboard, for our cleaning the hut, and for our 'periods', for that is what they call them. The next day we were on the square for the first period, after the camp had formed up and been inspected (we were part and parcel of the parade). We were on the parade ground for over an hour, then we had a break. It was not long enough to go to the NAAFI so we changed into fatigues and then sat around talking and smoking.

Every time we had a break, everyone wanted to get into our company. We knew that we had to accept this, but after the experience with the bully I wanted to be more selective with my choice of pals. I told Terry this and he agreed. We went to the rifle range this time, and did the same sequence as with the Bren, only starting at fifty yards then crawling up to 500 yards, slow then rapid. We were all getting on well with the NCOs and the platoon officer, whose name was Barrett.

We came back from the range dog tired. We had our tea, then we washed and cleaned our kit. I then lay down on the bed. Terry joined me, and we were both lying on my bed talking away about the past couple of days. Then a couple of the lads joined us. We stayed there all the night just talking, until lights out. Most nights Terry pulled his bed by mine and then threw his arm over me. Most of the boys knew this happened, but they did not say anything, for they knew we were twins.

The bugle woke us up with reveille, so the beds were back in place, should anyone have come in. The day after the parade, we were on actual field manoeuvres. A section on how to work in battle, involved crawling on your hands and knees, and I swear to this day Sergeant Moorland, in his wisdom, picked the muckiest field in the UK. We also did river crossing, exciting stuff. He was throwing thunderflashes at us. They would drop in the water, and when they went off you got soaked. It was an exhilarating day, and we all enjoyed it, because the sergeant was great, loving a joke. When we finished we were too tired to move. After doing kit and tea, and washing, Terry lay alongside of me, and we both dropped off.

The next day we were in the barracks, doing drill and gas and PT. We noticed the discipline was very lax there, and there was more wit in evidence than down in Cardiff. We did map reading, which I thought was very interesting. I said to Terry, 'I feel a lot stronger now and, I tell you what, I am enjoying it.'

'And I am,' Ter said. We sat on the bed talking about the merchant navy. 'I am glad I finished,' Terry said to me.

'I am, too. That last trip was a swine. I wonder if that Captain... What was his name? I cannot remember. Well, whatever, he was cruel, and I hope they hang him when the war finishes.'

'I wonder where the Norwegians are, and that German soldier? I hope they did well by our country. Do you know, now and then I see that hole we were in, I cannot get it out of my mind.'

'Forget it,' Terry said and changed the subject, for he knew I would crack up if we kept talking about it.

We were to go on Christmas leave for five days, then come back for our last week of training, then manoeuvres. We were going on the Thursday and reporting back on the Tuesday at 2359 hours. We had told Mam that we would not be buying Christmas presents this year, for we hadn't got the money. We heard that when we finished our basic training we would be going out for days and nights with the other regiments, doing manoeuvres.

On the Wednesday we were out with the PIAT (projectile infantry anti tank) – what an awesome weapon. You had to grip it very hard, otherwise you would break your shoulder. We were allowed to have two shots with that, with training shots. Thursday begin with drill parade. After that we put our beds for inspection with all the kit that we would now take with us.

Pay parade was at midday. Then we were on our own. We were lucky living in Cardiff, for a three-tonner was going down there. We picked our pay up, boarded the three-tonner and were on our way, without waiting for dinner. We arrived home at 1600 hours, knocked on the door, and Mam opened it. She was very excited when she saw us, kissing both of us at the door. There was no one else in the house, so we sat down and had a chat. 'The girls are both courting strong,' Mam said. 'Brian is a well-educated boy, studying to be an accountant. Ivy is very happy with him. He comes down the house a lot.' Mam said, 'Ivy won't bring him down now, for you take the mickey, but when you are away, she brings him down. Tony is down here all the time. He stays down most weekends, but sleeps on the settee in the middle room – and stop tormenting her,' Mam said.

'I only do it because I love her,' I said.

'By the way, your friend that you went to sea with, Timmy, called round. He has been round a few times. I think he is interested in June.'

'She is too young for him,' I said. 'Anyway, I don't want him as a brother-in-law. I had a hard time with him on the Russian trip. Mam, I think I told you that we will not be buying presents this year, for we haven't got the money.'

'Don't worry,' Mam said, 'we understand. As long as we've got you here, that's all that matters.'

They all started to roll in around five. First June – she gave us both a smacker – then Thelma and Tony. Dad was next. When he saw us his eyes lit up, and after a few minutes he said, 'Where are we going tonight?'

Terry looked at me. 'Snooker hall, John?'

'Yes, that's great,' I said.

'You can have one game before you come down Mac's,' Dad said, 'what do you think?'

Mam chipped in. 'They are not going round the pub, they haven't got the money.'

'I will stand them.'

'They are not going.'

'What do you say, boys?'

'We'll come round with you,' we both said. We had had all intention of going round, but we wanted to play Dad along.

Ivy came in. Mam said, 'Where have you been? You're late.' Ivy did not answer. She switched to us, came over and gave us a kiss. That was to get out of giving an answer.

We went upstairs after a wash and lay on the bed, thinking of the girls. 'Are you going to court?' I asked. Terry was quick and said, 'Are you?'

'No, I am not,' I said.

'Nor am I,' Terry said. 'I will never wane in loving you.'

I said, 'And that goes for me. Always remember we must not argue, for up to now we have never had a cross word with one another.'

The next thing we heard was Dad shouting, so we walked with him around to Mac's. All the same boys were there, and we put a knock on.

Vince had not come in. I asked Dad if he were all right. 'Yes, he has a small party with his works, so you won't see him tonight.' We won our first game and we stayed on the table, and had a pint each.

When we got up the next day, Christmas Eve, I said to Terry, 'I am going to give Mam a hand with the cooking,' for she was making puddings and Christmas cake.

'Well, I will give you a hand,' Terry said.

'Great,' I said. After breakfast, we read the papers. There was a big push by the Germans in Belgium, and they are forcing us back. 'Let's not talk about it,' I said, 'for it upsets Mam.' So we got stuck in and prepared the chicken. It was a very big one.

Terry was doing all the veg, cleaning and peeling. I stuffed the chicken and put it in the oven before Mam grabbed it for the cakes. The postman came. There was a lot of letters and cards for the house. There were a few cards for Terry and me. We opened them. One envelope was from the Prides, a card each for the two of us. In each one was a white fiver. There were cards from Captain Brecon, one each, one with a oncer in the cards for us, and we had a card each from Vince with a oncer in it. I said to Terry, 'Let's put the cards in the middle room.' When we shut the door, Terry said, 'What if we give Mam one of the fivers and we keep the rest?'

'Good idea,' I said, 'but I will give the three girls a oncer each.'

'Well, let's make it between us.'

'Good idea,' I said.

We went back into the kitchen. Terry said, 'Mam, we didn't buy any presents, so this is between John and I.' He kissed Mam and I did the same. When the girls came in, I made Terry do the same with the girls when he gave the money to them. Don't forget, a oncer was a lot of money in those days. The girls were excited at this attention from Terry and me. They gave us all a kiss. June was Terry's favourite. Dad came in, and Mam said to him, 'This is the first time in my life that every-thing is ready for tomorrow. I can take it easy.' We pulled Tony to one side, and explained to him about the money. 'Don't even think of it,' he said, and 'thank you.'

'Where we off to tonight, boys?' Dad said. 'We will be with you.' That shook him – well, we were not going to miss Christmas Eve in the pub. When we walked in, Mac's face lit up. He put a pint on the counter for us and, when we went to pay, quietly said, 'On me. Merry Christmas.'

We had our favourite seats in the pub now. It seems that everyone had a personal seat in the pub, and no one else sat in them.

Vince came in and we thanked him for the card and money. 'Have a nice Christmas,' he said. 'I hope you are coming round to the house to the party in the evening.'

'We will be there.'

As we sat down, I said to Terry, 'I told you they were cooking up something, didn't I?'

We had a great evening around Mac's and we more or less staggered home about 1 a.m. Mam played hell with Dad for keeping us out, and I was soon teasing her. The girls were out, apart from June. They had asked Dad for permission to stay out late, as they were both going to parties. We had just gone to bed when they both came in. For us, undressing was very hard. Eventually we were in bed, and fast asleep, with Terry doing his party piece, arm across me.

We stayed in bed till ten, and we were still under the weather. I said, I am not going out till dinner time, and we both stayed in. We came downstairs after washing. The girls had bought us two lovely presents between them, two leather cases with the full shaving gear in them. I was not shaving yet, and Terry was shaving only once a week, but the kit was ready for when we needed it. I had bought Terry a gold chain with a disc on it with his army number and name, and he had bought me a fountain pen and a pencil, in a case. I knew it was expensive, for I had been going to get the same for Terry. As always, Mam had been to buy them, so one boy didn't know what the other was doing. We bought Dad a box of Cuban cigars, which you could not get, but we did! We didn't have coupons, so the girls chipped in and bought for us, for Mam a twinset. She was over the moon with it.

Thelma had a very expensive camera. She insisted that we put our uniforms on so she could take some photos of us. We had to go in the girl's bedroom, for there was a dressing table there. She wanted us to sit at either corner, more or less facing each other, one leg on the floor, and the other on the table, with our hand on the leg. Of course, we were acting the goat, but she took a few, and one of each of us on our own. She said if they came out all right she would get them printed.

Dad went around to Mac's on his own. 'Where's the warriors?' they were asking. 'Getting over last night,' said Dad. When he returned we all sat down to dinner, and we all enjoyed it. We then sat in the kitchen for a while. Tony came round about 1500 hours. We went upstairs while they went in their room. Ivy had gone to Brian's, and she had to walk a fair distance, to Llandaff North. We heard the King's speech, and then went for a lie down. I felt a lot better than when I had woken up.

'I will never wear that gold chain while I am in the army,' said Terry.

'Nor will I,' I said. 'I will keep all our treasures home, in case we lose them to the thieves – and if we get captured, the Germans strip you of all your valuables. I am taking my watch now. There is no need to take yours, seeing that we are always together. Mine will do. But when we go abroad, I am leaving that home as well. You heard me ask Mam not to let anyone stay in our bedroom, and I mean it. As much as I like Tony, I don't want anyone in there.'

Dad called us around 8 p.m. and we all strolled round to Vince's house – that means June, Mam and Dad, and us two boys. Vince lived very handy to Mac's and to the works. He lived in a double house in Wellington Street, just a throw from the pub. Vince had a boy about thirteen and a girl about fifteen. Mac and his wife were already there. Also there were a few of the boys that drank with us, with their wives and a couple of children. We were introduced by Vince to everyone there. There were also his two brothers, all that was left of his family. We planted ourselves down and had a very enjoyable evening, going on till just after 2 a.m. I will say this, Vince knew how to throw a party. There was plenty to drink and eat. We sat with his boy and he was great. He liked us, you could tell. It was a good job that we had a couple of days off after that party! We got up at midday on Boxing Day. We could not go to the cemetery as there were no buses. We got up, washed and came down. Dad was there, and Mam, but not the girls. Thelma had gone to Tony's house, Ivy as usual to Brian's, and June was at over her friend's house. So we sat talking to Dad and Mam. He was quite worried. He knew that we were coming to the end of training, and would be going aboard soon. 'Just take care of one another,' he said. 'Don't do anything rash, think before you act. I want you boys back to come round the pub with me. Now, promise me that you will look after one another.'

Terry said, 'Dad, we are not going yet. We still have a couple of weeks up at Brecon. Also we will have embarkation leave before we go. Don't worry, Dad, we will look out for one another.' We started to talk about the girls. 'Thelma, I think, will be getting engaged soon,' said Mam.'

'Well, let's hope that we get an invite. I like Tony,' I said to Mam, 'he looks a good man for Thelma. I hope they do get engaged. I love Thelma, and Ivy with her boy, though we don't see him.'

'That's your fault,' said Mam, 'for you are always teasing them. Ivy will not bring him here, for she knows that you will have a go at Brian.'

'My lovely little sister – how old is she now, Mam?' Terry asked.

'She is coming up to fourteen. She is Terry's blue-eyed girl,' I said, 'and she loves Terry. She is doing well at school and becoming a fine woman.'

That night, Dad was going to the club. The pubs don't open on Christmas Day and Boxing Day. We were glad, for I was knackered, and Terry the same. So we went into the middle room and played records and talked. Dad was on his way, and Mam said she was going around her mother's. About nine thirty Mam came back, and at the same time June came in. She sat with us playing records. Just after ten we had a sandwich and tea, and we went to bed.

Lying on the bed, we decided that we would go to the cemetery, for this would be the last chance for a while. We decided to go in the morning, then we fell asleep.

We left home about 10 a.m. There were plenty of buses about, so we were not hanging about. True to the workers' word they had kept the grave tidy. There was even a wreath of holly on it. Terry started to cry. 'Come on,' I said, and I shouldered his head. 'Leave it go, Ter,' I said, and he gripped me very hard. I said, 'Come on, say a few words. I will first, then you.' I said the Lord's Prayer, and I walked away. Terry joined me after a couple of minutes, and we caught the bus home. We put no flowers on the grave, because there were no fresh flowers about. I said, 'I won't pay for flowers that will die before we get to the grave.'

We had not been in the house five minutes before my mates called for us to go to the snooker hall. 'Yes, we will go with you,' I said, 'but we will follow you down, as we have just come back from the cemetery.' While we waited for dinner, Terry said, 'We should answer the letters.'

'Yes, we will do that when we come in for tea, and then we can post them.' Ivy had picked our photos up on the Saturday, but she had forgotten all about them, so she gave them to us just as we were going down the snooker hall. We looked at them and they were good. We gave the girls one each and Mam the other one. We had only three, with the negatives.

We went with the boys to the snooker hall. Two of them had to go for their medical, on different days, in two weeks' time. We told them that we loved the army. I said, 'Are you called up or volunteers?'

'We are called up.'

'Keep your fingers crossed,' I said, 'army or the mines, eh?' Both said they didn't want to go down the mines. I said, 'That is why we volunteered.'

We got home from the hall and, after tea, went for a wash. I said to Terry in the washroom, 'How much money have you got?'

He told me £3. 'The same as me,' I said.

'Are we going out with Dad tonight?' asked Terry.

'No, I think we should save it for when we go back, otherwise we will not have any money. I know Dad will say, "Come on, I'll pay," but I think we had enough from them over the Christmas.'

Dad wanted us to go with him, but we both declined. We didn't say that we had no money, we just said that we wanted to go to bed early, as we were tired. We wrote the letters downstairs. There was no one in the house, so we had a bit of peace. We were talking in the kitchen till about 9 p.m. Mam came in with June. We sat talking with June and Mam about one thing and another, and went to bed about 10 p.m. after a cup of tea and a sandwich. We got into bed and talked for a while, then off we went.

The next morning I said to Mam, 'We will be going back at 4 p.m. for we have to catch our lorry at 6 p.m. We stayed in the house talking. We would not see Dad or the older girls before we went back, only June would be there. We were going back and we had just come home, the time had gone so quickly. We kissed June and Mam and we were off. We arrived at the barracks at 1700 hours and sat in the NAAFI till it was time to go. The NAAFI wasn't open, so we just talked. A few of the boys were early like us, and they were in a ring around us. The lorry was on time, and we boarded when we were told. They had a check – one missing. We waited about ten minutes, but there was no sign of him. While we were there, we did not see our old NCOs which was a pity. I would have liked to have seen them. Then we were off.

The chap we had waited for never turned up. Nobody said anything, everyone was talking about Christmas. We answered questions when they asked us anything. It didn't seem long before we got to Sennybridge. We made our beds, got our kit ready for the morning, and went to sleep. Terry put his bed alongside mine. A few of the boys were getting nosey. They wanted to know why he did it, and why he put his arm across my chest. 'Let me tell you this,' I said. 'On my mother's life there is a reason, and I am not going to tell you. So if you don't mind, please let it drop.'

The next day we out for two days, to train us in the dark and combine our regiment with other regiments in manoeuvres. There would be outside troops acting as enemy. These outsiders were the Monmouth Regiment. We would be trained to make defensive positions, attack in darkness, and how to feed ourselves in these circumstances.

We left the barracks at 0900 hours in our three-tonner. Altogether there we nine lorries. We were dropped right out in the countryside of Brecon, which is called the Brecon Beacons. We arrived at 1300 hours, and we were given a cooked meal, something like goulash. It was nice, but not very hot. Then we were dispersed into defensive positions. We were spread out right across a mountain. We put our Bren on fixed lines, in good cross-firing positions. We had to dig holes and then we were well concealed. That was the worst part, digging the holes. We were two to a hole. I and my brother were together, and we kept a watch on the skyline.

Everyone had their holes done in about an hour, then we were all paired off. We were already paired off, so they didn't say anything. It was just getting dark, around 2200 hours (we were into double British Summertime during the war). When the enemy was sighted, we waited for the order to fire. We had blanks. We didn't know that there were marksmen firing live ammunition at our supposed enemy. The battle lasted for an hour. It was pitch dark by now. The boys could rest, but must keep their eyes open for infiltrators, and no smoking. For those who smoked, it must have been very hard going all night without a fag.

At 0600 hours we had to move out. We advanced in extended line. These were all things that we had been trained for. At about 1150 hours we were halted. It was all over. Everybody seemed pleased.

We met the lorries at a certain point and were taken back to camp. This took about ninety minutes. We were all starving, for we had had no breakfast. This was in line with the training – to go without food for a couple of hours. When we got back to camp, we washed and cleaned and toileted. Then it was dinner call, and we were glad of it, for we were all starving. We had plenty to eat and a variety of food.

We had exams the next day, in Bren guns, two- and three-inch mortars and grenade throwing. We had a full day in the camp, and that was good. I enjoyed firing the Bren and the mortars. The instructors very pleased with us. By 1500 hours we had finished for the day. As a matter of interest, the chap who had missed the lorry had still not shown himself. We were going out map reading the next day, and they were going to drop us in pairs well away from the camp. We were, according to the officers, to be out all night. After the weapons exams, we got ourselves ready for the map reading. I was glad I had brought my watch. They told us that we could take our greatcoats, and an extra pullover. I said, 'I am not taking anything like that, for it will slow us down.'

We decided to stay in. Brecon was too small a place for the Fusiliers and us. It had just the one cinema, and if you couldn't get in there were only the pubs there. There was always a lot of trouble in the pub with the other regiment. So we were better off staying in and going to the NAAFI. First we lay on the bed talking. I asked Terry what had made him go into the merchant navy. 'There was no decent work about and I wanted adventure.'

The other boys by now had started to drift to our bed. 'What time are you going to the NAAFI?' they asked. So we got up and walked to the drinking hole. We had a pint of beer, which was the first time on our own. As you know we only ever had a drink with Dad. It was Terry's idea for us to drink beer in the NAAFI, as we would look a little silly just having cups of tea. We had two pints each, that was enough, and we filled our faces with sarnies and cakes. It seemed the same three boys were always with us. I thought they were the best of the squad: Malcolm James, Ben Thomas, and Rat White. If we sat on the bed, they came over. If we went out, they were with us. Even on exercises they were with us, but Terry and I stayed together.

After breakfast we all had to form outside the company office, where we were paired off. We were given a map each for the pair of us, and two corned beef sandwiches, and they were to last till we got back. The rule was to get back as quickly as you liked, by any means, but causing no damage to civilian property.

We were taken in the three-tonners, with the back pulled down so we could not see out. There was a sergeant in the back with us to make sure that we do not cheat. I asked the sergeant what the time was when we got on the lorry (I had been going to bring my watch but had forgotten all about it when we left home). He told us, and I was to remember this.

When we got to where we were to get off, Terry asked him the time, and the sergeant told him. We were getting off in twos, fifteen minutes apart. We had no idea where we were, but we knew we were going down country lanes, by the whine of the tyres and the changing the gears all the time.

When Terry and I got off, Terry again asked the time. I said to the sergeant, 'We were having a talk in the back, you might have heard us – are the three-tonners governed to do just a certain speed?'

'Yes, thirty miles an hour,' he said.

'Thank you,' I replied, and we left. We sat down, got the map out. I said, 'We were on the lorry for two hours and ten minutes.' We spread the map out in the lane. Terry had a penny (the old currency) and measured the diameter, knowing that the average thumb one inch from the knuckle to the tip. This way we found that the penny was just over an inch.

We then put it on the map to the camp, and drew a line around the penny, all the way around, so the map looked around Brecon, there were five rings. We measured this to the scale on the map. This way we had an idea where we were. Now we found the right direction, by looking at the sun. It was dry and warm day. Then we knew where we were.

We walked down the country lane – a beautiful place, if we had been on a picnic. We eventually came to a crossroads. We stopped a lorry and asked the driver where we were. 'Merthyr Cynog.'

'Where's that?' we both asked. He could see that we had a map in our hands.

'On exercise, are you?' he said. We both answered yes. 'Jump on and I will give you a lift down to the fort just outside Cradoc. But I have to pick up some churns on the way.' So we helped – at every farm, on the platforms, there were full milk churns.

It took us ninety minutes to get to Cradoc. We followed the road the lorry driver put us on, taking three-and-a-half hours to Trallong. We decided to get back to camp rather than stay out all night, for in the night it did get cold. We decided that we would sit and have a rest, and eat our sandwiches. Trallong was five miles from Sennybridge. Fit again after the sarnies, we carried on till we got to the camp, securing another little lift on the back of a lorry, which put us back at camp around 2130 hours. When we walked into the guardroom, they would not believe that we had been on the map reading exercise.

We were told to get back to our billets. After we had washed, we would have something to eat, for which we were told to go to the cookhouse when we were ready, where late meals would be on the hot plates. But they had not expected anyone back at this time, so we were early. We were quizzed after the meal by an officer and two sergeants. 'We were in the army cadets, and we learnt map reading with them.' They looked at us with wry faces. 'I don't think they believed us,' Terry said.

'They didn't,' I said.

The hut was empty. It seemed awfully strange. We went to bed, Terry pulling his bed to mine.

We talked for a while. Terry said, 'Don't take offence at what I am going to say or ask, will you, John?'

'I won't, I never have,' I replied. 'What is it?'

'You know all the valuables that we have in the house? Say that we might get killed, the two of us together – what about making a will?'

'That's a cracking idea,' I said. 'What made you think I would take offence at your suggestion?'

'Well, I thought of us getting killed – you wouldn't like me saying it.'

'Come on, Terry, we can both think and suggest. There is no reason to row over it, and I won't argue with you. But your idea is great. Let's think about it till we go on leave.'

'Also,' Terry said, 'we have the negatives of the photos at home. What about sending the Prides, and Captain Brecon, one each? Also we should go and see Captain Brecon when we are on embarkation leave. If we write and tell him we will be over with his permission. We will suggest another Sunday, and tell him just before we come on leave, and we can give him the photos when we go over there. I'll tell you what – say that we write and ask one of the girls to get the negatives developed. Then when we come home everything will be ready for us to post them off.'

'Good idea,' I replied.

Terry then asked, 'Are you happy in the army, John?'

I said, 'I love it. What about you?'

'Yes, I love it.'

'Don't forget, we stay together all the time.'

Terry said, 'Don't worry, I will never leave you.' The reason for this conversation, I think, was to reaffirm our commitments now we were in the army. We both fell asleep happy.

Sergeant Moorland came in the hut in the morning, and said, when he had heard that the twins were back, he could not believe it. 'I had to see for myself,' he said. He said, 'We don't expect to see anybody back till about dinner time. How did you do it?'

'Oh, just luck,' Terry said.

'Come on,' Sergeant Moorland said, 'that isn't luck. How did you do it? Where's your map? They must be handed in. The sergeant opened the map, still talking, and then noticed the rings around Sennybridge Brecon. 'What are these rings around the map?'

'I don't know,' Terry said.

'Come off it. These maps were clean when they were given out. You had some way of working out the route.'

'We don't know what you are on about,' Terry said. Terry did all the talking, for he was the oldest, and we had to keep the seniority right.

The sergeant said, 'You have had experience before, map reading.'

'We haven't,' we both said. He turned and walked out. He went to see the Company Sergeant Major, and he, Mr Hill, could not believe that we were so quick. 'I want to see them,' he said. 'I will get them now,' Sergeant Moorland said.

When Sergeant Moorland left us, I said to Terry, 'We have dropped a clanger by being back so quick.'

'Don't worry,' he said, 'we will tell them that we learnt to map read in the Army Cadets. After sitting down discussing the situation, we will keep to the same story about the army cadets. Don't worry,' Terry said.

Just then Sergeant Moorland came in. 'You are both to report to the Company Sergeant Major, down company office.' We both got up and followed Sergeant Moorland down to the Sergeant Major's office. He invited us in after we knocked on the door. On the desk before him was the map that we had used on the exercise. 'Now, tell me the secret of your success. You are brothers, aren't you?'

'Yes, sir,' we said.

'Right, where did you learn to map read?'

Terry said, 'In the army cadets in Cardiff.'

'They must be good,' he said to us, and Terry, still doing the talking, said, 'Yes, sir, they are.'

'How old are you?' he said to Terry. Terry told him. 'What about you?' he said to me.

'He is the oldest by a couple of hours. In other words he is the boss,' I said, trying to bring a smile to their faces, so that we could forget the serious talk.

'Where are you from?' he asked. 'Yes, I remember, there was a case a while back about some twins and a bully. Were you them?'

'Yes, sir.'

'Tell me what happened,' he asked. 'I only heard that a new recruit was sent to Colchester for bullying two boys that were a lot smaller than him. So we told him, or I should say Terry did. I didn't want to talk too much in case I said the wrong thing. After Terry finished, the sergeant major said, 'He got his deserts. I don't hold with that,' he said as he got up. Then he turned to us and congratulated us for being so quick. We were dismissed. We were crowing like two cockerels on the way to our hut. As yet there was still no one back.

Terry said, 'We have a couple of hours. Let's write to Mam and Dad.' Our practice by then was that I would write a few pages, and Terry would carry on with the same letter. There were about four pages between us. We didn't know when we would be home, but we asked again for one of the girls to get our photos developed. As Terry was writing he said, 'Have you thought of giving Vince a photo?'

'No, I haven't,' I said, 'that's a cracking idea, seeing how good he has been to us.' I said, 'Let's put them in a frame each, and parcel them up, and give them to him in the pub, not to be opened till he gets home. I know he would appreciate them.'

It was well in the afternoon before we saw the first of the boys, and when we told them that we were back the previous night they would not believe us. Come lights out there were three pairs missing. We were told in the morning that they would be given till midday; if they were not back by then, there would have to be a search. By midday one pair had returned. There were still two pairs missing, and now the army was showing some concern. So, after dinner, we were taken out to retrace their steps. We were dropped in the areas these boys were dropped in. They thought that we would not get lost. This time we knew where we were, and speed was not important.

We were dropped around Llandefalle Hill, the place where these boys had been dropped. There were no recruits in the party other than Terry and me. The army would not risk letting the other recruits back out, for they had all been late. We arrived at the starting point and were to make for Llandefalle village, where we would get in touch with Army HQ. If they were not found by then, we would carry on. By now the camp was on red alert over the missing boys.

Terry and I made our way to the village, where we were to meet some NCOs. But by the time we got there it was getting dark, so we stayed in the three-tonner for the night. There were blankets in the truck, put there as a precautionary measure, in case the boys needed to be wrapped in them. Anyway, we used them now. We set off in the morning, after having a wash and a hot cup of tea, provided by a farm that we were stationed outside. The quartermaster sergeant had arranged this with the farmer. We were told to keep our eyes open in the air – for if they had been found, a Very pistol flare would be fired green. Then we were to make our way to the starting point, the farm in other words.

We had been out about an hour when the four boys returned to the camp. So we had that flare telling us to get back to the starting point. We got back about an hour after the flare. We were the last back. The quartermaster sergeant thanked us and everyone on the party.

I don't know what was said to the missing boys but, as I said to Terry, they had done themselves no favours by being late. After a day it was forgotten, for we were going on leave. We had done the advanced training in four weeks, and I had enjoyed it. My brother said the same. We would have gone home earlier, but for the missing boys. We were not blaming them for it, it was just bad luck. We packed our kit. We were going by lorry to Whitchurch Barracks, where we would leave our kit.

We were to have ten days leave before reporting back to Whitchurch Barracks on Sunday, 6 February. We were going to Battersea for street fighting. I was looking forward to that. We arrived at Whitchurch Barracks at 1130 hours. We were given our pay and travel warrants.

We arrived at the house at 1400 hours and only Mam was there. She was delighted to see us. She said, 'I had your letter today, and Ivy, who works in town, said she would collect them, the photographs.' Mam made a nice cup of tea. I went around the chippy, and Terry came with me. We bought some pie and chips, came home and had some bread and butter, and we got stuck into them. They were delicious.

We sat talking about Dad. 'Do you want a bet?' Terry said.

'What is it?' I enquired.

'I bet Dad will say after he comes in, "Where we going tonight, boys?" '

'No, I am not betting, for that is a certainty.'

We decided we would be going into town the next day, looking for some frames for Vince. We told Mam what we were going to do. I said to Mam, 'He has been very good to Terry and me, and it is only a little thing.'

'By all means, Mam said, 'he would love that.'

'We will take June out to dinner from school,' I said.

'She will like that as well.'

I said to Terry when we went upstairs, 'Mam gets awfully excited when we come on leave. She grabbed us and kissed us as if we had been away for a year.'

'When Dad comes in and asks us where we are going tonight, we will say to the pictures, we will string him along.' Terry didn't want to do that, seeing that he had not long been adopted. 'Come on,' I said, 'he likes a joke, you must have seen that.'

We were right. After Dad hugged the both of us, he said, 'Where we going tonight?' I looked at Terry, and Mam shouted, 'They are going to the pictures – stop encouraging them to visit the pub.

I said, 'If there is a good film around Mac's I will come.'

'Having me on again,' he said.

'He doesn't have to encourage us, Mam, we have a pint in the NAAFI now and again. We just can't go in there with the boys, they have a pint we have a cup of tea – we would look ridiculous.

'There you are,' she said, turning on the old man, 'you have made drunks out of them.'

I said, 'Funnily enough Terry, was blind drunk, and I had to put him to bed.'

'I wasn't, Mam, honest. He's lying – another wind up,' he said.

Mam said, 'Stop tormenting him,' meaning Terry.

The girls came in just after we had our tea, and I started on Thelma. I said to Terry, 'The baby snatcher's in.'

'Mam, stop him,' she said.

'How is my little baby?' I said.

'I am not talking to you.'

'By the way, we want the middle room tonight,' I said.

'You are not having it. Tony is coming down.'

My father was not saying a word. Ivy was very quiet. I think she was waiting for me to start on her. 'Have you got a boyfriend?' I asked her.

'I am not telling you, she said.

'All right, when he comes in, I am going to ask him how old he is, also if his mother knows he is out.'

Terry chipped in, 'Come on, let's go upstairs to the bedroom.'

Dad shouted, 'Are you coming?'

'Won't be long, Dad.' We had both fallen asleep on the bed – it was just gone 8 p.m. Downstairs, Thelma was in the room with Tony; Ivy had gone out, having said to Mam, 'I am not letting John see Brian, for he will rag him silly.'

We both came downstairs. 'Fell asleep, boys?' Dad said, taking the mickey, for we were late, in his eyes, for the cinema.

I said to Mam, 'Did Ivy get the photos?'

'Yes,' Mam said, 'but she wasn't going to give them to you if you started to torment her.'

'Now, would I do that? Ask her when she comes in, and I promise I will not torment her, for at least a couple of days.' McDougall saw us as we walked in. 'The conquering heroes have arrived,' he announced, so all in the bar heard. The pub was very quiet that night. Vince wasn't there, so we played cards, and came home when the pub closed. We sat talking to Dad, near enough to 2 a.m. We told him about the map reading and about the boys who had got lost, and how we had been out looking for them.

'I'll tell you what we will do tomorrow, or rather today,' I said to Terry. 'We will go to the cemetery in the morning, take June to dinner from school, go into Woolworth's, then send the telegram to Captain Brecon. We will go on the Thursday this time, and that's what we will say.

'I am not taking any of our presents back to the army, I treasure them too much to lose them, and if they were stolen or taken off us, it would break my heart.' The watches were very expensive. In those days, watches were only for the well-to-do, in other words we would not have been able to buy one. Our names were on them.

We had not heard from the Prides since the last letter we sent, but there again it was very awkward with the war.

June loved coming to dinner with us. She adored Terry, I could see that, and I was delighted. We took her back to school, and then we went to Woolworth's and bought four frames, two for Mam and two for Vince. We got the frames and we then sent the telegram.

We went to the cadets with the boys. When we walked in we were the centre of attraction; even the officers made a fuss. We told the officers about the map reading. 'Would you like to tell the boys?' we were asked. 'If you want.' So they all sat in the desks in the classroom, and Terry and I told them about the map reading. We told them about the penny and how we had asked the time, also about the supposed argument about the lorry's speed being governed. This had been just to help us calculate the distance from where we were to the camp.

Terry told them about us getting back a day before anyone else, and how the company sergeant major and the sergeants could not believe that we were so quick. Terry said, 'We told them we learnt map reading in the army cadet force in Cardiff.' We went around the chippy when we came out of cadets, with all five of my mates, just like old times. Mrs Doodies from the chippy made a fuss of us all, which she did all the time.

On Sunday night we played cards at the house of one of the boys, Paddy's. We came home about 10 p.m. We went to bed before Dad came in. We sat talking about the merchant navy. Terry asked me about the *Tri-Mark*. He had heard only bits and pieces. So I went through the story, from being torpedoed to the Gibraltar escape. After two hours we went asleep.

We did not bother to get up early on Monday. We stayed in bed till about 11 a.m. We came downstairs together, after washing and toileting. Terry still seemed a bit coy. He waited for me everywhere. We went back upstairs after reading the dailies, and we started to make our wills out. Actually, we made the one will for the two of us, and that took some doing. Terry did the writing, and he was a good writer, it took us two hours to write it.

We did not put it with a solicitor, for in those days it wasn't heard of – only the rich people did that. Now we were at a loss, for whom were we going to give the will to? We decided that, if possible, our bedroom would never be used by other, with a padlock put on it at all times. We wanted the room as we left it, with just the bed covered. The will would on the dressing table, only to be opened if anything happened to us. We would give the keys of the lock to Dad.

On Tuesday we did nothing, just stayed in bed most of the morning. We were both awake. Terry was asking about Timmy, I told him about the Russian convoy, how he had sulked and made it very hard for me, for those convoys were sheer hell. I also told him about the donkeyman coming in the showers when Timmy and I were in there, which was against the rules of the ship. 'That was just after we left Cardiff. He was taken off the ship at Liverpool. My two friends Mike and Ted saw to that, I think I told you that a long time ago. They were great, they looked after me, just as you have done. But Timmy just sulked. "I needed someone like you," I said, "to talk with so we could comfort one another, but all you do is sulk. You are in a shell of your own." When we came home we just split up. He has been down the house a few times while I have been away – let's forget it. I have my very special friend.'

We were going to the snooker hall with our mates that evening, and the next day we were going into town. I said, 'I want to get the girls a little present.'

'I will come half with you.'

'Fair enough,' I said.

So that's what we did. We had them wrapped up. When Tony came round (I liked him, he was a smashing kid) we went to give the present to her. I walked into the middle room and said, 'A kiss for this parcel.' I was tormenting her again. In the end I had my kiss. I gave her the parcel, and I said, 'From Terry and me, we both paid half.' She then went and gave him a kiss. I said, 'You want to watch her, she fancies Terry.' He started to blush, and Thelma did as well. Tony just looked on sheepishly. We had the photos from Ivy, and we framed them, two for Mam and two for Vince. We wrapped the two for Vince, and Terry wrote, 'To be opened when home.'

I decided to have an early night, for I felt dog tired. We went up about 9 p.m. and talked for about an hour. I said to Terry, 'Tell me about your parents.'

'Well, Dad at first objected to me going to sea. Mam said, "Leave him go, it will do him good. It will teach him how to mix with people." My father was all right nothing like Dad here, very solemn. There was no go in him really. My mother was too fussy. I have seen your – I mean our – family now, and there is no likeness at all. There is more fun here, and the girls are great.'

'I told you that when we were at sea. I know I torment them, but I love them.'

On Wednesday night we went out with Dad. Terry carried the photos. There would be no way that Vince would know what they were. We sat down with Dad, and we put a knock on. Then Vince walked in, and Terry got him a pint. 'By the way,' Dad said, 'I don't want you buying every Tom, Dick and Harry pints. You can't afford it. I saw that bum the last time we were here asking you for a pint. You don't do it.'

Vince sat down next to Terry, who gave him the parcel. 'What's in it, then?' He read the writing on the parcel. 'All right,' he said, and we heard him ask the old man what was in it.

'I really don't know,' Dad said. 'You will have to wait till you get home.' We came out at 11 p.m. and walked home. Mam knew we would be going to Bristol the next day, so we asked her to give us a shout about 8 a.m.

We went over to Bristol. We knew where to go, and when we knocked on the door the captain's wife answered it and invited us in. We were talking, till the captain came in, about three hours after we got there, and he made a right fuss of us.

He insisted that we stayed the night, and that we went with him to Bristol zoo. I was delighted by the idea, so was my brother. Captain Brecon's daughter and son came in and also greeted us warmly. We told them about our experiences in the army, including the bully.

The captain asked us if any questions had been asked about our age, and if anyone had remembered us from the photographs. We told him about the sergeant querying the photos with us, though we denied knowledge of them, so they just dropped it. They knew, but they kept their mouths shut. We told the captain that we kept to ourselves. That way we would not slip up. Terry did the talking. Terry then asked where his coat had been put, and he was shown to it. He put his hand in the inside pocket and brought out the photos, in an envelope, and gave them to Captain Brecon. When he saw the pictures, one of Terry and two of me, he was full up. He got up and left the room for a second. 'Sorry, boys,' he said, nothing else.

The bed we slept in was really lush. The home itself was six rooms including two bay sitting rooms. The next day we went to the zoo. All the captain's family came. His son was taking to us all the time, a smashing lad, and his sister was a very nice girl. We were lucky enough to go by car. It had been given to him by the shipping firm he worked for. He was grounded; he dared not go back to sea, for his name was notorious among the Germans. So he got a plum job. He said, 'When you come out of the army, let me know and I will get the two of you a job. Now, don't forget,' he said.

We had a glorious day out. We had dinner in a restaurant, and the captain really looked after us. He saw us off at the station, and thanked us for the photographs. We thanked him for the wonderful time. We told him that we were going out with the boys, my mates from way back, and that's what we did. We got home about 5 p.m. and went to the snooker hall.

On Saturday I said to Terry, 'We will go with Dad tonight, for we have to go back tomorrow.' So we just hung about during the day. We did go around to see our grandparents, and came home and had a lie down till tea time. Mam shouted for us, and we came down, had tea, and talked to Tony and the girls, with no teasing. After about an hour we went and washed, and talked in the bedroom till Dad shouted for us. On the way, I said, 'Terry, we are going to confirm with Dad about our will. Also I want a padlock on the door. I am not worrying about the family, but if ever there is a party in the house, I will know nobody can go in the bedroom.' So we did just that. We both asked Dad to look after our valuables, and to put a stout lock on the door.

Thelma and Ivy were in. 'When is Brian coming down?' I asked.

'Never,' she said, 'for you take the mickey.'

'I won't,' I said. 'I don't do it to Thelma, do I?'

Thelma said, 'Not much!'

'When we bought the present for you, you just wouldn't stop kissing us.'

This was our last day home for a while. We sat with Dad, and he said again, 'No drinks for the lay abouts.' We played cards, and were knocked off again first time. If you get knocked off, there is not much chance of you getting back on.

In the Army (Battersea)

Sunday came and I said to Terry, 'Come on, let's make a move.' We had the same performance from Mam and Dad, both of them hugging us. Dad said, 'Watch out for one another,' which he knew we would do. Thelma came out, and Tony, who seemed more relaxed in the house now. Thelma kissed the pair of us, and Tony wished us all the best, and shook hands. June started to cry. 'Come off it,' we both said. 'We won't take you to dinner,' I added, 'if you cry like that.'

We arrived back at Whitchurch at 2000 hours. There were a few of the boys there. We made our beds, cleaned our kit and then went to bed.

At 0900 hours we were all outside our hut in full kit, ready for inspection. The three-tonners were ready, two of them to Chelsea Barracks. We were going for four days for the street fighting. Chelsea Barracks was a staging post for the Guards when they were on duty at Buckingham Palace. Also the MPs (Military Police) were stationed there. We were told that if we went out in the nights we must be in by 2359 hours. The gates would be closed if we were late, and we would not be admitted till 0630 hours, classed as AWOL.

We had tea, and Terry and I cleaned our kit. We were not going out. We just stayed in the dormitory, entirely different from the Nissen huts.

After breakfast we were inspected. Then two of the three-tonners took us to Battersea. I was shocked to see the state of the place. All the houses had been blitzed, ideal for learning street fighting. We were there till about 1530 hours. We had two corned beef sandwiches each and they brought hot tea around. I was enjoying this. I think, really, everyone was enjoying it. The instructors were outsiders, although we had our own with us, and these outsiders were good. They liked a laugh, and they would pull all sorts of stunts on us.

In the evening we decided against going out, so we sat on our beds. We were not allowed to close the beds together, so I lay on Terry's bed, and we talked about the girls and their boys. I thought Thelma's boy was younger than me, though Thelma was a year older than me. Brian, who was chasing Ivy, was young. They were a really nice couple of boys.

Two of the boys that we had got friendly with came over and sat on the beds. We talked till lights out, 2215 hours.

All the walls in the room had battle honours painted on them. This was the Coldstream Guards' barracks. When they cleaned their kit it was an organised clean, not like ours. We would finish at a certain time before tea, and then the night was ours.

That night we cleaned our kit and we decided to go to the NAAFI. We didn't know where it was. We stopped a guardsman and asked where it was. He said, 'When you talk to a guardsman, stand to attention.'

'Balls,' I said, and carried on walking.

At that precise time a sergeant from the Red Caps was passing and he heard me. 'What's the trouble?' he enquired.

'Nothing, sergeant,' we replied.

'Well, what was the abusive language for?'

'Nothing,' we said.'

'I heard it. What was it for?'

'The guardsman was standing to attention saying nothing. Terry said, 'Are we supposed to stand to attention to a guardsman?'

'No, you are not,' the sergeant said. 'You are dismissed. Guardsman, stay where you are,' he rumbled.

'What?' the guardsman said.

We don't know what happened but I bet the guardsman did not do that again.

We found the NAAFI (Navy, Army, Air Force Institute). It was huge. There were quite a few soldiers in there. We had a pint each. As we got our drinks, Whitley and Mac came in. They sat down with us. We didn't buy them a drink. They were counting their pennies, as we were. I don't mind buying people drinks, but we never had the money. We only wanted two, for we were just learning to drink, so two was plenty. We came out at 2200 hours, for they closed then. We got in and into bed just in time.

We had breakfast at 0730 hours, and we were on the square and away before the guardsmen formed up (for the Guards this is a ritual.) When we got to Battersea, we had a lecture. Then we were shown booby traps that were planted all over the place. 'Be very careful,' we were told. 'They don't hurt, but they can make you deaf for about ten minutes, especially in a very confined place.' If you were near in a darkened place, it would also blind you for a second.

We had a good week there, with no mishaps and plenty of excitement. I enjoyed it. Although Corporal Evans and Sergeant Moorland were with us, we were under two sergeants, Butt and James. The best laugh was that there were some soldiers dressed as Germans. We had plenty of fun with them. Everyone took it in the spirit of the training. It was a pity it had to end, but we were on our way back on the Friday afternoon. We got back at 1600 hours, so we stayed for tea, made our beds after a wash and brush up, and Blancoed our kit.

Terry and I went home. Dad's eyes lit up when we got in. 'We are only home for a couple of hours,' Terry said. 'We have to be back by 2359 hours. We went to the pub with Dad. I noticed now that Terry had really settled in with us, and he got on superbly with Dad. Dad treated us both the same, which is what I wanted. I said to Mam, 'We will not be back, we have to go back to barracks.' We left Dad just before 2200 hours, and caught the two buses that would take us to the camp, as trained soldiers we were allowed out in the evening after the periods finished.

In the Army (Whitchurch)

We fumbled our way into bed. Lights out was at 2215 hours, and it was pitch black in the hut. We were up early in the morning on reveille for the camp drill parade, which was held every Saturday. After that we could apply for a weekend pass, or travel back each night. We applied for the pass. We got home around dinner time, had something to eat, and then went and watched Cardiff City lost Aberaman. Then we had tea. In the evening all the girls and their boy friends were going to a dance. So while Tony was waiting for Thelma to get ready, I said, 'Let's go in the middle room,' to Tony. I gave Terry a wink. We all got up and walked into the middle room.

My mother said, 'Where are you going?'

'Only in the room,' I said.

'Now, leave Tony alone,' she said. Dad was sitting reading the *South Wales Echo*.

'We are only going to play records, aren't we, Ter?' I said.

'Yes,' he said.

'You are as bad as him,' Mother said.

In the middle room, I said to Tony, 'Now that you got your feet under the table, you are expected to take Dad out for a drink. He hasn't said so much yet, but you can see he is getting frustrated that you have not asked him. Now more so, since we are away a lot. He told me he likes you, didn't he, Ter, round the pub when we were talking, so you must do your part.'

Thelma came downstairs and couldn't see Tony. 'Where is Tony?' she enquired.

'In with the boys,' Mam said.

'Oh,' she said, 'what did you let him go in there with them for? They will poison his mind!'

'Leave him alone, he has got to stand on his own two feet,' Mam said. 'The more you shelter him from the boys, the more they will torment him.'

'Tony!' Thelma yelled out.

I said, 'Your master's voice is calling you.'

He jumped up and went through the door.

'Stay away from them,' she said. 'If they encouraged you to go in there, they are up to something.'

We could hear Thelma. I said to Ter, 'Come on, we will stir it a bit more.' We walked out, and I said to Tony, 'We will be going around the Duke at around eight fifteen. Are you coming?'

'Certainly not,' Thelma said.

'Come on, let him have a pint of wallop. It will do him good, it will make a man of him.'

'Dad, speak to them, will you?' Thelma said.

'Don't take any notice of them,' Dad said, 'they are only winding you up.'

'Eight fifteen,' I said to Tony as he was walking out with my sister.

Tony said to Thelma after they shut the front door, 'I like them, they are great.' No more was said about us boys by Tony, for he knew he was treading on dangerous ground.

Terry and I went with Dad round the Duke. All the cronies were there, buying us pints, and there was a good old sing-song going on. Vince walked in, and he thanked us for the photos. He thought they were good, and his wife loved them.

We stayed on after the doors were locked at closing time. We all went into the smoke room, and there was a tidy crowd there. We left at midnight feeling under the weather, both tight.

We were right under the influence, wobbling on our way home. The girls were in bed when we got home. There was only Mam in the kitchen. We had some sandwiches that Mam made, and we went to bed after a fashion. We had the usual performance trying to get undressed, but in the end we managed to get into bed, laughing all the time. A couple of times Dad shouted, 'Are you all right?'

'Yes,' we said, then we would be back to square one, laughing and falling about.

Next morning Mam had a go at us for the noise we made, but merely to impress the girls. We had dinner and in the afternoon we played cards. Then we had tea before going back to barracks. I told Mam and Dad that we would probably be home the next week. But meanwhile we went down to Porthcawl for training on the dunes. We had plenty of laughs down there. We went on the Monday and came back on the

Thursday, and we were all sent home on embarkation leave, to report back on 14 March.

The night we came home Dad was as always delighted to see us, but this time we declined to go to the pub. We stayed in and played cards, having my usual banter with the girls, and when we went to bed.

During that leave there was not much for us to do. We wrote letters to the Prides, and the captain, and went to down the snooker hall a lot. We went drinking with Dad the first Saturday we were home, but only once in the midweek and Saturdays, for we just had not got the money.

We went to the cemetery on the Saturday afternoon. The grave was immaculate condition. We put our flowers there. I said my little piece, and walked away, and Terry said his. He came up and hugged me, but said nothing. I think he was a bit emotional. We got home and had tea, and talked with Thelma and Tony. I heard a sly whisper that Thelma had got the photos that she took with her Christmas camera. As for the one with the two of us sitting either end of the dressing table, with one leg on the floor, looking at one another – she had had a large portrait of us being painted by a professional artiste. According to Mam it was costing her a tidy couple of bob. I asked Terry if he had any photos of his family. 'No,' he said, 'I am not forgetting what they looked like.'

'Come on,' I said, 'they would wish you all the happiness in the world. They don't want you to be miserable.'

'I am not,' he said, 'but it upsets me every time I visit the cemetery. That's why I always want you to be with me, for you have a good sense of humour.'

Before we knew it, we were making ready to go back. I said to Dad, 'We will have a drink tonight.'

'I love the pair of you,' Dad said. 'One must look after the other. Don't tell your mother that you are going abroad, either of you, for it will break her heart if anything happens to either one of you.'

'I won't, I will look after him,' Terry said. 'I know you will, son,' Dad said. 'Don't forget you are both sacred to me. Another thing, on a lighter note: I won't have anyone to go to round the pub with.'

'That's all right, Dad,' I said, 'I told Tony he has got to take over,' and we all smiled. We walked round the pub, and I started to feel choked, and wanted to cry. 'Terry,' I said, 'I'm frightened.' My father's walking in front started to upset me, for I loved him, and thought of what he had said.

I gripped Terry by the arm. He could see now that there was something wrong. Dad turned round and saw it. 'What's the matter, John?' he said, taking hold of me. I managed to say nothing. It was a good job it was dark, but Dad being so near could smell rather than see something was wrong. 'Come on, let's get a brandy down you,' he said, and I clung to Terry, 'All right, John, all right,' he kept saying.

We got to the Duke. Dad went in and asked McDougall if we could go into his quarters. 'Take him in here,' said Mac, pointing to a door. The room was empty. Dad sat me down. I still grabbed hold of Terry's arm, and would not let go.

'What's the matter, John?' Dad asked.

'Nothing,' I said. 'I just felt queer. I came over in a sweat, and I panicked.'

Dad went out with McDougall. I said to Terry (for we were on our own), 'As I saw Dad walking in front, the ship came into focus, and I started to panic like when I was trying to get out of the hold.'

Terry said, 'Stay with me,' and I would not let him go.

Mac brought the brandy in, and his wife came in, and she wanted to fuss. I said, 'I am all right now,' after drinking the brandy, which really tasted awful. Mac's wife gave me some codeine tablets, and after about thirty minutes I was feeling a lot better. I told Dad I was going back home. He wanted to come. I insisted he stayed. Terry said, 'I will take him home.' I thanked Mac, and we then came home.

Terry opened the door with the key that was behind the letter box. Mam put one there for us while we were home. I said to Terry, 'I am going straight upstairs. I am not going in the kitchen, for to be truthful I could not face anyone. So Terry went into the kitchen. Mam was there with June, Ivy and Brian.

'What's the matter?' she said to Terry. He wanted to call Mam into the hallway, but she knew without being told that something was wrong. She asked where I was. 'Just gone to bed,' Terry said. 'Let me go first to make sure that he is in bed.' He did so, then he called Mam, who dived in straight away, and the girls followed her.

'Get out,' she told the girls, 'while I see to him.' She had the draught that she used before from the hospital. She made me take it and said, 'Let him sleep.' Terry said, 'I am stopping with him, and with me holding Terry's arm, I dropped off to sleep. Terry had also fallen fast asleep, when Dad popped in. He didn't say anything he just looked in and went back downstairs. Mam asked what had happened. 'I don't know,' he said. 'I turned around, for I was in front of them a pace, and John was crying and gripping Terry. I could see, although it was dark, that something was wrong.

'We got him to Mac, and Mac let him stay in the sitting room for a spell. He gave him some brandy and some tablets, and then John came home.' Dad said to Mam, 'I think it is the same thing that happened before – something must have sparked it off. He won't leave Terry go. You know why – because Terry stayed with him, comforted him and saved him when he was really in distress.'

'He has got to go back tomorrow, hasn't he?' Mam said. Dad said yes. Mam said, 'I will send a telegram saying he is bad.'

'No, don't you dare do that, John would not forgive you. Let's see what he is like in the morning. I'd better go up and tell Terry to get into bed. He's fast asleep in the chair, with John holding his arm.' Dad went and woke Terry up and told him to get into bed. Terry did not argue. He waited for Dad to leave the room, then took all his clothes off and got into bed, putting his arm across my chest.

In the morning I woke up, but Terry was fast asleep. *I feel fine now*, I thought to myself, *though I have a headache*. I got out of bed gingerly so as not to wake Terry, then came down. Father had gone to work, June to school; Mam was reading the morning paper, which she had got about an hour ago. It was nine thirty.

Mam asked, 'Is Terry awake?'

'He is still fast asleep.'

'How are you feeling?'

'All right, other than having a headache.'

Mam got up and fetched a few codeines and some water, gave them to me, and then asked what I wanted for breakfast. 'Just some toast,' I said.

'Are you going back tonight?' Mam asked.

'Of course I am. I have to.'

Terry came in. 'How are you feeling?' he asked me.

'All right, thank you.'

'Are you gong back tonight, John?' Terry asked.

'You are the second one to ask that. Of course I am.'

Terry looked at Mam, but she just shrugged.

'What will you have?' Mam asked Terry.

'Just some toast, Mam, please.'

After breakfast, Terry and I went down to the snooker hall, at my suggestion. As we walked down at about 11 a.m., Terry asked me again if I was all right. He was still worried about me.

'Thank you, yes,' I said. 'I came over queer. I saw Dad walking in front, then I saw us on the ship. I was really frightened – everything came back, I went cold. Terry, I am scared. This is the second time this has happened. I am frightened this will happen on active service.'

'Don't worry,' Terry said, 'I will look after you.'

'Thanks, I know you will,' I said.

No more was said about it, not even by Dad. We went back home at 1 p.m. and had pie and chips. I loved this as a meal. We then sat in the middle room, playing records and talking. We decided that we would catch the seven thirty bus. That would give us plenty of time to make the beds and Blanco or belt and gaiters.

We had a bath each after tea, packed what little kit we had, and then we were ready to go. I was feeling a lot better now, and would be glad for us to be on our way. Waiting about was nerve-racking.

When it was time to go, I said to Mam, 'We will probably be home in the nights before we go but, if you don't see us, we will be up in North Wales, training.' I said that not to worry Mam, hoping she would think North Wales was where we were. We both kissed Mam and June; the others had not come home yet. Dad hugged the pair of us and said, 'Let's have some letters from you. Look out for one another, and take care.'

When we got back into the Nissen hut we were lumbered with our beds by the door. It was all right, for we would only be there for one or two days We Blancoed our kit, cleaned our boots, and did all the other things that we needed to do. It was about 2200 hours. We didn't take our watches with us. They were priceless to us. Nearly everyone else had a watch, so you could always find the time. The rumours had started that we were shipping out on Sunday, going to Dover to go to Ostend. We would take no notice till we were officially told.

Next morning we were lined up right at the back of the parade, about forty of us. When the parade finished we were marched to the company office of Three Company. We were told we would be moving out on the Sunday. We were to finalise everything before we went, leaving at 1600 hours – they didn't say to where.

We came home on the Friday and stayed in talking to Mam and Dad, Dad went out a little later than usual, the girls and their boys already having gone out, so we stayed in and played records. Thelma had bought some new ones – she would have gone mad if she knew we were playing them. We returned at 2200 hours and got back to barracks by 2300 hours. Next day we were allowed out at 1200 hours. On the way out we met Sergeant Hillard. 'Still in the army, are you?' he said.

'Why shouldn't we be?' we asked.

'Come on, the mug shots were yours.'

'We don't know what you are talking about,' we said.

'Shipping out Sunday, aren't you? Well, take care.' He shook our hands, and wished us the best of luck.

We got home and did nothing in particular, other than answering the letter we had from the Prides in South Africa. They were missing us, and glad that we had settled in to the new life in the army. Mr Pride made reference to us being too young. We wished him and his wife the best from both of us. Then we wrote to the captain, telling him we were about to go abroad, and wished him and his family all the best.

We went to the pub and had two pints with Dad, leaving about nine thirty. Dad followed us to the door of the Duke, and he hugged us both. I had never seen my father the way he was. He was full – he had a job to speak and he would not let us go. We did get away and the pair of us were equally full up. We got back home and picked our kit up. Only Mam and June were in the house. We kissed June and Mam and were gone before the flood gates opened.

In the Army (Continent)

We got back to camp. Nothing had changed, we were still going on Sunday. Six boys were still absent at 2300 hours. By the time deadline came, there were still four missing. We never saw them again. It was as if they had walked off the end of the world as far as we were concerned.

We had breakfast and dinner. We did nothing but talk. During the talk Terry and I had, I said, 'Now I am feeling a lot better, thanks, Ter, but I am scared stiff about going back on a ship, for that is how we are going to go to the continent.' The call went out for us to assemble outside company offices. Sergeant Moorland, Corporal Evans and another corporal were with us. The new corporal's name was Thomas.

We boarded the lorries, and at 1545 hours we were on our way. I was sitting with Terry towards the back, and I had to grab his arm. I was upset about leaving. Leaving to go on exercise is entirely different from going abroad not knowing what faces you. I was doing my best to hold myself properly. I whispered, 'Sorry, Ter, I feel like a kipper.'

'Hang on, I will try and get to the open end.'

'No,' I said. 'Let's not draw attention to ourselves, but I am petrified about going down into the bowels of the ship.'

'Let's wait and see what happens,' Terry said.

We arrived at Southampton at 2200 hours. We debused and went straight on to a passenger ship. Luckily we were the last on, so we were one deck from the top. As soon as we got under way we were allowed on deck, and that's where we stayed all night although it was cold, we sat in the companionway to the engineroom. It was warmer, and there was no one else about. It seemed everyone was asleep. We dropped off to sleep with my head on Terry's shoulder. When we pulled into Ostend you could see that some heavy fighting had been going on there. We were taken to a transit camp just outside. We were given a hot meal and a bed.

The next day we were up, had breakfast, and were given iron rations and two bully beef sandwiches. We left at 1030 hours on the road to God knows where. We were moving into the middle of Belgium, passing Brussels, going through Jodoigne, then into Holland. We didn't really know which places we were going through for it was dark, and we were all dozing off to sleep. When we had boarded the lorries from Ostend, Terry asked our mates that we were chummy with, Ben, Whitley and Mac, to get on the one side, so I could face out. Terry told the boys that I didn't like being in the back for I suffered from claustrophobia. They let me sit right by the tailboard of the lorry, and I was all right then, talking away. When I felt drowsy I just tucked myself into Terry. Now Terry was more comfortable knowing that I was comfortable.

Our new corporal sat on the opposite side of the tailboard. He was quite good, chatting away. He had been in the army for two years. 'I am known as RC – that is my Christian initials, Roman Catholic Thomas.' Everyone started to smile. 'You are young,' he said to us twins. 'Yes, my father looks young,' I said, 'about thirty when he had us two.'

Changing the subject, Terry asked, 'How long before we get to where we are getting to?'

'I don't know,' he said. 'What do you know?'

We said, 'Nothing.'

'That's exactly what I know, nothing. I am only a buckshee corporal.'

In the Army (Holland)

We could hear gunfire in the distance as we got out of the trucks. 'What regiment?' someone asked. The sergeant, who had now joined us, said, 'The Welsh Regiment.'

'Follow me.' We walked down a street. We found out later, that we had just crossed the Dutch frontier. The sergeant said as we came to the houses, 'Ten in there.' Terry and I were nearly split up, but good for Whitley, he dropped out for me to go with Terry.

Next day we were on parade. We were split into different companies. We were going into 3 Company. There were six of us altogether, including Sergeant Moorland. They kept Terry and me together with Mac. They were strengthening the companies, to bring the 4th Battalion up to strength. They had just come out of the line for a week's rest. This would be a good chance to get to know our new mates. You should have seen the attitude of some of them. They frowned on us, for to them we are just rookies. Others of them were all right.

If there were any dirty jobs to be done, we would end up doing them, for they wanted you to know that they had been in the fighting and you had not. Guard duties were done by the replacements, fatigues was done by the replacements – in other words we had to do everything. But that still didn't hide the fact that everyone had to do drill parades when they were called. Discipline was the same for them as us. On the whole we got on all right with them.

The battalion was returning to the line the next day, so we were writing our last letters in case. We had agreed not to take chances, and always be ready to be able to take cover. We decided to watch some of the old hands, then we wouldn't go far wrong.

The one thing that worried me was, what if something happened to Terry? How would I react? I had written a little note to be found on me if I should 'buy it', asking that if Terry and I got killed, we wanted to be in the same grave together. Without me knowing, Terry had done the same, just on a slip of paper, for we were only allowed to have our dog tags on us, nothing else.

I said to Terry as we were writing our letters, 'We are not telling the family that we are going into action tomorrow. Are you afraid?' I asked.

'Yes,' he said, 'what about you?'

'You know me,' I said, 'I am always afraid. I know I will be all right with you alongside me.'

'Same here,' Terry said, 'we will stick together.'

One of the old sweats came across to us. 'All right, boys?' he asked.

'Yes,' we said.

'Don't worry, just stick by me. It's simply a matter of confidence. I am as frightened as you. There is no one in this world that can say they are not frightened, even the Germans. Don't show yourself, and don't do silly things. Stay with me, I'll look after you.'

'Thanks,' we both said in nervous voices.

I went to bed on the floor. We were all kipping on the floor, and Terry and I were close together. I was facing him, and I said quietly, 'I am going to say a prayer. You go first and I will after.' His arm came across my ribs, which he had done since the ship *Bensmark*. 'I pray that the Lord will look down on Terry and me, guide us and make it safe for us. God bless our family and protect them. Thank you.' Terry said his prayer, which I didn't want to hear, so I closed off from his whispering. It was pitch dark outside. We could hear the rumbling of the guns, and it seemed a long way from us. At 0530 hours we were woken and told to take just our mess tins, field dressing, make sure they were in the pocket provided, our rifles and bayonets. We were to pick up two thick corned beef sandwiches, which we put in between the mess tins.

As we boarded the lorries, each man was given 100 rounds of ammunition, one smoke grenade and three Mills grenades. There were about a dozen lorries, if not more – there was no way we could determine the exact number, for we were at the front of the convoy. We were on the move for about an hour. The lorries were moving very slowly, as there was a lot of traffic on the road, including tanks. We debused just outside a village, having no idea of its name. There were no signs. But we had been told that we were not far from Tilburg, a moderate-sized city, not far over the border from Belgium.

The whole battalion was spread out. We were in the unit on the edge of the village. It was rather a large village in comparison to the ones at home. We were about two miles from the outskirts, and we had to move very slowly and carefully. We came across a large open field. In front, on our left, was a large pillbox. To the right of the pillbox were some trenches with Germans in them. Our two-inch mortars were laying a smokescreen. We then took the trenches on. But as we neared them through the smokescreen, the pillbox, which had accounted for two of our boys, was taken, and, when we were about to charge, the Jerries raised a white flag.

There were a dozen Russians fighting for the Germans, and they gave themselves up. So we had achieved our first objective. We then came across a low wall that we had to duck behind. There was another machine gun in the first house of the village; it was in our area.

The old sweat came up to us on his belly. 'Keep your heads down, don't volunteer.' Some of the company round the other side took the house from the back. Next thing there was a shout: 'Tanks!' We had our PIAT, but only had one in our section. We crawled away to the right of the PIAT to allow the gunner to position himself for a hit. But with these to be fairly accurate you have to allow the tank to get as near as possible, also without being seen.

He allowed the tank to get about 100 yards away. The gunner fired, which just tickled the tank. But now the gunner was in trouble. He and his mate, the ammo-carrier, belted sideways towards us. We all thought, the silly sod, why didn't he reload and try again? To reload a PIAT is tricky: if it is not held firmly, it will not recock itself. Also it could dislocate or even break your shoulder. But luck smiled upon us. Our tanks, which were stationary as we took our positions to attack, were now supporting us, just in time. The PIAT gunners would certainly have bought it without the tanks. The offending German tank was on fire after two shots.

We were lucky in more ways than one. When we arrived in Belgium and we joined the battalion, the snow was heavy on the ground and it was very cold even now. The Ardennes operation had fizzled out, a few weeks earlier. We had missed that (thank God) but we were in Holland now chasing the Germans. We were to try to breach the defensive line that the Germans were holding.

We were moved forward to a lead section. We were in extending line going across turnip fields. The wind was really howling, and swirling the snow as we were kicking it up from the ground. Our covering artillery fire had ceased. Now we were out of range of our own guns, and Jerry guns started to open up. We were in a very embarrassing position. We all scarpered to a ditch at the end of the field. We didn't know it was there, but you could pinpoint the separation of two fields. When we got in the ditch I was looking for Terry.

He was not in the ditch, and I was screaming his name. Sergeant Moorland and Corporal Thomas came running to me. 'Where's my brother?' I was shouting. Everyone was looking down the ditch. Let's face it, if he had been there, he would have made it known. We just could not see him. 'Can I go back?' I asked Sergeant Moorland. 'You go on,' he said, 'be careful.' I dived out of the ditch and I was running and shouting, 'Terry, Terry!' Just behind me was Mac. He had asked for permission to accompany me. I found Terry – he was on the ground, his clothes and his pack standing out against the snowy background. 'Terry!' I was shouting, waiting and hoping for a reply, for I was still a fair distance away from him. 'Here!' he shouted, and I was joyous at that reply.

When I got to him, I hugged and kissed his cheek. 'I was worried,' I said. 'I didn't miss you till we got to the ditch.'

'I think I have broken my leg,' he said to my enquiries as to why he was on the ground.' I went into a pothole as we started to run, when Jerry was shelling us. I could not move, and still cannot,' he said.

Mac grabbed his arm. 'You'll be all right,' he said. 'I was worried,' he then said.

'So was I,' I added.

'Stay here while I go back to the ditch to see if there is a medic there,' Mac said. Mac got back and reported to Sergeant Moorland: 'John has stayed with him, to keep him company.' Sergeant Moorland reported to the platoon officer, Barratt, who said there was a medic down the ditch. The sergeant sent a soldier down to get the medic, who came up and reported to Lieutenant Barratt, who with Sergeant Moorland told him where the casualty was. He said, 'Let his brother stay with him.'

The artillery from the Germans had stopped. After about two hours, the platoon moved out. When they got to their objective, they found that the Germans had gone – they had actually pulled back across the Rhine, but for northern Holland, where they held a line to stop the British getting to north Germany. They had evacuated all their forces to prepare for the final assault.

The medic got to Terry. He was on his own, so I helped him carry Terry on a stretcher that he had brought with him. We got to the ditch just as the company was to move off. The platoon officer told me that I could stay with my brother. Sergeant Moorland said, 'You look after him.'

'I will,' I said, and the platoon was gone. Other than Terry being injured, no one else was hurt during the advance.

We were together now, and with Mac we were a happy bunch. We met the other two, Whitley and Ben, in the canteen that had been put up for us, then we left at 2200 hours for bed. Terry had not broken his leg, but it was badly bruised. It was strapped up well, and after a couple of days, he was walking a lot better. I had stopped worrying over him, for I had been scared stiff that I would go away and he would still be in the camp.

But now we were together I was happy. All five of us were a good bunch. The other three looked after Terry and me, and we had got to like them tremendously. We didn't see much of Whitley and Ken. They were in another company, and only at night in the canteen might they come and sit with us on the beds. The Canadians were not far from us. They were, according to the grapevine, going north over the Rhine to take the north of Holland. We did not know exactly where we would be going into Germany, or when. It was all hush-hush.

In the Army (On the Rhine)

The camp was a former police barracks. We were not allowed out for fear of information being given away. Spies were probably still around. By March, Terry's leg was better. He was back on duty, for which I was glad. If he had gone and I had stayed it would have broken my heart. The weather was still very cold, with a wind that went right through you.

We were practised river crossings and house-to-house fighting. They were putting us through it, but now we were ready for that. Passing the camp were many lorries and guns going forward. We now knew that we would be moving out soon, not through having been told, but through seeing everything for the assault going by. At 1400 hours we were told to pack our kit, for we would be on the move by 1500 hours.

We got into our lorries and were off straight away. We travelled for an hour. Admittedly we never moved far, for there was so much movement on the roads. Vehicles were jammed packed. We got to a crossroads and were told to debus. We were lined up both sides of the road and then we moved off.

We came after about two miles to the Rhine, and you could not see anything forward. There was a big smokescreen on. We had not reached it yet when we were stopped. All of a sudden the guns let loose – what a din! – and the Germans were firing back with their big guns.

The guns fired for the rest of the day. They hardly stopped, there were only brief pauses to allow the launching of the attack to feel out the enemy strength. At 2000 hours our guns were silent, but not the German guns, which had zeroed in on the banks of the Rhine opposite them. They had caused a few casualties. When it was our turn to go across, most of the German gunfire had ceased. They had been overrun by our countrymen. But to my surprise, as we were going across the Rhine the whole area was lit up by our side. They were shining the searchlights to a cloud, and the reflection would beam back down, and light the whole area up. We got across safely, and we linked up with the other boys who were already there. Then we advanced to take our positions.

Next day there was a sight I will never forget. It seemed that thousands of planes came over above us. In the distance you could see the parachutes opening, and the gliders were landing all over the place. There were quite a few gliders shot down, with the full complement of men in them. They never had a chance. We were told to get a move on to quieten the guns. We moved at a terrific pace.

Jerries were sniping at us, but they were soon taken out. We got to the guns and fell upon the batteries that were shooting down our planes. We took the Germans completely by surprise. But our paratroops were dropped too near us. The idea had been to try to trap the German 7th Army.

As we were moving forward, we could see the cost of the air drop. There were scores of paras lying around dead. Quite a lot of them were still hanging from trees. Also there were quite a number of German dead, outnumbering our boys, and dead cattle everywhere. As we moved towards Reesfeld, the different nationalities fleeing towards us blocked the roads: Poles, Dutch resistance and French, and even Germans trying to escape by changing into anything that was not recognisable as a uniform.

When we got there the place was empty of Germans, so we went through to the other side. We could see the plains in front of us. We were halted to have a break, for we had been on the go for thirty-six hours. We had hot tea and something to eat. I still had my sarnies in the mess tins. We sat on the side, and then we heard the rumble of tanks coming through the small town, the tanks of the Guards Armoured Division, the Coldstream Guards.

Following them with our eyes, we could see them joining up with another lot of tanks, from what regiment we did not know. They were already on the open plain. We were on hold. Jerry prisoners were streaming through the area, being taken back across the Rhine. We had orders to move out. We were to take a village this side of the Ems Canal in the direction of Wilhemshaven. We moved sharply to the village to be confronted with remnants of the German Parachute Regiment – and they were fanatics.

We arrived just outside the area at 2200 hours. It was decided to hold off until we had tank support, so we stayed well back from the village for the night. We had hot food and drink, and we could wash and shave, and then we bedded down. Mac and four others of the section slept alongside Terry and me. We were woken at 0600 hours, and told we were to attack at 0700 hours. We started out spread across the open field. Then we were hit by a machine gun fire. No one was hit, but we dived down, and Number 2 section did a flanking movement. They ran into lethal fire, and the whole attack west of the village was held up. We could not get near them. We were told to engage them with rifle fire.

When the tanks came in we could move behind them. The old soldier who had told us not to take any chances came along with us, and he was talking all the time, encouraging us. The Jerries were holed up in the houses. As we tried to walk down the main street, Mr Barrett decided that we would have clear houses both sides of the street. Sergeant Moorland told Terry and me to 'face the house across the road, and if anyone pokes their head out, shoot. You take upstairs,' he said to me. 'Terry, you take the downstairs. This will be for five houses. Then you will go in on the next five on this side, while the other section covers you, as you cover them.' In the first house there was nothing, but, as we went into the second house, a machine gun opened up on the two boys going into the house opposite. Both were killed.

'Put a grenade in that bedroom window!' the officer shouted. Terry pulled the pin out and lobbed it right through the window, killing the three Germans manning the gun. The rest of the five houses were empty. It was now our turn. Sergeant Moorland came up to us and said, 'When you go in the house, as you open the door, the first one in fire your rifle. The second man will cover you. If the downstairs is empty, fire into the ceiling, four shots in each room. This way will safeguard you, for anyone hiding will do one of two things – panic and surrender, or fire back at you the same way through the floorboards. If that arises, throw a grenade. Right, go on!'

So we run into the first house, and we caught a Jerry coming downstairs. It was quiet, so he had thought that we had retreated after the machine gun fire. We injured him in the arm, and his carbine fell to the ground. There was nobody else in the house, so Terry picked up the carbine, slung his rifle over his shoulder, and fired into the ceiling to make sure it was working.

We went into the next four houses. There was no one in them, but across the road there was Jerries. As we attempted to go into the fourth house we nearly had it. One of the boys across the road heard some Germans talking, so he lobbed a grenade into the bedroom window.

This probably saved us, for there were four Germans in there. Two were killed and the other two were injured. We cleared the village, and I and Terry were really satisfied we had come through.

We carried straight on through the roads and fields till we came to a crossroads and machine gun and mortar fire opened up on us. We lost six of the boys, including Whitley from the other company. We didn't know this till later on, when we were deeply upset by it. We cleared the crossroads eventually. It took two companies to achieve it.

The enemy came up with some Tiger tanks, of which there were quite a few. Our CO ordered us to withdraw. He called for artillery support. The shells started to come over for about ten minutes. Although they hit one tank it was not enough to stop them, and the next minute we saw some Guards' armoured tanks rumbling across the fields. We withdrew far back as the tanks had a go at one another. There was a right old battle going on till it got dark. In the meantime we were all given hot tea, a sweet mess tin full. In the distance we could see the tanks. Sometimes one would blow up, and another would be in flames.

There were a lot of casualties on both sides. In the end we held the whip hand by sheer numbers. The Germans retreated, and soon after just packed it in. Our artillery had done a good job. They demoralised the Jerries and inflicted a lot of casualties, including the horses the Germans used for pulling their guns and stores. Also there were a lot of shattered guns, tanks and lorries. The place was a right mess. As soon as the Germans retreated, we were told to carry on. It was around 2200 hours. As we advanced we were spread in a line. Although now it was dusk, there were a lot of casualties from our tanks – a grisly sight, bodies half in and out, either burnt or shot as they tried to evacuate the tanks. I said to Terry, 'They are proper steel coffins. I would never go in them. I feel safe with the sky above me.'

We came to another village, and we used caution going through it. Just outside the Germans had made a defensive position, using all the old people, who were armed with the new type of Panzerfaust. They were sacrificed to allow the proper forces to fix up a more substantial defensive position further back. These old people more or less told us where they were – we were nowhere near them when some trigger-happy soldier disclosed where they were, and the whole perimeter where they were opened up.

Hitting nothing, we laid our two-inch smoke mortars. After our three-inch explosives had softened them up, it was carnage. We were not to know that there were old people and kids there, and we went in, full force of the battalion. It was now dark and if you saw a movement, you would fire, provided that it was in front of you. The German line offered no resistance when we got to them. They were fully demoralised. They were lying where they were, either blown to shreds or wanting to give in. It was terrible.

Terry said, 'There is no sense in this. I am really upset.'

'So am I,' I replied, 'but there again they opened up first.'

'They were frightened, you can see that in their faces.'

We carried on right through them. They were sorted out by the reserve company behind us. We went about two miles, before we were stopped, because Jerry let off a terrific artillery bombardment. We were told to dig slit trenches. 'Get in them, cover your faces with your helmets and lie down the best you can.' The helmet idea was to stop shrapnel on your face. We were in the forward positions. One would try to have some shut-eye, while one kept a lookout for possible enemy attack. Just before I dropped off asleep – Terry wanted me to go first – we ate our sandwiches and had some water, although it was still very cold – it was chilling but refreshing. I kept talking to Terry, but he was telling me to get to sleep. I eventually did drop off and had three hours' kip, so Terry had his turn for sleep.

The Jerries bombarded us for five hours. It was deafening and there was much shrapnel flying about everywhere. We were trying to sleep. Believe it or not, we were that tired that we did sleep. Dawn came, and it was at 0630 hours that the shelling ceased altogether. All hell broke loose. The Germans attacked with full force, tanks, the lot. We were ordered to withdraw.

How we got out was anyone's guess, but we were well clear before the Jerry tanks came in. We had a couple of near misses, Terry and me. At one point we stopped for some reason – a kind of premonition. There were four of us, withdrawing as fast as we could. Alf, the older type of chap who liked us, shouted. 'In here!' The front door of the house was completely off its hinges, so we all dived in there. About where we would have been, a three-inch mortar shell landed. We would all have been killed.

We ran through the house, through the back into a lane. There were Jerries firing at us from the end of the lane. We dived back into the house, and Alf said, 'Over the walls!' Luckily they were not too high, and easy to scale. Over we all went. We repeated that till we cleared the last house. We could see some of our chaps running like hell in front of us. We ran and then came to a large ditch. When we got there the ditch was full. Alf said, 'Follow me!' and he started to move along the ditch. Everywhere we went it was full of our boys. We were in trouble unless the tanks of the Guards came.

All of a sudden the artillery opened up. They bombarded the village-cum-town. We watched from what we thought was a safe place. Around dinner time some troops from another regiment were coming through us. We were being withdrawn. We had been on the go for two weeks and we were all tired. Other than little catnaps we would snatch when we were being shelled, we had been without sleep for quite a few days.

In the Army (In Germany)

We marched for about two hours single file each side of the road, until we came to a German small town. We boarded three-tonners and were taken to Emmerich, this side of the Rhine. There was a Bailey bridge which our boys had built, the REs (Royal Engineers). We drove straight across and were on the lorry for another four hours, until we came to the Dutch town of Breda. There we debused, and went into a former German camp.

We were to stay there for seven days, during which time we were allowed to go to Brussels for the day. Although it had been liberated for only a few weeks you should have seen the shops. They were full of practically everything. We had a good day, there were just the four of us: Mac, Ken, and me and our kid. We had a few bottles of beer. There were British Army places where you could get a meal. In all we had an enjoyable day. We had to catch our lorry back at 2200 hours, for we had a three-hour drive, for we were based in Holland, and Brussels was in Belgium. I bought presents for the girls and Mam and Dad. Everything seemed to be cheap. We had a slap-up meal before we left, and it was a great day.

By the time we got back to the camp we were all dog tired. We arranged to meet our other pals the next day in the canteen that had been set up for us. Also it gave us a chance to read and write our letters. We had one from Captain Brecon for both of us. Although Terry had had nothing to do with him, he had accepted Terry with me, knowing that we both wanted to be treated the same. We had a couple of letters from Mam and Dad to both of us, and the girls had written to us as well.

Thelma wrote and told us that the photograph that she had taken, and had had painted, was wonderful. It was 16 in x 40 in, and she had got Dad to make a stand for it. It was on our table in our bedroom. Tony was very serious with Thelma, and I hoped they would marry.

I said to Terry after reading Thelma's letter (he had the same), 'What are we going to do when we find a girl that we might like, and want to go serious with? Perhaps you might, perhaps I might… What are we going to do then, for we have been very close, and I don't want to lose you?'

'Nor I to lose you. We will worry about that after the war,' said Terry, 'So let's forget it for now.'

Our leave soon came to an end. We did nothing at all, which was great. The camp had organised pictures and laid on a concert, which was rubbish. But the canteen was open all day, with hot and cold foods.

We left camp on 5 April. When we got to the line, we took over from another regiment. I didn't know the name, they would not tell us, so that if we got caught, we would not be able to say which regiment had been taken out of the line. Our objective was Emden. We were on the road to it, but was still a very long way to go. The opposition was very strong now. We were meeting the cream of what was left of the German armies. We were following the autobahns to the north, and I marvelled at these roads. They went as far as the eye could see.

We were in the fields, moving slowly on account of the strong resistance. We came across a section of fields that had plenty of hedgerows. We were in the front line, and we became bogged down. The Jerries had fixed firing positions there.

They got us in a crossfire, through which we lost three chaps. We still had Alf with us, and he told us what to do and what not to do. Then our mortar section opened up, and he said, 'Keep to the ground with your heads. Don't look at what the mortars are doing, stay pinned to the ground.' Our mortars were after the machine guns that were on a fixed line in the hedgerow. The firing lasted ten minutes, and they were massacred. We advanced among them. There was no killing for the sake of killing; we helped with the injured, and we rounded up the fit ones that were left.

I was surprised to see that there were a lot of arrogant Jerries, looking at us in disgust, for capturing them. Those that were a bit cocky were handled more roughly, than those who accepted that their war was over. We comforted the many wounded as best we could, but we had to move on.

We covered about two miles before we came upon a displaced persons' camp, or concentration camp. The inmates were not in as bad health, as at the most notorious concentration camps. These prisoners were used for labour. The camp itself was not all that big, but there were a lot of poorly inmates. They needed food, and we had to try to hold them back. They were hell-bent on retaliating against the German population.

We were now officially on stop, so we bedded down for the night in the barns of a farmyard. There were five such large buildings. It seemed that a lot of the displaced people were working there.

We threw ourselves into the straw that was kept there for the herd of cows. The straw was in a storage place and had been there for about a year, but it was clean, and we didn't care. We had very little sleep. There was screaming and shooting going on all the night. When we got up and went outside, we had to control the DPs and move them back. Apparently there had been a lot looting and raping going on during the night. There was no way we could stop it. These people were getting their own back. There were Russians and Poles, plus a few Frenchmen there.

We were on the move just after 1100 hours. We went through a small town and came out into the country, where we met the full blast of freezing weather from the east. It was very cold for twenty-four hours, then it eased off. But we still carried on till nightfall. We then stayed in the ditches skirting the fields. We could not dig in, but Terry and I were all right because we couched into one another. I said, 'I wonder where we would have been had we gone back to sea.'

'Forget it,' Terry said, 'you will only start feeling sorry for yourself and having doubts in your mind.' We were lovely and snug. Had anyone else done what we were doing they would have been on a charge, and to make things worse, Terry still insisted on putting his arm across me.

'I bet the old man is having his daily tipple now,' I said to Terry.

'I wish I was with him,' Terry said. In no time everyone was asleep, other than the sentries.

We are on stop five days, and it was bloody freezing. We were getting hot meals and sweet tea, which made something to look forward to, but we could not walk outside the ditch. We asked how long we were going to be there for; 'We don't know,' the answer was. Terry started to cut some branches with his knife. He said, 'Come on, we will make a canopy.' We cut the thick branches for the framework, then put the thin ones with leaves to go on top. Although we were in the wrong time of year for such things, we found some and made a nice, cosy shelter. We then cut some for the floor and to make beds with. Before you could say anything, everyone was doing it. It also helped to keep us warm by working.

We still had to go out on patrol. We were told to venture out for no more than two hours, farthest point, then return.

We were now into mid April. We did not know what the other fronts were doing, if we were advancing or not, but we knew that we had been making good ground so far.

We were checked out medically while we were on stop. It was not an examination, just a look to see if our feet were all right. Each man had a fresh pair of socks to change into, so we were reasonably comfortable.

We were called to on the Friday, the fifth day, and we carried on. There were a lot of planes overhead, going in the same direction as us. I said, 'Some poor sods are going to get it.'

We then met serious crossfire, which stopped us in our tracks. The three-inch mortar of ours opened up, but there was no letting up. Then the Germans began pounding with their artillery. The order came to withdraw. We could not get out quickly enough. We waited for about two hours. Then some Mosquitoes came and pounded the Jerry artillery to pieces. We could see in the distance the damage these planes were doing, for near enough every second there would be a big explosion.

'Don't feel sorry for them,' Terry said, 'don't forget the islands – what they did to us on the ship. A lot of Germans are like that. When we shelled that last place, there were a lot of arrogant sods there, so really we should not feel sorry for them.'

We were on the move again after the planes went. We still met a lot of rifle fire and machine gun fire but we pushed the Jerries back. We came to a large village. It was too small for a town, but it was a large place. The houses infested with Germans. We had already lost seven men through sniper fire. The Germans started to use three-inch mortars. The call was to fall back. We were right up front against the walls of the houses, keeping a very sharp eye open for snipers, but it seemed the Germans were shelling their own people so they could stop us. As we turned and started to run back, a mortar shell dropped about seven yards away, and a splinter from the shell caught Terry in the back.

Terry shouted, 'John!' as he went down. I turned round and saw a big hole in his back. I moved a pace to him, for we were right together, I just a fraction in front. Then a sniper hit me in the back of the neck. I fell directly in front of Terry, face to face, the thickness of a playing card separating our noses.

In the Army (In Heaven)

Terry lay on his chest, with his back exposed. John had fallen on his left side. Terry was looking straight into John's eyes. John was dead. Terry, dying as he was, made every effort to close John's eyes. Despite the agony he succeeded. He crawled up with his hand across John's shoulder, and rested his arm where it stopped. Terry said, 'I—' and died.

The section finally got out of range of the guns. 'Where are the twins?' somebody asked. The entire platoon was looking around for the two boys. Alf shouted, 'No! No!' and he run forward to try to find them, or to see them. He was called back, but he did not hear the orders. He was oblivious to anything other than the twins – he loved them.

He came round the corner, and it was only the shooting of the Germans that halted Alf. But he did catch a glimpse of two bodies in khaki, slumped against the wall of a house halfway down the street. Alf broke down and cried. Others from the platoon came up to Alf. He didn't have to say anything. Mac, who was a mate of the twins, cried out loudly uncontrollably. Nearly all the platoon was weeping, even Corporal Evans.

Sergeant Moorland came over, and wanted to know what the hold-up was. He immediately assessed what was wrong. 'Come on, on your feet,' he said, but no one was willing to move. Mr Barrett came up and started to have a go at the sergeant for not moving the men out. When he saw the state of the men weeping like children, he was taken aback. On enquiring, he found out that the twins were dead, and even he was in a poor state.

Mr Barrett immediately went to the company commander and stated that the morale of his platoon was very low, explaining that the twins had copped it. Mr Allsopp, the company commander, ordered Mr Barrett to get the reserve platoon section 2 and replace them with 3 from the line.

Mr Allsopp was thinking that, in the state of mind that they were in the moment, further action would be committing them to their death.

So the twins' section was withdrawn. But they all sat around where they were, on the end of the street where the boys were killed, while heavy artillery from our lines smashed the resistance that the Germans were trying to hold.

About two hours after the brothers were killed, the place was cleared. The men all dived down to see if the boys were still alive, knowing in their hearts that they were dead, but hoping. 'Look at them,' someone said, 'as if they were asleep.' Mac said, 'Terry always threw his arm over John. It must have been because of something that they had done before. They just lived for one another.'

About an hour later the medics came. They were gently put in the ambulance together. Sergeant Moorland asked the ambulancemen where they were going now. 'There is a cold storage place about ten miles away. They will be kept in there for a couple of days, then taken across the border to be buried.'

'I want to make a request to you,' said the sergeant. 'If you have the authority, would you please ensure that they are put in the grave together, as you found them, preferably on a door, or some planks of timber. I want them buried as you found them.' They went through the boys' pockets, and they found the bits of paper that the boys had written requesting that they be buried together if they were killed.

All the section was helping with the bodies. Everybody was saying how young they looked. Alf had gone to pieces. He was quite uncontrollable, and they had to send him to hospital. He was kept there for a week, then transferred to a mental hospital. Alf never really recovered. He had had very little to do with the twins, but he always wanted them to look to him for advice. He thought a lot of them, as if they were his own sons. Alf was thirty-six years old. He thought the twins were too young for this game, and he had been determined to look after them.

The boys were taken to one of the larger places that they had come through, and were put together from the ambulance into the cold storage building. They were kept there together for three days, then taken across the border and buried in a temporary British grave, till the British government had permission from the Dutch government to have their own British cemetery.

True to the word of the ambulance driver, the boys were buried as they were found. They were put on a door, and covered over with canvas, and lowered into the grave, with Terry's arm across John. The British graves authority had given way on this one request.

The biggest battle the battalion went through was just outside their objective, Emden. On the plains, the Germans were lining up in a last-ditch stand. Up to Emden the battalion had taken 100,000 prisoners. Ken had been lost in the progress to Emden, besides quite a few of the other boys. In early May, just before the battle started, there were all kinds of rumours that the Jerries were packing in.

On the other fronts, the British Army had met the Russians at Vismar, so there now seemed no hope for the Germans. Hitler had committed suicide on the last day of April.

The battle that the battalion had lined up for started and proved to be nothing in comparison with what everybody was expecting. The RAF pummelled them and softened them up. All fighting in the north stopped where they surrendered. German commanders met Montgomery on Luneberg Heath, to discuss terms of surrender. Hamburg had already surrendered to the British.

The war was over. The twins' battalion had suffered a lot during the battles that they had been involved with in Europe. The British graves commission had been given a plot just outside Groningen, Holland. Now they had to assemble all the little plots where soldiers were buried on a temporary basis, to be gathered all into the one area.

The battalion had been given guard duties for the prisoners and installations, for there was talk that the Germans were going to start underground warfare. They were calling themselves 'werewolves'! But they were easily caught. The place was alive with displaced persons, and the battalion had a job to control them, for in the nights they were bent on revenge. Although efforts were made to keep in their camps, they got out, and there was rape, murder and arson going on all the time. Also there was a shortage of food to feed the Germans.

Dreaded Telegram

It was 23 April at 3 p.m. with Thelma ill, June in school, Ivy and Dad at work. At Ninian Park Road, a telegram boy was knocking the door of the Morgans' house. Thelma, having got up dinner time, was sitting in the kitchen when the knock startled her, for she was miles away thinking of her forthcoming engagement. When she jumped up to answer the door, Mam shouted, 'Don't you go to the door like that,' for she had only her nightie on. 'I'll put a coat on,' Thelma said back to Mam.

On opening the door, she saw the young telegram boy standing before her. It took her by surprise, for she had thought it was somebody canvassing. The boy said 'Morgans?' Thelma said, 'Yes.' He handed her the telegram, turned and went. Thelma, not knowing the significance of such things during the war, turned shut the door and went in. Mam enquired who it was. 'I don't know. It was a telegram. I expect the boys are coming home.'

Mam took the telegram from Thelma and opened it. She let out a terrible scream. 'Go and get your father,' she gasped. He worked across the road, in the Canton sidings. Thelma, still in her coat, turned. As she was about to go, she said to Mam, 'What is it?'

'The boys,' she said. She couldn't say any more. Thelma rushed to the weighing office Dad worked in, and she said, 'Quick, Mam!' as soon as she saw him. 'What is it?' he asked, but she was gone, so Dad chased after he as best as he could.

When he came into the kitchen he saw Mam slumped in the chair, still holding the telegram. 'What is it?' he said as he took the telegram from Mam. The first words he read were 'I REGRET TO INFORM YOU...' He went white and started to shake. 'Get dressed,' he told Thelma, 'and go and get your grandmothers.' Thelma got changed in very quick time.

Thelma flew around to both grandmothers, and said, 'Dad wants you – the boys, I think,' and she was gone. They both came round to read the telegram; one was earlier than the other. Thelma had now found out, and was screaming all the time. Dad's mother hit her to stop her screaming, for she was uncontrollable. As much as John pulled her leg, she really loved him, and Terry, who was the quieter of the two.

The continuation of the telegram was that Terry and John had been killed in action, nothing else. Mam was very ill when the implication of the telegram sank in. She would not speak; it was as if she were in a coma. Dad went out to the toilet. He was out a really long time. When he came in his eyes were really red from where he had been crying. It was tea time now and June would be home from school. Ivy would be another hour yet. When June came in, she could see that something was wrong, and when told she started to cry.

Ivy saw straight away that something was wrong, for the two grand-parents were still there and, other than the crying of Thelma and June, the place was very quiet, with no one talking. When Ivy heard she went crazy.

There was no tea as such. The grannies made cups of tea and sand-wiches. In the meantime Ivy had gone up with the other girls, and all three were crying, and all three uncontrollable. Mam had not said a word, and Dad was not much better. He was in a terrible state. Dad's mind went back to when he had had his birthday, when their mates had spiked his drinks, and the row the two of them made getting into bed, for they were drunk. They were never any trouble. They were really good boys, and they had been taken away. Dad was thinking of all the good times. There were no bad times. He could not contain himself, and he broke down and cried. At six thirty Tony came in. When Thelma told him, they were in the middle room. He started to cry.

The grandmothers stayed till about 11 p.m. When they left, they both said that they will be around in the morning. Dad did not go out that night. Someone in the pub said that there was something wrong, for 'the daughter came over the office, and he went straight away – and for him to miss his pint there must be something wrong.' They were all saying that in the pub. Nobody gave a thought to the idea that it could have been the boys. They guessed that his wife was ill, and she really was after the grandparents went.

Mam and Dad just sat in the kitchen not saying a word, both deep in their own thoughts about the boys. Thelma came in from the middle room, where she and Tony had been together crying. 'Will it be all right for Tony to stay?'

Dad said, 'No, he must go home, for his parents will be worried about him.' So Tony walked into the kitchen, and said to Mam and Dad, 'I am very sorry,' with tears coming from his eyes again. He turned and went.

There were no house telephones in the working-class areas, so Dad would have to go on his bike to tell everybody the next day. Dad asked Thelma how the girls were taking it. It was a good job Brian had not come down that night. Thelma said, 'Ivy has cried herself to sleep with June. Ivy said that she was not going into work tomorrow. Nor am I,' Thelma said.

Thelma went to bed after making a cup of tea for Mam and Dad. The time was just gone midnight. Mam had still not said anything, and Dad was now worried. She was in a state of shock. So Dad and Mam stayed up all through the night, both looking at one another but not talking, and every now and again. Dad would start crying again.

They were still like this at 8 a.m. They did not bother with the children. But when it was 9 a.m. Dad called Ivy to go round and get the doctor. The doctor arrived at eleven fifteen and told the grandparents that Mam must go to bed, as she was in a state of shock. He gave her some draughts and tablets to take three times a day.

The word soon got round, and the knocking on the door was unbelievable and unbearable, until Dad pinned a note asking people not to knock through illness in the house. Dad went to see Vincent down at his works, the lumber camp. When Vincent heard he went white, and was as near to tears as anyone could be. 'I'll call down the house in a couple of days' time,' he said. 'Is there anything I can do, or anything you want?'

'No, thanks,' Dad said, as he cycled away. After Dad had ridden round telling everyone that needed to know, he came home and went upstairs to see his wife, who was still in bed. The girls had just about stopped crying.

Thursday, in the local paper, there was a big story on the front page, relating to the previous story about the boys from the merchant navy. It now related the double tragedy that had fallen on the Morgan family, saying the boys were heroes for what they had been through. The next day the dailies from London all carried the stories.

By 28 April Mam was feeling a lot better. She was up. None of the family had gone back to work that week. Although the notice on the door was still there, many people and friends who knew the family were coming to the house. Vincent had been round to commiserate with Mam, and it was he who persuaded Dad to go out.

'Vince,' Dad said, 'if you see people coming up to me to say how sorry they are, nip them in the bud. Stop them, for I know how bad it is, but I don't want people coming up all night saying how sorry they are.' The grandmothers were still coming around the house for, as good as the girls were, the grandparents knew what to do, and what they were talking about.

They Will not be Parted

The war was over, and the battalion was on guard duties, as well as escorting DPs from Hamburg and Lübeck. The Poles were to go back to Poland on ships, and a battalion section would be the escort on the ships that would carry about 2,500 DPs back, a trip lasting about ten days. Just before departure, Sergeant Moorland had permission to see the commanding officer of the battalion, for he wanted permission to go to the War Graves Commission in The Hague. He had been asked by all the members of the battalion to make sure that the twins were buried together.

Sergeant Moorland wanted to go to Groningen, northern Holland first, to see the cemetery.

The Commanding officer listened to what he had to say, and agreed that it would be the right thing, to make sure the boys were buried together. He gave Sergeant Moorland permission to go after he had been to Poland. 'You make sure that they are together,' the commanding officer said.

Sergeant Moorland made the trip. There was no trouble to speak of, except that, when the Poles were going on the German ship, they were thought to be men only, Sergeant Moorland caught two females dressed as men trying to get on. He stopped them. It looked as of an ugly incident was about to happen. When the officer in charge confirmed that they were not allowed on, and the rest of the section was in position to enforce the rule, they gave in. The other minor incident concerned the food. They were allowed to send a few men from each hatch to collect their communal food, one hatch at a time. No. 2 hatch complained that their food was cold, there was not enough of it, and they didn't like the Germans cooking it!

Other than that, everything was all right. Coming back from Stettin they brought Germans back, having no trouble with them. Having left on the Monday, they were back on the Wednesday of the following week. The following morning Sergeant Moorland went to see the RSM (Regimental Sergeant Major) who knew all about his request to go to

Groningen and The Hague. He was given a Jeep and a driver, more or less to look after the Jeep, and leave the sergeant to concentrate on his errands.

He was given all the official papers for his journey, as well as the driver's papers. They left at midday. The plan was to go into army barracks wherever possible. 'You make a good job for the twins,' said the RSM, 'and the best of luck.' They got down to Vessel, and stayed the night in a German barracks, that had been taken over by the British. They were given food and shelter for the night, and carried on in the morning, after crossing the Rhine, to northern Holland, arriving at 1600 hours at Groningen. They were directed to a large house where the War Graves Commission was situated. They were given food and shelter, but the WGC insisted that all work would be done in works' time. Sergeant Moorland and the driver went out and had a few drinks with a couple of British soldiers, then went to bed.

The driver's name was Trevor, and he looked after the sergeant well. They were called at 0700 hours, had breakfast after washing and shaving, and at 0830 hours were ready to meet the person in charge. He held no army rank, but the sergeant addressed him as sir. We explained the situation. 'Yes,' said the official, 'I have the necessary papers here with the request from your battalion. I am afraid that this is not permissible. We don't bury two people in the same grave, only the name individual.'

'But this is a special case,' the sergeant pleaded. He then related what he knew about the boys, how old they were, and the contents of the newspaper article Sergeant Hillard showed him. 'These boys are special to our battalion. To everyone they were exceptional.'

'I will have to consult my fellow officers,' said the man in charge. 'I will let you know in the morning. As a matter of fact these boys will be brought in during the week.'

'I would like to stop till they are buried,' Sergeant Moorland said, 'if you don't mind, sir.'

'Yes, that's all right with me.'

They waited ten days for the bodies of the Welsh Regiment to be brought to be interred. They saw the bags the boys were in, and they were still together, on a door as the sergeant had suggested.

Permission was indeed granted that they should be together. Sergeant Moorland and Trevor were alongside the grave, when the boys were lowered into it. They had had to make the grave a little wider; they lowered the door which the boys were on. The sergeant wanted to ask if it was possible to look at the boys, but he was so upset that he said nothing.

As soon as the grave was filled in, Sergeant Moorland went outside, intending to buy a big bunch of flowers, but the lady in the shop gave them to him. He thanked her and went straight back to place them on the grave. He was surprised to see that the headstone was already in place: Terry and John Morgan, with their army numbers on each stone, side by side. He could still see their faces. He knelt down, though the men preparing the other graves were still there, and said a prayer.

According to the headstones they were nearly eighteen. But all their commanders had thought that they were younger than that. They would not let on; they wanted to be in the army. The sergeant came away with tears in his eyes. The driver said, 'Where to now, Sergeant Moorland?' He was brought to reality and said, 'In the morning we will make our way back to the battalion. I have their grave number – 701. I will always remember that number for the rest of my life.'

Sergeant Moorland turned to the driver, Trevor, and said, 'You didn't know them, did you?'

'No, I joined the battalion after they were killed.'

'They were very young at heart, and in looks and age. They were lovely kids. Everyone liked them, they were always obliging. I loved them.'

Sergeant Moorland left the next day at 0830 hours and arrived back at camp at 2000 hours, for the roads were still very bad, with heavy traffic and columns of refugees.

He reported to the RSM and assured him that the boys were buried together. He gave the plot number, which was the same for both, and was told to stand down for the day. But wherever he went, everyone wanted to know if the twins were together. 'Yes, they are,' Sergeant Moorland said, 'they are.'

Although the war in Europe was over, the battalion was now going to prepare itself for the Far Eastern conflict. They were going to be taken from Europe, to be kitted out and trained to be with other regiments, to be the assault troops on Japan. The time to move out was the end of August, to go to America for training, but first they were all going on leave, in batches from Germany. Sergeant Moorland and Corporal Evans's platoon were to be second draft.

Sergeant Moorland had every intentions of going to see the boys' family, and he wanted there to be a memorial service. When he got home on leave, he was going to see Sergeant Hillard and go down with him to the family home, to have a frank talk about the boys with their mam and dad.

Captain Brecon saw the news in the London morning papers. He went cold. 'Why those boys?' he said to himself. 'They have been through everything. Why them?' He sat down and cried. The house was empty, fortunately, for he could not control himself. He remembered the last time the boys were in his house, and he knew his son doted on the two of them. He would go to pieces when he found out, thought the captain, so would the rest of the family.

'They have been through everything,' he repeated. He made his mind up to go over to Cardiff. That's the least I can do, he thought. He decided to go over on the Sunday, over a week after it had been in the morning papers. He could not phone to make an appointment. He would take pot luck, and that's what he did.

Just after 2 p.m. Mrs Morgan opened the door. The captain introduced himself. 'Oh,' she said, 'the boys have talked about you. Please come in.' She showed him into the middle room. On the wall was an image of the two boys sitting facing one another. It was a wonderful photo taken by Thelma and Tony a long time ago. Captain Brecon stood in front of the picture frame, and said, 'This is how I remember them.'

Mr Morgan walked into the room. They shook hands after they were introduced by the boys' mother, and they sat down. Mr Morgan said, 'Would you like a cup of tea?'

'Yes, please,' the captain said. Then they talked about the boys, and their father said, 'Yes, they would have still been here. It was the thought of John being underground as a Bevin Boy. John, to be on the safe side, decided that they would volunteer for the army by advancing their ages. John was a very bright boy. He would pick things up fast.

'He packed in the sea, for he was twice prisoner of the Germans, and twice he was in confined spaces. John suffered badly from claustrophobia, and he talked it over with Terry, and they decided that they would go in the army now. If they were called up at the proper time, they would have ended down the mines, perhaps one or the two of them, but they did not wanted to be separated. We never interfered with what they wanted to do. It was their decision.'

The captain told the Morgans what John had done when he was a prisoner the first time – how he had been the main actor in their taking over the ship and escaping to Gibraltar. 'He was certainly brave, but he said the other boy was not with him at that time.'

Mr Morgan told him the story of how, on the last trip, they were in the same cabin together, Terry as a cabin boy and John as galley boy. 'They struck up a firm friendship. They would not argue, and they were very close, for John looked on Terry as his saviour, and Terry loved John for everything that John did for him, like giving him a home. They would do everything together. If one didn't want to do it, the other would back him up.'

Mr Morgan told the captain about the time they were in the army cadets. 'John was a full corporal, and he handed his stripes in, for he would not give orders to Terry. They were always together, always. When they were taken prisoner they stayed together, and when they went into that devil ship John needed comfort, for he was down the dark hold. So Terry befriended him and, when they slept, Terry his put his arm over John every night – even when they were home, and I bet you anything that Terry still did that in the army.

'John never forgot Terry for that. And when the Germans scuttled the ship, Terry saved John's life.' He told the captain what had happened, how John had survived because of Terry, and how they had stayed in South Africa as the guest of the Ambassador, who had brought them home.

'By the way,' Mrs Morgan interrupted, 'we will have to drop him a line and tell him.'

'Sorry,' Mr Morgan said to the captain, 'as I said, he brought them home. When they got off the train, Terry, who lived around the corner, left John to go home. About an hour after John came home, the bell went on the door. It was Terry – all his family had been killed in the very last blitz on Cardiff. All wiped out, including his father's brothers and families. He had nowhere to go. John said, "You are staying here." What could I say? He saved my boy's life a couple of times. So we took him in. We treated him exactly like John. What a wonderful boy he was. I worshipped the two of them. They have broken my heart.'

He explained how the boys had determined not to go back to sea. So as not to be separated, they had become brothers, and the family had adopted Terry at John's insistence.

'John loved Terry and I know Terry loved John. You could not separate them. Don't give anything to John unless Terry has the same. They slept together. Terry every night put his arm over John, it was a normal thing. They were very happy. I am glad that they both went together, for I could not see one lasting without the other.'

It was tea time now, and the girls made some sandwiches. The captain was invited into the kitchen around the table. He ate just as if he were home. He always said that if people take the trouble to make you feel at home, enjoy their hospitality.

'I don't know how to put this,' the captain said to Mr Morgan. 'Can I write a book about them? We will share whatever money that will be made. I will donate my money to the Merchant Navy Fund.'

'I'll look forward to reading it,' John's father said.

'There will be a lot of questions I will have to ask you, from time to time,' the captain said.

'Tell me, Captain, will it be possible to bring my boys home, and have them interred in Cardiff cemetery?'

'I am afraid not,' the captain said.

'We will at least will be able to go over to the cemetery in Germany?' Mr Morgan did not know where they were buried, for it had not yet been disclosed.

'It won't be Germany,' the captain told him, 'no British servicemen are buried in Germany. It would not be allowed. They will be buried to the nearest country to that they were killed in, which would be Holland.'

'They would not be buried in Germany.'

'That's good,' John's father said. They finished tea. Mr Morgan said, 'I would like you to see their bedroom. No one will ever sleep in this room again. We are holding it as a shrine. We are leaving everything as they left it.' He said, 'You bought them a watch each, didn't you?'

'Yes, I did,' the captain said, 'but it was from the men on the first German boat that we were on. They wanted to club together for some memento.'

Mr Morgan opened two drawers, one of each of the boys, and brought out the envelopes that were in them. He opened them and their worldly possessions fell out: the watches from the captain and the

Prides; in John's envelope there was the gold ring that Terry had bought him, and in Terry's was a gold bracelet with his name on it from John. 'That will tell you how much they thought of one another,' Mr Morgan said to the captain.

They went back down to the middle room, and they talked away, making arrangements for the book. The captain wanted to talk to people involved with John from all four ships. The two that would have been best able to help were both dead, Mike and Ted. 'You make a note of anything that your boy may have told you,' the captain said to John's father.

Later that week, on the Tuesday night, there was a knock on the door just before Mr Morgan went out. June answered the door, and a young voice said, 'Are your Mam and Dad in?'

'Who is it?' Mrs Morgan asked.

'I think it was the boy that John went to sea with.'

Mrs Morgan went to the door. Timmy was there. 'Come on in,' she said.

Timmy walked in said, 'Sorry, I have come to give my sympathy about the loss of John. I am very, very sorry,' he said. 'I would have been around before. My mother and father insisted that I come around and see you, and I kept holding back, for I was nervous. But now I am glad I came. I am really very sorry, I hope that you will understand.'

John's parents sat with Timmy for about an hour. Mr Morgan asked him, 'Did you know Captain Brecon?'

Timmy said, 'No, he was involved with John on the first trip.'

'Well, he is going to write a book about John. Now, I would like, if it is possible, you to make notes of the trip that you and John had. Try to relate everything. His two mates Mike and Ted were both killed when John was out East, so you are the only one who we know that could help. Captain Brecon will be over in a fortnight's time. If you could possibly have something for him, anything that involved you and John, that will be invaluable, for you were the best of mates on that trip. I know that you were no longer talking, but you were both young, and never understood one another.'

Timmy left, promising to write what he remembered about the trip.

In June came another knock on the door. Three army sergeants were there, Hillard, Morgan and Prince. This time Mrs Morgan answered, and they asked if the Morgan family lived there. 'We were the sergeants who controlled the destiny of your sons while they were in the army,' said Sergeant Hillard.

They were invited into the middle room. The first thing that they saw was the photograph of the boys facing one another. Sergeant Moorland said, 'Just like them, a beautiful portrait.'

John's father came in and they all introduced themselves, and Mrs Morgan went and made a cup of tea. The sergeants related how each one of them had been involved with the boys. Sergeant Hillard, the senior of the three, mentioned the write-up in the papers. 'Do you know,' he said, 'they looked me in the eyes and denied it was them. After they left the hut I was willing to bet anyone a fiver that it was them.

'They were so innocent, and I will tell you now they were well liked in the regiment. Sergeant Moorland was their platoon sergeant, and was with them when they got killed. They died a second behind one another.

John's father explained about Captain Brecon and how he was going to write a book about the boys. Sergeant Hillard promised he would compile what he knew of the boys' time in the army and let Mr Morgan have it for the captain. They left with a promise that they would come back. 'I would love that,' Mr Morgan said, 'for the boys' sake. They never said a bad word about you NCOs.'

The next day the Morgans had a letter from Mr Pride, saying that he was coming over on government business. He would like to call on them, with their permission. He said he would be over towards the end of July. So Mr Morgan wrote back and asked Mr Pride if he could remember a couple of things the boys might have done or said while they were with him.

Thelma and Tony had now decided that they wanted to get engaged, to marry in a year's time, Thelma told Tony straight, they would live with her mam for a while, for she wanted her father to take to Tony, as he had to the boys. She thinks it would help her mam and dad.

Tony was due for call-up, having finished his deferment as an apprentice. He had had his medical when the boys were killed, something that was hushed up at the time.

At the end of July a letter from the War Department informing Mr and Mrs Morgan that the boys had been buried in Groningen. It stated that they had been buried together. Mr Pride came down a day or so later. He was invited to the middle room, where he stood for about five minutes looking at the photos of the boys on the wall. 'What a lovely photo,' he said to Mr and Mrs Morgan. 'I don't suppose that you have a small photo of them, have you?'

'We'll ask our daughter when she comes in from work.' Mr Pride talked about the boys as if they were his – in a way they were, for the time that they were with him, for he loved them. He explained that the Prides received the daily newspapers from Britain, two days after they were published, in the diplomatic bag. They had seen the first article about the boys, and the story that had been all over the front pages, and then they saw the tragic news that the two of them had been killed.

'It devastated the two of us. Even the chauffeur was very upset, for the boys liked him, and he was always talking to them.' Mr Pride stayed till 9 p.m. He even had tea, a good old-fashioned English tea. Thelma had come in with Tony, and was introduced to Mr Pride. She said she would get some photos printed for Mr Pride.

Mrs Morgan told Mr Pride about Captain Brecon, and he said he would be delighted to send over his memories as soon as he could.

The battalion was nearly finished, with everyone having leave. They would be going to America in August, to train for assault landings. Everyone was looking forward to that, but not to Japan. But as the last draft was reporting back, the war with Japan ended. As Corporal Evans said, 'They could have waited another week – we would have been on the seas then.'

Everything was cancelled for America. Everyone was downhearted, for now they were on guard duties all the time. But a platoon was going home for a memorial service they were holding for the twins on Thursday, 14 September. This was the boys' own platoon, including the officers and NCOs. They had to rehearse what they were going to do; the papers and wireless were to carry the story.

The service would be held in Llandaff Cathedral – ticket only. Mr Morgan kept two tickets for Mr and Mrs Pride if they should want to come. Also a handful of tickets was sent to Captain Brecon for the officers of the first ship that John had been a prisoner on. There were not enough tickets for the number that wanted to come.

An unexpected visitor knocked on the door, just a week before the memorial: the cook with whom John had worked with on the Topley, Wayne from Grangetown. John really liked Wayne; they got on well together, and Mr Morgan knew this, for John had often spoken about Wayne. He was invited in and the Morgans talked with him for about two hours. You could see Wayne was upset. He also spoke well of Terry, recounting that it was Terry who has brought him back to life, in the escape from that hell ship. Wayne had not long previously packed in the sea.

The day of the memorial arrived. Mr Morgan was now very upset. Vince proved his friendship; he helped him all the day at the ceremony and after. The service started at two thirty. There was a vast crowd outside, and the cathedral was filling up inside.

The family and near relatives took their positions at the front. The service started with Captain Brecon giving a glowing speech: how John had saved them from captivity, how he was alone in the lifeboat, 'and don't forget he was not fifteen then,' and about the U-boat that picked him up. He finished by telling the congregation that he had seen Terry and John about six weeks before they were killed. He stated that John had served on four ships, being captured twice, and it was Terry who had saved John's life on the last boat the two served together on.

After Captain Brecon's speech came a hymn. One of the three priests said something about John's age. Sergeant Hillard mentioned their dry humour, and said to finalise his speech that they had served their country above and beyond their duty, all before the age of eighteen, and emphasised how Terry and John lived for one another.

The last speaker was Mr Pride, the ambassador. He related the state of the boys when they had been rescued by the Royal Navy. 'They were very thin, and they looked like two little boys. I was asked to help to nourish them back to health. If you had seen them then, you would have cried. They enjoyed their stay with us, and they started to get better. They were with us for nearly seven weeks, and we loved having them. They were very respectful to everyone they met, and my wife was very upset when it was time for them to come home.'

The service lasted two hours. Mrs Morgan was deeply distressed, as were the girls. Mr Morgan was trying very hard to maintain self control. He still had Vince alongside of him, which was a good job, for he comforted his good friend.

Captain Brecon came over a fortnight after the service. He brought his son, as he had promised, and the Morgans were delighted. He had received all the little stories from the different people that had served with the boys. He told John's father that the book would be called *Steel Coffin*, relating to the submarine and the hell ship.

The Morgans all noticed that June was rather keen on Captain Brecon's son, Matthew. She waited on him hand, foot and finger! They left after tea on the Sunday night, and Matthew said he would like to come again. June spoke for the family when she said, 'You must.'

When the book was finished, John's father asked Captain Brecon if, at the end of the story, he could put a short poem that he had written. The captain was only too delighted to agree.

Tony had been called up, and had joined the Welsh Regiment at Whitchurch Barracks. Timmy still kept coming round to the house. He did not mean any harm. He was looking for some sort of understanding. Perhaps Terry had stolen the limelight from him. Mr Morgan was really bemused over Timmy, but he did not want to upset the boy. Timmy had been called up, and was hoping to go into the Tank Corps. He came to say his farewells on the day before he went. He said, 'I'll keep writing, and I will see you when I come home.'

The proofs of the book were brought over at the end of November, for Mr Morgan's OK. Matthew was with Captain Brecon. He had kept on to his Dad, 'When are you going over? Can I come?'

'Don't worry,' Mrs Morgan said. 'Let him come. We love to see him. Also I think someone else loves to see him.' John's father read through the book inside the week that Captain Brecon had allocated. Then he gave Captain Brecon his poem to finalise the book.

> Their country first was their belief;
> To die together was some relief.
> To die too young was to bring much grief
> Their lives cut short by Death, the thief
> For wherever they go they'll be together.
> Please God our Lord, keep them from the devil for ever.
> Although they shared the joys of life,
> To die so young was just not right.
> To die so young was the price to pay,

To keep them together to this day.
Mam and Dad
God Bless You.

Tony decided to make a career in the army. He married Thelma, who was blessed with the birth of twins, who were called Terry and John. Thelma loved the boys, and so did Tony. He was very loyal to his wife, allowing her to stay home with her mother, an old promise that she had made to her parents. Mr Morgan lasted till 1951, when he died through ill health brought on by a broken heart. He was never the same after the boys went. Ivy and Brian got married, and now live in London, for Brian has a very good and well-paid job. Ivy came down with her two babies, boy and a girl, the boy named after Mr Morgan, and the girl after Mrs Morgan. June is still home, courting but not married to Matthew. She is getting engaged very shortly. Captain Brecon keeps in touch through his son.

The book was a bestseller thanks to the publicity in the papers.

In 1955, Ivy, June and Thelma decided to go over to the cemetery in Holland. Their mam wanted to go, but knew it would distress her too much. But she did make Thelma promise that she would take some photos of the plots. Tony, still in the army, was stationed in Germany. He arranged to meet them in Groningen, for he was taking some leave in order to look after them over Holland. They left the children at home. John's mother looked after the twins, and Brian's mother took care of Ivy's two. Matthew, at the last moment, wanted to come over with the girls. His father, the captain, made him promise to take photos as well.

When Thelma and Tony paid their last visit to the British Cemetery in Groningen, they took the twins, who were now sixteen years of age. When the lads saw their names on the headstones, they were shocked. They were told the full story at the graveside. Thelma wanted them to understand how she felt about her brothers. She broke down, and Tony finished telling them. Thelma said, 'You have seen the photos of the boys in the middle room – well, this is their resting place.'

Just after the boys were killed, Mr Morgan put a lock on their bedroom door. He called the family together, and said, 'This room will be locked for ever.'